Novels of
The Masks of Aygrima
from E. C. Blake

MASKS
SHADOWS
FACES*

MASKS

E. C. BLAKE

DAW BOOKS, INC.

DONALD A. WOLLHEIM, FOUNDER

375 Hudson Street, New York, NY 10014

**ELIZABETH R. WOLLHEIM
SHEILA E. GILBERT
PUBLISHERS**

www.dawbooks.com

For Alice, my beautiful daughter:
dancer, future chemist, and devotee
of sword-fighting princesses.

◆ ◆ ◆

Acknowledgments

Much of this book was written during my tenure as writer-in-residence at the Regina Public Library. My thanks to the library and its staff and administration and to the Canada Council of the Arts, which provides funding for the writer-in-residence program at the RPL, the longest-running program of its kind in Canada.

Thanks as always to my editor extraordinaire, Sheila Gilbert, who knows what works and, more importantly, what doesn't—and isn't afraid to tell her authors. This book is far better than it would have been without her insight and experience.

Also, thanks to my agent, Ethan Ellenberg, who looked at several pages of ideas I was toying with and immediately said *Masks* was the one to focus on. As always, he was right.

And last, but most importantly, my deepest love and gratitude to my wife, Margaret Anne, and daughter, Alice, the center and ground of my life.

PROLOGUE

Pain and Fire

F ROM ATOP A NAMELESS MOUNTAIN, the Autarch of Aygrima watched another of his villages
burn.

The mountain had no name because it deserved none.
Its peak was not distinctive; no towering cliff face set it
apart from its fellows; no spectacular fall of water cascaded down its stony flanks. It was not even particularly
tall; little more than a hill, really. What it *did* offer was a
clear view of the far more spectacular mountains to the
north, and, down its eastern slope, a clear view of the
village of Starbright.

Or, or least, it *had* offered such a view, when Starbright still existed. Nothing now remained of it but
crumbling walls, charred beams, smoking embers, and
the tumbled, bloody corpses of its residents, even now

being dragged through the streets to the mass grave scarring the once-lush grass of the village green.

The acrid tang of smoke stung the Autarch's throat, but he ignored it, though it made Keltan, his white stallion, stamp and blow. Behind him the black geldings of the six Sun Guards were likewise restless. He ignored them, too; a similar entourage had surrounded him all his life, even before his father's agonizing death from the poison of the now-defeated rebels.

Had he turned to look at the Sun Guards, he would also have seen the ocean, stretching out to the infinite western horizon. Four or five centuries before, there might have been a reason to look that way, to watch for the sails of ships from the myriad kingdoms of the West, sailing to Aygrima to trade for the magic that only the Autarchy could offer, bearing away Healers and Engineers and enchanted tools, weapons, and amusements to distant, exotic ports.

But then had come the Sickness, brought by a ragged ship with a dying crew. The Sickness had raged across Aygrima, felling hundreds, but in the end the Healers, through prodigious expenditure of magic, had gained the upper hand and snuffed it out. The historians believed it had been far more devastating elsewhere, for that plague ship had been the last vessel from overseas to ever make port in Aygrima.

At the moment, however, the Autarch was not interested in history. He was interested only in the dying village below, and the man now riding a bay mare up the winding path from the valley floor: Perris, his Guardian of Security—his *new* Guardian of Security, for Floccias, the old one, had died, courtesy of the Autarch, as agonizing a death as the Autarch's father, the man he had failed so spectacularly to protect.

"Mighty One," panted Perris as he arrived at last. "As you commanded, we questioned everyone—man, woman, and child—then put the village to the sword and torch. No one escaped to tell the tale."

"I don't care about the village," the Autarch snapped. "Did you learn anything? Anything about the girl?"

Perris swallowed hard. *Good,* thought the Autarch fiercely. *He fears me. As he should. As all should. Fear is my protector.*

Fear . . . and the Masks. They should be ready by the time I reach Tamita. Soon, everyone will be Masked, every Mask telling the tale of the wearer's thoughts to my guards, the soldiers I have already renamed Watchers . . . there will never be another rebellion.

Never!

"They were . . . remarkably unwilling to talk," Perris said. "They feared us. They feared what we could do to them . . . what we *did* do to them. But they feared *her* more." He shook his head. "They said *we* could only kill their bodies. They said *she* could reach inside them and take their souls."

A worm of fear entered the Autarch's heart. *Then it's true! She has the same Gift as I. The worm turned, metamorphosed into a pang of a different sort. She would understand. She alone would understand. If things were different between us . . .*

But things were *not* different. He hardened his heart against fear and regret alike. The girl's father had been a leader of the Rebellion. And though she might share his rare magical Gift, she had used it against him, time and time again. A series of ruined villages had preceded this one: villages she had attempted to make into her stronghold, villages from which she had been routed by the Watchers, with sword and flame and magic.

Starbright is the last, the Autarch thought. *She is pinned against the Great Mountains. Here she falls, here she dies: and with her dies the Rebellion. Once and—thanks to the Masks—for all.*

He let nothing of his thoughts show on his face. "Superstitious nonsense," he said. "There are no souls, and if there were, magic could do nothing to them. Did you manage to break through their fear of *her* with the fear of *me?*" He leaned forward and let his voice fall to a venomous growl. "*Did you find out where she is?*"

Perris swallowed again. "Yes, Mighty One."

"Then I suggest you lead the way, Guardian Perris."

Guardian Perris nodded and turned his mare. The Autarch and the Sun Guards thundered down the mountainside in his wake.

As they rode through the ruins of Starbright, the Autarch ignored the tumbled walls and burning beams, ignored the Watchers dragging the bodies of men, women, and children toward the mass grave. The villagers had harbored the girl, Arilla. Arilla was all that remained of the Rebellion. The Rebels—her father, and those like him—had killed the Autarch's own father, had almost killed him. They deserved nothing but pain and fire, and pain and fire he had brought them . . . as he would to the girl herself, now that they had her cornered.

On the far side of the village, a larger force of Watchers waited. Fifty-strong, they rode with Perris, the Autarch, and the Sun Guards up the other side of the valley, onto the flanks of the Great Mountains, which raised their unscalable, snow-streaked peaks far above.

An hour out of Starbright, Perris raised his hand, bringing the column to a halt. The Autarch surveyed the mountainside. The day was growing old, and just half an hour before clouds had shrouded the sky and begun to drop listless, spiraling flakes of snow, but he could still make out a narrow ravine, a split in the rock, choked with dark green trees. "In there?"

"So the villagers said," Perris replied. "Unless she fled elsewhere before we arrived. But I have sent out scouts in both directions, and there are no trees up here to give her cover. They would have seen her."

The Autarch grunted. "Then let's root her out." He turned in his saddle. "She is Gifted," he warned the Watchers. "And dangerous. But not invincible. Her Gift will not turn aside an arrow she never sees, a sword swung from behind. And you all have your own magic to draw upon, or you would not have been assigned this task. Show no mercy. Kill her on sight." He turned forward again, peering up at that dark slash in the mountain. "Advance," he said, and dug his heels into Keltan's flanks.

He thought he knew what to expect, and was prepared to counter it. He thought that, as she had in the past, Arilla would hurl boulders at them or flaming trees, perhaps try to bring down a landslide . . . although, truth to tell, the mountainside above the ravine looked much less steep than was typical of the Great Mountains. *A pass?* the Autarch thought, and felt a chill. "She may know a way through the mountains," he warned Perris. "We must not let her escape!"

"We won't," said Perris. They were almost to the mouth of the ravine. The Guardian of Security turned to address the troops. "We—"

His voice died in a little *whoosh!* of expelled breath, and he toppled from his horse: as did every other Watcher surrounding the Autarch, from the commander of the Sun Guards to the lowliest private. They thudded to the ground like overripe fruit falling from trees.

The Autarch felt a tug, like insubstantial yet powerful hands trying to pull from his body something his body did not want to release. The feeling lasted only an instant; then he sensed rage and a force of magic being hurled toward him, and threw himself from his stallion— just in time: Keltan screamed, reared . . . and exploded, showering the Autarch with blood and bits of bone, flesh, organs, and hair.

Dripping gore, the Autarch scrambled to his feet, his own rage swelling. He needed magic. Arilla had pulled her magic from Perris and the Watchers, so he could not draw on that—but he didn't need to. He could feel magic all around him, the magic contained in the black stone urns that every member of the Watch had carried to the mountainside. The girl had not touched that store: perhaps their Gifts differed more than he'd thought, and she could not.

But he *could*.

He raised his hands, and the magic poured into them, encasing them in multicolored light, glowing gauntlets of red and blue and green and gold and colors he could not even name swirling and shifting over their backs, palms, and fingers. He knew where that powerful attack had come from. He could sense it, could sense *her*. *There*, just inside the ravine . . .

He stretched out his hands, and released the magic.

It leaped from his hands, the colors melding into blinding white light that illuminated the mountainside more powerfully than any lightning bolt from any summer thunderstorm that had ever scored its side. It struck the mouth of the ravine. The trees within burst into flame, exploding in great gouts of red-orange brilliance and black smoke. The mountain shook. Deep, booming cracks echoed across the hillside. And then, the ravine . . . closed. Its sides heaved and shuddered and fell apart into massive boulders that rained down into the burning forest, smothering the flames beneath tons of dirt and stone.

The earth shuddered, again and yet again . . . and then all was still.

The Autarch, breathing heavily, fell to his knees on the snow- and blood-covered rocks. *It's over*, he thought. *She's gone*. Fierce satisfaction swelled within him. *I promised you, Lady Arilla. I promised you pain and fire. And I always keep my promises.*

After a long moment, the Autarch climbed heavily to his feet. Without a backward glance at the sprawled bodies of his erstwhile bodyguards, he began trudging back to Starbright. Perhaps he would come across one of the spooked horses of his slain escort. Perhaps not.

It did not matter.

The last threat to his power had been eliminated. He was young, he was powerful, he was the Autarch of Aygrima, and he had nothing to fear: not here, and not back in Tamita, the city where his throne awaited him.

With Arilla out of the way, no one remains who can threaten me. And once I return to Tamita, I will proclaim the Masking. From that moment on, no one will ever threaten me again. I will not die like my father.

Holding that thought in his mind like a good-luck charm, the Autarch of Aygrima trudged southward.

I will not die!

ONE

Tests

ON THE DAY SHE TURNED SIX YEARS OLD, Mara held tight to her daddy's hand and looked doubtfully at the darkened doorway before her. "It's all right," her daddy said, his voice deep and reassuring. She looked up at him and saw his blue eyes shining at her through the eyeholes in his Mask of burnished copper. The torches illuminating the staircase they had followed down from the surface into this strange underground hallway struck bright-red sparks from the diadem of rubies across his forehead and spirals of rubies on his cheeks, the unique insignia of the Master Maskmaker of the Autarchy of Aygrima. Through the mouth opening she could tell his lips were curved in a smile. "The First Test is nothing to be frightened of."

"I'm not frightened," Mara said. And she wasn't. Well,

not *really*. After all, she wasn't little anymore, she was six years old today, and she was with her daddy. But the room she had to go into all by herself looked so awfully dark that she suddenly found herself reluctant to let go of her daddy's hand.

Instead, he let go of hers. "Go on," he said. "Tester Tibor is waiting inside. Remember, I introduced him to you yesterday at home."

She remembered. She'd liked Tester Tibor, a big round man with a bright yellow Mask. He'd given her sweets he'd bought in the market on the way to their house, and he'd made her laugh. He was nothing to be scared of, either. And she *wasn't* scared.

I'm not scared!

All the same, her lower lip trembled a little as she walked forward on her own, leaving her daddy behind, and stepped into the dark room.

Well, not *completely* dark. The door was open, after all. But it had no windows, and very little light made its way in from the torches in the stairway.

She could just make out the Tester, seated next to a small covered bowl made of black stone, set atop a pedestal so short that even a little girl like herself could look down at the bowl. She was glad she'd met Tester Tibor the day before. Otherwise she might have been frightened by his dark, shadowy bulk. But now she wasn't.

I'm not afraid.

"Hello, Mara," Tester Tibor said in the deep, kind voice she remembered. "Happy birthday!"

"Thank you," she said, because her parents had taught her to always be polite.

"There's nothing to be afraid of," the Tester said.

"I'm not afraid," she said, out loud this time.

"Good!" Tester Tibor leaned forward, resting his elbows on his knees. "You know how this works. I'll lift the lid of the bowl, and you tell me what you see."

Mara nodded.

"Ready?"

She nodded again.

"Here we go!" Tester Tibor took hold of a small handle at its center and lifted the cover off the bowl.

Mara gasped.

Light filled the basin—light of every color she could name, and lots more she couldn't: so many beautiful colors, all swirling and mingling, painting the walls, the floor, the ceiling, the Tester's yellow Mask and robes and her own white dress in ever-shifting hues.

"It's so pretty!" she breathed.

Tester Tibor chuckled. "It is, isn't it?" he said. "And that's it, my dear—you've passed the Test."

He put the cover back on the black stone bowl. Mara gave a little "Oh!" of disappointment as the beautiful colors vanished.

The Tester stood and took her by the hand and led her out to where her daddy waited in the dim hallway. "She's Gifted," he said. He looked down at Mara and smiled. "Not that I ever thought there was much doubt she would be."

"Thank you, Tibor," her daddy said.

"My pleasure, Charlton. Tell the next child to come down, will you?"

Daddy nodded, and Tester Tibor went back into the darkened room.

"Was that magic, Daddy?" Mara asked as her father led her back up the stairs to the little room where three other children, two girls and a boy, awaited their turns with the Tester.

"Yes, Mara."

"It's so beautiful!"

He looked down at her, blue eyes glittering like sapphires behind the copper sheen of his Mask. "Yes, it is. Almost as beautiful as you."

"Does this mean I can be a Maskmaker like you when I grow up?"

"I hope so, Mara. I hope so."

Together they walked out into the sunlit morning.

• • •

Two weeks before her eleventh birthday, Mara Holdfast sat on a padded bench in the tutorhall's lecture room and heard about the Lady of Pain and Fire for the first time.

She was listening with just half an ear: the main topic of the lecture, after all, was the wonder and glory of the Autarch, and over four years of schooling she had, in between learning how to read, write, do sums, build a fire, cook a simple meal, and sew, been told over and over (and over and *over*) how their magnificent leader had squashed the rebels who had murdered his father, instituted the Masks to ensure no one could ever rebel again, established the Watchers, who watched the Masks for the magical signs that the wearer might pose a threat, and blah blah blah perfect society blah blah blah practically a god blah blah blah.

But when Tutor Ancilla mentioned the Lady of Pain and Fire, she blinked and looked up from the Mask designs she'd been doodling on her slate. "Who?" she asked.

Tutor Ancilla wore the plain white Mask of the un-Gifted, marked in black with the insignia of an open book on each cheek, symbol of the teaching profession. Her mouth, just visible, turned down into a frown and her eyes narrowed. "The Lady of Pain and Fire, Mara," she said. "Did you not read today's assignment?"

Mara bit her lip and looked down. "No, Tutor," she answered.

On her right, her friend Mayson, a skinny boy with shaggy blond hair, sniggered quietly. Tutor Ancilla's gaze immediately shifted to him. "From your reaction, Mayson, I assume you *did* read it. Perhaps you would care to fill in Mara on what she obviously overlooked?"

Mayson's snigger died. "No, Tutor Ancilla," he said. "I . . . I mean, I read it, but I don't . . ." His voice withered into silence in the heat of Ancilla's tutorial glare.

"As I thought," Ancilla said. Her gaze shifted to Mara's left, where her best friend Sala sat quietly. "Sala? I know *you* did the reading."

"Yes, Tutor," Sala said demurely.

"Then please stand and tell the class what you learned."

With an apologetic glance at Mara and Mayson, Sala stood, her bright red hair, too fine to ever be entirely controlled by a ponytail, forming a wispy halo around her head. "In the aftermath of the Great Rebellion," she said, clearly reciting (Mara exchanged a resigned glance with Mayson; they'd both long since gotten used to the annoying fact that Sala could memorize anything she read almost instantly), "our glorious Autarch faced a terrible trial: an evil sorceress called The Lady of Pain and Fire, who hated everything the Autarch had done to make the Autarchy such a safe and wonderful place. She used her terrible magical powers to destroy entire villages in the north, razing them to the ground and slaughtering everyone who lived in them, men, women, and children. The Autarch personally led a force of Watchers to root her out of her stronghold in the foothills. He threw down a mountain on her head, and she was never seen again, for her dark sorcery was no match for our glorious Autarch's mastery of the magic of purity and light." Sala stopped. "Was that all right, Tutor?"

Tutor Ancilla gave Sala an indulgent smile, clearly visible even through her Mask. "More than all right, Sala. Thank you."

Sala gave Mara another apologetic look and sat down. Mara resisted the urge to stick out her tongue.

"The Autarch's defeat of the Lady of Pain and Fire occurred sixty years ago today," Tutor Ancilla continued, "and that is why—"

The noontime gong shivered the lecture-hall air. Tutor Ancilla glanced through the open windows into the street, brightly lit by the autumn sun. "That is why class is over for the day. Enjoy your half-holiday, children, and

I will see you tomorrow morning. Those of you who have not yet done so," she gave a pointed look to Mara and Mayson, "should take time to finish reading Chapter Five of *The Annals of the Autarch: From Triumph to Triumph*. Dismissed."

There were twenty-three children in the lecture hall. Within a minute, all of them were outside, scattering to the four winds. Sala, Mayson, and Mara didn't have to ask each other where they would go: they headed downhill toward the Outside Market.

"Tutor's pet," Mayson said to Sala, but without any real rancor, as they went down the first flight of stairs that led from the fifth terrace of Fortress Hill to the fourth.

"If you'd just do the assignment," Sala pointed out.

"I did," Mara said. "Or at least I tried to. But . . ."

"But it's boring!" Mayson complained. "We've heard it all before. The Autarch is wonderful. The Masks are wonderful. We live in a wonderful time. Isn't it wonderful?" He made a face. "I can't wait until the Second Testing," he said. "Then we can start learning real stuff—how to use magic."

Mara shot him a frowning look; he caught it, blinked, and suddenly blushed. "Sorry, Sala, I didn't mean . . ."

Sala giggled. "You may have more magic than I do, but I've clearly got more brains."

To Mara's relief, Mayson just laughed at that. Mara grinned, glad her two friends hadn't argued this time. Sometimes they went at it like cats and dogs, with her caught in the middle.

"What do you want to do when you grow up?" Mara said. "You're lucky. At least you'll have a choice. Once Mayson and I have the Second Testing and find out what kind of magic we can see and use . . ."

"I think I'd like to be a glassblower," Sala said.

"Stand aside, please," said a gruff voice behind them, making Mara jump. She turned to see a baker descending the steps with a huge tray laden with bread, his beige

Mask marked on each cheek with stylized loaves. The three children squeezed to one side. Mayson mimed reaching out and snatching one of the delectable-smelling loaves from the tray as the baker passed, but Sala slapped his hand. He stuck out his tongue at her.

With the baker safely past, they continued their descent. "Why a glassblower?" Mara asked.

"Glass is so beautiful," Sala said, face alight. "And you can do a lot more than just make bowls with it. My mother and I were shopping in the Inside Market along Processional Boulevard last week and saw an amazing display in a shop. It looked like a garden, but everything was made of glass! Reds and greens, silvers and golds, it was so beautiful . . ."

"So boooo-tiful," Mayson said, and now it was Sala's turn to make a face at him.

"No need to ask you what you want to do when *you* grow up," Sala said to Mara. "You've said so often enough. You want to be a Maskmaker like your father."

"More than anything," Mara said. "What could be better than being apprenticed to your father?"

"Not being apprenticed to your father?" Mayson said, an edge of . . . something . . . in his voice. Mara exchanged a guilty glance with Sala. Sala's father was dead, but she was very close to her mother. Mara loved her parents and doted on her father and couldn't imagine what it would have been like to grow up without them. But Mayson . . . Mayson seldom mentioned his parents. And more than once he'd come to school with a black eye or a sore shoulder. Mara thought she knew why, but she didn't know how to talk to him about it.

"What do you want to be?" she said instead, though she already knew; he'd said so at least as often as she'd said she wanted to be a Maskmaker.

"A Watcher," he said promptly.

As if on cue, a pair of Watchers crossed the street ahead of them: black-Masked, black-helmed, black-cloaked, wearing mail and heavy gloves and high, polished black boots. Their Masked faces turned toward the children for a moment, and as always, Mara found herself running down a quick mental checklist of her recent activities to make sure she hadn't been up to anything that might get her in trouble. She hadn't, but still, there was something about those blank, black Masks that sent a chill up her spine.

"Why?" Sala asked in a whisper; she'd obviously had a similar reaction to Mara at the sight of the Watchers.

"They're not scared of anybody," Mayson said; and then, as if he'd said more than he'd intended to, added, "And neither am I," but somehow, Mara knew that wasn't true.

• • •

A month before she turned thirteen, Mara once more sat in the lecture hall. This time, though, she was alone with Tutor Ancilla, and the Tutor sat on the bench with her and talked quietly to her instead of lecturing. "In a month," Tutor Ancilla said, "you will turn thirteen years old. And that means ... ?"

" ... my Second Testing," Mara said dutifully. It was hardly a surprise: she'd known about it for years. *Could any Gifted twelve-year-old* not *know about her Second Testing?* she wondered. It seemed unlikely.

"Your Second Testing," the Tutor said, nodding. "In preparation for which, I am required to ensure that you understand what the Testing is all about. So ..." She tilted her head to one side, her bright brown eyes locked on Mara. "Tell me."

They'd learned little enough about magic in their lessons, but what they had learned, she knew by heart. "The Gift of magic is a rare and wonderful thing," she said. "Very few people have any measure of the Gift, so those who have it must serve the Autarch in whatever fashion their Gift best suits them for and the Autarch sees fit. Because of that, all children are Tested at age six. If they can see magic, then they are Tested again at age thirteen to see what kind of magic they can see, and how strongly they can perceive it."

"Very good," the Tutor said. "Apparently you *do* pay attention once in a while."

Mara shot the Tutor a startled glance. Was Ancilla actually making a joke? If so, the straight line of her lips behind the mouth hole of her Mask did not betray it.

"What is the difference between the First and Second Tests?" Tutor Ancilla continued.

"At age six, Gifted children can see all colors of magic," Mara said. "But by age thirteen, their Gift has settled and they can see only one or, rarely, two—and even if they can see two, one is always strongest."

"And the color of magic seen reveals what?" Tutor Ancilla asked.

"What kind of magic the Gifted child will be able to use," Mara said.

"What are some of the colors of magic, and what do they mean?"

Mara hesitated. "You only taught us a few, Tutor . . ."

"Oddly enough, I am aware of that," said Tutor Ancilla. "Only a few colors are permitted to be known. But tell me the few that you know."

"The Gift of Healing presents itself as blue," Mara said. "The Gift of Engineering—"

"Which is?" Tutor Ancilla interrupted.

"The ability to use magic to move and shape objects?"

Ancilla nodded. "Correct. Continue."

"The Gift of Engineering presents itself as blood-red."

"Any others?"

"The Gift of Enchantment—the Gift of imbuing inanimate objects with magical traits—" (Mara was rather proud of herself for remembering the word "imbuing") "—the Gift of the Maskmakers—reveals itself as a coppery red-gold color." She stopped. "That's all you told us, Tutor."

"Only the Autarch and members of the Circle know them all," the Tutor replied. "As it should be."

Mara said nothing. The list of things only the Autarch and his Circle of advisers and ministers were permitted to know was a long one and not something it was wise to ask too many questions about: Tutor Ancilla had made that clear long since.

"It sounds like you are well prepared for your Second Testing," said Tutor Ancilla. "Once the Tester knows what color of magic you see, you will be pre-apprenticed to a Master of that particular Gift. Although you will continue to attend thrice-weekly classes with me—" Mara saw her lips tighten in what she thought might be a smile "—which I am sure is a great joy to you, you will also begin spending several hours a week with your assigned Master. He or she will teach you what it seems good to him or her to teach you about the use of that Gift, although of course you are absolutely forbidden from using magic or even *seeing* magic until you are Masked, on your fifteenth birthday. Once that occurs, you will become a full apprentice and will be taught the complete use of your Gift in the service of the Autarch."

Mara nodded.

"Very well. You are dismissed."

Mara went out into the bright sunshine and stood there, blinking. She looked right, farther up Fortress Hill: up there, on the last terrace below the golden walls of the Palace itself, stood her house, though she could not see its bright green tile roof from this angle. *I should go home,* she thought. *It's almost suppertime.*

But instead, she turned and headed down Fortress Hill, toward the city wall. She knew Mayson had had his own conversation with Tutor Ancilla just before she had: he turned thirteen the very next day. And there was no way Mayson would have gone home right away: not to *his* father. Which meant . . .

Sure enough, she found him at their favorite spot atop the wall, seated, his bare feet dangling into space. She plopped down beside him and hung her own feet over the edge, unconcerned about the fifty-foot drop to the cobblestones of the Outside Market below. "Where's Sala?" she said.

"Dunno," he said. "'Course, she didn't have to have a little chat with Ancilla about Second Testing. Lucky."

Mara shot him a startled look. "Don't you *want* to be Gifted?"

"Only if I can be a Watcher," Mayson said. He made a face. "But I don't even know what color of magic I need to see to be a Watcher. What if I end up a Healer? Poking sick people. *Old* sick people." He shuddered. "*Naked* old sick people. Yuck!"

Mara laughed. Mayson shot her a look. "Aren't you worried about what color you might see?"

"My daddy says the Gift of Enchantment runs very strongly in our family," she said. "His grandfather was a Maskmaker—one of the first Maskmakers, right after the Autarch ordered everyone to be Masked—and his father was a Maskmaker, and he's the Master Maskmaker. I'm sure I'm going to be a Maskmaker, too."

"You *can't* be sure," Mayson said.

"I'm *sure*," Mara said stoutly, and told the butterflies in her stomach to settle down and believe her . . . but they didn't pay attention.

A sudden blast of trumpets off to their right startled Mara. She gripped the edge of the wall and leaned out a little. "It's the Autarch!" she said in amazement.

"What's he doing in the Outside Market?" Mayson wondered.

"Beats me," Mara said, but there could be no mistake: no one else had an entourage like the Autarch, not even the members of the Circle. To begin with, there was the horse: Keltan, the famed snow-white stallion the Autarch had ridden since he was a boy (which meant Keltan was either amazingly long-lived or the fourth or fifth of his name, Mara thought). Scarlet tack bedecked Keltan: gold bedecked his rider. A golden cape hung from the Autarch's gold-armored shoulders and draped Keltan's hindquarters; the Autarch's golden breastplate glittered with rubies; golden gauntlets encased his hands, and golden greaves protected his legs. Even his boots shone gold in the late-afternoon sun.

A jewel-encrusted cap of gold hid his hair—*or probably the lack of it*, Mara thought, mouth quirking; for all his glory, the Autarch was at least eighty—and then, of course, there was his Mask, the only one in all Aygrima permitted to be made of gold. From her perch high above, Mara could see very little of it, but she knew what it looked like: stern, handsome, given an unearthly sparkle by a dusting of tiny diamonds.

It was, truth be told, a little gaudy, and Mara thought, as she usually did, that her father could make one far better, should the Autarch ever need a replacement.

The Autarch and his entourage passed through the Outside Market like a moving seam in the patchwork quilt of the vendors' brightly colored awnings. The cream, white, gray, and beige Masks of the ordinary citizens, crowded together on either side of the main boulevard to make way for the Autarch, moved in unison to watch him pass. Here and there a Mask of red or green or blue stood out, marking their owners as Gifted.

What color will mine be? Mara thought uneasily, and pushed the thought away. *Copper, like Daddy's. I'm sure of it.*

"Look at those country yokels," Mayson said scornfully. "They don't know what to do with themselves."

Mara had to agree, grinning to herself as she watched the vendors scuttle out of the way of the approaching ruler. She could easily pick the country women out of the Masked crowds below by their simple, unadorned hair. No city woman would be seen in public without an elaborate headpiece, feathered and silvered, gilded or jeweled. But country women . . . *If they wear headscarves above their Masks, they think they're popinjays.*

Mara herself was a city girl through and through, born and raised in Tamita, capital city—*only* city—of Aygrima. She couldn't imagine living in the rolling green countryside, dotted with cattle and sheep and sleepy little towns, which stretched to her left, west, all the way to the distant western ocean and its tiny fishing villages. She thought it would be even worse to live in one of the lumber towns scattered through the forested hills to the east, or one of the distant mining towns in the lower ranges of the snow-capped, impassible peaks that formed Aygrima's eastern border and, curving west, the northern one. As for the flat prairie to the south, mile after mile of wheat and barley and oats, eventually giving way to orchards and plantations and finally the salt marshes of the southern shore ... she shuddered at the thought, even though her own mother had grown up in the south. *What is there to* do *out there?* she wondered. *Play with cows? Dig holes?*

She glanced over her shoulder into Tamita, climbing in terraced ranks up Fortress Hill. From their perch she had a straight view up Maskmakers' Way to the red roof of the tutor hall she had just left, the emerald-like gleam of their own home's tiles, the golden dome of the Maskery, where in two years' time she would don her Mask. Looming over all there was the Autarch's Palace itself, a vast, many-towered pile of yellow stone, aflutter with blue pennants from which the sun struck occasional golden sparks as it glinted off the golden emblem of the Autarch.

"Here come the Child Guards!" Mayson said, and she looked down at the market again. "Lucky brats!"

There they were, a dozen slim and silent youths following in the wake of the Autarch, dressed in identical white robes, wearing identical silver Masks, riding identical white mares, the six girls sidesaddle, the boys astride. Membership in the Child Guards, instituted just five years earlier, was the greatest honor the Autarch could bestow on a young Gifted. The youths, from across the Autarchy, spent their days in close company with the Autarch himself, learning to use their magic in his service. When they turned twenty-one, they took their place in the court. Someday, it was said, some of them might join the ranks of the Circle.

The whole village celebrated when a country youth became a Child Guard, Mara had heard. It offered hope to even the lowest commoners that one day a child of theirs might ascend to the nobility. But looking down at those silent, white-robed, silver-Masked youths, she shivered. *Might as well be in prison!*

Most of the Child Guards kept their Masks turned resolutely toward the Autarch; but one, a boy riding in the last rank, looked about him as he rode. His gaze traveled up the city wall ... and stopped on Mara and Mayson, sitting high above.

Mara stared boldly back. *What must his life be like?* she wondered. *Always in the presence of the Autarch Himself, living in the Palace ...*

She also wondered what he saw when he looked up at *them.* And then she suddenly remembered she was wearing a short tunic and he was looking *up* at them, and felt herself blushing. She squeezed her knees together.

"What's *he* staring at?" Mayson demanded, and Mara blushed harder but said nothing, not wanting to put any ideas into his head.

The silver-Masked boy's gaze finally slid away as the twelve silent youths rode on in the wake of the Autarch. Behind them came six of the Sun Guards, the elite force of Watchers that guarded the Autarch day and night.

"Look at those!" Mayson said, voice tinged with admiration.

He seemed to find the Sun Guards fascinating. Mara found them frightening—though less frightening than regular Watchers, she supposed. Most Watchers wore all black: black Masks, black armor, black surcoats, black capes. But although the Sun Guards' Masks were as black as any other Watchers', their helmets, armor, and cloaks were gold like the Autarch's, and their surcoats white as snow. Blue-and-white banners fluttered from the shining silver tips of their long black lances.

A respectful distance behind the last pair of Sun Guards, the rigid lines of the crowds dissolved into the ordinary bustle of the marketplace. Mara, glancing left, saw the Autarch's procession reach the main boulevard of the Outside Market and turn toward the Market Gate.

She shook off her momentary self-consciousness. It was getting late. "Guess I'd better head home," she said. "Good luck tomorrow."

"Thanks," Mayson said. His eyes were still on the receding figures of the Sun Guards. "But I'm sure I'll get what I want."

Mara said nothing. Mayson wanted to be a Watcher. *If he* does *get what he wants, how will we still be friends?*

"'Bye," she said, gathered her feet up under her, and headed for the guard tower whose stairs would take her back down to ground level, and the road home.

• • •

A month later, on her thirteenth birthday, Mara once more stood in the darkened hallway outside the Testing chamber, holding her father's hand; but this time she held it, she told herself, only because she loved holding it, loved the feel of his callused fingers in hers, loved being close to him. It had nothing to do with being afraid. After all, this time she knew what she would see.

Well, sort of. She knew she would see magic. But . . .

"What if I don't see the right color?" she asked. She looked up at her father's Masked face. She didn't have to look up as far as she had when she was six, but far enough: her father was very tall, so tall he was always easy to pick out in a crowd, even from behind, while she was still rather short for her age. "What if I don't see the red-gold color I'm supposed to see?"

"There's no 'supposed to' about it," Daddy said. His lips curved in a smile. Wearing the ruby-studded copper-colored Mask and his favorite rust-red hat, he looked the same as he always had, although she knew well that the Mask hid a few more wrinkles and the hat a lot more gray hair than the last time he had brought her to the Testing chamber. "You'll see what you see. There's nothing you can do to change it." He squeezed her hand. "But if it makes you feel better, both Tester Tibor and I feel sure you'll see red-gold, the color of Enchantment. Some skills tend to run in families, and Enchantment is one of them. And as you know, both your great-grandfather and grandfather were Maskmakers, too. But whatever color you see, the Autarch . . ." For some reason he paused. "The Autarch," he finished, his voice a little rough, "will still find a use for you."

That wasn't a comforting thought. Mara hadn't seen Mayson again since the day a month ago when they had sat together on the wall, watching the Autarch pass beneath them. Whatever it was that the Testers looked for in Watchers, Mayson must have had it: the very day he had been Tested, he had (Mara had heard secondhand) moved out of his parents' house, accompanied by much shouting and cursing from his father, and climbed up the hill to the Palace and the barracks of the Watchers which nestled inside its outer wall. Though he would not receive his black Mask for another two years, his training had already begun.

The Autarch had found a use for *him*, and Mara wondered if she'd ever see him again.

What would happen to her if she saw a different color of magic than the one that would allow her to fulfill her dream of being her father's apprentice?

The door to the Testing chamber swung open, and Tester Tibor stepped out, lips curled in a smile behind the mouth opening of his yellow Mask. "Come in, Mara, come in."

Mara let go of her father's hand and stepped into the darkened room. Everything was just as she remembered, except the pedestal on which the bowl of magic rested seemed much shorter.

"Now," said Tester Tibor. "Ready?"

Mara nodded.

The Tester lifted the lid of the basin.

Mara stared into it, heart beating fast, and her breath caught in her throat.

"Which color is strongest?" Tester Tibor said.

Mara didn't know how to answer. She'd been frightened she wouldn't see the red-gold of Enchantment, the color that would mean she could be a Maskmaker. She'd worried that her Gift would have faded, as they sometimes did, so that although she might be able to see magic, she wouldn't be able to make much use of it: that was, after all, what had happened to her mother, whose Mask of pale blue proclaimed her to be Gifted with Healing, but whose Gift was so weak she could do nothing with it and thus had not been called upon to use it in the service of the Autarch.

What had never occurred to her, because she had never heard of such a thing, was that she would see *exactly what she had seen as a six-year-old*: the basin filled with seething, swirling colors, every color of the rainbow and every combination between, breathtakingly beautiful . . . but *wrong*. At thirteen, she was only supposed to be able to see one color, maybe two. *Is something wrong with me?*

"Go on," the Tester said. "You can tell me."

Mara swallowed. She thought her heart might burst right out of her chest, it was pounding so hard. She knew she should tell Tester Tibor the truth, but what would that mean to her dream of being her father's apprentice?

Faced with the rainbow maelstrom of colors, she thought back to what her father had said . . . and lied. "Red," she said. "Well, more like an orangey red. Red-gold, I guess you'd call it?" *It's not a* total *lie*, she thought. *I can see those colors.*

Just a lot of others, too.

"Excellent," the Masker repeated, making a mark in a small leather-bound notebook. "And as I expected. These things usually run true."

"My father is hoping . . . I can be apprenticed to him,"

Mara said. Her heart was pounding. *He's going to figure out I'm lying. He's going to find out . . .*

"Pre-apprenticed, certainly," Tester Tibor said. "Of course, it may still be that you do not have the Gift in strong enough measure, something which cannot be determined until you are Masked and allowed to start using magic yourself. But you answered with such confidence, I think that's unlikely." He gave her a big smile, teeth flashing behind his Mask. "Congratulations."

Mara managed a small smile, though she thought she might be sick. She turned and went out to join her father, who was waiting in the hallway.

"A happy result all around, Charlton," Tester Tibor said to him. "You have a new apprentice!"

Her father whooped and gathered Mara up in a huge bear hug. Mara hugged him back, but inside her mind wailed, *What's wrong with me?*

It wasn't too late. She could still tell the Tester the truth, tell her *father* the truth. She knew that was what she *should* do. But then she thought of the Autarch, trailed by the silent Child Guards, the Autarch who could snatch her away from her father tomorrow if it would suit his purposes, and she said nothing.

"Let's go home and tell your mother," her father said, and she nodded mutely, took his hand, and left the Place of Testing.

TWO

Changes

MARA'S MOTHER WAS AS THRILLED as her father had been by the apparent success of her Test, and cooked a special celebratory dinner of fresh fish and mashed redroots. Mashed redroots were Mara's favorite food in the whole world, and yet they tasted like ashes in her mouth that night. She didn't like lying to her parents. But she didn't dare tell them the truth. *I'm just late developing my true Gift*, she thought. She glanced down at her flat chest. *Just like I'm late developing, period. It will come. And when it does, I'm sure I'll see red-gold, just like I said. The Gift runs true in our family. My father said so.*

Still, she had trouble sleeping that night, and as a result, overslept. Late the next morning she came yawning down the stairs in her thin nightdress to find a Watcher standing like a shadow on the landing by her father's workshop. Her heart skipped a beat. *He knows I lied to the Tester!* But though the Watcher's blank black Mask turned toward her, eyes glittering behind the eyeholes, mouth set in a stern frown, he said nothing. She hurried past him, feeling naked. At the bottom of the stairs she glanced back. He was still staring at her.

She went about making breakfast for herself, heart still beating fast, listening for the heavy tread of the Watcher's feet on the stairs, but he stayed where he was. It wasn't until she was holding two slices of bread on a toasting fork over the fire that he descended, and he wasn't alone: with him came a woman wearing flowing white robes and a Mask of green. She had no idea what kind of Gift that represented.

The two passed into the front room without a word to her, and a moment later she heard the door open and close, releasing them into the street. She breathed a sigh of relief, pulled the hot toast from the fork, and was sitting at the table spreading butter and jam when her father came down the stairs. He wasn't wearing his Mask, though she knew he would have donned it while the visitors were in the house. She frowned up at him. "I didn't expect to run into a Watcher on my way to breakfast!" she said accusingly.

Her father laughed. "Special delivery," he said. "I ran short of magic last week. A lot of Gifted to make Masks for." He smiled down at her, blue eyes twinkling in the early morning sunlight streaming through the window above the sink. "Masks you'll soon be helping me to make."

Feeling a pang of lingering guilt, Mara took a big bite of jammy toast and pushed the plate bearing the other slice toward her father. He waved it off. "No, thanks, I already ate." He sat down across from her and watched her.

"What?" she said nervously, uncomfortably guilty under that gaze.

"Nothing," he said. "I'm just thinking how wonderful

it will be to have my beautiful daughter as my apprentice, and how relieved I am everything worked out all right."

She gave him a shocked look. "You said both you and Tester Tibor were *sure* I'd see red-gold!"

He grinned at her. "I might have been a little more reassuring than I was assured," he said in a conspiratorial tone. "I admit that I did worry a *little* bit that you might not have the right kind of Gift."

Mara felt another pang of guilt, but she said nothing. *It'll turn out all right,* she told herself. *It has to.*

"I'm already thinking about *your* Mask," her father continued. "I know it's still two years away, but ... well, I want it to be special. Copper for a Maskmaker, of course. But for decoration ..." He frowned in thought.

"It's strange to think that in two more years I'll be wearing a Mask," Mara said.

Her father smiled at her. "Scared?"

"A little." Mara wiped crumbs from her mouth with the back of her hand. "I mean ... what if it ... changes me? I like who I am. I don't want to be someone different."

Her father sat down across from her and leaned forward, forearms on the table. "It won't," he said seriously. "The Masks don't change you. They just show what's inside you. The magic that's put into them—that *I* put into them, on behalf of the Autarch, and once you are Masked, you will, too—protects us all. You've learned all this in school."

"Because of the Rebellion," Mara said. She closed her eyes and recited from memory, thinking that Tutor Ancilla would be proud—and probably a little surprised—to hear her do so. But she really *did* pay attention ... at least, *some* of the time. "And when the last of the traitors had been executed, the young Autarch made a decree: Henceforth all citizens of Aygrima would be Masked in all public places. For all the long years of the Rebellion powerful Gifted in the service of the Autarch had been secretly developing the magic of the Masks, and now at last they were perfected. Never again would the people of Aygrima suffer as they suffered during the Rebellion. Never again would innocent blood be shed by murderous traitors, for the Masks would reveal all traitorous thoughts to the Watchers, protectors of the people, trained to use their Gifts to read the message of the Mask. Those who would defy our great and benevolent Autarch in future would be discovered and punished before they could act on their traitorous impulses. Blessed be the Autarch. May he guide and protect us forever." She opened her eyes again. "Did I get it right?"

"Perfect," her father said.

"Can the Watchers *really* do that?" she asked. "See what you're thinking?" She thought about Mayson. *Will he someday be able to read my mind?* It was an odd and unsettling thought.

"Not exactly," her father said. "As I understand it, it's more . . . they get a . . . a sense that certain people may be a danger to the regime." He shrugged. "To tell the truth, Mara, I don't know exactly *what* they see when they look at a Mask of someone who might threaten the Autarch. It's a secret, as you'd expect. But whatever it is, if they see it, they will question the wearer of the Mask. If they don't like what they hear . . . well." He grimaced. "Then Traitors' Gate awaits."

Mara flinched. She couldn't help it. She had been forbidden to ever go near Traitors' Gate, which of course meant she'd sneaked up there with Sala, and she'd had several nightmares since involving naked, rotting corpses impaled on spikes. She had no intention of ever going back. The thought she might actually end up as one of those corpses . . . she shuddered.

Her father, though he didn't know she'd been to Traitors' Gate—at least, she *hoped* he didn't—smiled reassuringly and put his hand on hers. "Now, now, you certainly don't have to fear *that*."

"I heard," Mara said, wanting to change the subject,

"that sometimes, if someone does something bad enough, the Mask just . . . shatters."

Her father nodded. "Yes. An outright betrayal of the Autarch would do that. And sometimes, of course, a Masking fails. Almost never for the Gifted," he hastened to add, squeezing her hand. "But sometimes, someone has something wrong, inside, something that makes them bad, or makes them a threat to themselves and others. And the Mask . . . the Mask knows. It refuses to attach itself to that person's face. And he or she becomes one of the unMasked, and we don't see them again." His face turned grim for a moment. She could tell there was something he wasn't telling her—she could read his face like one of her schoolbooks—but then he forced a smile and squeezed her hand even harder. "But none of this is anything to worry about. As beautiful as you are, inside and out, your Mask will always be beautiful, too, to anyone who sees it, from the lowliest peasant all the way up to the Autarch."

Mara smiled at him, but inside she quailed. *And what happens to someone who lied to the Tester about the magic they saw?*

It wasn't a question she could ever ask.

It will be all right, she told herself again. *It will be all right.*

It has to be.

●　●　●

On the night before Sala's fifteenth birthday and Masking, with three months to go until her own, Mara, naked and giggling, shouted to Sala, "Race you to the other side!" and dove into the reflecting pool in the courtyard behind the Waterworkers' Hall. She had a good two lengths' advantage over her friend when she started, but out of the corner of her eye she saw Sala pulling even with her, long limbs flashing in the moonlight, and by the time they reached the other side, Sala was two lengths ahead. Sala pulled herself out, dripping, and turned to sit on the edge of the pool. In the dim light, her red hair looked black. "Hurry up, slowpoke!" she called to Mara as she finally reached the edge, too. Mara lifted herself up, and sat on the marble ledge that surrounded the pool, the stone cold under her bare bottom even though the night was so warm she felt no chill on the rest of her body.

She sighed. Her body was the reason she couldn't beat Sala at swimming, or running, or much of anything else. Oh, her face was pretty enough, she thought—she hoped—at least, boys did take a second look at her in the street. But she was still short and rather . . . she glanced down . . . flat. Sala, on the other hand, was, well, *statuesque* was the word Mara supposed applied. Certainly there were strong similarities between Sala's current appearance, nude and shining, and some of the statues along Processional Boulevard, which led from the main gate of the city up to the Palace.

"Are you scared about your Masking tomorrow?" Mara asked. She kicked at the water, splashing it up in shining silver sheets.

"No," Sala said. She gave Mara a grin. "At least I know I'll have a beautiful Mask."

Mara grinned back. "You'll love it," she assured her friend. She and her father had labored long and hard over it. Mara herself had carefully laid in place the silver filigree that traced twining vines along its gleaming white cheeks and forehead. In the almost two years since her Second Testing, she'd learned everything there was to know about the making of Masks except how to infuse them with magic. She would not learn that until after her own Mask was in place in six weeks' time. Then she would be fully apprenticed to her father, and begin her adult life as a Maskmaker.

Assuming her Gift had finally settled, and assuming that Gift had run true, as her father had seemed so certain it would. She had not been allowed to see magic since her Second Testing.

What if she still saw all the colors? Or no colors?

She shivered. Suddenly she did feel a little cold, although the air remained as milk-warm as ever, unusually so even for late summer.

"Don't worry," Sala said. "We'll still be friends. And you won't be very far behind me, you know. In six weeks, I'll be able to come to your Masking."

"I wish I could come to yours," Mara said, but she knew that was impossible: children were not allowed into the Maskery, the circular temple of white stone, topped with a golden dome, where the Masking ceremonies took place.

"I do, too," Sala said. She shrugged. "But it really won't change anything. It won't change *me*. I'm not Gifted. I've already learned a lot about glassblowing. I'll just keep learning and improving. All it means is I'll have to wear my Mask whenever I go out."

"No more sneaking out at night, though," Mara said. She grinned at her friend, but she felt a strange pang. Tonight wasn't the first time she and Sala had gone skinny-dipping in the Waterworkers' pool, but it would be the last. It was a minor offense for a child to be caught out after curfew. For a Masked citizen . . .

For a Masked citizen, the consequences could be dire. Prison, or . . .

Mara shuddered. *Or Traitors' Gate.*

To be caught out after curfew *probably* wouldn't earn a citizen a one-way trip to the gallows, but there were no guarantees. The one *certain* way to be sent there was to be caught out in public unMasked. From tomorrow on, Sala would never feel the outside air on her face, except in the closed and concealed courtyard of her own home.

"No, no more sneaking out," Sala said. She shrugged. "But we have to grow up sometime."

Mara looked down at herself again, and sighed. "That's what they say."

Sala stood up. "Race you again? I'll spot you four lengths this time."

Mara scrambled to her feet. "You're on." But before she could dive into the water, a voice—a male voice—boomed from behind them.

"Hold it right there!"

Both girls squealed and jumped into the water... from which they were hauled a few moments later by black-Masked Night Watchers who draped them in cloaks, handed them their clothes, and, once they were dressed, separated them and, silent and disapproving, took them to their own homes.

As she endured an endless lecture from her mother about how horribly embarrassed she was and how much disgrace Mara had brought on the family—"And your father the Master Maskmaker, at that!"—Mara's main regret was that she hadn't had a chance to say good-bye to Sala and wish her good luck in her Masking.

I'll see her again soon, she thought as she climbed the ladder to her attic room. *She's just being Masked. It's not like she's dying.*

And soon I'll be Masked, too.

She shivered, and the thick blankets of the bed into which she burrowed a few minutes later did nothing to warm her.

• • •

A week before her fifteenth birthday and her Masking, Mara sat once more on the city's north wall. She remembered sitting there with Mayson before her Second Testing, watching the Autarch and the Child Guards proceed below them through the Outside Market. *By now he's Masked, too, like Sala. A Watcher.*

Glad he wasn't a Watcher yet that night Sala and I got caught skinny-dipping, she thought. Bad enough to be seen naked by strange men. But if *Mayson* had seen them . . .

She shook off the thought. Her bigger worry today was that her *mother* might see her, dressed as she was in what her mother would consider a scandalously short tunic that left her long legs bare and had a tendency to slip off of one suntanned shoulder. Her mother had taken to insisting she wear a proper long skirt and long-sleeved blouse when she went out. "You're not a child anymore, Mara," she'd said. "You'll soon be Masked, and then you'll be an adult. It's time you started acting like one."

Mara glanced over her shoulder, looking up Mask-makers' Way to the green roof of their home. She could see her parents' bedroom window. She wondered if her mother were looking out. *Well, even if she is, it's not like she can pick you out at this distance*, she reassured herself.

She sighed. Her mother would have preferred Mara not to leave the house at all, but she couldn't bear spending day after day locked up there, especially now, with her Masking so close—and the workshop off-limits.

Ever since Healer Ethelda paid a visit, she thought.

She'd been in the workshop, mixing the special clay for a new Mask, when her father had suddenly come in. "Leave that, Mara," he said. "Go downstairs and get something to drink. The Master Healer is here to speak to me."

Obediently—and willingly enough; she *was* getting thirsty—she'd put down the stirring stick, taken off her leather apron, and left the workshop. On the landing she'd come face-to-face with a small woman—only a little taller than herself—wearing a blue Mask (bright blue, unlike the pale blue Mara's mother wore), decorated with green gems. Her robes were that same sky-hue. Even her eyes were blue: they looked at Mara gravely as she gave a small curtsy. "Healer Ethelda," Mara said.

"Mara," said the Healer. "I hope you are well?"

"Very well, thank you."

"Go downstairs, Mara," her father repeated, and she descended to the empty kitchen—her mother was out shopping. She helped herself to bread and cheese and drew a glass of cold water from the pump, wondering what the Healer had come to talk to her father about. *I hope she doesn't take too long*, she thought. *That clay isn't going to mix itself.*

But she'd never finished mixing that clay. Ethelda was closeted with her father for a very long time. She was still there when Mara's mother came back. Mara helped place the bags of meal, jars of oil, onions and redroots, and other foodstuffs from the market into the pantry. She'd washed dishes. She'd weeded the garden. The day had slipped away, and it wasn't until suppertime that Ethelda at last descended, said a brief hello and good-bye to Mara's mother, and slipped out into the darkening street.

Her father came down the stairs soon after. He looked ... shaken. Mara's mother frowned at him. "Charlton?" she said. "Is everything all right?"

"It's fine, Karissa." He gave his wife a brief smile, then turned to Mara. "Mara," he said. "It's only a few weeks until your Masking, and I've decided ..." He stopped and took a deep breath before continuing. "I've decided you should stop helping me. Just until after you're Masked and you're a full apprentice."

She'd been shocked, hadn't known what to say. "But, Daddy, the Masks I'm working on ... that Engineer's Mask is ready for the—"

"I can manage just fine without you for a few weeks, Mara," her father had said. "I've decided it's time to start working on your Mask, and I don't want you to see it."

"But—"

"You heard your father, Mara," her mother said, though Mara did not miss the uncertain glance she'd given her husband. "I'm sure I can find you plenty to keep you occupied around the house."

And that had been that. She hadn't been back in the workshop since. That was bad enough, but worse was the fact she'd hardly seen her father. He spent hours locked in his workshop. He'd stopped coming up to her room to say good night, as he had every night of her life before.

And he'd stopped coming to eat with his daughter and wife, not even for breakfast, which had always been one of their favorite times together as a family, sharing porridge or bread and bacon in the morning sun, sometimes laughing over silly jokes and wordplay, sometimes just sitting in sleepy, silent companionship. *He might as well be in Silverfall*, she thought bitterly: the mining town high in the eastern mountains was famously the most inaccessible place in all of Aygrima, snowed in most of the year.

"He's just busy, Mara," her mother insisted when she asked. "And one of the things he's busy with is your Mask. He wants it to be very special."

"I know," Mara mumbled, but inside she thought, *Busy with my Mask for* weeks? He'd only taken ten days to create a Mask for Stanik, the Guardian of Security and the most powerful man in the Circle, and Guardian Stanik was his *boss*, overseer of all the Maskmakers of Aygrima. *Of course, he had my help*, she thought; but she knew she hadn't been *that* much help to him. She hadn't really done much more than mix glazes and watch the kiln.

It was all very strange, and very disturbing, and strangest and most disturbing of all was the fact that in a week's time, she would be Masked and she still didn't know if her Gift had run true, and if, in fact, she could do the magic required of a Maskmaker.

And that was why she was sitting on the city wall as she had so often in the past, once more dressed in the simple tunic of a child in blatant defiance of her mother, who had seen her go out wearing her staid skirt and blouse, but hadn't seen her slip into the gardening shed and exchange those clothes for this, and leave her sturdy shoes behind to once more run gloriously barefoot. It was her last chance to be a child, after all. In a week, everything would change forever.

Although, she admitted to herself, she might have thought twice about her current attire if the weather had already turned cool. But though harvest had come and gone and the damp, chill Tamita winter must surely follow, for now the sun, beating down from a bright blue sky, still had real heat in it. On a day like today, who could bear to be wrapped up in a woolen skirt and scratchy blouse?

But she glanced uneasily over her shoulder and up the hill again at her green-roofed house, and decided it was time to move. Just in case her mother *could* see her.

She pulled her feet up, stood, and trotted easily along the wall, unconcerned by the sheer drop to hard stone just steps to either side, until she'd reached the next tower, safely out of sight of her house.

With one hand on the tower's smoothed yellow stone, she looked down into the Outside Market again—and froze. That bright-red hair, that blue dress, it had to be . . . !

"Sala!" she yelled at the top of her voice. A birdfruit vendor, a little girl in a long red skirt, and a shirtless boy in a green kilt all looked up at her, but the object of her shout kept walking without so much as a glance her way.

Mara dashed into the tower and down its narrow winding stairs. She burst out through an archway onto the Great Circle Road that made its cobblestoned way all around Tamita just inside the wall. A cart horse snorted and balked, earning her a curse from its driver, but she ignored him and ran as fast as she could to the Market Gate. She dodged through it and then, twisting and turning, slipped through the crowds in the Outside Market like a snakefish through seaweed. Masks of every sort turned her way, some smooth and beautiful, chased with designs that spoke of their occupation (here the red scrollwork of a lawyer, there the crossed silver hammers of a blacksmith); some dull and gray, all decoration long worn away. One or two Gifted looked her way: a blue-Masked Healer, a red-Masked Engineer, his Mask set in a permanent smile but his real lips beneath pressed into a disapproving line.

The black Masks of two Watchers talking to a trembling gray-Masked knife sharpener turned toward her as she ran past, but an instant later she rounded a papermaker's stall and was out of their sight. An old woman whose Mask looked like a bleached skull screeched and swung her cane, but Mara dodged with the ease of long experience and didn't lose a step.

She reached the lane. Sala had been walking in *that* direction. Mara stood on tiptoe, trying to see over the throngs, and glimpsed red hair and blue cloth in front of a baker's stall a hundred feet distant. She dashed that way, and reached the stall just as the red-haired girl dropped a silver coin into the baker's hand and turned away with her basket full of rolls.

"Sala!" Mara gasped out with what little breath she had left, then doubled over, hands on her knees, panting.

Sala turned, and Mara looked up at her snow-white Mask and the red hair, once so flyaway, now piled in an elaborate, coiled coif above the gleaming clay covering her face. Shining silver grapevines curled across the Mask's forehead and down its cheeks, where the red circles on the cheeks marking her as a glassmaker would be added once she had finished her two-year Masked apprenticeship. Mara hadn't seen the Mask since she had applied that silver filigree, and she felt a surge of pride as she looked at it now. *It really is beautiful*, she thought. As it well *should* be: her father, tasked as he was with making all the Masks for the Gifted, only rarely made Masks for the non-Gifted, and those he did were so expensive only the wealthy could afford them, but for his daughter's best friend he had not only made an exception, he had done so free of charge, insisting that Sala and her parents accept the Mask as a gift from Mara and her family.

"Oh," said Sala. "Hello, Mara."

Mara frowned. Sala's voice sounded different: not just slightly muffled, but almost *embarrassed*.

Embarrassed to talk to me? Mara thought. *That's crazy. We've been best friends forever.*

"I haven't seen you since the night the Watchers hauled us out of the Waterworkers' pool," Mara said, her breath coming more easily now. She straightened up. "How's the apprenticeship going? What's Masked life like? I want to know *everything*."

"I am enjoying my apprenticeship very much, thank you," Sala said. "Esterella is an excellent mentor." Her voice remained cool and detached, as though she were making small talk at a party. "And I have become quite accustomed to the Mask. Please thank your father again for me for such a wonderful Masking Day gift." She looked over her shoulder, the now-orange light of the westering sun turning the silver vines in her Mask into lines of fire on the white glaze. "And speaking of Esterella, she must be wondering where I am. I must catch up to her." She glanced back at Mara. "It has been good to see you again, Mara. Once you are Masked, we must get together some time." And then Sala turned and walked away.

Mara gaped after her, as unable to speak as if her breath had been knocked out of her. "Sala!" she finally managed to call, but her friend, already twenty feet away, didn't turn around. "Sala!" she shouted louder, and took a step after her, but a heavy hand landed on her shoulder, restraining her. She twisted around and saw the black, blank mask of a Watcher, eyes glittering deep within the eyeholes.

"Don't bother the citizen, girl," he growled.

She's my best friend! Mara wanted to shout at him, but even as upset as she was, she knew better than to talk back to a Watcher. "Yes, sir," she said. The Watcher lifted his black-gloved hand, and she swallowed, turned, and walked as unhurriedly as she could back toward the Market Gate, certain she could feel his gaze on her the whole way.

Her stomach roiled inside her like the time she had foolishly eaten one of the tiny round chokeberries that grew on the bushes in their backyard. How could Sala have changed so much in such a short time? Just three months ago they'd been laughing together at the Waterworkers' pool. And now Sala was all, "It's been very good to see you again," and "Once you are Masked, we must get together."

Mara felt her face heat. *Not bloody likely. You think you know someone . . .*

It's the Mask, she told herself as she began climbing Maskmakers' Way. *She's got herself a Mask, and now she thinks she's better than me. Even though* everybody *gets a Mask. It's not like they're anything special. I'll have one myself in a week, and it's not going to change me!*

But not for the first time, she wondered if that were really true.

THREE

The Colors of Magic

MARA HOPED AGAINST HOPE that her father would be sitting at the dinner table when she got home, but his place was empty. "Where's Father?"

"At the Palace." Her mother didn't turn from the counter. "Another meeting with Ethelda."

Mara's heart fluttered a little. Her mother claimed all the hours her father had been spending with Ethelda had to do with some changes to the Masks assigned to Healers—a new shade of blue, additional ornamentation— but Mara couldn't help wondering . . .

"He's not . . . sick, is he?" she asked softly, her voice breaking a little. Afraid of the answer, she hadn't dared ask the question before. But with her Masking so close . . .

But to her relief, her mother turned at once and came

to her. She wiped her palms on her yellow apron, then took Mara's hands in her own. "No, darling! No, it's nothing like that. It's just work. That's all."

"Are you sure?" Mara felt her lip trembling. "It's just . . . I've hardly seen him in weeks. And my Masking is coming. He . . ."

Her mother pulled her into a tight, encompassing hug. "It's all right, Mara," she murmured, stroking her hair. "He's not ill. And he misses you, too. He's just busy." She released her, stepped back. "All right?"

Mara, biting her lip, looked into her mother's eyes. She thought, after almost fifteen years, that she would know if her mother were simply telling her a comforting lie. She saw no sign of it.

Of course, her mother could read her face as well as she could read her mother's. "There's something else bothering you, isn't there?"

Mara nodded. "I saw Sala today."

"Did you?" Her mother indicated the table. "Go on, sit down. Your dinner is getting cold."

Mara pulled out her chair and sat down. Back at the counter, her mother spooned mashed redroots onto a plate, poured gravy over them, laid a slice of ham along-side, and turned to the table. "And how is Masked life treating Sala?" She put the steaming plate down on the polished brown wood of the table and went back to the counter for a tumbler of water and a knife and fork. "Is she enjoying her apprenticeship to the glassmaker?"

"She seemed well," Mara said reluctantly, picking up the utensils. "And she said Esterella is an excellent mentor. But she was . . . different."

"Well, she's a grown-up now, Mara."

"It's not just that, it was . . ." Mara hesitated. "Mother, the Mask doesn't change you, does it?"

Her mother, who had just turned around with her own dinner, stopped in surprise. "Mara, you know the answer to that. You're a Maskmaker's daughter, for stars' sake! You've made Masks yourself!"

"Only the outside," Mara said. "I haven't put in the magic." She poked at the ham as her mother sat down opposite her. "I know what I've been told, Mother, but ..."

"Told by your *father*, Mara," her mother reminded her. "I hope you're not suggesting that he hasn't been telling you the truth!"

"No, of course not, I just ..." *I just I wish I could talk to him about it*, she thought, falling silent again. She took a bite of ham and chewed mechanically, hardly tasting it. True, "The Masks don't change you," her father had told her back when he was still talking to her. And yet ...

Sala *had* changed.

It couldn't have been the Mask, Mara tried to reassure herself. *Mother's right. It's just that Sala is working now, she's an apprentice, she has grown-up things to worry about. She could be married and pregnant by this time two years from now!*

And so could I, she realized suddenly, but *that* was such a strange and scary thought that she hurriedly pushed it aside. *It's only ... I miss my friend. And it feels like the Mask took her away.*

Maybe I'll get her back when I'm wearing a Mask, too, she thought; as she would be, in just a few days—well, whenever she was in the street, anyway. *And no more sneaking out in short tunics,* she reminded herself. *From now on it's going to be proper dresses and proper cloaks and proper shoes and proper manners.*

Only a week left to be a child. And after that ... an adult. A new school, new classes with other newly Masked Gifted, in which one of the powerful magicians from the Palace would teach them about the permissible and impermissible uses of their Gifts, the laws restricting magic to the service of the Autarch, and more. *At least I'll be fully apprenticed. I'll learn the final secrets of making Masks. Daddy and I will be working side by side again ...*

Provided I really do have the right Gift ...

That fear never really left her; it hadn't really left her for two years, and it was returning fourfold now that the day of her Masking was so near.

The next time she looked at magic, what would she see?

I could find out. There's magic in Daddy's workshop. Daddy's at the Palace. I know where he hides the spare key. I could sneak in and . . .

The thought shocked her. She couldn't believe she'd had it. Sneak into her father's workshop, when he'd ordered her to stay out of it? Uncover the basin of magic, which he had always refused to open in her presence, explaining that it was expressly forbidden for the un-Masked Gifted to even be in the presence of uncovered magic except during their Tests?

It was wrong.

But it was also tempting.

It wouldn't hurt anything. How could it hurt anything? I wouldn't do anything with the magic. I'd just look. No one will ever know.

She could picture the magic basin clearly in her mind: a bowl of thick black stone, as wide across as her forearm was long, atop a three-legged stand of bronze, its contents hidden by a heavy stone lid. It would be a simple matter to push that lid to one side, not too far, and get a glimpse of the magic within . . .

. . . see what color it was . . .

She found herself, without being aware she had decided to do so, getting up from the kitchen table, the chair legs squawking on the stone floor. "Excuse me," she muttered. Her face felt hot, and she was certain her mother would figure out what she was up to. But her mother just said, "Of course," and kept washing dishes without looking up.

Mara hurried up the smooth-polished stairs of dark brown wood to the closed door of her father's workshop at the first landing. She knelt down in front of it. There was a loose floorboard, up against the wall where no one would tread on it accidentally, with a thin crescent of wood missing along one side, remnant of a knot in the original tree. She stuck a fingernail into that small opening, lifted the floorboard, and from its underside unhooked a big brass key. She'd seen her father take it out of there one very late night when she'd woken to hear a noise downstairs and had crept out of her room to peer into the darkness below. Her father had been at some function in the Palace at which, she guessed, a great deal of wine had been served, and although he had probably thought he was being quiet, in fact he'd been stumbling and banging and grunting enough to wake the dead. Mara doubted he even remembered coming home that night. He certainly had no idea she'd been watching.

But she had, and now the key he had inadvertently revealed to her slipped easily into the lock. She turned it, and it made a snicking sound that caused her heart to leap to her throat; but her mother continued clattering dishes in the kitchen and after a moment of frozen terror she took a deep breath, turned the brass doorknob, pushed the door open, and stepped into her father's workshop.

Ordinarily the yellow light of the oil lanterns hung from the rafters gleamed off the racks of unfinished Masks, spools of gold and silver wire, pots of clay and glaze, the giant kiln in the corner, and the array of tiny blades and hammers and pliers placed neatly above the long workbench of smooth golden wood. But tonight the only light was a faint, faint glow through the window at the far end of the narrow room . . .

. . . and a glimmer, almost invisible, but definitely present, from the basin of magic in the middle of the workshop.

If she had never been in the workshop before, Mara would have hesitated to step into that darkness, afraid of banging her shins or sending something crashing to the floor, alerting her mother to her transgression. But Mara had spent many, many hours in the workshop watching her father craft Masks, learning, in fact, all there was to know about them except for the secret of imbuing them with magic. She knew exactly where everything was, even in the dark. And so she stepped forward, cautiously but without terror, and made her way to the faintly gleaming basin.

The lid sealed it as tightly as always. The faint glow came from the stone of the basin itself, as though it were covered with a thin film of luminescent oil.

Taking a deep breath, Mara reached out with both hands and slid the heavy stone disk away from the edge of the basin.

She looked down, and caught her breath in delight, with dismay close on its heels.

Magic seethed inside the basin. To Mara it looked like a liquid, a liquid heavy as quicksilver, an endlessly shifting mass of twisting, twining color . . .

. . . but still, all colors: none stronger than the others. Her Gift still had not settled. She still could not be certain she would have the ability required to craft Masks like her father.

And her Masking was only days away.

But as she stared down into the magic, her dismay faded, while the delight remained. *It's so beautiful!* Her heart ached at the thought that someday all that beauty would vanish forever, replaced by only one or two colors instead of the endless variety before her now.

Then her dismay returned full-force: not because of what she saw in the magic, but because of what she heard downstairs—the sound of the door opening, and her father's voice, "Karissa?"

"In here, sweetheart," her mother said.

Mara whispered a word she'd heard on the street but never dared to use in her own house before, and quickly pulled the stone lid back over the basin. She hurried to the door . . . then froze. She could tell by the sound of his voice that her father was at the base of the stairs. He'd hear her for sure if she opened the door now.

"Where's Mara?" he said.

"Upstairs in her room," her mother said. A pause. "She misses you," her mother continued, so softly Mara could barely hear her through the door. "She doesn't understand why you won't talk to her." Another pause. "I miss you, too." Yet another pause. "I don't understand, either."

"I told you," her father said. *He sounds worn out*, Mara thought, her breath catching in her throat. *As if he's at the end of his strength. Maybe he really is sick!* "I'm busy. Working on her Mask. I can't—"

"You're always working on a Mask," her mother interrupted. "I don't see why this one should be—"

"I don't want to discuss it," her father snapped. "Is there anything to eat?"

A very long silence followed. "Bread. Cheese," her mother said. "Nothing hot."

"Fine." And then, to her relief, Mara heard her father's steps move away from the base of the stairs. Quick as a frightened mouse, she nipped out, closed the door of the workshop silently behind her, locked it, put the key back in its hiding place, and fled: up the stairs, down the upper hallway, then up a final flight of stairs as steep as a ladder and through a trapdoor into her own room.

She closed the trap behind her and sat down on her narrow bed, beneath the thick black beams that supported the roof, sloping down sharply to her right. Head in her hands, elbows on her knees, she stared at the tiny blue flame flickering inside the glass tube of the gas lamp in the corner. The pilot light illuminated nothing but itself, but she left the lamp turned down, content to sit in the deepening dark, leavened only by the fading glow through the skylight window over her bed.

Warning bells rang in the streets, deep, slow, ominous: curfew for the children of Tamita, and a warning to the Masked that they must hasten home or else make their way to the well-lit boulevards lined with shops, restaurants, and theaters that were the only streets in the city where even the Masked could congregate after dark.

The Night Watchers not only patrolled the boulevards, they patrolled everywhere else, ensuring that no one lurked or lingered in the darkened alleys and winding lesser streets. The Watchers' black cloaks, Masks, and clothing made them almost invisible in the darkness. Some said they carried magic that could *really* make them invisible, but Mara had watched the Watchers patrolling the shadowy streets too many nights to believe they had mystical powers: not only the night she and Sala were caught skinny-dipping, but many other nights when they *weren't*.

Of course, all Watchers *supposedly* had enough of the Gift to read Masks, but Mara wondered if that were true. She remembered what Tutor Ancilla had told them. "There are maybe twenty thousand people in Tamita," she'd said. "An enormous number. But at any given time there are no more than two hundred who have the Gift. Only half of those have it in great enough measure to actually use magic. And fewer than half of *those* can use it to any great purpose."

"Aren't you special," Sala had whispered to Mara, who had stuck out her tongue at her.

Of course, the ability to read Masks might not require enough Gift to actually *manipulate* magic like that gathered in the basin in her father's workshop. But even so, there were hundreds of Watchers. They served as police, army, and bodyguards. They could not possibly all have the Gift, even in small amount.

The trouble was, Mara had once overheard one adult mutter to another after a Watcher had passed by, casting the customary chill on conversation, you could never be sure whether the one staring at *your* Mask had it or not.

Still, Gifted or not, the Watchers couldn't be everywhere, especially at night. And so sneaking out into the night—at least as long as she was still unMasked—held no terror for Mara.

Quite the opposite, in fact.

She rose, turned, and stepped up onto her bed, which

sagged alarmingly under her weight in a way it hadn't just a year previously. *Another peril of growing up,* she thought. Reaching overhead, she took hold of the wooden frame of the skylight window and pushed it sharply to the left. *On the other hand,* that's *a lot easier than it used to be.* The window shifted, there was a click, and then the heavy wood-framed glass came loose in her hands. Mara tugged it free of the skylight, bent over to set it carefully onto her bed, then straightened again and took a deep breath of the cool evening air flowing down from above. But before she went out . . .

She jumped down off the bed, pulled off her skirt and blouse, tossed them on the floor, rummaged in the trunk at the foot of her bed for a tunic like the one she'd worn that afternoon—only even shorter, she discovered as she pulled it on—then stepped back up onto the mattress. A jump, a wriggle, a scramble, and she was crouched on the rounded green tiles of the roof. Careful not to dislodge them and send them skittering to noisy destruction, she crept down to the eaves. From there it was an easy step to the top of the wall that ran past the house on that side, closed off the backyard, and stretched a full fifty yards farther along the alley past other houses and yards.

Bare feet sure and steady on the familiar stones, she ran the length of the wall, swung into and down from a handy tree at its end, and then paused, barely even breathing hard, in the shadowed alley. She looked both ways for Night Watchers, saw none, and started running.

She didn't have a destination. She just wanted to run, to be free, to be a child, to take deep breaths of air unblocked by the Mask that would soon cover her face whenever she went out, marking her as a grown-up, marking her as a full-fledged citizen . . .

. . . marking her, if she did not conform, did not obey, did not do everything a responsible member of the community was expected to do, as someone to be watched, someone not to be trusted . . . someone the Watchers might decide at any moment to remove from the community for good.

All her life she'd looked forward to her Masking. Or *thought* she had. But now that it was so close ... now, it felt more like an impending prison sentence, as if she were enjoying her final few days of freedom before bars of propriety, harder and colder than any steel, imprisoned her forever.

And so she ran with nowhere to run to, cautious enough to keep an eye out for Watchers, not cautious enough to worry about exactly where she was ... until she suddenly turned a corner into a dead end, three tall blank walls towering in front of her ...

... and heard echoing behind her, in the street she had just left, the unmistakable sound of boots on the cobblestones.

Mara swore. Her mother would *never* forgive her if she were dragged home by the Night Watchers this close to her Masking. Last time she'd had to scrub every floor in the house on her hands and knees ... twice. This time ... her imagination failed her, which was probably just as well: whatever her mother came up with was likely to be far worse.

She looked wildly around, and saw a door—a trapdoor, really. Square, about three feet on a side, set waisthigh, black as the wall all around it, it obviously opened into someone's coal chute.

Praying it wasn't locked, she ran over to it and shoved at it with the palms of her hands. It didn't move.

The footsteps echoed closer. The Night Watchers would turn the corner any second ...

She rammed her shoulder into the door. Wood splintered, and it swung inward. She held it open against the force of the spring trying to close it. Staring at the pitchblack square leading who-knew-where, she hesitated; then she heard a man's voice from the street say, "Did you hear something?" and in sudden terror threw herself headfirst through the opening.

The door banged shut behind her. In absolute darkness she slid down a metal chute, arms outstretched and legs spread to try to slow her descent.

She shot out of the chute and fear wrenched a scream from her as she fell—

—not, fortunately, very far; but all the same, coal really wasn't the softest thing in the world to land on. She tumbled over and over in a welter of rock and finally came to rest on a hard stone floor, bruised, breathless, no doubt filthy, but not seriously hurt. Making good use of several more interesting words she'd learned on the street, she sat up.

Then she yelped in terror as a voice out of the darkness said, "Who's there?"

FOUR

The Boy in the Basement

FOR A MOMENT Mara didn't answer, too shocked to say a word.

"I know you're there, I heard you," the voice said: a young voice, a boy's voice. "I warn you, I've got a knife—"

"So do I!" Mara squeaked. A lie, of course, but *he* wouldn't know that. "What are you doing down here?"

"What are *you* doing down here?" the boy countered. Mara thought he was about ten feet away. His voice didn't echo much; the cellar must be small.

"It's after curfew," Mara said. "There were Night Watchers coming."

"You're not Masked?" The boy sounded relieved.

"No," Mara said. *Not for another week.* "Are you?"

"No!" The word exploded from him. "No! And I won't be, either."

Mara stared at the place where the voice came from. "But—"

"The Masks are evil. The Masks are . . . are wrong. I won't wear one."

"But when you turn fifteen—"

"I *am* fifteen," the boy said. "I turned fifteen a week ago."

"But then—"

"I ran away. The night before my Masking. I've been hiding ever since."

Mara gasped. "But—but if they catch you—"

"They won't catch me," the boy said. "This is my last night here. I have a way out of the city."

"You have to be Masked in the country, too!"

"Watchers can't be everywhere," the boy said. "There are places you can go. People who . . ." He stopped. "Who are you?" Suspicion flooded his voice. "Are you a spy for the Watchers?" She heard a shuffling sound, and then his voice sounded much closer. "What are you doing out after curfew?"

"I'm not a spy!" Mara protested. If this boy had run away from his Masking, he probably really *did* have a knife . . . and if he thought she might turn him over to the Watchers he'd probably *use* it, too. "Honestly! I just sneaked out. For fun."

"Fun for you," the boy growled. "Life and death for me if you led the Night Watchers here."

"If they'd seen me stuff myself into that chute, they'd be down here already!"

Silence for a moment. "I suppose so." Another pause. "What's your name?"

Mara hesitated, but saw no reason to lie. "Mara," she said. "What's yours?"

"Keltan," the boy said instantly.

"Keltan?" Mara blinked. "That's the name of the Autarch's horse!"

"You don't think I'm going to tell you my *real* name, do you?" "Keltan" countered. "Besides, it's a beautiful horse. The only good thing *about* the Autarch is that horse."

Mara gasped. She'd never heard *anyone* criticize the Autarch before. *But I suppose if you're already risking your life . . .*

"Why wouldn't you take your Mask?" she said. "Why would you run away? You'll be a fugitive the rest of your life if you—"

"Because," the boy said. "The Mask changes you."

Mara, hearing her own fears coming from someone else's lips, fell silent.

"Oh, they *tell* you it doesn't. They say it only shows what's inside you, that it's for public safety, so the Watchers know who's a threat, blah blah blah. 'You'll be the same person afterward,' they tell you. But it's not true!" The exclamation came out like a curse. "My best friend was Masked two months ago. *And he's not my friend anymore.*"

Like Sala, Mara thought, feeling a chill that had nothing to do with the dank cellar. "He'll be a full apprentice now," she said, echoing her mother's words. "More responsibility. He's an adult. That's all—"

"That's *not* all," Keltan snarled. "He's not acting like an *adult*. He's acting like *a completely different person*. He acts like we never did all the things we did. Like he doesn't remember all the fun we had. All the secrets we shared. He . . ." He stopped. "He told me to go away and quit bothering him. He said he didn't want to see me again. That was the day before I was supposed to be Masked."

"And that was enough to make you run away?" Mara said. "To risk your *life?*"

"There are other reasons," Keltan said. "But they're none of your business." Suddenly he was right beside her. His hand found her wrist in the dark and squeezed it so hard she gasped in pain. "My knife is right here," he said. "Now tell me why you're *really* here, 'Mara.' If that's your real name. And don't . . ." He jerked her arm, hard. ". . . lie."

"I told you the truth!" Mara squeaked. "I just came out for fun. We used to do it all the time—"

"We?" Keltan jerked her arm again.

"My friend Sala and me!"

"And where is *she?*"

Gone, Mara thought, remembering how Sala had cut her dead in the market that morning. *Like your friend.* "Masked," she said out loud. "Masked."

Keltan let go of her as suddenly as he had grabbed her. She rubbed her sore wrist. "Then you *know.* They're lying to us. The Masked ones. The grown-ups. The Mask-makers—"

"No," Mara said. "My father—" She bit off her defense before it fully emerged, but not soon enough. Suddenly Keltan had her wrist again.

"What about him?"

"Nothing!"

He squeezed so hard she couldn't stifle another gasp. *"What about him?"*

"He's a Maskmaker," she yelped. "I'm going to be his apprentice."

His hand loosened on her arm. "You've got the Gift?"

"Yes! And I *know* the Masks don't change you. My father told me so."

"And you believe him?"

"He's my father!"

Keltan snorted. "All the more reason not to trust him. He *wants* you to change. He wants you to be a good little drone in the Autarch's hive like him, like all the rest of them. *Especially* if you have the Gift. You *have* to be obedient, and the Mask will make sure you are."

"But my father is making my Mask himself."

"So? Doesn't he wear a Mask?"

Mara said nothing.

"You see? It's a perfect scheme. The Masked creating more Masked, while the Autarch rules with an iron fist and nobody is ever able to challenge him, or even *think* about challenging him. Except for the . . ."

He stopped again.

"The–the what?" Mara asked in a small voice.

"The unMasked Army," the boy said, barely whispering.

If he'd shouted obscenities Mara would have been less shocked. "They're a myth! A tale from a storybook!"

"No," Keltan insisted. "They're real. And I know how to find them."

"How would—"

"I'm not telling you anything else." He moved away from her. "Get out of here. Go."

"Love to," Mara said fervently. "But how, exactly?"

His voice came from even farther away. "You might try the door." A click, and for the first time, light entered the cellar: faint, flickering, but bright as a torch to her eyes after so long in the dark. "I can get you back on the street. After that, you're on your own."

"I can find my way home," Mara said. She scrambled to her feet, stray bits of coal clattering to the floor.

But Keltan still blocked her way, a black silhouette in the doorway. Something in his hand glinted as he pointed it at her. He hadn't been bluffing about the knife. "Don't tell anyone you met me. I'm warning you—"

"I won't tell," Mara said. "Who would believe me? I don't even know your real name."

She squinted at him, but with the light behind him, she still couldn't see his features. He was a good head taller than she was and his hair stuck out in all directions, shining blond in the illumination behind him.

"You'd better not," he said. He pointed the knife at her. "And don't think you can send anyone back here to find me. I won't be staying. I've got other hiding places."

"I already said I won't tell anyone," Mara snapped. "For one thing, I'd have to admit I was out after curfew!"

Keltan turned abruptly. "This way."

The light came from a barely alight gas lamp at the end of a short corridor and the bottom of a flight of stairs. Keltan led her up the steps to a landing. The stairs turned and continued up, but he stopped there, by a bolted wooden door. He put a finger to his lips. She could see his face a little better now. Thin and freckled, it was punctuated by a sharp nose. He wore a short black jacket over a nondescript white shirt above equally ordinary trousers and plain brown boots. Coal dust smudged his face.

She looked down at herself. Her tunic, arms, legs, and feet were every bit as black. *How am I going to hide all this from Mother?* she thought in a bit of a panic, then pushed the thought away. She'd worry about her mother once she'd gotten past the Night Watchers.

Keltan eased the bolt back and opened the door a crack. He peered out. "All clear." He pulled the door further ajar. "Go," he said. "Get home." He paused, looking at her, his gaze traveling from her face down the length of her skinny body to her dirty bare legs and feet and back up again. She felt herself blushing and wished she'd worn a longer tunic. "You're older than I thought," he said, looking into her face once more. She found herself wondering what color his eyes were; she couldn't tell in the dim light. "Your Masking must be soon."

"Pretty soon," Mara said.

"Think about what I've said," Keltan said. "You won't be the same person after you're Masked. You could run, too. The unMasked Army would—"

"The only place I'm running is home," Mara said. "Good-bye." She slipped out into the street, looked up and down its length to make sure it was deserted, then turned and said, impulsively, "Good luck." Then she darted away.

She had no more encounters with Night Watchers, and now that she was paying attention, quickly found her way back to familiar streets. Soon she was clambering up through the tree onto the wall behind her house; a moment after that she was on the roof and letting herself down onto her bed. She lifted the skylight window back into place, then stepped quietly down onto the floorboards to avoid any thump, stripped off her soot-stained clothes, and stuffed them under her bed to dispose of later. Then she washed herself as best she could with the cold water from her basin, pulled on a clean nightgown, and climbed beneath the covers. Her stuffed cat Stoofy, who had shared her bed since she was a baby, lay by her pillow; she pulled him to her chest and held him tightly, staring up at the square of stars she could see through the skylight's glass.

Keltan's warnings about the Mask uncomfortably echoed her own doubts. But . . . *run away?* If she missed her Masking, she'd be sentenced to death. Whatever life was like behind the Mask, it had to be better than no life at all!

She hoped Keltan was right, and an unMasked Army was waiting to take him in. Because otherwise . . .

. . . otherwise, his naked body might soon be hanging from the gallows by the Traitors' Gate.

She shuddered. No. *She* would not run. She would take the Mask, just as she was supposed to, join her father as his apprentice, and put away her childhood. There really was no other choice.

Besides, she thought muzzily as sleep at last claimed her, *Father has been working so hard on my Mask . . . I can't let him down.*

And I can't wait to see it.

FIVE

The Masking

THE NEXT MORNING Mara stumbled down to breakfast, yawning and stretching, once again wearing the staid blue skirt and white blouse her mother preferred, though she hadn't gone so far as to put on shoes. To her delight, her father stood at the counter, his back to her.

"Daddy!" She ran up behind him and threw her arms around him. "Eat breakfast with me!"

She felt him stiffen, freezing in the middle of whatever he was doing. She squeezed him tighter.

"Let go of me, sweetie," he said, his voice a little hoarse.

She gave him a final squeeze, then let go and stepped back. He turned around, a steaming mug of black-bean tea in his hand, and she almost gasped: unshaven, with dark shadows under his eyes, he looked like he hadn't slept in days. "I wish I could, Mara, but I've got too much work to do." He didn't seem to want to meet her eyes: his gaze slid past her, and he started toward the stairs.

"My Mask, right?" Mara called after him.

He stopped, one foot on the stairs. "That's right," he said after a moment.

"What does it look like?" Mara knew that by tradition no one knew what their Mask looked like until the moment it was presented to them, but she was desperate to keep her father talking to her, starved for the sound of his voice. "Is it beautiful?"

From where she stood, she could just see the mug of tea in his right hand. It trembled. "It is what it is," he said at last, still without looking at her. Then he resumed climbing the stairs. A moment later she heard his work-shop door close—and lock.

Mara blinked back tears. *At least when I'm Masked, I'll have my father back.*

She went to the sideboard, where her mother, who seemed to be out, had left cheese and bread and a couple of hard-boiled eggs. She took an egg, a chunk of cheese, and a slice of bread back to the table, poured oil into a small bowl, dipped the bread into it, and chewed on her breakfast while also chewing over the conversation with the boy in the cellar the night before. By morning light, his fears about the Masks seemed silly, and so did hers. So Sala had been a bit standoffish. So what? People changed. Sala really *did* have more responsibilities now. She was officially an adult, and adults *were* different than children, weren't they? It wasn't a bad thing. It was just the way things were.

Before you know it, she'll be married, she thought. *Before you know it, so will I. And then we'll have children of our own . . .*

Again she pushed that uncomfortable thought aside. Time enough to worry about *that* later.

Much later.

The important thing was that when they were both Masked, she and Sala could be friends again. As for all that stuff about the Masks changing people . . . nonsense, and she knew it. Her *father* was making her Mask, and he would never make something that would harm her. He might be a bit preoccupied right now, but she knew he loved her. She had a lifetime of memories of cuddles, of storytelling and laughter, of running to Daddy for comfort when she'd skinned her knee or been stung by a bee, to prove it. *Whatever he makes for me will be beautiful*.

As for "Keltan," well, he was . . . delusional, that was the word. *All that crazy talk about the unMasked Army. The unMasked Army is a myth!* She felt sorry for the boy, risking his life for nothing. And she *would* keep her word and not tell anyone she'd met him. He might be crazy, but she didn't think that would matter to the Watchers, and she didn't want him to end up hanging on a gibbet outside the Autarch's Palace.

She shuddered at the thought. Ugh. Not the best thing to think about at breakfast. She pushed away what was left, half a slice of oil-soaked bread and a good-sized chunk of boiled egg, got up, and took the dish to the sideboard. She put the leftover food into the compost, then pumped water into the bronze sink and fired the rock-gas burner underneath it. As the water heated, she looked out at the bright blue sky. *Another warm day*, she thought, and her arms and legs itched at the thought of wearing a long skirt and long sleeves. But she felt guilty about sneaking out the night before, and promised herself she'd be extra-good all day to make up for it.

Besides, she only had two short tunics: one was wadded up in the garden shed, and the other was crumpled up under her bed, black with coal dust.

The water wasn't as hot as her mother would have made it, but hot enough for Mara. She turned off the burner, took the hog's-bristle brush from its hook just below the windowsill, and began scrubbing her dirty dishes. *I'll have to figure out some way to wash that tunic*, she thought. *And my sheets. They were black when I—*

"Good morning, Mara," her mother said from behind her. She jumped, then turned to see her mother smiling at her from the archway leading into the front room.

Mara forced a laugh. "You scared me!" She hoped she didn't look as guilty as she felt. "Good morning, Mother."

"Come in here," her mother said. "I have something to show you."

Mara dried her hands on the blue towel hanging on a peg beside the window and went over to her mother. "What is it?"

"Close your eyes," her mother said.

Mara blinked at her, then giggled and said, "All right." She closed her eyes. Her mother took her hand and led her into the front room.

"Now . . . open them."

Mara opened them, and gasped.

In a patch of the bright morning light that poured through the diamond panes of the tall windows stood a dressmaker's dummy, wearing the most beautiful dress Mara had ever seen.

Shimmering green, sparkling with tiny glittering stones sewn into the fabric, it seemed almost to float above the dummy. It had a high waist and a low back and no sleeves. A shawl, so delicate it might have been made of blue smoke, its fringe glittering with more of the tiny gems, more drifted above than hung from the shoulders. On the floor beneath the dummy rested two silver shoes, with open toes and high heels.

Mara took it all in with an open mouth, then suddenly remembered to breathe. "For me?"

"For you," said her mother. "For your Masking."

"Oh, Mommy!" Mara flung her arms around her mother and squeezed her tight. "It's beautiful!"

"Would you like to try it on?" her mother said.

"Would I!"

She dropped her skirt and blouse where she stood,

then, wearing only her thin drawers, pulled on the dress. Her mother watched her, a strange expression of mixed amusement and sadness playing around her lips. When Mara had everything on, tottering a bit on the heels, the shawl over her shoulders, her back feeling daringly exposed, she looked at her mother and said, "How do I look?"

"You're beautiful," her mother said. Her eyes suddenly filled with tears. "My little girl . . ."

"Get Daddy," Mara said happily. "He should see—"

Her mother wiped her eyes, and shook her head with a smile. "No. He won't tell me anything about your Mask. Says he wants it to be a surprise. Well, let's make *this* a surprise for *him*. The first time he sees you in it, let it be on your birthday."

Mara laughed. "I can't wait to see his face." She looked down at herself. "I wish I had a mirror."

"Milady has only to ask," her mother said. Mara had been so taken with the dress she hadn't even noticed the tall, cloth-covered object in the corner. Her mother pulled the cloth away, revealing the full-length mirror that normally stood in her parents' room, a marvelously clear glass that had been a gift from a wealthy merchant in appreciation for a particularly fine Mask made for his Gifted daughter.

Mara looked at herself, and her breath caught in her throat. "I look like a grown-up!" *Well, a very* skinny *grown-up*, she amended. She needed to fill out quite a bit more in certain crucial areas before she could *really* show off the dress to its best effect.

"Wait until we have your hair done properly, and add a necklace and bracelets," her mother said. "And then the Mask . . ." She paused. "You know that the Autarch will likely be present for your Masking."

Mara's breath caught. "What?" She turned to look at her mother in wonder.

Her mother nodded. "It's true. For the last few months he has made a point of attending the Maskings of the

Gifted. Your father attends many as well, of course, as a guest of the family, and in appreciation for his work. He has seen the Autarch many times." She started to say something else; then stopped. "Many times," she repeated after a moment.

Mara stared at her. "I never dreamed . . ."

"It is a great honor," her mother said.

In that moment, Mara's fears about the upcoming Masking evaporated. And the next few days, passing in a whirlwind of preparation, left no time for doubt. There were visits to the hairdresser, the manicurist . . . after which she began wearing shoes; she didn't want to damage her toenails, which suddenly looked prettier than she'd ever imagined toenails *could* look . . . and the caterers. Two other children would be Masked at the same ceremony, but each family would hold its own separate reception afterward: and since Mara was the daughter of Tamita's Master Maskmaker, *her* reception had to be top-tier, indeed.

Yet through all the planning, the decorating of the house with strings of silver sequins and garlands of preserved passionflowers of red and yellow and white, one person remained conspicuously absent: her father.

"Are you *sure* Daddy is all right?" Mara asked her mother as they worked in the kitchen just two days before the Masking. "The last time I saw him, he looked so tired."

Her mother, polishing silver at the washbasin, remained silent for a moment. "I told you," she finally said. "He's not ill. He's just . . . preoccupied." She put aside a gleaming knife and picked up a tarnished fork. "And I think I know why."

"Really?" Mara had her own polishing task: to make sure none of the crystal goblets had even the tiniest water spot to mar their glittering perfection. She lifted the one she held up to her eyes, peering critically through it at the window. "Why?"

Her mother moved on to a spoon. "It's you."

"Me?" Mara put down the goblet and stared at her. "Huh?"

"You're his little girl," her mother said. "But after the Masking . . . well, you'll still be his daughter. But you won't be a little girl anymore. You'll be an adult. You'll wear your Mask whenever you go out, and before you know it there'll be some young man courting you, and then . . ." She sighed. "It's the way of the world, and there's nothing to be done about it. But it's hard. Hard for me, too. But I think it's even harder for your father. For *all* fathers."

Mara picked up the next goblet and rubbed it with her soft white cloth. "Was it like that for your father?" Mara had never known her grandparents, who had died before she was born, but knew her mother's father had been a dye merchant, the success of his business bringing the family north to Tamita just before her mother was Masked. His warehouse still stood down by the Gate, although she didn't know who owned it now: she'd seen big black wagons roll out of it, but had no way of knowing what they carried.

"Yes," her mother said sadly. "He was different, after I was Masked. Like he didn't know how to talk to me anymore. And I guess I didn't really know how to talk to him after that, either. And before we ever figured it out, he and Mom got sick, and . . ." She pressed her lips together, and resumed polishing the silver, harder than ever.

Mara said nothing more about it, but in her heart she swore she wouldn't let that happen to *her*. *The Masking won't change me*, she promised herself. *And it won't change our family. We're still a family. We'll* always *be a family. Nothing can change* that.

And then, as if time had suddenly leaped forward, it was the day of the Masking itself.

Mara saw her father again at last, in the front room as she and her mother came down that morning after spending an hour on Mara's hair and makeup. His expression when she appeared in her beautiful dress was not at all what she expected. She saw a flash of the pride and wonder she'd hoped for, but then it vanished, as though shutters had been slammed closed across a brightly lit window. All that remained was the same withdrawn look of fatigue she'd seen a few days earlier at breakfast.

"You're beautiful," he said, but almost as if the words hurt him.

"Isn't she?" her mother said. "My little girl. The Autarch will be—"

"The Autarch won't be there," her father said. As Mara's mother gasped, he turned away and picked up his Mask from the stand by the front door.

"What?" her mother cried. "But the Autarch has come to almost all of the Gifted Maskings for the past—"

"Almost all," her father said. "Not quite all. And this one . . . he has chosen to stay away from." He settled his Mask on his face, and only then turned to look at them again, his expression hidden by the smooth copper surface. "But there will be another distinguished guest," he continued. "Ethelda, the Chief Healer of the Palace. Healer of the Autarch himself. She will attend in the Autarch's place."

"Ethelda?" Mara's mother said, sounding hurt and bewildered, and Mara couldn't blame her. *Daddy is already spending as much time with Ethelda as he does with us. Now she's coming to my Masking?*

A horrible thought struck Mara. Could her father be . . . be unfaithful? Her stomach fluttered at the very idea. No. It couldn't happen.

But then why wasn't the Autarch coming to her Masking? Why was Ethelda coming instead?

It's because I lied about the magic I see, she thought suddenly. *The Autarch knows. Maybe this Ethelda does, too. Maybe Daddy does, too. Maybe that's why he's been so distant. I don't have the Gift at all. Or at least, not enough. Maybe I won't be able to use it all. I won't be able to be my father's apprentice. . . .*

All those thoughts raced through her mind in an instant, in the time it took her mother to press her lips together and then lift and don her own her Mask, pale blue with a pattern of white stars on the cheeks. Their true expressions hidden behind faint smiles of magical clay, Mara's parents led her outside, and for the last time, Mara stepped into the cool morning air with her face uncovered.

They climbed silently up Maskmakers' Way to the Maskery's walled compound. The bronze-bound wooden gate in the tall stone fence stood open. Inside, rather than the cobblestoned courtyard she had expected, Mara saw a riot of color, flowering bushes growing in profusion on manicured lawns beneath tall trees whose leaves rustled in the light breeze. Liquid trills of birdsong filled the space, as though avian composers had been specially commissioned to mark the august occasion.

The midmorning sun glinted off a path of crushed white stone that led to the Maskery, a circular building of white marble, topped by a golden dome and surrounded by a slender-columned portico.

The other two children being Masked that day already waited by the Maskery door: a boy and a girl Mara had never met. Though they obviously shared a birthday, they hadn't shared a tutor. The girl, far more buxom than Mara, wore a shamelessly low-cut red dress that hugged her hips. The boy, all in black from head to toe, looked more like a twelve-year-old than someone who had just turned fifteen. A heavy dusting of freckles stood out in stark relief on his paper-white face, framed by big ears. He kept swallowing and clenching and unclenching his fists. Mara just hoped he wouldn't be sick. *That* would certainly take some of the shine off the proceedings.

She didn't feel nervous at all, she told herself, even as a bead of sweat slid down her exposed back. And she had a much nicer dress than the other girl, even if she didn't fill it out in quite the same way.

Two Watchers in expressionless black Masks flanked

the Maskery door. The door itself, though twice as tall as Mara, was so narrow that only one person would be able to pass through it at a time. Solid bronze, bearing high-relief images of four Masks, one above the other, it gleamed dully in the sunlight, far outshone by the Masker waiting in front of it: like Tester Tibor, he wore yellow, bright as a daffodil, from his Mask to his hooded robe to his sandaled feet. Even his toenails were painted yellow, Mara noted, then quickly raised her eyes and looked straight ahead again, feeling it must be somehow improper to be examining the toes of a Masker.

They all formed a line in front of the door, the Masker at the head, then the boy, the other girl, and Mara. The witnesses—her parents, a younger couple that seemed to be the girl's parents, and an older couple she thought must be the boy's grandparents—brought up the rear.

They stood there in silence for what seemed to Mara a very long time, until a final witness came up the white stone path from the Gate.

The newcomer, not much taller than Mara, wore a long white robe, belted with blue. Blue shoes slipped in and out from beneath the robe's blue-embroidered hem as she walked. Blue also Masked her face; green gems glittered on the forehead and cheeks.

Ethelda. Mara's gaze swung to her mother, who took one quick look at the newcomer, and then turned to face forward again. Mara wondered what expression lay beneath the shining pale blue surface of her Mask.

"Healer Ethelda," said the Masker, gravely. "You are here as a witness for the Autarch, long may He reign?"

"I am," Ethelda said. Her voice sounded slightly breathless, as though she had run most of the way from the Palace, whose tall golden walls loomed above them atop the crest of Fortress Hill.

The Masker nodded, then turned toward the door. Though he didn't touch it, it swung silently inward. One by one, they stepped inside.

The first thing Mara noticed was the sound of running

water, issuing from the dimness beyond the door. As her turn came to enter the Maskery, she discovered the source: just inside, a bridge arched over a shallow moat about five feet wide, filled with water that tumbled foaming out of golden spouts, shaped like the heads of mountain cats, set at regular intervals around the Maskery's curved white marble walls.

Between the spouts burned white torches in golden sconces, their yellow flames the only source of light — except for the eyes of the golden mask at the very top of the dome, fashioned exactly, Mara saw at once, like the Mask of the Autarch. (Although on those rare occasions she had seen the Autarch, his eyes had not actually blazed with light like the eyes of *this* Mask, lit from behind by a skylight.)

At the center of the chamber rose a circular dais perhaps ten feet in diameter and two feet high, covered with gleaming white tiles that contrasted with the blue tiles of the main floor. Beyond the dais, white-tiled stairs led down through an opening in the floor. More torchlight flickered in the underground corridor beyond.

Mara had been told what would happen, so she knew to follow the Masker to the edge of the dais, but not to step up onto it until called. The three candidates stood side by side while the Masker took his place in the middle of the dais. The Watchers stood to either side of him. The Witnesses spread out behind the candidates, several steps back.

On a table beside the Masker rested three lumps, each covered with cloth of gold. Mara looked at them and licked dry lips. One of those, she knew, was her Mask.

The Masker looked down at the three children. "Perik Adder, come to be Masked."

The boy jerked forward so suddenly he almost tripped over the edge of the dais, but caught himself just in time and stepped up onto the white tiles. He faced the Masker, his hands, Mara saw from behind, working more convulsively than ever.

The Masker turned to the table and pulled the cloth off the nearest lump. A white Mask, its cheeks and forehead marked with red stars, stared sightlessly at the ceiling. *Not one of ours*, Mara thought disapprovingly. She made a mental note to never make anything that ugly.

The Masker raised the Mask in both hands, and turned back to Perik. "Perik Adder, you have reached the age of fifteen years. It is now the will of the Autarch that you become a full citizen of Aygrima, with all the duties and responsibilities that entails, and that you serve him and his heirs for the rest of your life. Do you accept the will of the Autarch?"

Of course he does, Mara thought. *He has to get his Mask. He can't leave here without one.*

"I do," the boy said.

"Should you prove false, the Mask you are about to receive will reveal your treachery to the Autarch's Watchers," the Masker warned. "Serve the Autarch well, and you will live a long and happy life in his service. But be untrue, and that life is forfeit. I ask you for the second time, in the full knowledge of these truths, do you accept the will of the Autarch?"

Was it Mara's imagination, or did the boy hesitate? But it was only for a second, if he did.

"I do."

"So that there can be no mistake, for the Autarch does not want in his service those who do not come to it freely, I ask you for the third and final time: do you accept the will of the Autarch?"

The eyes of the golden Mask overhead dimmed suddenly as a cloud passed in front of the sun.

"I do," said the boy.

The Masker inclined his head. "Then I welcome you to full citizenship, to adulthood, and to the service of the Autarch; and in recognition of your thrice-made vow, I present you with this Mask, symbol of your devotion, guardian of your thoughts."

He turned the Mask and settled it gently onto the

boy's face. The boy gasped. Though it appeared to be made of glazed, fired clay—though in fact, as Mara knew well, it *was* made of glazed, fired clay—the Mask *squirmed* as it touched Perik Adder's face. Then, abruptly, the movement stopped, and the Mask looked exactly like his face had looked—except, of course, in white clay. The boy swayed for a moment, then straightened; he turned to face the Witnesses. Polite applause pitter-pattered through the domed chamber. Mara glanced behind her, and saw the older couple hugging.

"You may join your family," the Masker said, and Perik Adder stepped down.

The other girl—Jilna Patterner was her name, and a very silly name it was, too, Mara thought—was next. Her Masking proceeded exactly as Perik's had. She stepped down from the dais, wearing a white Mask like the boy's, though hers was marked with little pink roses on the cheeks (Mara didn't roll her eyes at the sight, but she wanted to).

And then ...

"Mara Holdfast, come to be Masked."

Even though she'd known that call was coming, Mara's heart skipped a beat. Bearing herself as straight and proud as she could, she stepped up onto the dais. The Masker turned to the table and pulled the cloth off the last lump there, and Mara gasped. She had never seen a more beautiful Mask: gleaming, copper-colored, with rubies forming a fiery tiara across the forehead, more rubies sparkling like flickering flames on the cheeks. Tears started in her eyes. *Oh, Daddy!*

The Masker lifted that magnificent Mask and turned to face her. "Mara Holdfast, you have reached the age of fifteen years. You have been tested, and found to have the Gift." Mara couldn't turn around to see, but she hoped Jilna Patterner's eyes had just narrowed in jealousy inside her silly rose-painted Mask. "It is a precious thing, the Gift of magic," the Masker went on. "Precious, for it enables you to serve the Autarchy in ways that those without that Gift can only dream of. With your Gift in particular comes great responsibility, for you, Mara Holdfast, are apprenticed to your father, Charlton Holdfast, Master Maskmaker of Tamita." The Masker nodded over her shoulder in the direction of her father. "Someday, your Masks will adorn and glorify the faces of generations yet to come."

Mara shivered, goose bumps running up her bare back and down her arms. She'd never thought of it in quite such grand terms.

Doubts and fears forgotten, she felt only awe and gratitude. She focused her eyes on the beautiful Mask her father had so lovingly crafted for her. The skin of her face seemed almost to have a mind of its own, a mind that yearned for the touch of the Mask's smooth clay . . .

"Mara Holdfast," the Masker intoned, returning to the vow he had already administered twice. "You have reached the age of fifteen years. It is now the will of the Autarch that you become a full citizen of Aygrima, with all the duties and responsibilities that entails, and that you serve him and his heirs for the rest of your life. Do you accept the will of the Autarch?"

It was hard to even say "I do" through the lump in her throat, but all too soon, it seemed, the oaths were over, and the Masker stepped forward with the beautiful copper-colored Mask in his hands. "Then I welcome you to full citizenship, to adulthood, and to the service of the Autarch: and in recognition of your thrice-made vow, I present you with this Mask, symbol of your devotion, guardian of your thoughts!" The Masker raised the Mask in both hands and settled it onto Mara's face.

It was the most beautiful, wonderful, joyful moment of her life . . .

. . . and then it all went wrong.

The Mask writhed, like the others; but unlike the others, *it did not stop*. It squirmed and wriggled like a basket full of snakes, faster and faster and harder and harder. Mara gasped in terror, then screamed in pain, as she felt the skin above her cheekbones rip open, the skin of her forehead split, her nose break. She fell to her knees, eyes squeezed shut to try to protect them, scrabbling at the Mask with both hands, tearing at it with her fingernails, but it wouldn't come off, wouldn't come off, wouldn't come off, *it was going to kill her—*

The Mask shattered, the thunderclap of its destruction making her ears ring. A dozen pieces fell away from her face and crashed to the dais. Her blood, shockingly red, splattered the white tiles. She coughed and choked and spat out scarlet-laced saliva and mucus.

Yellow toenails in white sandals stepped into her vision. Gagging, she looked up through bleary eyes to see the Masker looking sternly over her head at the Witnesses behind her. "This candidate has failed the Masking," he intoned. "She cannot be made a citizen. In the name of the Autarch, clear this place!"

She heard her mother screaming her name. She wanted to get up, go to her, beg her father to help, to do *something* . . . but the room swayed around her, and the thunder of the falling water seemed to pound down on her, pinning her in place.

What's happening to me? Nothing made sense. *Is this a dream?*

The door to the Maskery slammed closed, cutting off her mother's screams.

SIX

An Uncertain Future

FOOTSTEPS SOUNDED BEHIND HER. Black-gloved hands seized her arms, pulled her upright. Her head swam and her vision grayed. Her neck seemed boneless. She couldn't look up.

A hand lifted her chin. The Masker's yellow Mask swam in her blurred vision. "Another failure of one of the Gifted," he said, his voice strained. "Until two years ago I had never seen even one. But recently . . ."

"If I may?" said a woman's voice behind her.

"Of course," said the Masker. He stepped back.

Ethelda took his place. "Hold still, child," she said. From a leather pouch hung on her blue belt she took out a flask of black stone. A metal clasp bound the stone stopper in place. She undid the clasp, pulled out the stopper, and dropped it back into her pouch. Then, holding the flask in her right hand, she upended it above her left palm.

Magic flowed out: glimmering, shining, heartbreakingly beautiful . . . heartbreaking, because Mara, staring at it with blurry eyes and a mind fogged with pain, knew that she would never, ever, learn to use it to make Masks with her father.

Would never see her father again . . .

Tears rushed to her eyes. She gasped out a sob, and choked again on the blood still flowing into her throat from her broken nose.

"Hush," Ethelda said. "Lift your face to the light."

Mara did so. The movement made the wounds on her cheek gape, and she felt a new rush of warm, fresh blood, pouring down her face to drip from her chin.

"Nasty," said Ethelda. "But nothing that can't be put right."

"It hurts," Mara whimpered.

"I know," said Ethelda sympathetically. "And I'm sorry, but so will this." She lifted her hand, coated with magic, no longer shifting and shimmering in a multitude of colors, but glowing a deep, sapphire blue, like some kind of elegant glove.

For a moment Ethelda held herself absolutely still, brow furrowed. Then she took a deep breath, opened strangely unfocused eyes, and reached out toward Mara's face. Mara forced herself not to pull back, though she couldn't help going cross-eyed . . . and then the Healer touched her, and she gasped, too shocked even to scream, as pain such as she'd never imagined froze the breath in her throat and made her heartbeat go suddenly unsteady.

If it had lasted more than an instant, she would surely have fainted; but almost before she registered it, the pain vanished: *all* the pain, not just the pain of the Healing but all the discomfort she had been feeling since the Mask had torn her face and broken her nose. Her face tingled, a feeling like the pins and needles she felt in her calves when she sat cross-legged too long. She raised trembling hands and touched her cheeks and nose, feeling smooth, unblemished skin beneath the slick of blood, the same straight and slightly upturned nose she had always known. Tears of relief sprang to her eyes: tears that in another instant turned to full-fledged sobbing. She threw her arms around the Healer's neck and cried as if she would never stop.

"Shhh," said Ethelda, patting her on the back. "You're unharmed."

Unharmed? Mara had heard what happened to those who failed their Masking. They were banished—no one knew where. And their faces . . . crisscrossed with scars, noses crooked . . .

She drew back shakily from the Healer. "Will I . . . am I . . . scarred?" she whispered.

"Not with me doing the Healing," Ethelda said. She seemed unconcerned by the blood Mara's hug had smeared across the front of her white robe. "You were fortunate I was here to represent the Autarch. Most who fail the Masking are sent to *Healer*"—she made the honorific sound more like an insult—"Ruddek."

"Healer Ethelda," said the Masker from behind Mara. "Is the girl healed?"

Ethelda turned her head toward him. "You can see that she is."

"Then your work is done. She is now one of the un-Masked and no longer your concern."

Ethelda nodded brusquely. "Of course. I will return to the Palace and inform the Autarch of this lamentable occurrence." She leaned forward and whispered, so low Mara was hardly sure she'd heard it, "Be strong. Don't give up hope." Then she straightened again, turned, and walked out of the Maskery, over the footbridge that crossed the foaming moat and out the bronze door, which swung silently open at her approach, letting in the morning sunshine. Mara heard a snatch of liquid birdsong, felt a breath of cool air on her still-tingling face, and then the doors slammed shut behind Ethelda with a sound like a coffin lid closing.

She turned to the Masker. "Now . . . now what?" she said, her voice barely above a whisper, her throat still raw from screaming and choking.

The impassive yellow Mask regarded her for a long moment. Then the Masker glanced back at the Watchers. "Take her," he said.

As one, they strode forward, the sound of their boots echoing from the domed ceiling, seized her arms, and dragged her from the dais. Mara, helpless in their grasp, looked down at the blood splattered across the once-shining green dress. *It's ruined,* she thought. For the moment, that seemed the worst catastrophe of all; everything else that had happened, that was *still* happening, was too enormous, too horrible, to even contemplate.

Down the white-tiled stairs they went, her feet thumping nervelessly on each step. "Walk, damn you," snarled the Watcher to her left. "It's a long way to the warehouse."

The warehouse?

"Walk, I said!" the Watcher snapped, and Mara struggled to get her legs to move, to put one foot in front of the other, and managed it after a fashion, though she felt so weak and shaken she knew if the Watchers let go of her arms she'd collapse where she stood.

She couldn't think, couldn't grasp what had just happened. The Mask had rejected her. The Mask *her own father* had made for her had rejected her. And then her parents had *abandoned* her, left her in the Maskery with no one to turn to. If Ethelda hadn't been there . . .

Ethelda had healed her. Ethelda had told her to be strong, to not give up hope. But Ethelda was gone, and Mara didn't feel strong, and she didn't feel hope. She felt only numbness and despair.

Children whispered horror stories about those whose Maskings failed. Some said they died on the spot, that their ghosts haunted the city's dark alleys at night, and that the curfew for children and the laws forbidding even Masked grown-ups from traveling most of Tamita's streets at night were to protect the city's people from the vengeful spirits of those whom the Masks, and therefore the city and the Autarch, had rejected.

But she hadn't died, and she wasn't a ghost. *Not yet, anyway.* She was still Mara. Mara, in shock, head swimming, stomach churning . . .

. . . stomach heaving. Her insides convulsed, and she threw up onto the white tile floor, the bread and fruit she'd had for breakfast spattering her bare toes. The Watchers swore and pulled her along faster. She did her best to keep up, but her legs felt like rubber and her stomach continued to roil.

After twenty yards or so the corridor turned sharply right for a few yards to meet up with a cross corridor, this one lacking the gleaming tiles but instead chopped out of solid rock, lit by torches at widely spaced intervals. To the right, the corridor ran in the direction of the Palace; to the left, it ran in the direction of the Market Gate, and it was to the left that the Watchers took her, from pool of flickering light to pool of flickering light through long stretches of darkness. Periodically, they descended flights of stairs.

Mara's thoughts also traveled long stretches of darkness, with far fewer patches of light. *The warehouse?* she thought. *It can't really be a warehouse. Is it a prison of some sort? Am I going to spend the rest of my life in a cell?*

But I haven't done anything wrong! she cried silently. *I did everything right! I welcomed the Mask, I wanted the Mask.*

Maybe something was wrong *with the Mask . . . ?*

No! She rejected that idea instantly. *My father made my Mask. He's the Master Maskmaker. He could* never *make a mistake like that.*

It's my fault. It has to be. And then it came to her. She

suddenly knew exactly what she had done to poison her Masking; she had to swallow hard to keep from throwing up again. *That boy, Keltan, I didn't tell anyone about him, even though he was a criminal, on the run from his Masking . . .*

I should have turned him in. I should have told the Night Watchers where to find him. But I didn't. And the Mask knew. The Mask knew I had already *betrayed the Autarch.* That's *why it rejected me!*

Guilt crashed down on her, black as the darkness between the flickering torches, more painful than when the Mask had wounded her, more painful than when Ethelda had Healed her. She'd wrecked *everything.* Everything her parents had worked for, everything they'd hoped for her, their only child. Everything she'd hoped for herself.

Her life was over. She'd just turned fifteen years old, and her life was already over.

She wished then that she really *was* dead, but wishing didn't make it so. She kept breathing. She kept hurting. She kept walking.

By her reckoning, they had descended far enough, and walked long enough, to have almost reached the city wall, when the tunnel at last ended in a door of rough black wood, bound with rusty iron. One of the Watchers unlocked the door with a large key from his belt. The other Watcher pushed the door open. Together, they ushered Mara through.

She winced and flung her arm across her eyes as she stepped into a beam of bright sunlight, slanting down from a window high up the far wall of the building they had entered. The next instant she was in darkness again, but, dazzled, she still couldn't see much of the building's interior. From the echo of the Guards' booted feet on the flagstones, though, she thought it must be enormous. *It really is a warehouse,* she thought. *One of the warehouses by the city wall, like the one that used to be my grandfather's.*

As her guards led her out into the middle of the vast

room, she had the distinct impression she was being watched. She glanced around. The contrast between the patches of sun on the floor and the deep shadows everywhere else still made it hard to see, but as her eyes adjusted, Mara realized cells made of iron bars lined two walls of the warehouse, six on a side. Both of the other two walls were mostly taken up by huge double doors, large enough for wagons to drive through. There were no windows except the small ones high up under the eaves.

Most of the cells were empty, but not all.

Some of them held children.

She counted three girls and a boy, each locked inside a metal cage maybe ten feet deep and eight wide. Besides the child, each cage contained only a covered bucket and a narrow wooden bed. She couldn't see the children's faces clearly, but their watching eyes gleamed wide and white in the gloom.

A fourth girl stood in a beam of sunlight in the middle of the room, in front of a seated fat, bald man who wore a plain gray Mask. He held a pad of paper in one hand; the other grasped a long piece of charcoal that scratched the page as he stared at the girl.

Taller than Mara, the girl wore a gray, shapeless smock that had been pulled down to expose her dark brown shoulders, which shone like polished wood in the patch of sun. One hand clutched the smock at her breast to keep it from slipping off. She stood very still, her head tilted back, staring up into an empty corner of the warehouse ceiling.

She was beautiful—or had been; as the Watchers brought Mara right up next to her, she saw the half-healed scars, white and pink, crisscrossing her dark skin.

The girl's brown eyes flickered in Mara's direction as she approached, but otherwise she didn't move.

The fat man looked up at the Watchers. "You're in my light," he complained. Then he saw Mara and his eyes widened inside the gray Mask. "Her face," he breathed. "It's unmarked!"

"She had a better Healer than most," said the Watcher. "But she's yours now. She's to go out with the others."

"Tomorrow," said the fat man. He leaned forward, never taking his eyes off Mara's face. "UnMasked, and unscarred," he murmured. "I must draw her!" His eyes snapped to the other girl. "You, back in your cell."

The dark-skinned girl's gaze snapped down. She nodded without speaking, gave Mara an unreadable glance, pulled her smock back up over her shoulders, then turned and walked away, not hurrying, to one of the cages whose door stood open. She stepped inside, turned and gave the fat man a haughty look, and pulled the door shut. The metallic click echoed in the emptiness of the warehouse.

"You're good, then?" said the Watcher who hadn't spoken yet. "Don't need us no more, right?"

"Yes, yes, on your way," said the fat man. He got to his feet as the Watchers, without another word, went back the way they had come. "First things first," he said. "Follow me."

Mara, stumbling a little in the high-heeled shoes that had seemed so beautiful and now seemed sad and ridiculous, followed him into a dim corner of the warehouse, furnished with a few chests and a table on which rested a chipped white basin and a blue pitcher full of water. A couple of rough towels lay beside the basin. "Take off your dress and shoes," the man said, "and wash off the blood."

Mara turned toward him, shocked. "What? Here? Now?"

"You heard me. Yes, here. Yes, now. Dress is ruined, but I might make a silver or two off the shoes." The fat man had turned away to fling open one of the chests. He pulled out a gray smock like the one the dark-skinned girl had been wearing. "Put this on instead. Then I want to draw you." His gaze moved over her body from head to toe. "With your clothes on, I think. It's your *face* they'll be interested in, not that skinny body. When you're ready, come back to the chair." With that the fat man turned and strode away.

Blushing furiously, Mara turned to the basin. She gripped the edges of the table for a moment and then, hoping it was too dim in the corner for the fat man or the boy she had spotted in one of the cells to see, convulsively stripped off the bloodstained green dress, letting it puddle to the ground around the silver shoes, which she stepped out of a moment later. Wearing only her drawers, naked from the waist up, she kept her back to the fat man and the cages and scrubbed the blood from her chest and belly. Then she pulled on the rough gray smock. It was slit alarmingly far down the front and too big for her. All that kept it from slipping off her shoulders were two strings at the neck that she tied tight.

Dressed—or at least half-dressed—she turned and walked barefoot across the warehouse's flagstones to the pool of light around the wooden chair, where the fat man waited, pad of paper open to a fresh page on his lap. "Stand there." He pointed at the patch of light. "Let the sun fall on your face."

Mara stepped into the sunbeam, and closed her eyes for a moment. The warmth of the sun felt good on her cheeks after the damp chill of the long tunnel from the Palace and the cold-water scrubbing.

"Eyes open," snapped the man. He stood up, dropping his pad of paper on his chair, stepped forward and, before she realized what he was about to do, had untied the neck of the smock. Then he grabbed the shoulders and tugged. Mara gasped as the smock slipped down to her waist. She snatched it just in time to keep it from falling off entirely, and pulled it back up, cheeks flaming with embarrassment. But the fat man hadn't even looked at her body; his eyes were on her face. Holding the smock like the other girl had, her exposed shoulders cold in the warehouse's chill, she endured the fat man's touch as he took her chin and tilted her head this way and that.

"Perfect," he breathed. "Now stand still, or you'll ruin everything."

He returned to his chair and picked up his charcoal and paper. Mara, clutching the top of her smock, stared into a corner just like the dark-skinned girl had done.

The fat man kept her standing there for an hour, though he had her move twice to follow the sunbeam as it slowly slid across the floor. But finally he stopped drawing, and looked at his picture critically. "Excellent," he said. "I can charge double for that. Maybe triple. Never had a completely unmarked face before." He snorted. "Only thing you've got going for you."

Mara lowered her head, shrugged her smock back up onto her shoulders, tied it tight, then rubbed a crick in the back of her neck. "May I see?" she said. No one had ever drawn her picture before.

"No," the fat man snapped. "Come with me."

He led her across the floor to an empty cell and locked her in. In the cell to her left the dark-skinned girl lay on her cot, one arm across her face, apparently asleep. In the cell to the right stood the boy, huge and muscular, almost the size of a grown man. As the door clanked shut and the fat man strode away, the boy gripped the bars and grinned at her.

Mara didn't like the looks of the boy; wouldn't have liked them even without the vivid red scars slashed across his cheeks and forehead. He hardly looked as if he'd been Healed at all. Ragged stubble speckled his upper lip and chin.

"What's your name?" the boy said. His grin twisted into something more like a leer. "I'm Grute."

"Mara." She looked past Grute; the cell on the other side of him was empty. There were only the three of them on this side of the warehouse; the other girls were invisible in the shadows across the broad floor. "All of you failed the Masking?"

"Sometime in the last month, yeah," Grute said. "Now we're just waiting."

"For what?"

"For them to take us where the unMasked go," Grute said. "Looking forward to it, myself. I've heard some things. I'm gonna do all right there. Better than I ever would have in Tamita, anyway."

He hadn't taken his eyes off her since she'd started talking to him; she found his gaze unnerving. "What are you staring at?" she snapped.

He snorted. "Your face, of course. You don't have these." He lifted one hand and traced the contours of one of the scars slashing across his cheek. His smile/leer widened. "And you're pretty, too. Or will be once you flesh out a bit."

"I was cut up, too," Mara said. "I just had a better Healer."

"Yeah? Why did *you* rate?"

"Just lucky," she said. It was the only answer she had. Why *had* Ethelda been there? Representing the Autarch, she'd said, but why? Why hadn't the Autarch himself attended? She was the daughter of his Master Maskmaker. Why had Ethelda come in his place?

"Gifted, were you?" Grute said. "Think *that* makes you special?"

"Yes, I have the Gift," Mara snapped. "What's it to you?"

"*Have* it?" Grute's voice dripped vicious glee. "*Had* it, you mean. You ain't got it no more."

"What?" Mara stared at him. "What do you mean?"

"I mean," Grute said, "that when a Gifted's Mask fails it takes her Gift away from her. You got no more Gift than I do. Or the fat man out there." He jerked a thumb in the direction of the chair in the middle of the warehouse floor. "You ain't no better 'n anyone else, now."

Mara's stomach flip-flopped. "I don't believe you!"

"Ask *her*," Grute said, pointing at the sleeping, dark-skinned girl. "She had the Gift, too, until a month ago when her Masking failed—right in front of the Autarch, too. She knows she ain't got it no more. Masker flat out told her. Gift don't survive when the Mask fails." He jerked his head in the direction of the cells on the far side of the warehouse. "'Nother girl over there, same thing. *They* know the truth. Now you know it, too: there ain't nothing special about you at all, not anymore." His gaze traveled over her body, and she felt herself blush. "And I do mean *nothing*." Then his eyes moved back to her face and his voice dropped to a low growl. "Except you got no scars. *That's* special. That could make you *real* popular where we're going. Men'll probably be fighting each other over *you*."

Mara swallowed. For the first time, she wondered if the Healer had done her a favor. "What's with lard butt out there?" she said, wanting to change the subject. "The drawing. What's with that?"

Grute snorted. "Don't get out much, do you? *Big* black market for drawings of the unMasked. Girls, mostly, though there's a market for boys, too." He leered. "You're just lucky he didn't make you take *all* your clothes off. He usually does. Probably would've, if you had anything much to look at. But you don't. Saw that much when your smock slipped down." The leer became an evil grin that almost split his face. He was missing two teeth. "No, it's your face he cares about. UnMasked and unscarred. Must be a first."

Mara gaped at him. "That's disgusting! I don't believe you."

"Ask *her*," the boy said, again nodding at the sleeping girl. "Made her take all *her* clothes off, first day here. Couple of the other girls, too. I watched." He leaned forward, eyes locked on Mara, and said in a thick whisper, "I didn't find it disgusting at *all*."

If Mara hadn't already been on the far side of the cell from him, she would have backed away. "Leave me alone!"

Grute rattled the bars of the cage. "As if I have a choice." He grinned again. "For now." He mimed a huge kiss, then went to his cot and flopped down onto it, his back to her.

Mara stared at him. She looked back at the dark-skinned girl, but she remained asleep. She looked out through the bars at the fat man. He seemed to be putting the finishing touches on a drawing. *Mine?* She imagined men buying it from shadowed stalls in the city's back alleys, and felt dirty. "How did this happen?" she whispered to herself. "*How did I end up here?*"

No one answered her.

The day wore on into evening, gloom gathering in the warehouse as the sun slipped too low to shine through the windows. She desperately needed to relieve her bladder, but there was no way she was going to do *that*, in the bucket, while there was light enough for Grute to watch her, which she was sure he would.

Not that *he* had any qualms about it. She had to avert her eyes twice during that long afternoon.

The fat man gave them each a loaf of bread and some water as the windows turned orange. When the room was all but pitch-black, Mara finally felt her way to the bucket and did what she needed to do. But when she returned to her cot, she found no rest.

It wasn't just the lumpy mattress or the chill in the air that the thin blanket could not ward off. It was the fact that in the dark she was completely alone with herself, her thoughts . . . and her memories. The excitement of donning the green dress. The anticipation of the Masking celebration to come. Walking to the Maskery in the cool morning air. The sound of birdsong in the courtyard. The wonder of seeing the beautiful Mask her father had made for her, his love for her apparent in every beautiful bit of it . . .

. . . and then the tearing pain as her face split, the crunching agony as her nose broke, the blood, and, worse than all of that, her mother's screams . . .

Now here she was, locked in a cell, unMasked, de-graded, cast out, sentenced to who-knew-what fate.

I wish the Mask had worked, she thought, as tears ran down her face onto the smelly cover of the straw-filled mattress. *Even if it really* does *change you. I wish it had worked. Because nothing could be worse than this. Even my Gift is gone. I'll never see magic again, ever. . . .*

And then her eyes, squeezed shut against the tears, flew open.

Ethelda had Healed her face with magic—and *Mara had seen it*, clinging to her hand like a glowing blue glove. *Maybe the Gift doesn't vanish instantly when the Mask breaks*, she thought. *Maybe it fades slowly. Maybe it's gone now.*

But maybe, just maybe, it *wasn't.*

"Be strong," she whispered to herself, echoing Ethelda's last words to her. "Don't lose hope."

Clutching the faint possibility that her Gift had not deserted her, as tightly as the night before she had clutched Stoofy, she finally found sleep.

The shouts of the jailer jolted her awake what seemed an instant later. She lay confused and frightened, heart pounding. Why was she so stiff and cold? What had happened to her bed, her cozy room, the skylight?

Then, sharp as a slap, everything that had happened the day before rushed back. She gasped, and raised her head.

The fat man strode from cell to cell, slamming a long wooden club against the iron bars. "Wagon is here," he shouted. "Say good-bye to your luxurious accommodations, my sweets."

Luxurious? Mara thought with a mixture of outrage and lack-of-sleep befuddlement. Grute stood in front of his bucket, peeing. He winked at her. Mara closed her eyes. *If this is luxurious*, she wondered, *what comes next?*

She found out half an hour later when, having used her own bucket as modestly as she could, scrubbed her face in cold gray water from the basin, and choked down a handful of dates, she blinked in a sudden flood of light as the big doors at one end of the warehouse crashed open.

A tall black wagon, pulled by two huge, shaggy-footed, dappled gray horses, clattered in over the flag-stones. The hairs stood up on the back of Mara's neck. It had a brutal look: thick wooden slats, rusty iron studs, tiny barred windows high above wheels that stood as tall as Mara herself.

But the worst of it was that she had seen wagons like it before, had wondered what they were for and where they were going; had seen them because she had sat on the city wall staring down at this very warehouse ... *the warehouse that had once belonged to her mother's father.*

She felt sick.

Two Watchers flanked the driver, a slight man wear-ing a dull-gray Mask, nondescript clothes, and calf-high boots of scuffed black leather. He stayed put, holding the reins of the blowing, stamping horses, while the Watchers jumped down, boots slapping against the stone, and went around to the back of the wagon. Doors swung wide, and then the Watchers moved to the first occupied cell on the far side of the warehouse. The fat jailer opened the cage door, and the Watchers escorted out a trembling girl who looked too tiny to be fifteen. They led her to the wagon. She was too short to climb up into it, so one of the Watchers grabbed her, swung her legs up, and shoved her in feet-first. The other two girls from the far side of the cell, one about Mara's height but much more rounded, the other taller and tough-looking, were rousted out next, and climbed in under their own power.

The Watchers crossed to Mara's side of the ware-house. They opened the cage of the brown-skinned girl. She crossed the warehouse floor with her head high, and climbed in with no difficulty.

Then it was Mara's turn. She padded on bare feet across the cold flagstones. She, too, was able to climb up into the wagon's dark interior without help.

Like the cell, the wagon was lined with straw. Unlike the cell, it didn't have a bucket, only a small hole in the center of the floor. The interior stank of mold and sweat and urine, and Mara shuddered at the touch of the rotting straw under her hands and bare knees as she crawled in.

The other four girls had huddled together in a corner. Mara instinctively joined them, so that they were shoulder to shoulder when the Watchers came back with Grute. He jumped easily into the wagon, which rocked under his weight. His head barely cleared the ceiling as he stood looking down at them, hands on his hips. "Well, well," he said, face twisted into the leering grin Mara had already come to hate. "This could be fun."

The doors closed, plunging them into darkness. Mara felt the brown-skinned girl, who had been sitting to her right, get up. The wagon jerked on its springs. Grute gave a high-pitched, almost girlish shriek, and the wagon jerked again as something heavy thudded to the floor. The next moment Mara's neighbor was back at her side. The sound of moaning filled the wagon.

As her eyes adjusted to the faint gray light seeping through the tiny barred windows, Mara could just make out Grute lying curled on the floor, hands between his legs. Tears glistened on his cheeks.

Mara felt a smile turn up the corners of her mouth for the first time since her Masking. She turned to the girl. "My name's Mara," she said. "What's yours?"

"Alita," said the girl. She put her arm around the smaller girl. "And this is Prella."

"I'm Simona," said the buxom girl.

"Kirika," said the tough-looking one.

The wagon shifted again as, presumably, the Watchers climbed back aboard. And then they were rolling, the light brightening as they trundled out of the warehouse into sunshine.

They drove for hours without stopping. As the sun rose higher and higher, so did the heat and stench inside the wagon. Grute, once he had recovered enough to quit moaning, crawled away to the far corner of the wagon, where he sat, silently glaring, his eyes all Mara could see clearly in the semidarkness. They gave her a creepy feeling, but she kept watching them all the same. She wanted to know *exactly* where Grute was *all* the time. She doubted even Alita's . . . *forceful* . . . action would keep him at bay indefinitely. The boy was bad, and it was no wonder the Mask had rejected him . . .

. . . *just like it rejected me.*

She talked a little with the others. Alita and Prella, she learned, were—or had been—Gifted; Simona and Kirika were not. Alita had been destined for apprenticeship to a Healer and Prella to a Horsemaster. Simona had expected to go to work in her father's bakery. Kirika said nothing about what her plans had been.

But all of their plans and expectations had come crashing down in the same way: the writhing of the Mask, the pain, the blood, the screams of horrified Witnesses, the Watchers hauling them away down the long tunnel.

At both Alita and Prella's Maskings, the Autarch himself had been present. "Not that I saw him," Prella said. "He was behind a golden screen. But I saw the Child Guards." Her voice trembled. "I was so ashamed when the Mask failed. Failing like that in front of the Autarch!"

"The Autarch comes to the Maskings of the Gifted?" Simona said, sounding awed.

"He didn't come to mine," Mara said. "The Palace Healer, Ethelda, was there instead. I don't know why."

"Lucky you," Alita muttered, and Mara felt a pang of guilt. *Every time they see my unmarked face they'll know how lucky I was*, she thought. *I hope they don't resent me for it. It's not like I had anything to do with it!*

But then she remembered what Grute had said about how "popular" she might be among the men where they were going, and the pang of guilt turned to a worm of nausea that made her swallow hard. "Maybe not," she whispered, but she doubted the others heard her over the noise of the wagon.

Of the four, Kirika said the least, and nothing at all

about her background. Alita was slightly more forthcoming. Mara found out she was the daughter of a blacksmith, that she came not from Tamita but from one of the outlying villages, and that she was the first of her family to be Gifted. All Gifted were sent to Tamita to be Masked, since only the Master Maskmaker—*Father*, Mara thought—could make their special Masks.

"The week before my fifteenth birthday, the whole village feasted for three days. And when I rode out onto the road to Tamita with my parents, they showered us with flower petals . . ." She fell silent after that, and would say nothing more.

Simona said her father's bakery was located on the far side of Tamita from Maskmakers' Way, which explained why Mara had never seen it. Simona had been working in the bakery several hours a day, with her mother and only sibling, an older brother, since she was eight. The Masking had seemed a mere formality, just an annoying interruption in a well-established routine. "They'll miss me in the bakery," she said. "And there was . . . a boy . . ." She fell as silent as Kirika and Alita had become.

Prella, on the other hand, prattled. Her father was a tailor and her mother a dressmaker. She was the youngest of eight children. Her eldest brother was also Gifted, and currently working in the Corps of Engineers, building the city's new aqueduct from the eastern mountains. All of her siblings had been Masked without a problem, she couldn't understand what had happened, wasn't that warehouse an awful place, being drawn by the fat jailer, she'd never been so embarrassed, where did they think they were being taken . . . She talked enough for all the rest put together.

That suited Mara. She said only that her father was a Gifted craftsman—nothing about him being a Maskmaker—and that she was an only child.

"Your poor parents," Prella breathed when she heard

that. "I mean, my parents will miss me, but at least they've got seven more. What will *your* parents do?"

"I don't know," Mara said, against the lump rising in her throat. She swallowed and pressed her lips together. *I'm through crying,* she told herself fiercely. *Crying won't change anything. It just makes me look weak. And I can't afford to look weak. Not in front of Grute.*

But despite her resolve, more than a few tears found their way down her cheeks during that long ride.

A few hours after setting out, they stopped briefly and were let out of the wagon to stretch. Given hard bread, harder cheese, and carrots that were anything *but*, along with tin mugs of rather funny-smelling water, they sat with their backs to the wheels on the shady side of the wagon and ate their meager fare while gazing out over a wheat field. Smoke rose from the chimneys of a village in the distance, but no villagers were to be seen. *Know enough to stay away,* Mara thought.

She shot a glance at Grute, sitting well apart from the girls. *Are all unMasked boys like* him?

No, she answered herself firmly. She thought back to her encounter with the boy calling himself Keltan. *He* certainly wasn't like Grute, or she would never have escaped that coal room. *But he wasn't rejected by the Mask,* she reminded herself. He *rejected* it.

Even though she was half-convinced her failure to turn him in was one of the reasons she was where she was, she hoped fiercely that he'd escaped. She wished, even more fiercely, that she had accepted his offer to run away with him.

The Watchers soon ordered them back into the wagon. "Where are we going?" Mara dared to ask as she climbed in.

"You'll find out when we get there," one Watcher growled, and slammed the door.

After more hours of rumbling darkness, they stopped again. This time, emerging into early twilight, Mara saw that the landscape had changed: there were more hills, more trees, and no sign of human habitation except for a squat brick building with tiny barred windows. The Watchers chivvied all of them into it and slammed the thick black door behind them. Mara heard the rusty bolt slide shut and the heavy clank of a padlock.

As one, the five girls turned to see Grute leaning against the far wall, watching them. He leered. Alita clenched her fists and took a step toward him. He straightened, leer fading. "You won't do that again," he growled. "Caught me by surprise, is all."

"You're big," Alita said softly. "But there are five of us. You gonna try anything?"

Grute gave her a long, hard stare, then very deliberately turned his head and spat on the ground. "Don't flatter yourself." He grabbed one of the dirty blankets rolled up and stacked in one corner of the cell and spread it out on the stone floor. "I hope you all have sweet dreams tonight, ladies," he said as he sat down on it. "Nothing but nightmares ahead for you where we're going."

"Where is that?" Prella asked, her voice trembling a little. "Where are they taking us?"

Grute bared his teeth. "A mine," he said. "A deep, dark mine. Full of men. A whole lot of men . . . like me." He pursed his lips and made a loud smacking noise. "Like I said, sweet dreams." Then he lay down, rolled over, and ignored them.

"I can't work in a mine," Simona said, a hint of panic in her voice.

"Work or die," Alita said. "Me, I'll work."

"Me, too," Kirika said. Her voice held a strange hoarseness. She had sat down on the floor with her back to the wall and her bony knees pulled up to her chest. She was staring at the dark lump of Grute in his blanket.

"I'm scared," Prella said in a barely audible voice.

Alita put an arm around the smaller girl's shoulders, her movements and expression fierce as a hawk's. "I'll be with you," she said. "We can help each other."

"We can all help each other," Mara said, putting her arm around Prella's shoulders, too, over the top of Alita's. Simona joined them, taking Mara's free hand in hers.

Only Kirika stayed where she was. "The camp will be full of men like *him*," she said, still staring at Grute. Her voice dripped loathing. "Like . . ." Her voice dropped almost to a whisper. "Like my uncle."

Mara blinked, puzzled; then suddenly understood and felt sick inside.

"I miss *my* uncle," Prella said, oblivious, and Alita and Mara exchanged a half-horrified look of exasperation.

They broke apart so they could get blankets and spread them out in a line along the wall on the far side of the room from Grute. Then they sat in silence as the room grew darker, each lost in her own thoughts. It was almost pitch-black before Mara heard the bolt slide open. One of the Watchers came in with a lantern, which he hung on a hook by the door. The other followed, carrying a tray of food—hard black bread, thin gruel with stringy bits of beef in it, a pitcher of water. Then they went out again.

They ate by the lantern's dim light, Grute rousing himself to take his share—and more than his share—gobbling it down noisily before belching, peeing noisily into the filthy bucket in one corner, and then, giving them all a leer, settling down again on his blanket.

Mara hated to even touch the stiff, grim-caked wool, but it was better than the greasy black floor . . . though not by much. She lay down, staring at the lantern, which promptly sputtered out.

So far from home, Mara thought in the sudden darkness. *In so many ways*. Tears, hot in the chill air, rolled down her cheeks. She heard a muffled sob from elsewhere in the room and knew she wasn't alone in her grief. *How much farther? And what's waiting at the end?*

She didn't find out the next day, or the day after that, or the day after that. Four nights they spent in prisons just like the first, obviously built to house unMasked on their way to ... wherever. She learned a little bit more about all the girls except Kirika, who simply would not talk about herself, and far too much about Grute: his father a drunk, his mother a prostitute, his older sister following in her mother's footsteps. In the middle of the second night Simona woke to find Grute standing over her. Her scream brought the Watchers running, and they shoved Grute to the ground, cursing and kicking him; but when they'd left, Grute sat up, contemptuous. "I've been beaten bloody by better 'n them and never made a sound," he bragged, but he didn't bother any of them again that night, and after that they took to sleeping in shifts, one of them awake at all times.

On the fifth day, the road, which had never exactly been smooth, began tossing them around inside the wagon like seeds in a rattle. At one point Mara's head smacked the side of the wagon so hard she saw stars. Gingerly exploring her skull with her fingers a few minutes later, after the ride smoothed a bit, she winced as she touched a good-sized lump. Then the wagon lurched and she promptly smacked her head again.

The lunch break came as a blessed relief. This time, when they emerged into daylight, high, wooded slopes surrounded them, the rough track winding along the bottom of a valley. The air had a chilly bite. "We've climbed," Alita said, looking around. "We must be getting close to the mountains."

"Shut up," one of the Watchers ordered.

They ate, and clambered back aboard the wagon for more bone-shaking travel. Mara had no way to tell the passage of time, but she thought at least two hours must have gone by since lunchtime when she heard frantic, furious shouting. The horses screamed, the wagon jerked sharply right ... and then, almost in slow motion, tipped over onto its side.

Simona yelled as she slid down on top of Grute, kicking all the way. He threw up his hands to protect himself.

"Stop it!" he shouted, just before she sprawled across him.

Kirika and Alita slid down beside Mara in a tangle of arms and legs, and then the shrieking Prella landed right on top of her, knocking the breath from both of them. As they lay there, helpless, mouths agape like landed fish, the doors of the wagon were flung wide. Figures, black silhouettes against the sunlight, lurched forward, grabbed all of them by the arms, and pulled them out into the cool air.

Mara, doubled over, unable to straighten, supported by gloved hands on each arm, saw nothing but booted feet and rutted dirt. Her new captors dragged her off the road and propped her against a tree. As her breathing slowly returned to normal, she held the ribs bruised by Prella's fall and stared around, trying to figure out what had happened.

The wagon lay on its side in the middle of the road, which was completely blocked by an enormous felled tree. The driver was under the wagon, motionless, neck twisted at an unnatural angle. The Watchers were also dead, but not from the crash: one lay only a few yards from Mara, the feathered shaft of an arrow protruding from the back of his neck. The dirt beneath his body was dark and red. He stared sightlessly up at the sky. His black Mask had shattered with his death, its pieces lying in crumbling shards all around his dead face, streaked with the blood that had poured from his nose and mouth. Mara swallowed, and looked away.

She counted eight attackers in all, both men and women. All wore tunics, leggings, and jackets of forest green, brown capes, and high brown boots.

They did not wear Masks. The sight shocked her almost as much as if they had been naked.

She looked around for the other children. Alita, Prella, Simona, Kirika and Grute huddled together near the wagon in which they'd been riding, guarded by a tall woman with long red hair pulled back in a tightly braided ponytail. She held a drawn sword in her hand. Mara, for some reason, had been isolated.

Who are they? What do they want?

One of the attackers broke away from the group around the lead wagon and strode toward her. She looked up as he approached, then quickly looked away again. Except for her father, Mara had never seen a grown man unMasked. She could feel herself blushing furiously.

The man stood above her. She stared resolutely at his scuffed brown boots. "You're Mara?" he said. "Daughter of Charlton Holdfast, Master Maskmaker of Tamita?"

That brought her head up, shock erasing embarrassment. "How . . . ?"

The man looked about the same age as her father, which made it even stranger to see him without a Mask. "Never mind how we know. Just be assured you have nothing to fear. We will not harm you."

Mara cast her gaze down again. "Who are you?" she whispered.

"My name is Edrik," the man said. "Look at me." He knelt beside her, and his hand grasped her chin. Gently but inexorably, he lifted her head until she had no choice but to gaze once more into his blue eyes. "You must get used to looking at men and women without Masks," he said softly. "Because as of this moment, you are part of the unMasked Army."

Mara's eyes widened . . . and then flicked sideways as another green-clad figure trotted up. *His* face, freckled, framed by shaggy blond hair, she had seen before. "Keltan?"

"Hi, Mara," said the boy from the basement. He grinned. "Surprise!"

Edrik glanced at him. "So she *is* the same girl?"

Keltan nodded. "She is. I thought she must be."

Edrik's eyes returned to Mara's face. He studied her a moment longer, then got to his feet. "I'll leave her in your care, then," he said. "Stay with her while we finish up with the wagon."

He strode away. Keltan placed his back against the tree trunk and slid down it until he was sitting beside Mara. She glanced sideways at him. He grinned at her again. "Told you the unMasked Army wasn't a myth."

"Sorry I doubted you," said Mara. She looked back at Grute and the others. "Why aren't I with *them?* Was that your doing?"

Keltan snorted. "Me? I'm nobody. Just the latest—and least—recruit. No, you're here because you're special." She glanced back at him, puzzled. He spread his hands. "You're the daughter of the Master Maskmaker."

"Were you the one who told them that?" Mara asked. Then she shook her head. "No," she said, bewildered. "It couldn't have been you. I told you my father was a Maskmaker, but I didn't tell you he was the *Master* Maskmaker!"

"I had nothing to do with it," Keltan said. "I never mentioned your existence. I assumed you had gone off to your Masking like a good little girl and were lost to the service of the Autarch. But *he*"—he nodded in Edrik's direction—"somehow, knew different. He not only knew who your father is, he knew you'd failed your Masking and were coming our way on this wagon. When he told the unMasked Army the plans for this raid, he described you, and gave your name. Good thing, too! I wouldn't even be here if I hadn't said I thought I'd already met you, in that coal cellar when I was on the run in Tamita."

"But . . ." Mara stared at Edrik. "*How* could he know all that?"

"Wish I knew," Keltan said. "Presumably someone told him."

"You mean, like a . . . a spy? In the city?"

"Maybe. Probably. But I told you; I'm the least of the least. They're not telling *me*."

Mara rubbed her face with her hands. Her head still

throbbed from the wallop it had taken in the wagon, and her ribs ached.

A horse whinnied, the sound full of fear and pain. Mara looked up. Both horses had gone down in the traces. One, apparently uninjured, had struggled back to its feet and was being cut free. But the other remained on its side, flanks heaving, head writhing, eyes white and rolling. A woman who had been kneeling beside it shook her head, stood, and drew her sword. Mara closed her eyes for a moment, not wanting to watch.

The horse screamed, then fell silent. When Mara opened her eyes again, it lay still, blood spreading out into the dirt beneath it.

The sound of axes on wood rang out as the unMasked attacked the wagon, smashing the wheels and everything else they could. "Do they do this often?" Mara asked Keltan. "Raid the wagons?"

Keltan shook his head. "No," he said seriously. "In fact, they *never* do it. Their recruits have always been those who escape *before* their Masking. They don't trust those who fail their Masking. Too many of them have already gone . . . bad. Those kinds of recruits would be worse than useless."

Mara, thinking of Grute, nodded. "There's at least one like that in this group."

"That's why the others are still under guard," Keltan said. "But something is different. Maskings are failing more often." He nodded at the group of children. "Two or three times a month. And those failing the Maskings are no longer just those who are already twisted. Some are just ordinary children. And some are . . . were . . . Gifted. Until recently, the Gifted *never* failed their Masking."

Oh, good, Mara thought bitterly. *I'm special*.

"And somehow, the Army heard about the failure of *your* Mask, Mara," Keltan continued. "Somehow they knew the daughter of the Master Maskmaker of Tamita would be in this wagon, and for some reason that was enough for them to launch this raid."

"But . . ." Mara didn't know what to say. "What good could I be to them?"

"Don't ask me," Keltan said. "I told you—"

"Least of the least. Yes, I remember." Mara stared at the wagon, its wheels smashed to kindling, holes gaping in its side, roof, and bottom. It would never roll again. "They should burn it," she said venomously, thinking of that wagon and others rolling, month after month, from the warehouse that had once been her grandfather's, carrying children to a horrible fate . . .

"Can't risk the smoke," Keltan said. "The mining camp is still half a day down the road, but there could be hunting parties in the forest, and the next supply wagon from Tamita is due to pass this way in a few hours but could be ahead of schedule. We want to delay the Watchers learning about the attack for as long as possible."

Edrik, who had been examining the wrecked wagon, turned and shouted, "Time to go!"

A lead had been attached to the bridle of the remaining wagon horse, which obediently followed one of the unMasked toward the forest while others chivvied the children to their feet. Keltan stood up, too, then leaned down and reached out a hand. "Come on," he said. "Edrik will tell you more later. But for now, we have to move. We've got a long journey ahead of us."

Mara let him pull her to her feet. His hand lingered in hers as they walked past the shattered wagon. As she gazed at it, she felt a sudden fierce joy at the thought that no more children would ride in its stinking darkness to an unknown fate.

But there are other wagons, she thought. *The fat man is still waiting in the warehouse like a bloated white spider. The Maskery will see more blood and tears. More children's faces will be torn apart. More children's families will be torn apart.*

But the unMasked Army was proof that there was another way to live. Maybe, just maybe, they could put a stop to it all: all of the evil committed and suffered in the name of the Autarch.

And maybe, just maybe, she could help.

I'd like that, she thought fiercely, as they left the road behind and climbed the slope into the woods. *No, I'd love that.*

SEVEN

Cold Water

THE UNMASKED HAD LEFT their own horses, four in all, hidden among the trees above the road. To Mara, who had never ridden one, they looked intimidatingly large as she approached them side by side with Keltan (although she'd let go of his hand; at some point during the climb it had suddenly seemed embarrassing to still be holding on to it, and she'd released him with a muttered, "Sorry." Keltan had opened his mouth to say something, but then swallowed the comment unvoiced.)

Edrik stood patting the neck of the nearest horse, a rangy-looking gray mare. The mare turned and looked at Mara and blew out air between its lips—*Pbbbt!*—as if disgusted by the sight of her. "I don't think it likes me," she said nervously.

Keltan laughed. "It's just a horse."

"And I can't ride."

Keltan shrugged. "Don't worry," he said. "We won't be riding."

Mara blinked. "But . . . I thought . . . can't we ride double?"

"Not on *our* horses," Edrik said, turning away from the mare. "We don't have very many, and the ones we have are too valuable. Riding double is hard on the horse, because the second rider is sitting on the weakest part of the horse's spine. It's also harder for the horse to balance. And a nervous rider sitting with her legs dangling down onto the horse's flanks? No thanks. A spooked horse in the terrain we'll be going through would be no fun for anyone."

"But in stories—"

"Story horses aren't real horses," Edrik said. His mare chose that moment to let fall a sizable amount of dung. Edrik glanced at the animal. "Thanks for so pungently making my point," he said dryly, and Mara couldn't help laughing.

"Believe me," Keltan said under his breath as Edrik turned away to organize the rest of the group, "you're better off walking. I gave it a try. Better sore feet than a sore . . ." He grimaced. "Well, never mind. Let's just say I'd show you my bruises, but we don't know each other that well."

Mara laughed again.

The first thing the unMasked did was open their saddlebags and provide the rescued youths with clothes to replace the girls' prison smocks and Grute's thin pants and top. Behind a screen of underbrush that provided a modicum of privacy, Mara, Alita, Kirika, Prella, and Simona pulled on the same green leggings and tunics worn by the unMasked Army, plus warm brown cloaks and brown leather boots.

Warmer than she'd been since the warehouse, Mara joined Keltan again while the unMasked formed into a column. Edrik led the way on his gray mare, with two other riders behind him. Mara and the others from the wagon would walk behind the riders ("Watch where you step," Keltan said under his breath, and Mara laughed again), accompanied by two dismounted unMasked, plus Keltan. One other unMasked would lead the horse freed from the wagon, while the final mounted unMasked would bring up the rear.

The tall woman with the braided red hair walked next to Mara. With a friendly smile, she introduced herself as Tishka. Like the unMasked behind her, she led an animal on a leash: Grute, rope around his chest, hands tied behind his back. Somehow, Mara thought, the unMasked had already realized what Grute was like. *Maybe Alita told them.*

Grute, despite his bonds, showed no emotion as he looked around at the preparations except when his eyes flicked over Mara. Then, just for a moment, she thought she saw a flash of . . . something. Anger? She couldn't be sure, and already his gaze had moved on.

She decided, not for the first time, to stay as far away from him as possible.

The unMasked band trudged through the forest in a generally westerly direction. Every now and then the sun, sinking ahead of them, stabbed Mara's eyes through an opening in the tree, blinding her: but then, there wasn't much to see—just trees, more trees, and more trees after that.

Mara had never been in a forest before. She couldn't figure out how Edrik could find his way through it. After a couple of hours she began to suspect he *wasn't*, that he was as thoroughly lost as she. But no one else seemed concerned, so she kept her fears to herself.

She had another thought she *didn't* keep to herself, though, as she stepped around yet another pile of manure. "They'll be able to track us easily," she said to Keltan. "Won't we lead them straight to the unMasked Army?"

"We won't be leaving tracks much longer," Keltan said.

Mara glanced at him. "What?"

"You'll see," he said.

And she did, very soon. As the shadows deepened and the sun, no longer able to pierce the forest canopy, turned the treetops orange, they reached a broad, fast-flowing stream, foaming white in the gathering gloom. Edrik called a halt. "We'll follow the stream for the next few hours," he said.

"In the dark?" Mara whispered to Keltan, who just shrugged.

"You're crazy!" Grute shouted.

Edrik ignored him. The unMasked were rummaging in the saddlebags again, pulling out clay pots filled with . . . Mara sniffed, and blinked. Goose grease?

"Waterproofing," Keltan explained, and Mara understood. Tishka brought Keltan one of the containers, and the two of them began slathering the grease onto their boots. Mara wrinkled her nose at the smell and feel, but gamely covered her borrowed boots until they glistened. They were slightly too large and she was pretty sure she was getting a blister as a result, but bare feet would have been far worse on the rocky path they'd been following—and the thought of wading barefoot in the mountain stream before them made her wince.

Grute, however, continued to complain. "These damn boots you gave me are too tight," he snarled at Tishka. "My feet hurt."

Tishka shrugged. "So don't wear 'em. Your feet won't hurt once they've gone numb. Won't hurt at all after we've had to cut 'em off later."

Grute muttered something under his breath, but subsided. Tishka handed out sausage and cheese; Mara devoured both gratefully. After a few more minutes' rest, they all plunged into the stream.

The greased boots kept Mara's feet dry, but almost at once she felt a chill creeping into them. And the way the boots slipped around on her feet made the uncertain footing provided by the slimy, water-rounded rocks even more treacherous. She skidded and stumbled and felt every moment as if she were on the verge of turning her ankle.

As darkness descended and a full moon rose in a sky sprayed with brilliant stars, Mara, already exhausted, hoped, then expected, then *prayed* that Edrik would say they'd gone far enough and take them ashore to make camp, but instead they kept walking, and walking . . . and walking. Her feet felt like they didn't belong to her anymore, as if they had been cut off and replaced with stockings full of frozen sand. She staggered and almost fell; Keltan grabbed her arm to save her, and she leaned against him gratefully.

"How much longer?" she murmured. "I don't know how much more I can stand . . ."

If a voice could sound pale, then Keltan's sounded pale as he replied, "I know where he's taking us, but I don't know the path well enough to say how close we are to it. But we can't leave the stream until we get there. We can't risk Watchers finding our trail."

Mara glanced behind her. The bright moon and star-spangled sky provided more than enough light for her to see the other girls from the wagon clinging to each other in pairs, Alita and Prella together, even dour Kirika leaning on Simona. Only Grute walked alone, following Tishka at the end of his leash.

Look at that, Mara thought. *A horse's ass, but no horse.* The thought made her grin in the darkness despite her frozen weariness.

An interminable time later, Edrik finally stopped — but not, Mara realized with dismay, to make camp. "We can take a short rest break here," he said, coming back from the front of the column to address them. "Over there." He pointed left, his gesture clearly visible in the moonlight. "Bread and water for everyone. If you need to relieve yourself, do it in the river; downstream, if you please, so we can replenish our water and the horses can drink. If your horse leaves anything on the rocks, wash them. We want no trace of our presence. We're still too close to where we attacked the wagon."

Keltan led Mara to the riverbank, and she gratefully splashed out of the water and found a rock to sit on. The horses were variously ridden or led ashore, the un-Masked kneeling beside them to check their legs and ankles before going off, one by one, into the darkness downstream, adjusting their clothing as they returned after a minute or two.

"My turn," Keltan said, and he, too, disappeared downstream. Mara, whose bladder had been uncomfortably full for hours, made her own trip a few moments later. She squatted above the freezing water feeling embarrassed, undignified, but resigned: the body had its needs regardless of the circumstances, and if she could use that noxious bucket in the cell with Grute not ten feet away, she could manage this.

Shivering, she returned to the stony beach . . . and an argument.

"I've got to go," Grute said. "Untie my hands so I can go." He was glaring at Tishka. Then his face slipped into a leer. "Unless you'd like to help me."

"Take him downstream," Edrik snapped. "Untie his hands so he can relieve himself. But then tie him up again. And watch him the whole time."

"The *whole* time?" Grute said, eyes still fixed on Tishka.

"The whole time," Edrik said levelly.

Grute shrugged. Tishka, face twisted in disgust, gave him a shove toward the river, then walked behind him. They moved downstream until they were just shadows, only visible because they were silhouetted against the sparkle of moonlight and starlight off the rushing water.

Keltan handed Mara a chunk of crusty bread and a flask of water. As she nibbled and drank gratefully, she gave Grute no more thought . . .

. . . until she heard a sharp cry and a splash, audible even above the stream's constant burble. Along with everyone else, she looked downstream.

She saw two dark shapes strangely low in the water; a moment later they straightened abruptly, and then Tishka came splashing back upstream, holding Grute's arm bent behind his back with her left hand, her right forearm clamped across his neck. She threw him, coughing and sputtering, onto the stones at Edrik's feet. "Little beast tried to hit me with a rock," Tishka snarled. "So I half-drowned him." She put her boot to Grute's rear end and shoved him facedown onto the rocks. "Should have finished the job."

"Nice guy, this friend of yours," Keltan muttered.

"He's no friend of mine," Mara shot back.

Edrik glared down at Grute, still choking and shuddering. "Tie him up," he ordered, contempt in his voice. "He goes the rest of the way as baggage. Sling him over the wagon horse."

Keltan made a snorting sound. "And I thought horses were a misery to ride the *proper* way!"

Mara said nothing. She'd only known Grute for a day, but already felt certain that no amount of punishment would change him. *He's bad,* she thought. *Bad through and through. And the Mask knew it.*

But the Mask rejected me, too, and I'm not bad through and through . . .

. . . am I?

She looked at the other children, slumped together on the rocks. *Not unless Alita, Prella, Simona, and Kirika are, too.*

The call to resume the long slog through icy water came almost as a relief. Better the misery of that exhausting, freezing struggle than sitting and reliving the horror of her Masking yet again. But nothing, not the dark, nor the cold, nor the sound of rushing water, could blot from her mind the echoing memory of her mother's screams.

They pushed on for another eternity, then another, and then another. The bump on Mara's head throbbed counterpoint with her sore ribs. Toward the end, Mara only stayed on her feet by leaning heavily on Keltan, who had grown very quiet and grim, but gamely offered what strength he had to spare.

As they walked, the landscape changed, the banks rising higher and higher, lifting the forest with them, until finally they slogged between sheer gray cliffs, the only hint of the trees the sound of rushing wind far above.

At last Edrik pointed again, to the right, the gesture much harder to see this time, for the moon had long since vanished behind the towering stone walls, leaving only the light of the narrow strip of stars. They emerged from the water onto a shelf of rock. Even without the moonlight, Mara could see a dark split in the cliff wall. "Is that . . . ?"

"Our road home," Keltan said from out of the darkness. "Rocky, narrow, and almost impossible to find even if you know it's there. It would take a miracle for the Autarch's men to trail us now."

Mara nodded. That was good news, of course, but she couldn't dredge up much enthusiasm from the deepening black mud of her exhaustion.

"Fires," Edrik said. "Safe enough down here. A hot meal for everyone. Then sleep. We ride again at first light."

A rough and ready camp sprang up. Mara had wondered where the wood for the fires was supposed to come from, but the unMasked answered that by opening bundles of sticks that had been slung on the horses. The night was clear, so there was no bother with tents. There being nothing to graze on, the horses got feedbags. "Always see to the horses first," Keltan said, when Mara protested that the animals got to eat before they did. "They've already drilled *that* much into me!"

Two fires flickered to life. Mara immediately went to the nearest and sat as close to it as she could, soaking up the glorious heat as if she could never get enough—which, at the moment, she didn't think she could. Keltan was busy elsewhere, and Simona and Kirika already slept, despite the stony ground, stretched out near the second fire, but Alita and Prella joined her. The smaller girl cuddled close to Alita and promptly dozed off. Alita stared into the flames, her face drawn and her dark eyes glittering in its unsteady light.

"So," Mara said. "We've been rescued."

"For now," Alita said. "But the Autarch . . ." She looked around to make sure she couldn't be overheard. "He won't stand for this," she said in a low voice. "They've gone too far. Sooner or later, he'll find this 'un-Masked Army,' no matter where they hide. And then it will be worse for us all."

Mara looked across the fire to the dark bundle of Grute, who, still bound and gagged, had been dumped unceremoniously on the cold gray stone. "I doubt it," she said. "This mining camp they were taking us to must be full of people like Grute. Would you really rather be *there* than *here?*"

Alita also gazed at Grute. A small smile flickered across her tired face. "Well, when you put it like that . . ."

After that they both fell silent, staring into the fire. Somehow Mara lost track of time: the next thing she knew she was being gently pulled upright by Keltan; she'd fallen over onto her side. He shoved a bowl of steaming stew with a spoon in it into one hand, and a hunk of brown, crusty bread into the other.

"Eat," he said. "And then sleep."

Like the good girl she'd always thought she was, Mara did as she was told.

EIGHT

Magic in the Dark

EDRIK WAS TRUE TO HIS WORD—or threat, Mara thought wearily, as at first light she was roused out of her bedroll, which had proved more comfortable than a couple of blankets spread across bare rock had any right to be. The bump on her head had subsided, she discovered, feeling it carefully, though the spot was still very sore. But a night in a cold, hard bed hadn't done much for her bruised side and she gasped, pressing a hand to her ribs, as she got stiffly to her feet.

After a hurried breakfast of bread and dried fish, the party moved on, leaving the rushing stream behind to climb up the narrow, winding gully. Only a trickle of water flowed down the middle of it, but rounded rocks and scattered driftwood spoke of past floods and made Mara wonder uneasily what they would do if one came roaring down on them now. She asked Keltan about it; he shrugged. "Drown, I guess."

She punched him on the arm for that and got a grin in response.

Edrik had relented enough to untie Grute that morning for a short period of time, but this time when he'd relieved himself he'd done so in full view of the entire camp, though thankfully his back had been turned. Mara sighed. It seemed that she was doomed, in her new un-Masked life, to watch Grute pee.

Once he was done, he'd been fed a chunk of bread and a chunk of fish, then gagged and tied again and once more thrown like a sack of meal onto the wagon horse, which Tishka led. "What will happen to Grute?" Mara asked Keltan as they left the river behind and began trudging up the gully.

Alita, walking nearby, snorted. "Who cares?"

Keltan glanced at her, then turned back to Mara. "That's up to the Commander."

"Edrik?"

"He's not the Commander."

"He's not?" Alita asked.

Keltan shook his head. His mouth quirked at some private joke. "You'll see."

"See what?" Mara asked, but Keltan wouldn't say anything more about it.

"Newest of the new, lowest of the low, remember?" he said primly. "Not my place to fill you in." And with that, Mara had to be content.

The second day's travel, though as miserable as the first, was at least miserable in a whole new way. Icy water no longer ran around their feet, but the tumbled stones of the gully threatened a twisted ankle with every step, and as the day went on, the way grew steeper, the little stream leaping down beside them in a series of miniature waterfalls. The riders led their horses: the only one mounted, if you could call it that, was Grute.

They climbed all morning. Just as the sun found them,

having finally cleared the ravine's rock walls, they toiled up one last slope to find themselves at one end of a small lake, out of which the stream they'd been following poured down toward the river they'd left behind. Sheer cliffs surrounded the lake, forbidding and black except where the occasional stunted tree clung in defiance of gravity.

Just beside the creek's outlet grew a tiny patch of yellowed grass, barely large enough to accommodate them all. While the horses pulled up mouthfuls of the scraggly growth, the humans rested and ate a meager lunch of dried meat, dried fruit, dry bread, and hard cheese. Mara thought longingly of mashed redroots, soft white loaves, tender roasts, and brown gravy.

I wonder what Mommy made Daddy for lunch today? she thought, and the claws of grief clutched her heart and squeezed her throat so tight she could hardly swallow, the pain far worse than the fading discomfort of her bumps and bruises. But she forced herself to keep eating. She had no idea how long they would have to walk before they got wherever they were going.

She glanced at the creek, tumbling down into the gully they had left, and wondered if, even then, black-masked Watchers were relentlessly climbing after them. Like Alita, she couldn't believe the unMasked could evade the Autarch forever. Children told each other that the Autarch's powerful magic allowed him to see everything that was happening in the Autarchy, everywhere at once; that he could actually look out of the eyes of any Mask he chose. Mara's father had told her that wasn't possible. But she no longer knew if what her father had told her was the truth, since the Mask he had crafted just for her had betrayed her so viciously.

It's not his fault, she told herself. *It's yours. For helping Keltan . . .*

But looking at the boy who sat beside her, munching unenthusiastically on his own rations, she couldn't wish she had betrayed him to the Watchers, even if it would have meant success at her Masking.

If it's my fault, then so be it, she thought defiantly. *And to hell with the Autarch!*

The seditious thought, surely enough to at least twist a Mask, if not shatter it entirely, sent a strange thrill through her. She shivered a little, grinned, and ate with more appetite.

Grute was untied and once again Mara found herself looking at his back as he peed. She groaned and turned to Keltan. "Where do we go from here?" she said. "It looks like a dead end."

Keltan shook his head and pointed. "Look again. Down at the far end."

Mara squinted in that direction as Grute's arms were seized and tied behind him once more. "He didn't wash his hands," Prella said from where she sat with Alita. "Yuck."

Yuck, Mara thought. *That sums up Grute in a nutshell, doesn't it?* She was gazing at the far end of the lake as she thought it, still not seeing whatever-it-was Keltan was pointing out . . . and then she did.

"Oh, no," she groaned. "Is that what it looks like?"

Keltan grinned. "If it looks like a cave, yes."

"And we're going in there?"

"Only for three or four hours. It'll take us to another ravine, and that one leads us the rest of the way to the Secret City."

"Secret City?" Mara stared at him. "How can there be a Secret City? How do you hide a whole city from the Autarch?"

Keltan shook his head. "Not—"

"—your place to tell me." She sighed. "I'm getting really tired of hearing that."

To get to the cave, they had to splash around the shallow edge of the lake. No one mounted. Even Grute walked now. His gag had been removed so he could eat and drink, and hadn't been replaced, but his wrists remained bound behind his back, and Tishka still held his leash.

By sheer bad luck, Mara found herself right in front of him as they reached the cave. "Mara," he said, voice hoarse and mocking. "I've still got plans for you, pretty girl."

Keltan spun and backhanded the other boy across the face, the crack of skin against flesh so loud that even the unMasked at the head of the column, just about to enter the cavern, turned to look. "Don't talk to her," Keltan snarled. "Ever."

Grute jerked his head back to face the other boy. Blood trickled from his split lip. He caught Mara's eye and licked the blood away, slowly, obscenely, then showed his teeth at her in a skull-like grin.

Mara looked past him at Tishka, who flicked Grute's leash. "Keep moving, you," she growled. "And keep your mouth shut. Or I'll gag you again. And I won't use a clean rag, either."

Grute gave her a glance over his shoulder, then pressed his lips together and started forward. Keltan and Mara moved aside to let him pass. Alita and Prella had been behind him. "He talks to you again, knee him in the knackers," Alita told Mara under her breath. "Works every time."

"What are knackers?" Prella asked.

Alita gave her a look. Prella blushed. "Oh," she said.

"Don't worry," Keltan said. "It's just talk. He can't hurt you. The unMasked won't let him."

"They can't keep him a prisoner forever," Mara said.

"Long enough," Keltan said. "Either he changes, or . . ."

"They should string him up," Prella piped up. "By the knackers!" She turned bright red as she said it, but stuck out her chin and looked defiant.

Mara couldn't help it; she burst out laughing. So did Alita. Keltan looked faintly alarmed. Mara found that even more amusing.

The glistening rock of the tunnel walls almost brushed the shoulders of the horses as the column passed through it, single file. Four of the unMasked carried torches. It wasn't nearly enough light, in Mara's opinion, but the flickering glow at least *usually* illuminated the rough places that could catch your feet or the stalactites that could split your scalp. The horses blew and stamped and shivered, clearly uneasy, but they kept moving.

After a couple of hours' travel, the party took a break in a large chamber from which several tunnels exited. Mara looked around uneasily. *If you went down the wrong one, you could wander in the dark forever!*

They carried on, until finally, after another couple of hours, the tunnel widened, the ceiling drew away, and they emerged into an enormous cave mouth, gray evening light flooding in through an opening as big as Mara's lost home. The view wasn't much—yet another towering wall of rock on the other side of yet another stream—but Mara thought she'd never seen anything more beautiful.

A blackened circle of stone near the mouth of the cave spoke of previous camps, and sure enough, Edrik called a halt. The riders stripped their horses of saddles and saddlebags and led them out of the cave and out of sight, presumably to some patch of grass. The other unMasked started unrolling bedrolls. Tishka lit a fire in the old fire circle, using wood from a stockpile in one corner.

"One more day's travel," Keltan said as he and all five girls from the wagon stood near the crackling flames, warming themselves. "And it's easier walking." He nodded to the outside. "That ravine runs downhill, all the way to the sea."

"And that's where the Secret City is?" Alita said.

Keltan nodded.

The sea, Mara thought, spirits lifting at the thought. She'd never seen it, could barely even imagine such a vast quantity of water. But then again, she'd seen a lot of things in the past three days she would have previously found hard to imagine.

Two corners of the cave, screened by rocks, had been set aside as latrines. "I'll be back in a minute," Mara told

Keltan and the others, and headed toward the women's side, grateful that at least in *this* camp Grute would be peeing out of her sight.

She did what she needed to do, trying not to breathe too deeply—several women had been in the space before her—then started back toward the fire.

Something caught her eye, a glint of light deep in the darkness of the cave's recesses. At first she thought it was a bit of shiny rock, reflecting the firelight; but as she watched, its color shifted, from red to blue to green to yellow and back again. She hurried over to it.

In a hollow atop a large boulder of black stone, magic had gathered.

There was very little of it, compared to the magic in her father's stone basin, or even the magic Ethelda had poured from her small vial onto her hands before healing Mara's face. But there could be no doubt that that was what it was.

She hurried back to the others. "Come see what I've found," she said excitedly.

Looking puzzled, they followed her. "What is it?" Alita asked. "An animal?"

"Gold?" Simona guessed.

"Diamonds?" added Prella.

"No . . ." They reached the place. Mara stared down at the seething color in the tiny pool, entranced. "Better!"

The others followed her gaze, then exchanged glances. "Um . . . Mara?" Keltan said. "There's nothing there."

"Just black rock," Prella said.

"*Boring* black rock," Alita added.

Mara stared at them, bewildered. She'd assumed that Grute had been lying to her about the Gifted losing their Gift when their Masking failed. Keltan, Simona, and Kirika shouldn't be able to see it, of course, but Alita and Prella had also had the Gift. "But . . ." Her voice trailed off.

Alita's eyes suddenly widened. "Magic? Is it magic? You can still see it, even after . . . ?"

"Yes," Mara said simply. "I can see it."

"Oh!" said Prella in a small, wondering voice. "Lucky..."

"But why?" Alita demanded. "Why can you still see it when we can't?" She sounded almost angry. "I'll bet it was that Ethelda, that Healer that came to your Masking. I'll bet she did something to save your Gift. While Prella and I..." She pressed her lips together.

Was that it? Mara thought. Had Ethelda healed more than her face?

It was the only answer she had. She looked at the resentment on Alita's face, and felt bad, but she couldn't wish she'd lost her Gift along with everything else.

Although she didn't know what she could do with it. She was supposed to have started training to use her Gift just as soon as she was Masked. Now ... who would teach her? Who would be able to tell her anything about magic or how it could be used?

Or abused, she thought uneasily. There were a lot of old stories about magic being used for terrible things, and stories about Gifted hurting themselves and others by sheer accident.

"What are you doing back here?" said a deep voice behind them, and Mara jumped—even though they were doing nothing wrong, that authoritative voice had triggered her naughty-child reflex—and turned to see Edrik frowning at them.

"Mara can still see magic," Prella piped up at once.

Alita shot her a disgusted look, but Mara, reminding herself again she was doing nothing wrong, said, "Yes, I can." She pointed at the tiny pool of color. "There."

Edrik glanced down, but clearly saw nothing. "Really," he said, sounding skeptical. "I don't see anything."

Mara felt a flash of irritation. "You don't have the Gift." It came out sounding much more insolent than she had intended.

Edrik raised an eyebrow. "True," he said. "But it is also true that your Masking failed. We have been told that those Gifted whose Maskings fail lose their Gifts."

Told by whom? Mara wondered again, but knew she wouldn't get an answer to *that* question.

"Why should you be any different?" Edrik continued, and Mara couldn't answer that question for him any more than she'd been able to answer it for the others. He stared down at the stone. "So . . . assuming you're telling the truth . . ."

"I don't lie," Mara snapped.

He raised a skeptical face. "Can you do anything with it?"

Mara felt a chill, her misgivings rising again. "I . . . I don't know. I . . ." She looked at Alita and Prella. "*We* were all supposed to start our training in the use of magic as soon as we were Masked."

"Convenient," Kirika said, the first word she'd contributed to the conversation. Mara glanced at her, and saw that her expression was closed and hard. *What's her problem?*

But her scornful tone had stung. Pushing aside her doubts, Mara reached out and touched the magic, remembering how magic had formed a glowing blue glove when Ethelda had poured it into her palm from the vial she carried. There wasn't enough magic in the tiny basin to cover her hand, but the instant she touched it, it transferred itself from the depression to her fingers. When she straightened again, her fingers glistened with shifting colors, like oil on water.

It didn't feel like oil, though. It felt . . . alive, somehow; as though she were holding hands with someone . . . with her father, or . . .

. . . or Keltan . . .

"I still don't see anything," Edrik said.

"It's on my hand," Mara said distantly, all her attention on the strange sight and sensation. *Now what?* she thought. *How do I make it do something? And what can I make it do?*

She looked at Kirika, who was staring at her fingers with a scornful expression Mara suddenly wanted to wipe off her face. Her gaze traveled down to the other girl's cloak. At some point during the journey Kirika had caught it on something, tearing a gash about six inches long. Easy to fix, with a needle and thread or . . .

Moved by instinct as much as by conscious decision, she reached out her magic-coated fingers and touched Kirika's cloak.

She gasped; it felt as if she had stuck her hand into a nettle bush, pain and prickling crawling across her skin. At the same time, the multiple colors of the thin sheen of magic faded away, leaving only a ruby-red glow that flowed into the cloak like a bloodstain.

Kirika jerked away. "Don't touch me!" she snarled. Mara lowered her hand. But she kept staring at the place she had touched. Red tendrils of light writhed across the tear in the wool for an instant, then vanished . . .

. . . as did the tear, mended so perfectly it might never have existed.

Kirika looked down at the repaired cloak, then back at Mara. Her eyes narrowed, but all she said, in a voice hard as stone, was, "Don't *ever* touch me without permission. Ever." She raised her eyes to the others. "Any of you."

Nobody was listening. They were all staring at the magically mended cloth.

"Wow," Keltan said at last, breaking the silence.

Both of Edrik's eyebrows were raised now. "It seems you're telling the truth." He glanced around. "Is there more magic here? There are other things that need mending . . ."

Mara shook her head. "I haven't seen any more. And I used it all . . ." She paused, then leaned over the basin. Yes, she'd used all the magic collected there, but she could see more already seeping into the basin, a tiny thread, insubstantial as gossamer.

Where does it come from? she wondered. *And why does it collect* here?

She had no answer. *Something else they were going to teach me,* she thought bitterly.

How many years had it taken that slender thread of magic to collect in the basin? And she had used it all up in an instant.

She straightened. "There's no more," she said.

Edrik looked thoughtful. "But if we could get more . . ." He stood silent for a moment, then shook his head. "A problem for another day." He nodded back toward the fires. "You should eat and get to sleep. We have another long walk tomorrow."

They walked back to the fire. Kirika took herself off and lay down, back to them. Alita's expression remained closed and resentful. Keltan kept stealing wide-eyed glances at her. Only Prella and Simona seemed unaffected by the news that she still had her Gift. Prella prattled on about how beautiful magic was and how much she missed being able to see it. Simona prodded the smaller girl along with questions but didn't ask Mara any. She seemed almost . . . frightened.

Mara didn't know what to think. She still had her Gift. Wonderful. But what good was it? She might never see magic again, where they were going. All she'd accomplished, as far as she could see, was mend a torn cloak, and in the process, frighten Simona, make Alita jealous, annoy Kirika, and . . .

She glanced at Keltan, who saw her look and immediately turned his gaze back to the fire, poking at it, completely unnecessarily, with a stray stick. "I'm not going to suddenly turn you into a pig, you know," she finally burst out. "I had the Gift when you met me the first time. I've had it all along. I haven't changed."

He started, then glanced at her a little sheepishly. "I . . . I know," he said. "It's just . . . I've never actually seen anyone *use* magic before. The way you just touched the cloak, and it knit itself up again . . ." He looked back into the fire. "It was creepy."

She sighed. "Well," she said, "you'll probably never see it again. That may be the last magic I ever see."

Keltan said nothing more about it, but at least he quit looking at her as though she'd sprouted a second head.

Despite her exhaustion—or maybe even because of it—it was a long time before Mara slept that night. It seemed she could still feel the magic, clinging to her fingers, waiting for her to use it . . . and now that she had felt it once, she found that she wanted to feel it again, and feel more of it.

What else could I do with it?

She didn't know; couldn't know without more magic. But someday, she hoped she'd find out.

The next day, at the end of a long but relatively easy walk down a broad ravine, they finally arrived at the Secret City.

NINE

The Secret City

NOT THAT MARA even *saw* the Secret City at first glance. She had eyes only for the ocean.

The ravine ended in a sandy cove, shaped like a horseshoe, surrounded on three sides by towering walls of black stone. Directly across from the returning party, perhaps a quarter of a mile away, water began, and what amazed Mara was that *it never ended*: at least, not until it met the half-set sun on the distant horizon. The sea rolled endlessly in toward the shore, breaking in long, shadowy waves, black against the orange fire pouring across the water from the sunset. Mara gaped. She'd never imagined anything so big or so beautiful: almost as beautiful as magic. The masts of a half-dozen boats pulled up along the shore speared the red sky.

But the sun made the ocean too bright to look at for

long, so she tore her gaze away and instead studied the cliffs. Thin tendrils of smoke, lit orange by the sun, rose from the cliff to her left, presumably from unseen chimneys or fissures high above. Narrow window slits punctuated the rock face at ground level and for three or four stories above that, and one large opening gave access to the cliff's interior from the cove. Other black openings gaped at the base of the cliff on the right, though none higher than ground level, and no smoke rose from that side of the cove.

Through the window slits to her left she glimpsed glowing lamplight and flickering hearth light and dark, moving figures. Then suddenly, from the large opening at ground level, men, women, and children poured out like ants from an overturned nest.

Mara drew back instinctively as people ran toward them, until she found herself back to back with Alita, Prella, and Simona. Kirika stood apart, fists and jaw clenched, as though daring anyone to come near. Keltan, on the other hand, moved forward. He clasped hands with another boy, a head taller and perhaps two years older, and brought the youth over to the rescued girls. Thin as a broom, with a thatch of black hair, he had startlingly blue eyes and white teeth. Both flashed in the last of the sun's light as he gave them a friendly smile.

"Mara, Alita, Prella, Kirika, Simona," Keltan said, "I'd like you to meet Hyram, Edrik's son."

"Hi," Hyram said. "Welcome to the Secret City!"

"City?" Alita said. "All I see is a bunch of caves."

Hyram laughed. "Well, what is Tamita but a bunch of man-made caves? People lived in caves a long time before they built buildings. In fact, they lived in some of *these* caves; we've found their wall paintings."

Prella shuddered. "I don't like caves," she said. "The one we came through on the way here was horrible. I don't even like the *idea* of caves. In stories they're always full of bats and snakes and bears and . . . and monsters."

"I can honestly say," Hyram said, smile widening,

"that I have never seen a monster in the Secret City. And I've lived here my whole life." He jerked his head toward the entrance. "Come on. I'll show you."

Mara hesitated, glancing toward Edrik. Were they allowed . . . ?

But Edrik, busy kissing the tall, black-haired woman who had her arms around his neck, seemed singularly uninterested in anything they might do.

Hyram followed her gaze, and laughed again. He'd already laughed a lot since they'd met him. She couldn't help smiling in response. "Don't worry," he said. "You won't get in trouble. Mom told me to get you settled."

"Your mother is beautiful," Kirika said unexpectedly.

Simona gave her a surprised look; Hyram laughed yet again. "Thanks," he said. "Too bad I don't take after her."

Mara, who had found it hard to keep her eyes from his finely honed features from the moment he had come over to them, opened her mouth to protest, then closed it again with a snap. If Hyram noticed, he gave no sign, instead just indicating the cave entrance again. "Follow me!"

He led them to the opening, half as tall as the Tamita city wall and as wide as the Market Gate—three wagon breadths, at least. "We call this the Broad Way," Hyram said as he led them into the cavern beyond, and Mara could see why: the wide cave mouth became an equally wide tunnel that extended into darkness. Lanterns hung on the stone walls cast periodic pools of yellow light. Here and there other tunnels joined the Broad Way. After a hundred yards or so it sloped down and out of sight.

"Storerooms and our water supply are all down there," Hyram said, pointing toward the Broad Way's hidden end. "Baths, too." He glanced at them and his mouth quirked. "I, um . . . *sense* . . . that you could all use them sometime in the not-too-distant future."

Mara took a sniff, and decided not to take that personally.

But that sniff also brought far more appealing smells

to her attention. Woodsmoke, of course, and a general sort of people smell; but also the really, really good smells of baking bread and roasting meat. Her mouth watered and her stomach rumbled.

Hyram glanced at her. *He heard*, she thought, face growing hot. "Food in a few minutes," he said. "But first, let me show you where you'll be sleeping."

He led them, not down the Broad Way, but into the first tunnel on the left. Clearly man-made, cut out of the rock, it changed almost at once from tunnel to staircase. They climbed up rough-hewn steps, past two lit oil lamps and one that had burned out, emerging into one end of another tunnel stretching away into the rock. Hyram, however, took them directly across that tunnel to a wooden door that he pushed open, revealing a good-sized chamber beyond. Thick black timbers shored up the roof and walls. A slit of a window, hewn through at least four feet of rock, let in cool salt air and the sound of surf. Shutters hung on the inside could close it off if need be. Half a dozen beds, the frames made of white-washed wood, the mattresses covered with warm-looking woolen blankets of blue and green, lined the walls. Each had a side table; lanterns burning on three of them filled the room with a cozy yellow glow. An unlit hearth was cut into the inside wall. "Girls' room," Hyram said.

Mara went over to one of the beds and poked at the mattress. It rustled and released the unmistakable smell of hay. She sat, then lay down. A week before she would have thought it unbearably prickly and lumpy. But after one night in the iron cage in the warehouse, four nights in the cold cells of the way stations, and two nights on the ground—all of those nights far too short—it felt like heaven. She felt her eyes closing and jerked upright again. Looking around, she saw that the other girls had picked out beds and were testing them, as well.

"Well?" Hyram said. "What do you think?"

"Better than I had at home," said Alita.

"A *lot* better," muttered Kirika.

"Not as good as *I* had at home," said Simona. She touched the thin scars lining her face. "But I'm not about to complain."

"I think it's perfect," Prella piped up.

Mara saw Keltan and Hyram both looking at her, as if only her verdict *really* mattered. "It'll do," she said, and both boys relaxed—and then gave each other a strange look she didn't know how to interpret.

"What about Grute?" asked Prella. "Where will he sleep?"

"Grute?" Hyram gave her a puzzled look.

"The sack of dung on a leash," Alita clarified.

"One of the *old* kind of unMasked," said Keltan. He told Hyram about Grute's attempt to hit Tishka with a rock, and Hyram's face stiffened. *And he doesn't even know what happened in the wagon*, Mara thought. *Or the warehouse.*

"You should execute him," Kirika said, voice cold and flat. "He's a waste of space. Not worth feeding."

Mara hated and feared Grute, but even so, Kirika's matter-of-fact bloodthirstiness shocked her.

"Not up to me," Hyram said shortly, but it sounded as if he rather liked the idea. He looked around at the girls. "There's one other thing you need to see up here. This way." He took them back out into the tunnel that ran in the same direction as the Broad Way a level below. A couple of other tunnels opened off of it left and right, along with several doors, but it ended in a chamber whose entrance was hung with a curtain of gray cloth, currently pushed aside to reveal, inside, a wooden seat with a hole in it, over an opening in the rock from which came the distant sound of rushing water. "Toilet," Hyram said succinctly.

Alita looked into the hole. "I hope that's not our water supply down there."

Hyram's smile vanished. "Of course not," he snapped. "All waste goes into the underground river downstream from where we draw our water, and the river empties straight into the ocean. We're not fools, you know."

Alita raised an eyebrow at him, expression cool, and Hyram flushed. "Sorry," he said. "I know it's all rustic, compared to Tamita. But we've been here a long time, and we've not only survived, we've thrived—free of the Autarch, and his Watchers . . . and his Masks."

Alita said nothing.

Hyram took a deep breath and turned away from her. "Speaking of water," he said, "now I think it's time I showed you the baths."

He took them back down the stairs into the Broad Way and down it, the main entrance disappearing behind them as they went deeper underground. After those first hundred yards, no more tunnels opened off the Broad Way, which suggested to Mara that the Secret City existed only near the surface of the rock face. Understandable; the amount of work required to create even what she had seen was mind-boggling, even if, as Hyram had suggested, some of it had been here for centuries. Anyway, who would want to live any farther inside the rock than they had to? She could almost feel the vast mass of stone above her pressing down.

The Broad Way became progressively less broad as they walked, until it was only a couple of arm-spans wide. Then, with no warning, it opened up again into a huge chamber. A dozen lamps on wooden poles struggled to light the space, their feeble illumination failing to reach the far wall, some unguessed distance away in the darkness, but their glimmer still revealed enough to make Mara and the others gasp.

They stood on the shore of an enormous underground lake, its water smooth as glass. Curtains and daggers of stone festooned the high stone ceiling, the lamplight waking tiny sparkles of golden light even in the deepest shadows: the whole cave, in fact, glittered as if studded with diamonds. Through the crystal-clear water Mara could see the bottom of the lake sloping gently away into dark depths.

"We get our water from the springs over there," Hyram said, pointing left, and Mara turned to see clear water tumbling down from a crack in the rock, splashing into a small pool that then overflowed into the lake, the flowing water mimicked by the flowing shapes of the sparkling stone over which it poured. "The stream you heard under the toilet empties out of the lake over there." He pointed farther to the left, toward a dark opening.

"We bathe in the lake itself. Girls over here . . ." He led them along the right side, around an outthrust shoulder of rock, to where an arm of the lake extended into a horseshoe cove. He turned and pointed back at the smooth surface of the lake, disappearing into darkness. "No one can see in, so modesty is preserved."

Mara knelt by the lake and put her hand into the water. "It's warm," she said, in surprise.

"Hot springs well up into the lake," Hyram said.

Mara stood and looked around, spotting gray lumps of soap in a natural depression in the rock. No towels, but she supposed there must be something in their room. "All the comforts of home," she said, trying to sound cheerful, though in fact she had suddenly been struck by a wave of homesickness so great she thought for a horrible moment she would burst into tears.

She wanted her *own* room, her *own* home, their enameled bathtub, her mother's cooking, her father's laughter . . . not this horrible place of stone and strangers, darkness and displacement. But she couldn't have it. She could never have it again.

Because of the Masks. Because of the Autarch. Because . . .

. . . because.

She realized that both Hyram and Keltan were watching her—again—and managed to dredge up a smile. It felt horribly false—*like the smile of a Mask*, she thought—but she held it in place. "Now how about something to eat?" she said. "I'm starving." She glanced around at the others. "Aren't you?"

Amid a general murmur of consent, they made their way back up the Broad Way, the smells of cooking growing stronger as they approached. "Big feast tonight to welcome everyone back," Hyram said. "In the Great Chamber." He led them to the opposite side of the Broad Way from the stairs they had climbed to the girls' room, and into a room that would have been breathtaking in size if they hadn't just seen the underground lake. As it was, it was merely impressive.

Wooden tables dotted its smooth gray floor. At hearths around the perimeter Mara could see cooks stirring and turning and seasoning and tasting sizzling sides of meat and the bubbling contents of countless cauldrons. As she watched, a baker pulled a long platter covered with loaves of bread out of a clay oven. Her stomach growled again and she thought she might drown in her own saliva.

"Let's find a table," Hyram said, but as she started to follow him, someone touched her arm. She turned to see Edrik.

"The Commander wants to see you," he said.

"But—" Mara looked longingly toward the food. "Couldn't it wait until . . . ?"

"I'm sure she won't keep you long."

She? Mara blinked.

Hyram and the others had stopped and glanced back when they realized she wasn't with them. Hyram took a step toward her, but Edrik shook his head, and his son stopped.

No rescue, Mara thought. Resigned, she turned her back on the good smells of the Great Chamber, and followed Edrik back into the Broad Way. He turned right, as though taking her to the underground lake, but only went a short distance before turning right again down a side tunnel, one that ran straight and flat, uninterrupted, for a very long way. It ended in a closed door, painted white.

Edrik rapped on the smooth surface with his knuckles. After a moment, a voice said, "Come in." Edrik lifted the latch and pushed opened the door, and Mara stepped through.

She felt as if she had somehow stepped out of the caverns into a luxurious tent. Heavy tapestries, colors muted by age, hid the walls of the chamber, about the same size as the one the girls would share. Filmy white cloth draped the ceiling. Thick, intricately patterned rugs in red, brown, and cream covered the floor.

A slit of a window above a large white four-poster bed at the chamber's far end showed only darkness, but let in the sound of surf, much louder here: this chamber, Mara realized, must overlook the ocean. An oval mirror above a wooden dresser to her left reflected the room back on itself; beside it stood a heavy wardrobe, taller than she was.

Lamps illuminated the room with a golden glow. A fire blazing in a hearth to Mara's right added a hint of woodsmoke to the sea air.

Mara took it all in with a glance and an intake of breath; then her gaze riveted on the woman at the center of the unexpected luxury, seated at a round table of polished yellow wood in one of the four matching chairs that surrounded it.

Tiny, thin, snow-white hair pulled into a severe bun, face deeply etched with wrinkles, she wore a heavy black cloak pulled close around her. Fur peeked out from under the collar, though Mara found the room stifling. The woman's hands, gnarled and knobby as old tree roots, rested on the table. But all the clues that spoke of great age were belied by eyes as bright, blue, sharp, and glittering as twin steel blades.

"Grandmother," said Edrik. "I have brought Mara Holdfast."

Grandmother? Mara shot a glance at Edrik, then

looked back at the woman. Now that the idea had been put into her head, she could see the resemblance: something in the nose, the line of the jaw, the height of the forehead, and definitely in the bright blue eyes, shared by Edrik and Hyram alike.

"Come here, child," said Edrik's grandmother, her voice cracked, but with a core of strength that brooked no disobedience. Mara walked over to the table. The old woman looked past her at Edrik. "Leave us, grandson."

Edrik bowed and went out, closing the white door behind him with a soft click.

The old woman studied Mara for a long moment, then said abruptly, "I am Catilla, Commander of the un-Masked Army. And you are Mara, daughter of Charlton Holdfast, Master Maskmaker of Tamita."

"Yes," Mara said. "But I don't understand how you know that."

Catilla shrugged. "It is enough that we do."

"And I don't understand how all *this*" — Mara waved her hands — "can even *exist*. Why hasn't the Autarch found you?"

Catilla's eyes narrowed. "Why should I entrust *you* with our secrets? You have not yet proved yourself a friend. And you have come to us under . . . unusual circumstances."

Mara felt a flash of anger. "You kidnapped me!" She thought of the blood-soaked ground beneath the slain Watchers and wagon drivers. "You *killed* to kidnap me! And now you don't know if you can trust me?"

"It is *because* we 'kidnapped' you— " Catilla's eyes narrowed further, "—although some might say 'rescued'— that I cannot be sure I can trust you." She pulled the cloak tighter. "Always before, our recruits have come to us of their own free will, fleeing their Masking."

"Like Keltan."

Catilla nodded. "Some few," she continued, "*very* few, have come *after* their Masking—long after, in some cases—fleeing the gibbet, knowing their Masks are about to betray their true feelings about the Autarch's bloody reign to the Watchers."

Mara blinked at that. She'd never thought of someone fleeing Tamita while their Mask remained intact. But if they had, they might still be able to get back into Tamita, or at least into some of the smaller towns and villages, once or twice more before their Masks betrayed them. She shuddered, thinking of the danger involved; but it was the only way she could imagine that the unMasked Army could infiltrate Masked society, and plant the rumors of their existence they needed to maintain the flow of recruits . . . *and perhaps to buy things they can't make themselves,* she thought, glancing at the dresser and mirror. *But if that's true, what does it say about this woman that she would have people risk their lives for her comfort?*

"However, we have never before snatched unMasked from the very clutches of the Watchers, en route to the mining camp," Catilla continued. "And so I find myself on uncertain ground."

"Then why did you do it this time?" Mara demanded.

Catilla's blue gaze did not waver. "The others are of no importance. We would never have risked discovery for ordinary unMasked, those who chose to go to their Maskings willingly rather than risk all to find us as others have. No. We did not set out to rescue *them*: we set out to rescue *you*, Mara, daughter of Charlton Holdfast."

"But *why?*" Mara asked again.

"We judged the potential reward outweighed the risks."

"*What* reward?" Mara cried in frustration. "I don't understand!"

Catilla regarded her. "Well," she said after a moment. "Perhaps I must tell you at least *some* of our secrets." She gave a wintry smile. "It's not as if we will let you escape to betray them."

Mara waited. The room was so hot, despite the open window, that a drop of sweat ran down her nose. She batted it away.

"Many years ago," Catilla said at last, "more years than I care to remember, when I was a young woman only a little older than you are now, the old Autarch died. He died suddenly, under suspicious circumstances, and, almost immediately, rebellion erupted. The old Autarch had raised taxes to ruinous levels, thrown countless people into debtors' prison when they could not pay, arrested those he suspected of crimes against the state—a category of wrongdoing which had a *very* broad definition in his mind—imprisoning or even executing them without trial, and on and on. The rebels sought to overthrow the Autarchy, to institute a new kind of government, one where rulers would be elected by the people, not born to privilege or seizing power by force."

Mara blinked. She'd never heard of such a concept. Catilla carried on. "But though many supported the rebels, there were also many for whom the old Autarch, for all his tyranny, had represented stability. Far from suffering, many of those people had grown fat under the Autarch's rule. They did *not* want change. And ultimately they prevailed."

Catilla sighed. "The Autarch's son, still a beardless youth, ascended to the Sun Throne upon his father's death. Even while open rebellion still roiled in the streets and whole villages burned, he summoned Aygrima's greatest mages and artisans. He wanted to be certain, once the rebellion was quashed, that he would never face another. He wanted a magical way to be assured, always and absolutely, of his subjects' loyalty, a way to root out treason and sedition before it could break into open revolt. He *especially* did not want to die like his father had, screaming in agony as poison ate him from the inside out.

"Within two years, the rebellion had been quelled. And while the last of its fomenters still hung from the gallows outside the Palace entrance known ever since as Traitors' Gate, the Autarch announced the solution his magic-workers had crafted: from the next New Year's

Feast onward, all adults of the Autarchy, everyone who had reached the age of fifteen, would be Masked—their faces encased, whenever they were in public, by a magical simulacrum of their features that would reveal their innermost being to a corps of Gifted warriors known as the Watchers, and betray them if they harbored rebellion in their hearts.

"Most of the Autarch's subjects submitted—but not all. Some fled into the Wild, pursued by Watchers who hunted them down like animals. There are still some—a dozen dozen, perhaps—who live as bandits in the woods, mostly those who committed some crime and fled the Autarch's justice. We have agents among them to ensure they never threaten our secrets, and to ensure they continue to raid villages and farms and murder the occasional Watcher."

"Why?" Mara asked, bewildered.

Catilla raised a white eyebrow. "Surely it's obvious? Because as long as the Watchers know those bandits are out there, they, and therefore the Autarch, will continue to believe *they* are the mythical 'unMasked Army,' built up by rumor and wishful thinking into something far greater than reality." She tightened her grip on her cloak again. "As I said, rather than accept the Masks, some ran to the Wild. A few, in desperation, boarded fishing boats and sailed deep into the Great Sea, over the horizon, in search of whatever lies beyond the ocean—if anything does. Myself, I think they drowned or fell off the edge of the world.

"But I had a better plan." She leaned forward. "My father was very high in the rebellion. When it all began to crumble, when he knew it was only a matter of time until he was arrested, he entrusted me with a great secret: the location of a hidden redoubt, a complex of caves inhabited and expanded by the ancients but abandoned for centuries. Late in the rebellion, he had stumbled upon it while fleeing the Watchers. He had hoped that it might provide a base where the rebels could regroup and from which they could eventually strike back. But by the time he returned to Tamita, he saw it was already too late: the rebellion, and almost everyone who had supported it, were dead." Her eyes suddenly turned bright and tears trickled down both cheeks. "As was he, far too soon: arrested and beheaded on the spot . . . on the front steps of our house."

She blinked and scrubbed her face with the back of her right hand, her left still clutching her cloak. "Damn the sentimentality of old age," she muttered. She leaned forward again. "I had married, at age sixteen, just before the old Autarch's death. My son was still an infant when my father was executed. My husband, only eighteen himself, frightened they would come for him next, disappeared, leaving me to care for our child alone. And then came the proclamation about the Masks . . .

"I would not don the Mask myself, and I most assuredly would not raise my son to be Masked. So I fled, with my son and a few like-minded associates, a week before the decree took effect. Ostensibly we were visiting friends in Snowdrift, but we never got there—never went anywhere near it. Instead, we came here, and here we stayed."

Catilla leaned back, and looked around the overly warm chamber. "I have slept in this chamber now for more than sixty years, for as long as there have been Masks. I raised my son here. His wife died in childbirth and he died shortly thereafter, and so it also fell to me to raise my grandson, Edrik." Again she wiped her eyes with an impatient hand, without pausing in her tale. "And slowly, so slowly, the unMasked Army has grown. Every year, there are some few who come to understand, before they are Masked or after, that to wear the Mask is to be a slave. They flee. The lucky ones make contact with us." Her face turned grim. "The unlucky end up with the bandits, or as naked corpses hanging from the gallows at Traitors' Gate."

"What about the ones whose Maskings fail? Like

mine?" Mara said. "They're unMasked, too. Why haven't you tried to rescue them, link them to your cause? Keltan said we're the first ones you've ever freed from the wagons!"

"Until recently," the Commander said, "most of those whose Maskings failed would have been worse than useless to us. Until recently, you could almost predict which children's Masks would fail. Even at fifteen, some youths have already gone well down the road of crime or violence. Others, though neither bad nor trending toward badness, were just . . . odd. Withdrawn, perhaps. A little slow. Developing a romantic interest in those of their own sex. Different."

Mara stared at her. "And even knowing *that*, even knowing they weren't all bad like . . . like Grute . . . you never tried to save them . . . *any* of them?" Mara heard the anger in her blunt accusation. Catilla heard it, too: her eyes narrowed. Mara wondered if she had just stepped over a line that would have her thrown into a cell like Grute . . . or maybe (horrible thought) *with* Grute. But the thought of all those children, children just like her, turning fifteen with a mixture of hope and trepidation, a little uncertain what life behind a Mask would be like, but happy, excited, party planned, friends invited . . . all those proud parents watching their children on the dais, half their thoughts on the celebrations to come . . . and then the terror, the pain, the blood, the screams . . . the anger surged higher. "Not even *one?*" She hurled the words at Catilla like a dagger.

Catilla's lips drew into a tight white line in her wrinkled face. "Don't you *dare* judge me, child!" Her voice, though barely above a whisper, conveyed deadly warning, like the venomous hiss of a snake. "My concern is not whether *this* or *that* child escapes the Mask. My concern is overthrowing the Autarch so that *no* child ever faces the Mask."

"And how's that going?" Mara snapped, while a part of her quailed and wondered, *What are you* doing? But only a *small* part. The larger part, furious, frightened, hurt, hungry, wary, weary, was more than halfway to *hating* this old woman, crouched at the heart of the Secret City like a poisonous spider at the dark center of a vast web. "The Autarch still reigns. The Masks are still made. *And children are still suffering!*"

Catilla's knuckles turned white as her thin fingers, clutching her cloak, curled into tight little fists . . . and then those fists relaxed. She took a deep breath. And then, to Mara's enormous surprise, she chuckled. "You have fire, little one. Good." She relaxed back into her chair. "And indeed, you ask the pertinent question, one I have asked myself year after year. How *is* our quest to overthrow the Autarch going? And the answer, year after year, is the same." Her mouth twisted in sudden anger. "It's going like shit."

Mara blinked. It wasn't that she'd never heard—and even, when away from her parents, *used*—that particular vulgarity before. She just hadn't expected it to come out of the mouth of the birdlike little old woman before her. But Catilla's frank admission of failure surprised her even more.

"We have never been able to strike an effective blow against the Autarch, because the very thing we wish to overthrow, the tyranny of the Masks, prevents us from infiltrating Tamita. Those who come to us with Masks— briefly—intact, we dare send only into the smaller villages, where Watchers are scarce, less observant, and less likely to be Gifted. They spread the rumors we want spread and bring back goods we need. But to send one such as that into Tamita would be a death sentence *and* reveal our existence to the Autarch. How can you foment rebellion when the rebellious, or any they convince of the rightness of their cause, are betrayed by their own faces?" She leaned forward again. "And *that* is why you were rescued."

Mara still felt angry. "I don't understand what use you think I can be. All those other children deserved rescue, too, and you stood by—"

"And would do again, and *will* do again, for there are wagons sent to the camp every month, and we will *not* strike at them again," Catilla snapped. "Once, we *may* get away with: the Watchers will, we *hope*, assume the attack was carried out by bandits and will simply redouble their efforts to track and kill them. But twice? The risks are too great. Not just for us, but for everyone." She slapped her open hand against her chest. "No one else stands against the Autarch. *No one*. If we are destroyed, no new rebellion will arise in your lifetime." She snorted. "Not that you are likely to have much of a lifetime, if we are destroyed."

Even through her anger, Mara could see the sense of what Catilla said, though doing so almost made her angrier. But something still bothered her. "You said you cannot infiltrate Tamita," she said slowly. "But you also said you had an ally there, someone who told you of me. How has he escaped detection?"

"*That* secret I will not share." Catilla studied her. "Edrik tells me you still have the Gift. *That* comes as a surprise."

"I'm glad something does," Mara muttered.

Catilla snorted. "It doesn't change anything. We have no store of magic here and no one to train you in its use if we did, and I have always heard that without training and use, the Gift withers. Yours will no doubt fade soon enough. There must have been Gifted children born here in the Secret City over the decades, but since we have had no way of either testing them or teaching them, what use have their Gifts been? None. No, what matters is not that you still have your Gift. What matters is that you can make a Mask."

And suddenly Mara thought she understood what Catilla wanted from her . . . and it terrified her. She jumped up. "No! I can't make a Mask. Why would you think I could make a Mask?"

"You are the daughter of Charlton Holdfast, Master Maskmaker of Tamita," Catilla said inexorably. "Maskmaker to the Gifted. Maskmaker to the Circle, to the Autarch Himself. You were pre-apprenticed to your father. We *know* he has already taught you much of the art. Don't deny it."

"I don't deny I was *going* to learn to make Masks," Mara said hotly. "What I deny is that I *have* learned! I don't have a clue how to put the magic into them, don't even know how to start—"

"But," said Catilla, "we don't *want* Masks with magic. Masks with magic are the *last* thing we want. What we want are clever forgeries." She pointed at the chair. "Sit down and *listen*, and I will tell you what we need, and what you will do for us." She leaned forward again, her eyes glittering in the candlelight, cold and reptilian. "For you *will* do what I ask, Mara, daughter of Charlton Holdfast. We have risked much to save you from death—or worse. You owe us, and you *will* repay us."

"Or what?" Mara said, defiance blazing up inside her even though she knew she was already defeated, that she would have no choice but to do what Catilla wanted.

Catilla, it seemed, knew that, too, for she smiled, the sudden warmth of it like sunshine breaking through snow clouds. "Why discuss something that will never happen? Sit, child. Sit, and listen to what I propose." She pointed at the chair behind Mara again. "Sit!"

And Mara, feeling strangely brittle, like a dry twig that might snap at any moment, sat and listened to what the unMasked Army demanded of her. But she couldn't help wondering what would happen if she failed.

TEN

"I'll Need a Few Things"

AN HOUR LATER, Mara sat with Keltan, Alita, and Prella beside a blazing driftwood fire on the beach, watching the surf rolling in, pale lines of foam appearing in the circle of flickering illumination, pouring over the sand, flattening, and then receding. The crackling of the fire and the endless wash of water on sand surrounded them in a private cocoon. No one could hear them out here.

The food Mara had eaten in the Great Chamber immediately after the interview with Catilla sat like a lump in her stomach. The others had peppered her with questions when she'd come back, but she'd said nothing, and Hyram, whether out of kindness to her or deference to his great-grandmother, had steered the conversation in other directions. Kirika had gone off by herself shortly after Mara returned, saying nothing. Simona had left next, announcing she wanted a bath more than anything. A few minutes later Hyram had been called away by his mother, and that was when Keltan, after a stealthy glance around, had opened his strangely bulky coat to reveal the two wine bottles tucked into its interior pockets and quietly suggested they take some mugs and go out to the beach. He now sat to her left, a wine bottle stuck in the sand between them.

She'd never had wine before in her life. Was it supposed to taste like that, fruity but not sweet, warming her throat and her insides? She hadn't much liked the first couple of swallows, but it seemed to get better the more of it you drank, and about the time she'd emptied her mug she'd found herself telling the others everything Catilla had said.

"She wants you to do *what?*" Keltan lowered his own mug to stare at her.

"You heard me. Make counterfeit Masks, so the un-Masked Army can sneak into the city and do . . . something. I'm not sure what. Try to assassinate the Autarch, maybe. She wouldn't tell me."

"Assassinate the Autarch?" Prella, seated on her right, stared at her wide-eyed. She'd taken one swallow of the wine, made a face, and passed it down to Alita, on the other side of Keltan. "You can't do that!"

Alita, who had drunk Prella's mug and her own and showed not the slightest sign it had had any effect, gave Prella another silent look. Prella subsided. *I think Alita still has some kind of magical Gift,* Mara thought. *Or maybe that's what comes of growing up surrounded by boys.*

Alita turned back to Mara. "I doubt that's what they have in mind. Someone else would just take over."

"Who?" Mara asked. "The Autarch is childless."

"So what? He must have cousins or other blood relations. The line of succession is a many-headed snake. You can't kill it just by cutting off one head; you have to kill the whole thing."

"Could be a lot of infighting if that happened, though," Keltan said thoughtfully. "Maybe even civil war . . ."

He and Alita continued in that vein, speculating what would happen if—or *when*—the Autarch died. Mara poured herself more wine and sipped it, saying nothing. She didn't know what to think. She'd grown up under the rule of the Autarch. She'd never really given it much thought until her Masking had failed so spectacularly. The Autarch just *was*, a force of nature, like the wind or the rain. *Somebody* had to be in charge, and in Tamita, that was the Autarch. If her Mask had worked, she would never have even considered the *possibility* of overthrowing the Autarch.

Of course, she wouldn't have dared to, while she wore the Mask; and that was part of the reason for overthrowing him, wasn't it?

Her mug was empty. She filled it again from the bottle by her side as Alita said, "Well, whatever they're up to, why now? The unMasked Army has been out here for what? Sixty years? The Autarch is an old man. He can't live much longer. Why act now, when they've done nothing for decades?"

"Good question," Mara said. She sipped from the refilled mug.

"I wouldn't say they've done *nothing*," Keltan protested. "They've provided a haven for those who fled their Maskings. Like me."

"Sure, great, wonderful—for *you*, and a handful of others," Alita snapped. "But what about the ones who tried to flee and were caught? I've sneaked up to Traitors' Gate. Haven't you?"

"No," Prella said in a small voice.

Alita ignored her. "Those weren't all grown-ups hanging up there. Some were boys no older than *you*." She pointed at Keltan. "And there weren't any girls at all . . . which tells me something about what the Watchers use *them* for."

Mara, mug at her lips, looked over it at Prella, half-expecting the smaller girl to say, "What?" and dreading what Alita would say in response, but for once Prella, though she still looked confused, kept her questions to herself.

"So I don't see how the unMasked Army is an 'army' at all," Alita continued. "It doesn't fight, it hides."

"Not anymore," Keltan shot back. "Or you wouldn't be here."

Alita grunted. "Doesn't have anything to do with *me*. They'd have left *me* and the rest of us to rot. It was *her* they wanted," and she nodded at Mara in a way that seemed like an accusation.

Flushing, Mara drank more wine.

"Which just proves Catilla finally has a plan to fight back," Keltan said.

"About time," Alita said. "But why now? What's changed?"

"The Masks," Mara said. She lowered her mug and looked down into it: it was almost empty again, so she drained it and reached for the bottle. Keltan raised an eyebrow at her as she refilled her mug for the third time. She gave him a big smile, and took three big swallows.

When she lowered the mug, she saw the others staring at her as if expecting her to explain what she had meant, so she tried . . . although for some reason her tongue seemed to find it harder than usual to form words. "Catilla told me. The Mash . . . Masks have changed. They're not just reflecting what people are like inside. They're changing pleople . . . people. From the inside out. Different. Keltan noticed. Old friends not friendly anymore. Me, too. And Gifted. Gifted Masks never failed. Now they do. More and more." She drained the mug again and reached for the wine bottle—there was still a little bit left in it—but Keltan pushed it away.

"I think that's probably enough," he said, and after that somehow she didn't really notice anything else that happened until she found herself lying in her bed in the girls' room, which was making slow circles around her. It was very strange, but after another moment she didn't notice it any more, or anything else until morning.

She woke to Alita shaking her. "Edrik is at the door," she said. "He wants you to come with him again."

Mara groaned. Her head pounded, each thump of her heart was accompanied by a stab of pain behind her left eye, and her mouth tasted like . . . like *shit*, she thought, because "dung" definitely wasn't a strong enough word. Alita looked down at her with a strange expression. "You only had three mugs of wine."

"Three too many," Mara said. "Take my word for it, it—"

"I had four," Alita said, not as if she was bragging, just stating a fact. "I'll tell Edrik you'll join him in the Broad Way in a few minutes." She turned and went out.

Mara sat up, the pounding in her head instantly switching from blacksmith's-hammer intensity to something closer to a pile driver. Prella sat on the edge of her bed, pulling on a pair of soft leather boots she certainly had not had the night before, any more than she had had that pair of brown trousers or that long-sleeved white blouse. Mara looked at the foot of her bed, where she had tossed the travel-stained clothes she'd been given after they were rescued by the unMasked: they had vanished, to be replaced by a clean blouse and trousers much like Prella's, though the trousers were dark blue and the blouse a light green. Even better: clean underwear. Particularly since at the moment she was wearing nothing at all. *Who undressed me?* she wondered. She decided she didn't want to know. Also lying with the clothes was a brown towel and, in place of the heavy travel cloak she'd worn the night before, a light leather jacket.

Mara massaged her pounding temples. "You shouldn't have drunk so much wine," Prella said with a bright smile that for a moment made Mara hate her. "I didn't have any. I didn't like the taste."

"I didn't either . . . at first," Mara muttered. She swallowed. "And I don't much like it now, either."

A clay pitcher full of water, a wooden basin, and a wooden cup rested on a low table beside each bed. Mara got up, pulled on the underwear—drawers and an undershirt—then poured water into the basin and splashed some of it on her face: its icy bite revived her a little. She took a few big gulps to wash the awful taste out of her mouth, ran her fingers through her tangled hair, wished desperately she had a comb, sniffed, and wished even more desperately she could take a bath.

But there was something else she needed to do even *more* desperately, and so she finished dressing in her new clothes, then pulled on the boots she found at the foot of her bed—made of black, well-worn leather, they fit far better than the ill-fitting goose-greased ones she'd worn on the journey from the wagon—and made her way to the little room at the end of the corridor Hyram had shown them yesterday. Hearing the rush of water far below her, she tried hard not to think about falling in.

Finally she descended to the Broad Way, where Edrik indeed awaited her, not very patiently. The moment she appeared, he took her arm and steered her to another tunnel and up a long staircase to yet another chamber that, if she were any judge, had to be directly above the girls' bedroom, close to the top of the cliff. As they approached its open door, she heard voices, though she couldn't make out what they were saying: they cut off as Edrik entered with her.

Daylight streamed in through three windows, wider and taller than the slit in the girls' room—albeit gray, not-very-bright daylight, since thick fog filled the stone horseshoe of the Secret City. Wisps of mist even drifted into the room from time to time, vanishing at once in the warmth of the fire crackling in the hearth at the far end, behind Catilla, who sat at the head of a long table of the same polished yellow wood as the one in her bedchamber.

Half a dozen others sat along either side of the table, three men on one side, a man and two women on the other. Pitchers of water, drinking cups, and scattered bits of paper gave the scene the general air of an interrupted discussion . . . or possibly argument; some of those at the table did *not* look happy.

Catilla didn't look happy, either, but Mara suspected she never did. As Edrik left Mara's side and took the seat at the end of the table nearest the door and farthest from his grandmother, Catilla's sharp blue eyes locked on Mara's face with the same disconcerting intensity as the night before, as though she were peering inside Mara's head, and not much liking what she saw. "I trust you slept well," she said.

The politeness of the query was so at odds with her predator-like gaze that it caught Mara off guard. "Yes, thank you for asking," she replied, the manners her mother had drilled into her for fifteen years providing the answer without her having to think about it. Feeling off-balance, both metaphorically and, thanks to the previous night's wine, literally, she looked around for someplace to sit, but all the seats were taken.

"I have just been telling the captains" — Catilla's eyes flicked briefly around the room — "about our conversation last night."

"Which part?" Mara said. Her head still hurt, no one had offered her a chair, and she didn't really feel like being cooperative. *Mother's not here to tell me to be polite*, she thought bitterly, *and she never will be again. So why bother?* "The part where you made excuses for not doing anything for *decades* to rescue children from failed Maskings?"

An angry murmur ran around the table, but nobody spoke except Catilla. "No," she said without changing the inflection of her voice one bit. "The part where you told me what you need to create counterfeit Masks for us."

Mara stared into Catilla's icy eyes, trying for defiance, but she couldn't hold it. She blinked and looked away and said in a much smaller voice than she had imagined herself using, "I told you. I don't even know if I *can* make a fake Mask that will fool anyone—much less a Watcher—even at a distance. But to even make the attempt . . . I'll need a few things."

"Go on," Catilla said.

Mara repeated the list she had given Catilla the night before. "Maker's clay. A set of shaping tools. A kiln. Pigments. A mortar and pestle. Silver or gold or copper for decoration. A crucible. Maskmakers' wax, to make the mold of the face. A . . ." She went on, listing everything she could think of, hoping they would see how impossible the whole thing was.

And at first she thought they had. "We have none of these," pointed out one of the captains, a big, burly man with a thick black beard.

"No," Catilla said. "But we know where to get them. Edrik?" She nodded at her grandson.

"Stony Beach," he said at once. "The Maskmakers' workshop is set apart from the main part of the village."

"It's too close," objected the black-bearded man. "They could track us back to the Secret City—"

"Why should they?" Edrik countered. "Maskmakers, as Mara has just pointed out, use kilns. Very hot. Prone to causing fires. More than one Maskmakers' workshop has burned. An unfortunate accident, one that destroys the workshop and all the Maskmakers' tools . . . very sad. But not particularly suspicious." He snorted. "After all, who would want a Maskmakers' tools? No one knows how to use them except for," he nodded at Mara, "another Maskmaker."

I'm not a Maskmaker! Mara wanted to shout. *I'm not even a full apprentice! I'm just a girl who learned a few things from her father.* He's *the Maskmaker!*

Her father's face came to memory so forcefully it closed her throat in a sudden, painful spasm. *And if I help these people, aren't I betraying him?*

Yet what choice did she have? She was at their mercy. And she wanted the Autarch overthrown, too. Of course she did . . .

But if that happened, what would become of her parents? The question had not occurred to her until now. Her father made Masks. If there were no more Masks, what would he do? And how much of the anger of the people rising up against the Autarch, if it ever came to that, would be directed at him and the others who had served the Autarch, willingly or unwillingly?

Her head throbbed, and again she wondered if she wouldn't have been better off in the labor camp, forgotten by everyone, instead of caught up in plots and rebellions.

The assembled captains had been arguing while she stood lost in her own miserable thoughts, but she looked up as the arguing abruptly ceased. Catilla had stood, and that simple act had instantly silenced the captains, twice the size and half the age of their diminutive Commander though some of them were. "It is settled," she said. "Edrik will lead a raid on the Maskmakers' workshop in Stony Beach to retrieve the tools and materials Mara needs to make counterfeit Masks for our use. Escha,"—she looked at the black-bearded man—"your company will assist." She turned her attention back to the others at the table. "Stamas, Misk, and Anna, conduct your usual patrols. Pentra, take your company up the gully. A scout returned this morning and reports that the overturned wagon has been found, but the Watchers lost the raiding party's trail at the river. Nevertheless, I want extra eyes looking in that direction for the next little while. Jarl, your company will garrison the Secret City. Dismissed."

The captains departed, talking in low voices, until only Edrik remained. Catilla nodded from Mara to her grandson. "You will tell Edrik precisely what you need, describing it in detail so there can be no mistake. We must not overlook anything. One raid like this we can, barely, risk. Two would be far too dangerous."

"It would be easier if I went with him, to show him," Mara said, thinking, *Maybe if I got out of here, I could slip away, get word to my father somehow . . .*

The half-formed and, if she were honest, suicidal plan evaporated as Catilla said flatly, "No. You are too valuable. You will remain here." And with that she swept out.

Edrik gestured Mara to the table. "Sit," he said. "Tell me again everything you need. Slowly."

For the next half hour, she listed everything she could think of, describing the various materials and how they would be stored so he could recognize them. When she came to the tools, she pictured her father's finishing sculptor's tools, nestled in the black velvet lining of his redwood tool case. Silvered and gilded, they shone like jewels in the glow of his workshop lamps. A village Maskmaker's tools would surely not be so grand, but they would just as surely have the same shapes and functions.

"There will be a series of scrapers," she said. "Some curved, some straight. The largest blade will be the size of my thumbnail, the smallest little larger than a hair. I would expect them to be together . . ." She went on. Edrik took no notes, but she could see him tucking away everything she told him behind his blue eyes, so reminiscent of his grandmother's, though not—quite—as cold.

When she had gone over the list three times, and answered all his questions, he stood and said, "Thank you. I think that will be all for now."

"Good," Mara said. As she got to her feet the room swayed around her and her head pounded anew. She grabbed the table's edge for support. "I . . . I think I need breakfast," she added weakly.

Edrik, to her surprise, actually looked guilty. "I'm sorry," he said. "My grandmother likes early-morning meetings." He made a wry face. "And late-night ones, too. I should have awakened you earlier so you could eat before you faced all this." His gesture took in the long table.

Mara felt a touch—just a *touch*—friendlier toward him. "I'm glad you didn't," she said. "I needed the sleep. But now, I *really* need food."

"I'll escort you," Edrik said. He offered his arm, and she took it. She only came up to his shoulder, but he walked as gravely with her back down the corridor and across the Broad Way as if he were escorting a noble Masked lady, and she felt more of her antagonism toward him fading as she made a grand entrance into the Great Chamber.

Of course, it was a shame there wasn't really anyone there to see that entrance except for Hyram, who turned from a sideboard, holding a steaming bowl of pink mush. "Good morning, Mara," he said, flashing his infectious grin. "I see I'm not the only one late for breakfast."

"And it is my fault in both cases," Edrik said. "In your case"—he looked down at Mara—"because of Grandmother's summons, and in your case"—he looked at his son—"because I told you to bring my company's horses down from the east pasture. Which I presume you did?"

"They're in the back-door stable," Hyram said. "Ready for saddling."

Edrik nodded. "Good. We ride out within the hour." He released Mara's arm. "I'll leave you in my son's capable hands," he said, and turned away.

Hyram's grin widened, and he leaned toward Mara. "Don't worry, he didn't mean that *literally*," he murmured, too low for his departing father to hear.

Mara blushed, which embarrassed her, which made her blush harder. To cover it up, she brushed past Hyram to the sideboard. She lifted the lid on the pot there and looked at the heaped pink mass inside. "What *is* that?"

"Mush," Hyram said. "Pink mush."

Mara laughed. "I can see that. But what *kind* of pink mush?"

"The pink mushy kind." Hyram grinned. "Sorry, I really haven't a clue. But it's not bad. Well," he said, taking a seat at the nearest table, "not *really* bad."

Mara looked around. Empty pots and dirty dishes stacked on the table at the far end of the chamber, nearest the kitchen, indicated there must have been more food earlier, but nothing remained except the cauldron of mush, some small loaves of bread, a couple of clay pitchers—filled with water, not wine, she saw with relief—and a few wooden cups. She ladled the mush into a bowl, stuck a spoon in it, poured herself a cup of water, and joined Hyram at the table.

"So how was your first night in the Secret City?" Hyram asked.

"Interesting," Mara said. She took a bite of the mush. It was warm, and filling, and had a slightly nutty taste that was all that kept it from being horribly bland, but she had a feeling she'd get tired of it quickly if it were all she had to eat. Resolving to be earlier to breakfast from then on, she took a bite of bread, washing it down with a swallow of water.

"I heard," Hyram said, "that you're going to make counterfeit Masks for us."

"It's not a secret?" she asked.

Hyram shrugged. "You can't keep secrets in the Secret City. Ironically enough. We're all stuck here with each other and there's not much else to do but talk. And chores, of course. Always lots and lots of chores." He sighed and shoveled another spoonful of mush into his mouth. "We call ourselves an army," he mumbled around it, "but we don't do much armying."

"Until now," Mara said.

"Exactly." Hyram swallowed and said, much more clearly, "The raid to rescue you is the most exciting thing that's happened in months. And now there's going to be *another* raid, to steal a Maskmaker's tools. And it's all because of *you*." He grinned at her. "I think I'm in love."

That was pretty much the most embarrassing thing anyone had ever said to her, and Mara didn't have a clue how to respond to it. So she didn't. "I don't even know if I *can* make believable Masks," she said. "What if I can't? All this risk and danger . . . it could be for nothing."

Hyram shrugged. "Then we'll try something else. At least we're trying *something*, at long last."

Mara sighed, and finished her bowl of mush. She pushed it away, and stood up. "There's still a lot of the Secret City I haven't seen," she said. "And it looks like I'm stuck here a while. Want to show me?"

Hyram shoved aside his own half-empty bowl. "Love to."

Over the next couple of hours he took her into every nook and cranny of the Secret City. She kept expecting to run into Keltan or the other rescued girls somewhere along the way, but they never did. It wasn't until she'd been in Hyram's company for an hour that she began to suspect Hyram knew *exactly* where the others were and was deliberately not taking her there, because he wanted her to himself.

Boys had never paid much attention to her, and she hadn't paid much attention to them, either. But Keltan had stuck to her like glue after the rescue, and now here was Hyram. He'd even said he was in love with her. Of course, he'd been joking.

Hadn't he?

We only met yesterday, she told herself firmly. *Of course he was joking.*

Still, she enjoyed his attention, and as a tour guide he was first-rate: not surprising, since he'd been born and raised in the Secret City.

"Only about two dozen people arrived here with Great-Grandmother," Hyram explained as he led her to the storerooms that opened off of the Broad Way. "Now there are more than three hundred men, women, and children. Around a hundred fighters."

Some of the storerooms were full of grain the un-Masked Army grew itself ("in a secluded little valley above the sea cliff"), others held racks of dried fish ("The boats go out every day, weather permitting"), beef, and mutton ("There's a small herd and flock up on top"), but one was stacked with barrels of wine, oil, olives, and honey—things the unMasked Army had certainly not produced itself.

"Where did all *this* come from?" Mara asked. She pointed at the hook-beaked profile of a bird on the side of a barrel of wine. "That's from Eagle Ridge Winery. It's fifty miles east of Tamita, up in the foothills. You're un-Masked. You can't exactly go shopping."

"The Masks don't reveal *everything* to the Watch," Hyram said. "They don't reveal under-the-table deals made by certain businessmen, who receive gold by mysterious means in exchange for misplacing the occasional wagonload full of goods."

"But how do you contact them?" Mara said. "Isn't the whole reason I'm supposed to make counterfeit Masks the fact that it's impossible for the unMasked Army to enter Tamita?"

"We don't go to Tamita," Hyram said. "But the larger towns and villages we can risk. Occasionally we send in someone who has just joined us and whose Mask is still intact, but that's rare and it's very dangerous for them to go anywhere near a Watcher. Mostly, we use children."

Mara gave him a startled look. He grinned. "Don't look so shocked! They don't do anything dangerous. But the Watchers pretty much ignore them, and an un-Masked twelve-year-old is perfectly capable of delivering a message . . . or dropping off a bag of gold. Even a teenager can get away with it if he's small and skinny enough. I did it myself until I, um . . ." He gestured at his rangy frame. "Sprouted."

"But where do you get the gold?" Mara said.

"Ah, that's later on the tour," Hyram said, and he wouldn't explain any more until they'd seen the armory, and the blacksmith's forge, and the stables.

The latter puzzled Mara, too. Hyram showed them to her, on the far side of the cove from the main part of the Secret City, carved out of the rock like everything else. But they were empty of horses, if not of their smell. She looked back across the cove. The thick fog of morning had burned away, and now bright sunshine poured down on the land between the two cliffs. People were moving out there, busy with various tasks—pulling turnips from vegetable patches, arranging fish on drying racks—but there were no horses. "Where are they?" she asked. "The horses?"

Hyram shrugged. "Gone. The raiding party has already set off, and the other companies are on patrol."

"They all went out the ravine?" Mara asked. "But we've been crisscrossing the cove for an hour and I never saw them."

"The ravine's not the only way into the Secret City," Hyram said. He took her down to the water's edge. "Look," he said, pointing north along the shore. She tore her eyes away from the endlessly fascinating, endlessly repeating lines of surf and saw that the cliffs did not rise directly from the water: instead, a narrow sliver of level sand ran beneath them. She looked south; the beach ran in that direction, too. "High water now," Hyram said. "At low water, it's a lot broader. But even at high water you can ride along it." And sure enough, looking closely, she saw signs of horses' passage in the portion of the sand that had not recently been pounded flat by the breakers.

"There are paths up from the beach to the top of the cliff," Hyram continued. "You'd be hard-pressed to find them up above, though, without knowing exactly where they are. Most are only footpaths, but there's one that horses can manage. It leads up to the farmland I told you about. If you'd been here last week, we'd have been in the middle of harvest."

Mara looked out to sea. "The Secret City may be hard to find from land," she said, "but it certainly isn't hidden from the water. What about boats?"

Hyram shrugged again. "In my whole life, the only boats I've ever seen out there are ours," he said. "Stony Beach is the nearest village and their fishermen don't come this far north. There are dangerous rocks and shallows along the coast south of us."

"That doesn't mean one won't show up tomorrow," Mara said.

"We have plans for such an eventuality," Hyram said. "But I doubt they'll ever be needed." He clapped his hands. "Now. You've seen everything except the source of our gold. This way."

He led her north along the beach. It narrowed rapidly, and Mara looked uneasily at the waves rolling in to her left. "Does the water ever come this high?" she ventured, as an extra-large breaker spent itself at her feet.

"In storms," Hyram said. "But remember, it's high tide now. The water will be receding for the rest of the day. Don't worry, you're not going to be swept away." He grinned. "Well, not by the water."

Mara felt herself blushing again. *Stop that! It doesn't mean anything. He's just being a boy.* But she stayed silent for the rest of the walk, which ended in—why was she not surprised?—yet another cave.

Stepping from sunlight into darkness, at first she couldn't see anything; but her eyes quickly adjusted—and then widened. White rock veined the cavern's walls, and within that rock glistened . . .

"Is that really gold?" she breathed.

Hyram nodded, as proud as if he'd put it there himself. "It really is. Before we found it, when my father was a boy, things were a *lot* grimmer in the Secret City. Nothing could be bought; very little could be stolen without risk; the unMasked Army had to live entirely on what it could grow, hunt, or fish. Which we still mostly do, but things are easier now that we can at least occasionally purchase tools and things we can't make, like wine."

Or the fine furniture in Catilla's room, Mara thought, but didn't say. "And the Autarch knows *nothing* of this?" She didn't try to keep the skepticism out of her voice.

"Rumors of black market dealings in the remote villages may have reached his elevated ears," Hyram said, "but I doubt it. The Autarch does not, by all accounts, personally concern himself much with anything that happens outside the walls of Tamita. He leaves that to his Watchers, and out here, his Watchers are mostly fat and lazy. We can't prove it, but we think they're mostly unGifted: they can't read Masks, all they care about is that they haven't cracked. So they let little things slide." He snorted. "The Autarch has become *too* dependent on the Masks, my father says. The Autarch and his Circle think that because the Masks will reveal to the Watchers anyone who might act against them, they've got nothing to worry about."

"No," Mara said; because, suddenly, she thought she understood. "They don't think that at all. And that's why the Masks have changed."

Hyram turned from running a finger along one of the seams of gold. "What?"

"The Masks are changing people . . . changing the way they think. They didn't used to. So that means the Autarch is worried. Maybe he's been listening to the rumors about the unMasked Army. Maybe he's beginning to think you're real. Maybe he's just old and scared he's going to end up like his father. So he's changed the Masks to *force* everyone to be loyal. Even though it means more Maskings are failing." *And Father knew it,* she thought. *He must have. He's been making these new kinds of Masks. He wouldn't have any choice but to comply. The one he made for Sala . . .*

. . . and the one he made for me.

And suddenly, belatedly, she thought she understood why her father had seemed so strangely distant during the days leading up to her Masking. He'd known the Mask he was making would change his daughter forever, take away her freedom of thought, make her no more than a compliant cog in the machinery of the Autarch's state . . .

. . . and so he deliberately made a Mask that would fail! He thought I'd be better off unMasked than forced into the mold the Autarch wanted.

Better off suffering whatever horrible fate awaited me at the labor camp? she thought angrily. *Better off in the hands of that fat spider drawing naked girls in the ware-*

house by the walls? By making your Mask fail, he put you in that wagon with Grute, heading to a whole camp full of Grutes! He didn't know you would be rescued.

Or did he?

"Are you all right?" Hyram asked, and she realized she'd been staring blankly off into space, for several seconds.

"Yes," Mara said automatically. Then, "No." Then, "I don't know." She shook her head. "It's just . . . can we go back now? I've seen enough."

Hyram nodded. They walked back to the Secret City in silence. Once they were in the Broad Way, Mara said, "Thank you for the tour. I think I'd like to be alone for a while."

"Of course," Hyram said. "I—"

Tishka suddenly dashed in from outside, flushed and out of breath. "Hyram, you were walking along the beach. Did you see Grute?"

"Grute?" Hyram looked confused. "That sack of horse shit my father dragged back? Of course not. He's locked up."

Tishka shook her head. "He *was* locked up," she panted. "He's escaped."

"How?"

"Pulled the door right off its hinges. Wouldn't have believed it if I hadn't seen it."

"Nobody was guarding him?" Mara demanded.

"He was locked up," Tishka repeated. "We didn't think we needed to guard him, too." But she looked a little shamefaced. "We don't usually have prisoners here. In fact we've *never* had a prisoner here. He was just locked up in one of the small storerooms. And bags of meal don't try to escape."

Mara looked around uneasily. "He could be any-where."

"He's not in the Secret City," Tishka reassured her. "We've searched every room and hallway, all the way down to the lake. He's out there, somewhere." She waved toward the tunnel entrance.

"But he knows where the Secret City is!" Hyram exclaimed. "If he tells the Watchers—"

"You think nobody else has thought of that?" Tishka snapped. "Jarl has the garrison out looking for him, but with so many out on patrol or off to Stony Beach we need everyone we can get. So—"

"Of course," said Hyram. He gave Mara a quick, worried smile. "Duty calls." Then he rushed off with Tishka, back out into daylight.

Mara stared after them. Grute on the loose *again*, she thought. You had to hand it to him. He might be a "sack of horse shit"—*she* wasn't about to argue with that description—but he was certainly resourceful.

But the risk to the Secret City if he got away . . . She shuddered. The village Watchers might be fat and lazy, but the ones in Tamita most assuredly weren't, *especially* the Autarch's elite Sun Guards. *They* were said to have magic capable of wiping an entire village off the map. The unMasked Army would stand small chance against *them*. If Grute revealed the Secret City's existence, and even its approximate location, they'd have no choice but to run.

Run where? Mara wondered, and had no answer.

She climbed up to the girls' room. It was empty; she still didn't know where the others were. *Probably doing chores somewhere*, she thought; she didn't get the feeling anyone was allowed to sit around feeling sorry for themselves in the Secret City.

Except, apparently, her.

She had been longing for one thing since they'd arrived, one thing that had always made her feel better, one thing, she hoped, that might also help her think more clearly.

She was going to take a bath.

She grabbed the towel that had appeared with her clean clothes that morning, and descended to the Broad Way.

For a moment she hesitated, looking up and down its

length, a little uneasy at being alone when Grute was at large. Tishka had said they'd searched the entire City, right down to the lake where she was headed, but still . . .

Maybe I should wait, she thought, but then she caught a whiff of herself, wrinkled her nose, and decided she really couldn't, not and live with herself. *What must Hyram have thought?* she wondered, and blushed again.

That settled it. Grute or no Grute, she had to have a bath.

She headed down the tunnel.

ELEVEN

Kidnapped

SHE MET NO ONE along the way, and that suited her fine. She really, *really* wanted the bath for its own sake—she was tired of her own scent following her around like a stinky stray puppy—but she also wanted it for a chance to be alone with herself and her thoughts.

The lanterns still glowed on their poles near the entrance to the vast water-filled chamber. More lamps burned to left and right along the shore. Mara listened carefully. Even though she had seen that the men's and women's bathing areas were separated and completely out of sight from one another, the thought of bathing when there were naked men splashing around within earshot, even if she couldn't see them, made her uneasy. She peered into the darkness at the far side of the lake.

Nothing disturbed the water: it could have been a single, enormous sheet of glass.

Finally feeling certain she was quite alone, she went around the corner to the girls' bathing area, put her towel and soap down on the rock, slipped out of her boots and clothes, picked up her soap again, and waded into the surprisingly warm water.

She sighed as the liquid wrapped itself around her limbs. She scrubbed herself thoroughly with the crude soap until her skin tingled, then plunged her head under the water and worked more of the soap into a lather in her hair, running her fingers through it over and over again until all the tangles were gone. Finally she ducked her head once more and scrubbed her scalp again to rinse the soap away.

Clean at last, she tossed the soap onto the rocky shore, put her head back, and let her feet come off the stony floor. With her ears underwater, all she could hear was the low rumble of her own blood coursing through her veins. She closed her eyes.

Floating free, only her own body and thoughts for company, she felt completely disconnected from the world. Still, she'd felt that way now for several days, ever since the horror of the Masking. That moment of blood and terror had removed her from her old life as abruptly—and painfully—as a blade amputating a limb. Her parents, the center of her short life, had been ripped away and were now separated from her by an impassable gulf. More than just her face had been crushed and mutilated by the horrible twisting of the failed Mask. So had her plans, her hopes, her dreams—everything that had defined who and what she was. She'd gotten her face back, thanks to Ethelda, but she would *never* get her old life back.

So I guess I'll have to make do with this new life, she thought, floating in the underground lake with her eyes closed. *And my new family. Keltan. Simona and Kirika.*

Alita and Prella and Hyram. Edrik and, I guess, Catilla. There's no going back.

And if there's no going back, then there should be no looking *back. It doesn't do me any good to pine for Daddy and Mommy and Stoofy and everything else the Masking stole from me. I can't get them back. Ever. The Autarch has seen to that.*

If the unMasked Army hadn't grabbed me on Catilla's orders, who knows what would be happening to me, or about to happen to me, in the labor camp? So why am I resisting what she wants from me? It's stupid. I should do everything I can to help the unMasked Army try to get rid of the Autarch, even if it seems impossible. Because they're all I have now. If they fail—if the Autarch finds and destroys them—then he will destroy me, too. And there will be no one to rescue me a second time.

She took a deep breath. *So be it. I'll—*

Someone grabbed her ankle.

She jackknifed, went under, gulped water, then surged to the surface, spluttering. Her sudden movement had pulled her ankle free, but as she straightened someone seized her arm and twisted it behind her. A thick arm crushed her breasts and pinned her tight against a hard, muscular body. "Guess who?" said a voice in her ear, and she stiffened in terror.

Grute!

"What are you doing here?" she demanded. It was a stupid question, but she couldn't believe that she was literally in his grasp. *Naked and in his grasp,* a part of her mind reminded her, but modesty seemed the least of her concerns. "They searched the Secret City! They said you'd fled outside—"

"Left some clues so they'd think that," Grute said. "And spent the night making this." He released the arm behind her back, but kept her pressed so tightly against him she still couldn't move. She could feel him fumbling in his pocket; then he held in front of her eyes a glistening cylinder: a candle, she realized, carefully hollowed out to make a tube. "Broke the door, dropped some bits of it along the Broad Way in the direction of the entrance, then turned around and came this way; popped myself under the water and breathed through this until they went away." He tossed the tube aside; it hit the water with a splash. "Deep in the heart of the 'Secret City.'" He snorted. "Won't be much of a secret once I get to the labor camp. Won't be much of a city, either, not long after that!"

"You're crazy if you think you can get out of here without being seen," Mara said.

"Oh, I can get out of here," he said. "Count on it. And *you're* coming with me."

"I'm not—"

Grute barked a laugh. "You are. Didn't plan on it before, but since you plopped right into my hands . . ." He propelled her toward the shore, never letting go. Once they'd waded up onto the rocks, he shoved her toward her clothes so hard she splashed onto her hands and knees in the shallows. She glared back at him. He wore the green and brown clothes the unMasked Army had provided, sodden and dripping. "Get dressed," he said.

"I'm surprised you wouldn't rather keep me naked," Mara said defiantly, but she scrambled to her feet and snatched up her clothes just the same, holding them in front of her.

"Too cold in the woods," Grute said. "I want you healthy when we get where we're going." He snorted. "Besides, it's not like you've got a lot to look at."

Mara blushed at that, then was furious at herself for blushing, especially when there wasn't the slightest possibility of hiding it. She dressed slowly, hoping someone else would enter, but Grute stepped forward and yanked her hair so hard she gasped. "Stop dawdling," he growled.

Defeated, she pulled on her boots and turned to face him. "You can't get out of here without going down the Broad Way," she said. "Someone *will* see you. And this time they'll hang you."

Grute laughed. "Do I look like an idiot? I wouldn't have come down here if I hadn't known I could get out." His grin faded. "And it's time we were getting." He strode forward, seized her arm, and half-dragged her along the shore. They passed the opening into the Broad Way. Mara looked down it, hoping someone else might be coming for a bath or fresh water, but the passage was empty as far as she could see.

"Don't even think about screaming," Grute breathed in her ear. "No one will hear you, and then I'll kill you."

He's only a boy, she told herself. *He's the same age as me.*

She believed his threat all the same.

He dragged her past the men's bathing area, and kept going, splashing into the lake and wading through its shallows. She heard a rushing noise; and then, in the flickering shadows ahead, saw a dark opening, water from the lake pouring into it. "You're insane!" she whispered. "You can't mean—"

"Yes, I can," Grute said.

"In the dark? You don't even know where it comes out—"

"Yes, I do," Grute said. "It pours out into the ocean a half mile from here, out of sight from the cove."

Mara blinked. "How?"

"I asked." Even in the near-darkness, she could see his smirk. "No harm telling the prisoner something like *that*."

Mara said nothing. Her mouth had gone dry; her heart raced. "I'll drown," she whispered. "I can't swim."

"You can float," Grute said. "I saw you."

"I can't float down *that*."

"So hang on to this." Grute bent over; when he straightened he was holding a log, cut and trimmed for the hearth. "Brought a couple with me when I ran," he said. "Lucky for you I thought I should have a spare."

"But . . . rocks . . . waterfalls . . ."

"That's enough!" Grute spat. "Shut up, take it, and jump in. Or I'll throw you in without it."

Trembling, Mara took the log. She hugged it to her breast as tightly as she used to hold Stoofy, wishing with all her might that it *was* Stoofy, that she was safely asleep in her own bed, that everything that had happened and was about to happen was just a bad dream. She stared down at the water rushing past her feet into darkness.

And then Grute's hands slammed into her back and she toppled like a felled tree.

She hit face first, almost lost the log, pulled it close instead, spluttered to the surface, and screamed as she hurtled through absolute darkness in the grip of the powerful current. She screamed again and again, over and over, as she spun this way and that.

A rock slammed into her leg, numbing it. Spray filled the air with so much water she choked as she breathed . . .

. . . and then the current strengthened and pulled her under.

Immersed in cold water, unable to see, unable to breathe, all she could do was hold on to the log while the pressure mounted in her lungs, the urge to breathe grew more and more unbearable, and the moment raced nearer when she would have to open her mouth, suck in water, and die, drowning in darkness and silence deep beneath the Secret City, her body doomed to float out to sea, a feast for fish and gulls . . .

But just when she knew that fatal moment was upon her, as her vision filled with stars and the pain in her chest could no longer be denied, she burst out into the open air and gulped a huge, wonderful, surprised breath before she hit the water once more and spun away into still-unrelieved blackness, clutching the log in a death grip.

She sensed a larger space around her. The current had eased. She could float on the surface now, taking deep breaths, and she thought she'd never felt anything half as wonderful as the unimpeded rush of air into and out of her lungs, breath after breath. But then she realized there was something almost as wonderful as breathing, and that was seeing: the darkness was no longer absolute. Shadowy rock walls slipped past, growing brighter and brighter . . . and then nearer and nearer as the passage narrowed.

The stream took her around a sweeping corner and suddenly she was blinking in full daylight, pouring through an opening in the rock, so bright she could see nothing beyond it. But that hardly mattered, because the stream hurled her at that opening as though anxious to be rid of her, and a moment later she spun out through the open air in a welter of spray and the sound of thunder, fell twenty feet, and hit so hard the impact finally broke her grip on the log that had borne her so far. She tasted salt as she struggled to the surface. She gulped air, flailed, sank . . . and then felt strong hands grab her.

Fighting the urge to kick those hands away, she let Grute pull her back to the surface, then swim both of them into water shallow enough to stand up in. Then she pushed him away with revulsion and staggered up onto the beach, turning and sinking down into the sand to sit, shaking, staring out at the endless lines of breakers rolling toward her across the blue expanse of ocean. She glanced up at the waterfall that spouted from the cliff and plunged into the sea; looked down and saw the sharp rock-teeth she must have just missed; then looked up at Grute, standing over her, hands on his hips, grinning his infuriating, leering grin.

"Still alive, are you? I figured it was even money you'd panic and pop out of the cave as a waterlogged corpse."

"We could have both been killed!" Mara snarled. "Don't you *care?*"

Grute shrugged. "Why should I? I'd *rather* be dead than a prisoner of that bunch"—he jerked his head back toward the waterfall—"and I don't care about *you* at all except for what you'll be good for once I get you to the camp." His grin widened. "Not everyone's going to care you're almost as flat as a pressed fish. They're just going to care you ain't got scars on your pretty face."

"You're going to sell me." Mara's stomach churned and she thought she might throw up. "Like a . . . a piece of meat!"

"You got it," Grute said. "And it's time I got you to market." He spat on the beach. "The unMasked Army is a joke, but that don't mean they're all brainless." He lifted his shirt, and Mara saw he'd wrapped a length of rope around his belly; he undid it, then, holding it loosely in both hands, stepped toward her. "Up!"

Mara got to her feet.

"Turn around." She glared at him. "*Turn around*," he snarled, and this time he grabbed her arm, spun her hard, and yanked her back toward him. His arms went around her waist. She felt a tug and a sense of pressure as he tied the rope around her. He stepped back, and she glanced over her shoulder to see that he now had her on a leash.

She raised her eyes to give him a glare she hoped was defiant, but he just smirked. "You won't be running away now," he said. "Let's move." He flicked the leash as though it were the reins of a horse. She gave him another glare, but really had no choice but to turn and start struggling south through the sand.

They walked in silence for an hour or more, Grute constantly searching the cliff face for a way up. Mara clung to the hope that he wouldn't find one, that they would be trapped along the shore until the unMasked Army finally came riding this way in search of them, as they surely would sooner or later, but that hope was dashed as the sun passed the zenith and began to descend toward the sea. He suddenly stopped her with a sharp tug on the rope. "Here," he said. "Start climbing."

Mara looked up, shading her eyes. The cliff looked just as forbidding here as everywhere else. "We can't climb that!"

Grute jerked the rope irritably. "Look again, idiot. There's a gap."

Mara lowered her gaze, and suddenly saw what Grute

had already spotted: a narrow crack in the rock, feathered with greenery. "What if it doesn't go anywhere?"

"Then we'll come back down and keep looking," Grute said. "Climb!"

Mara clambered up on the rounded boulders at the base of the cliff and slipped through the crack. It seemed barely wide enough for her, and for an instant she hoped it would be too narrow for the broad-shouldered Grute, but he grunted and squeezed through. She saw that he had tied a small loop of the rope around his wrist, so he could use both hands to climb but remain tethered to her.

She turned and looked ahead into the ravine. It seemed dark as a cave after the brilliant sunshine of the beach, but far overhead she saw a crack of sky. Rounded rocks covered the ravine floor and a trickle of water tumbled down its center. It sloped up steeply—but unlike the cliff, not so steeply it couldn't be climbed.

Grute had found his path up.

An hour's hard struggle brought them, panting, out onto flat (or at least flatter) land, the ocean lost to sight, trees all around. The little stream that trickled down the ravine wound away to the south, but Grute pointed to the northeast. "The mine is somewhere over there," he said. "Let's get walking."

"We don't have any food, any water—"

"Lots of streams," Grute said indifferently. "Lots of berries. We won't starve in two or three days. Move."

The rest of the afternoon passed in silent trudging through woods that never seemed to change. They would climb a ridge, descend the other side, splash across a stream, sometimes pausing to drink, and then press on. As the light began to fade, though, Mara thought she saw the shadowy forms of buildings up ahead, and her heart skipped a beat. The mine?

But as they drew closer, she saw that the buildings were mere ruins, and old ones, at that: nothing more than a few tumbled walls, collapsed cellars overgrown with weeds, the charred remnants of roofs. "An abandoned village, looks like," Grute said. He spat on the ground. "Not a roof to be had in the place, but it don't look much like rain." He peered around in the gloom. "Over there," he said, pointing to one of the taller bits of wall, tall enough it still bore the bottom half of the squared-off opening that had once been a window.

"We'll freeze," Mara muttered. The air already had a chill edge to it.

"We won't," Grute said. "Move."

They reached the broken wall in moments. The stones bore black scorch marks, and inside a few charred timbers lay half-hidden by scraggly weeds. The light had almost faded, but Mara could see enough of their surroundings to see that the two-dozen or so ruined buildings, some, like their chosen shelter, apparently small houses, some larger, like stores or stables, clustered around an open space where the grass still grew lushly, despite the lateness of the year, over a long, low mound. "What happened here?" she wondered out loud.

"Don't know," Grute said. "Don't care. Wish they'd left some food behind, though."

At the mention of food, Mara's stomach growled, but of course there was nothing to put in it. Yet she had been drinking water off and on all day, and though she'd been putting it off, she had to relieve her bladder.

"I have to pee," she told Grute. "Are you going to untie me?"

"No," he said. "Go ahead."

Feeling utterly humiliated, she went to the end of the rope, turned her back on him, and did what she needed to do. When she turned back, she knew he had watched.

And then, of course, he had to do the same. She closed her eyes until the sound of urine splashing on the ground had stopped.

As darkness descended, he had her lie down with her back to the broken wall, and then shortened the rope, leaving just enough slack that they could each turn over without pulling it tight. "I'm a light sleeper," Grute warned. And then, to her disgust, he reached over and pulled her close to him, so that her buttocks were pressed into his pelvis and his knees were in back of hers. She tensed, and he snorted. "Don't flatter yourself," he said. "This is just for warmth." But then he leaned forward and whispered, his breath hot in her ear, "Besides, virgins are very popular in the camp, I'm told. You're worth more untouched."

Shortly after that, his breathing deepened and his arms around her slackened, and she knew he was asleep. But she lay awake a very long time, her empty stomach churning, her heart pounding in her ears. It was just as well she'd had nothing to eat; she was sure if she had she would have vomited it across the ground.

Her body eventually took the rest it needed, but her sleep was troubled by strange dreams, filled with fire and smoke and screaming. She woke almost gratefully to the tug of the rope to find gray light all around and Grute, the rope lengthened, peeing.

Again.

He adjusted his clothing and turned back toward her. "Your turn," he said, and again she turned her back. When she glanced back at him this time, though, she saw that he hadn't been watching. Instead, his eyes were focused on the clouds scudding overhead, ranks of them, each thicker and grayer than the last.

Well, she thought, remembering the day before in the bathing pool, *he's seen everything I've got anyway, hasn't he?* The thought was less humiliating than infuriating now. The shock of yesterday had passed. She might be miserable, cold, and desperately hungry, but it was a new day. And today, she vowed, she would spend every minute looking for a way to escape.

"Weather's changing," Grute said. "We may need better shelter tonight. Come on."

As they passed through what had once been the village green, Mara saw something white sticking out of the low mound. Grute tugged her along impatiently, and that was fine: she didn't want to look any closer.

Unless her mind had been playing tricks, a human skull had been leering at her from the lush green grass.

It wasn't just the weather that changed as they walked that day. The terrain did, too, becoming steeper and rockier. Late in the morning they climbed a ridge that, for the first time, had no trees at the top, and got a clear view of what lay ahead.

Mara gasped. Ridge after ridge rose before them, each higher than the last: and beyond those, mountains, towering, blue, capped with vast fields of ice and snow. "We can't cross *those!*"

"We don't have to," Grute said. "The mine is in the foothills." He pointed east. "That way. Eventually we'll find the road. And then we'll find the mine." He stood gazing in that direction for a long moment, and then grinned. "Luck's on our side," he said. "I see some sort of hut on the next ridge, maybe five miles." He looked up at the sky; the clouds, unbroken now, streamed low overhead, looking close enough to touch. The wind had a nasty bite to it, and her thin jacket did little to stop it. She wished she still had her heavy brown travel cloak. "We'll need a roof over our heads tonight for sure. Let's go." He dragged Mara downhill again.

By the time they reached the bottom of the valley between the two ridges, a light drizzle was falling. By the time they were halfway up the ridge, already soaked to the skin, the drizzle had turned to a steady rain. And by the time they reached the top, the rain was mixed with snow, huge white clots that melted as they touched the ground . . . *but for how long?* Mara wondered.

Shivering, they trudged silently along the ridgetop. The world that had seemed so wide when Mara had stood on the top of the previous ridge, staring at the mountains, had shrunk to just a few yards of mist, rain, and snow. The rock grew slippery under Mara's feet. The wind picked up. More snow fell, and less rain. "Where's that hut?" Mara shouted at Grute. "We've come more than five miles. We've got to find shelter!" And in the back of her mind she couldn't help but hope that if the hut were occupied, she might have an opportunity to escape Grute's clutches.

"You think I don't know that?" Grute yelled back at her.

Mara opened her mouth to say something else, but all that came out was a wordless cry as, looking back at him, she put a foot wrong—and fell.

Her legs went out from under her and she hit the ground so hard it knocked out her breath. Mouth soundlessly agape, she felt herself beginning to slide down the slope to their right, and saw ahead in the fading light the sharp edge of a sheer drop-off, nothing beyond it but swirling fog.

Then the rope around her middle tightened with a jerk so sudden that if she'd still had any breath it would have squeezed it from her. Her head snapped back, and she found herself looking upside down at Grute, feet planted, hands gripping the rope, muscles in his neck standing out like thick cords. Jaw set, he began to pull her back toward him, dragging her over the rock inch by inch until at last she reached level ground. By then she was beginning to get a little air back into her emptied lungs, gulping small amounts. As breathing became easier, Grute plopped onto his rear beside her and looked at his hands. Both palms bore bright red welts. "Thank you," she managed to gasp out after a few more minutes.

Grute grunted. "If you went over the edge, you were taking me with you." He got to his feet. "Get up. It's only going to get darker and colder. If we don't find shelter by nightfall, we'd have been better off falling."

Mara nodded and got shakily back to her feet. Feeling slightly more favorably disposed toward Grute than before, even though she knew he was telling the truth about saving her only to save himself, she pressed on along the narrow, rocky ridge. Not ten minutes after she'd almost fallen to her death, they reached the hut.

It crouched on top of the ridge like an animal hunkered against the storm: small, square, and squat, just four slabs of stone, carved from the ridge itself, roofed with rough sheets of slate. Shutters closed the single window and a rusty padlock secured the ironbound wooden door, which Grute banged on with both fists. When no one answered, he took a step backward and slammed his shoulder against it. Wood cracked and splintered, and the door swung inward.

Mara looked inside and gasped in amazement. Then she shot a startled look at Grute as he grumbled, "Black as a whore's heart."

What are you talking about? she wanted to cry. Light *filled* the room: shimmering, sparkling, phasing from pale red to icy blue to the green of sunlight through leaves. But she bit off her protest just in time. *Grute can't see it*, she realized in wonder. *It's magic!*

She said nothing as Grute rummaged about. She watched him walk blindly into a table, cursing as he bruised his thigh, then feel his way along the mantel, his questing fingers finally finding the flint and steel Mara saw the whole time. He crowed and knelt in front of the fireplace, reaching out to touch the wood and kindling already laid in the hearth. As he set to work lighting the fire, though, her eyes weren't on that orange, ordinary blaze, but on the ever-shifting light streaming into the room from an open door leading into a second room at the back of the hut. She didn't move until the fire provided enough light for Grute to see it, too. Then she said, "What's in there?" and crossed to the door.

Grute pushed her to one side and peered in first. "Not much," he grunted. "Nothing we can use, anyway." He turned back into the main room. "Wonder if there's any food?"

As he knelt to open a cupboard in the corner, near the table and chair that, apart from a narrow bed, were the room's only furniture, Mara stepped into the back room, bright as day to her eyes.

She remembered her father, one day in his workshop, telling her that magic had to be gathered like precious ore, tiny amounts of it collected, brought together and transported to the Palace, where it was stored and allocated to those with the right and skill to use it, such as Maskmakers. He hadn't known exactly *how* magic was collected—or if he had, he hadn't told her—but now, she realized, she stood in one such collection facility.

In the center of the room rose a black pillar of stone, its top hollowed out to make a deep basin, much larger than the one in Father's workshop. Magic half-filled it, color ever-changing—more magic than she had yet seen in one place. On shelves at the back of the room rows of jars made of the same black stone stood silent sentinel: each, she suspected, either filled with magic, or intended to be filled with magic.

She remembered the black stone in the cave where the tiny pool of magic had gathered, the black stone of her father's basin. *There must be something special about the stone*, she thought. *Maybe it attracts magic. So you build a hut like this, some place where magic wells up naturally, and slowly the magic is drawn to fill the basin . . .*

She wondered how long it took for as much magic to gather as she saw here. A month? Two? More? Periodically one of the Autarch's magic-gatherers must come to the hut, fill the jars, and send them off to the storehouses of the Palace.

She had used that tiny pool of magic in the cave to mend Keltan's jacket. What could she do with *this* much magic at her command?

Grute clattered something in the main room. She glanced that way. If only she knew more about how to use it . . .

She resolved to think of something before she fell asleep. But in the end, thinking didn't really enter into it at all.

Trouble began with a whoop: the triumphant sound

from Grute brought her out of the back room to see him holding up a clear glass bottle, filled with an amber liquid. "Snowdrop Whiskey," he crowed. He took out the cork, slugged back a good long swallow. He coughed, then grinned. "*That* warms a fellow's bones."

He put the bottle on top of the cabinet and didn't offer her any, which suited her fine. Her eyes were more on the beef jerky and travel bread tucked behind the bottle. That Grute *did* share with her; only, she thought, because there was plenty for both of them. Sitting in the chair at the table, gnawing at the jerky, she felt almost human again: especially since Grute, in a fit of something approaching kindness, untied the rope and let her go to the outhouse, a freezing-cold wooden structure ten yards distant, though he stood in the hut's doorway and waited until she emerged and dashed back through the now thickly falling snow to the warmth of the hut.

As she sat steaming by the fire, Grute made his own trip out into the snow. She gave the briefest of considerations to making a run for it, but she remembered that terrifying slide down the wet rock toward oblivion, shuddered, and stayed where she was.

Once they'd eaten, Grute set to working his way through the rest of the whiskey, sitting on the bed he'd claimed for himself, though at least he tossed her a blanket. She lay on the hard wooden floor next to the fire with her back to him, and eventually, warm, lulled by the constant rush of the wind in the eaves and the crackle of the fire, she slept.

She woke in terror to find Grute pawing at her.

He reeked of alcohol so strongly she was amazed he hadn't gone up in flames just by coming so near the fire. It had sunk to embers, but the glow of the magic in the other room was more than enough for her to see him clearly . . . and to see that he was naked—and aroused.

"Face will be enough," he muttered. His eyes were wide, and he was breathing hard, as though he'd just run a race. "Nobody'll care if you're still a virgin . . ." He had hold of the blanket, was trying to pull it off her. Terrified, she kicked at him, heard him grunt as a flailing foot found its mark. He fell back and she managed to kick herself free of the blanket and scramble away backward, crablike. "Nowhere to run, bitch," he yelled, crawling after her. "Just you and me here. I'll have you, and you know it." He reared back on his knees, flaunting his nakedness. "You might as well lie back and enjoy it."

Bile rose in the back of Mara's throat. Choking, she turned over, stumbled to her feet, and dashed into the magic-gathering room. Grute appeared in the doorway behind her, clutching the jambs. He leered at her. "Dead end, bitch. And now you're mine."

He staggered forward. Mara turned and, gasping, plunged both hands into the basin full of magic. As he seized her shoulders, spun her around and pulled her toward him, she screamed in fury, fear, and hatred—and slapped her magic-coated hands against the sides of his head.

She only wanted to drive him away. She only wanted him to leave her alone. But she didn't know how to control the power she had seized from the basin, had no clue as to its real strength . . .

. . . had no clue what it was capable of.

She shrieked as agony seared her hands, as though she'd just plunged them into an open fire. But in that same instant, Grute's head . . . vanished. One moment it was there, his mouth open, his breath reeking of whiskey, his tongue half-extended as he sought her lips. The next, there was a sound like a thunderclap, the pain in Mara's hands vanished, and something hot and wet sprayed her face and chest. Blood fountained from the ragged stump of Grute's neck, shooting up around the jagged white end of his severed spine, and his naked corpse fell against her and then crumpled to the ground.

Covered in blood and bits of brain and bone, Mara staggered back against the workbench, turned, fell to her knees, and spewed the remnants of the beef jerky and travel bread she had eaten across the floor, the vomit mingling with the spreading scarlet pool of Grute's blood.

She didn't have the strength to stand. Instead she crawled back into the main room, dragging long streaks of blood across the floor, scrabbled her way to the door, and almost fell through it into the storm outside, rolling over onto her back to let the thick white snowflakes pour down on her, hoping they would wash away the blood, the stench . . . and the horror.

But within moments she began to shiver. She would freeze to death if she stayed out there, and there was no way, *no way*, after all this, she was going to die because of *Grute*.

Grute, dead at her hand.

She couldn't believe it; couldn't believe she'd killed him, couldn't believe the *way* she'd killed him, couldn't believe that magic could do *that*. But when she staggered back to her feet and stepped back into the warmth of the hut, there he lay in the back room, dead and headless in an enormous pool of blood. Mara swallowed hard at the sight, gagging on the stench of his voided bowels, but though her stomach threatened to heave once more, she managed to keep her gorge down. She stumbled across the room and closed the door. With Grute out of sight, only the trail of blood and her own blood-and-tissue-splattered clothes remained to remind her of what she had done. She couldn't do anything about the former, but she took off all her clothes, put them outside in the snow, and then wrapped herself in blankets on the bed and lay there, staring at the fire.

For a long time she just gazed at it, dry-eyed and numb, but then out of nowhere the sobs took her. She wept, great, body-shaking sobs: wept for her lost child-hood, wept for her parents, and even, a little, wept for Grute, thrown out of Tamita like the rest of them when his Masking failed.

But she couldn't weep forever; and eventually, she

had to deal with the body. She first went and retrieved her clothes, soaking wet now after being buried in a thick blanket of snow, and worked out the mud and blood as best she could by the fire, the water running brown and red onto the hearth, where it sizzled and popped.

Leaving the still-damp clothes to dry, she wrapped the blanket even more tightly around her and hesitantly approached the closed door of the back room. For a moment she just stared at it, all too aware of the horror within, but then she pressed her lips together and pushed open the door.

Grute's corpse lay where he had fallen, naked and headless, the pool of blood all around him darker now that it had congealed, but still glittering in the strange, ever-shifting light of the magic. There was far less of it in the basin than there had been, she saw, swallowing hard to keep from throwing up again—not that there was anything left in her stomach *to* throw up—but she hadn't exhausted it completely.

Which gave her an idea.

Cringing at the stickiness of the blood-coated flagstones beneath her bare feet, she went to the basin. Letting the blanket fall open, so that it hung loosely on her shoulders like a cape, she plunged her hands into the multicolored pool, welcoming the strange tingle of power. She swirled her hands around the basin, trying to gather all the magic it contained. And then, not really knowing what would happen, she turned and knelt, closed her eyes so she couldn't see him, and reached out to touch Grute's bare, blood-caked back, wishing with all her heart that somehow the magic could send his cooling corpse elsewhere, anywhere, just get it out of there …

That same burning agony in her hands, gone in an instant; then a soundless flash of white light penetrated her closed eyelids, turning her vision red.

She opened her eyes. For a moment, she couldn't see anything. The magic's ever-changing light had vanished, so that the only illumination came from the dim glow of the fire through the open door. But slowly her eyes adjusted, and she saw ...

... nothing.

Grute was gone, as though he had never been. Not a trace of blood remained behind; not a speck of flesh, bone, or brain. Instead, fine dust coated the floor, and her skin, and drifted from her hair as her head snapped back and forth. She scrambled to her feet in a cloud of dust, the blanket falling away completely, and darted naked into the front room.

Even the blood on the floor was gone. So were the bloodstains she had been unable to scrub from her clothes, though there, too, that dust lingered.

Grute's disappearance terrified her almost as much as the moment when his head had exploded between her hands. How had she done *that?* How had the *magic* done that?

The use of magic by the Gifted was tightly regulated by the Palace. Her father was licensed to use the magic he was given by the Palace *only* for the making of Masks. If he used it for anything else, he would be brought up on charges.

So what was the penalty for *killing* with magic, she wondered? She could only guess—and shivered, remembering corpses rotting on the gallows of Traitors' Gate.

A slightly crazed laugh bubbled up between her lips. She clapped her hand over her mouth to stifle the sound, but the thought remained: showing her unMasked face in Tamita would get her hanged just as thoroughly, and after all, they could only execute her once.

In any event, she wouldn't be using—*mis*using— magic anymore *here*. The basin was empty. She'd exhausted the supply.

And in the process, she'd exhausted herself.

She stoked the fire with fresh firewood. Then, leaving her clothes to continue steaming, she stood and glanced into the magic room. The blanket in there, covered with Grute-dust, she didn't want touching her skin. Fortu-

nately, there was a second blanket on the bed, which
Grute had hardly disturbed, since all he'd done was sit
on it and drink. She cautiously checked the mattress,
found that it looked reasonably clean and vermin-free,
and gratefully stretched out on it, pulling the remaining
blanket up around her. She blinked sleepily at the dying
fire once or twice; then her eyelids closed and she slept.

• • •

Light flooded the room, accompanied by a blast of icy
air. Mara woke with an uncomfortable start and jerked
upright, clutching the blanket to her chest.

A dark figure stood silhouetted in the snow-bright
rectangle of the open doorway.

"Who the hell are you?" boomed a man's voice.

TWELVE

The Camp

MARA GAPED AT HIM. "I—"
The man didn't wait to hear. He strode past her, ignoring her as she scrambled to keep herself covered with the blanket, and yanked open the door to the back room. He swore again. "Nothing! I make the trek all the way up here in this weather, and there's *nothing!*" He turned and stared at her. He wore no Mask, but his broad, black-bearded face was unscarred. "Except *you.*" He took a step, looming over her. Blankets clutched as tightly to her chest as she could hold them, she pushed herself away from him, pressing her bare back against the cold stone wall. "Who are you?" he demanded again.

"M—Mara," she said.

"Mara." His dark eyes narrowed. "And how old are you?"

"Fifteen," she said, and knew she had made a mistake as his eyes flew wide.

"You're one of *them!* One of the unMasked from the ambushed wagon!"

"But you're unMasked, too," Mara said.

He snorted. "No. I just don't bother with the dratted thing when I'm out here alone in the Wild. Who's to see?" He rubbed his chin as he studied her. "Maybe the trek wasn't for nothing, after all." He looked around, saw her clothes by the fire, strode over, grabbed them, then turned and threw them at her. "Get dressed," he said. "You're coming with me."

Mara pulled on her clothes under the blanket while the man returned to the back room. She saw him lean over the empty basin, heard his angry mutter, and then watched as his eyes scanned the darkened room. He strode over to one of the shelves bearing the black stone jars and ran his finger over the wooden plank, lifting it covered with white dust. He sniffed at the dust, made a face, and then wiped his finger on his clothes. He turned to glare at her. "What the hell happened here?"

"Nothing since I got here," she said, trying to sound as young and innocent as possible. "What are you looking for?"

"None of your business. Are you dressed?"

"Yes." She pushed aside the blanket, pulled her boots out from under the bed, and tugged them on. "Where are you going to take me?" she said.

"Where you should already be," the man said. "The unMasked labor camp. I know the Warden. He'll give me a fat reward for bringing you in." He jerked his head toward the door. "Let's go."

Mara emerged, squinting, into bright morning sunlight, made all the more blinding by a foot of fresh snow. She'd brought the blanket with her for additional warmth, but she still shivered as the air bit her nose, ears, and fingers. A big black horse tethered outside tossed its head and snorted at her. Next to it, a much smaller gray mule gave her a mournful look, flicking its long ears as the cold wind ruffled its mane.

"Get on the mule," the man said.

"I don't know how to ride," Mara protested.

"You don't need to ride, you just need to hang on. I'll lead the mule. He won't fall."

Mara walked over to the mule, feet crunching in the snow, but couldn't figure out how to mount it. Two large panniers hung on either side of its bony hindquarters; smaller leather pouches were slung across its withers. The man muttered under his breath, then came over, seized her roughly around the waist, and lifted her up. She swung her leg over more or less by instinct and found herself on the mule's back. She managed to tuck her legs, spread uncomfortably wide, between the panniers and the pouches. She saw no reins, so she grabbed hold of the leather straps crisscrossing the mule's back to hold its load in place. Feeling more or less secure, she watched the man swing easily up into the black horse's worn saddle.

"How far do we have to go?" Mara asked. Now that the light no longer brought tears to her eyes, she saw what she hadn't been able to see in the snow and darkness of the previous night: they stood on the highest point of a ridge, a miniature mountain peak, the ground sloping away in every direction. The *real* mountains, soaring up to the north, her left, were sheathed in snow and wreathed in clouds that came apart in tatters high overhead, shredded by the icy peaks into long white streamers that faded away into the blue sky that was everywhere else.

To the south, her right, the ground ran away in a series of ridges to the rolling territory she and Grute had traversed en route from the Secret City. She glanced over her shoulder. Even from this height, she couldn't see the ocean, but she knew it was back there somewhere, and so were her friends in the unMasked Army. She and the man were about as exposed as they could be at that moment. Anyone looking up from miles around might see them.

Was anybody looking? Had the unMasked Army's patrols come this way? Would they see her?

Would they rescue her?

She saw no movement in the dark forests all around, but that proved nothing.

Then the man clucked to his horse and the mule, and they started forward, and down. Almost at once, they dipped below the ridgeline and out of sight of any hypothetical watchers. But by that point Mara had forgotten all about the unMasked Army. Instead, all her attention was focused on not falling off the mule. Her momentary sense of security on its back vanished with its first step. Its body rolled beneath her like a barrel in a river, threatening to pitch her off at any moment, and with no stirrups in which to rest her feet she had to rely on the strength of her legs and her death grip on the leather straps to keep her in place. Both mule and horse seemed incredibly sure-footed on the narrow track. The man had been right. The animals wouldn't fall.

She wasn't nearly that certain about *herself*.

In stories, riding horses and mules always seemed as easy as sitting in a rocking chair. No one ever talked about how tiring it was, how hard it was to keep your balance, how sore your legs got, how sore *everything* got that was in contact with the mule, which seemed to have no padding on its spine at all. *Maybe it's easier with a saddle*, she thought, as she clung desperately to the straps, sliding first this way then that. *It must be. Otherwise nobody would ever do it.*

After half an hour that felt like half a day they reached the bottom of the valley to the north. On level ground, the mule's back didn't roll so much, and Mara was able to relax, just a little. Down here, the snow was already melting, great wet dollops of it dropping from the trees, making white splashes on the bare, sheltered ground beneath before fading away.

Of course, melting snow meant mud, which wouldn't have been so bad if only it had stayed on the ground, but despite their easy pace, a remarkable amount of it flew up all around her. Mud splattered her cheeks and clotted her hair, and one particularly annoying blot clung to the very tip of her nose, where she couldn't get at it without letting go of the straps—and there was no way she was going to do *that*.

The man took no notice of her except for the occasional glance back—to be sure, she guessed, that she hadn't fallen off. He didn't speak. They traveled without a halt until the sun stood high overhead. Then the man reined the black horse to a stop on a bit of rocky shore beside a rushing stream, and slid smoothly down. *For him*, she thought resentfully, *riding a horse really* does *look as easy as sitting in a rocking chair*.

For her, though . . . With difficulty, she disentangled her sore, stiff fingers from the leather straps. The muscles in her thighs and legs screamed as she swung her right leg over the top of the mule. And every other muscle screamed as she let herself slide to the ground, so that she had to grab a pannier to keep from simply crumpling into the mud. She clung there, panting, while the pain eased slightly. Then, feeling like an old woman, she hobbled over to the stream. She knelt beside it, thinking maybe she could crawl into it and let it wash the mud away, but one freezing, stinging touch told her that would be a bad idea. She limited herself to splashing water on her face. Even that made her gasp—but it also revived her a bit.

She stood and looked downstream. "How much farther?"

"Rest of the day," the man said, his back to her. He had opened the flap of one of his saddlebags and pulled out a round loaf of hard brown bread. After a bit more rummaging he also withdrew half a fat red sausage. Mara's mouth watered.

The man grunted as he lowered himself onto a flat-topped boulder. He pulled a knife from his belt, and, holding the bread on his lap, cut a thick slice of the sausage. He tore off a piece of bread and stuffed sausage and bread together into his mouth. She couldn't take her eyes off him.

He swallowed. "Well, come and have some, then," he said. "I can't stand you looking at me with begging-puppy eyes."

She dashed forward and sat beside him on the boulder. He ripped off a chunk of the bread and shoved it into her hands along with a couple more good-sized cuts of sausage. She took a bite of bread and another of the heavily spiced sausage and thought she'd never tasted anything better.

They ate in something approaching companionable silence for a moment. "What will happen when we get to the mining camp?" Mara asked at last, timidly.

The man took another bite of sausage, then swiped the back of his hand across his mouth. "Don't know," he said. "Nothing to do with me. I'll give you to the Warden. He'll decide." He didn't meet her eyes, and that gave her a bad feeling.

"What do the unMasked *do* there?" she asked.

"They work," the man said. "In the mine. With Watchers aplenty to make *sure* they work. And a few, whaddya-acallems, *trustees*—unMasked that have been there a long time, keeping the others in line, making themselves useful." He pointed his knife at her. "Want my advice, you stay on the good side of the Warden, the Watchers, *and* the trustees. Then maybe someday you'll be a trustee yourself, if you live that long."

That sent a chill down her spine that had nothing to do with the cold air. "But . . . but how long do the unMasked stay in the camp?" Mara said, while inside she asked the real question. *How long will I be there?*

The man shoved his knife into his belt and stood up. "What do you think, girl?" he said sarcastically. "You can't go anywhere unMasked. And you can't ever be Masked. So . . . ?"

For the rest of my life, Mara thought. The prospect turned the food she had wolfed a moment before into a lump of lead in her stomach. She looked down at the last piece of bread in her hands, turning it over and over but not really seeing it. *Life in prison. That's what the un-Masked Army saved me from. But now I'm headed there again.*

Will they save me again?

She glanced left, upstream, in the general direction of the Secret City: but she saw only shadowed forest and the ever-rushing water.

"Time to move," the man said, turning his back on her. She got slowly to her feet, quailing at the thought of climbing onto the mule again. The man heaved her up onto the animal. She winced as bruises renewed their intimate acquaintance with the bones that had made them, grabbed onto the leather straps with still-aching fingers, and they resumed their miserable journey.

Mara's first hint they were close to the mining camp came when, as the sun settled low behind them, the man paused, reached into his saddlebag, and pulled out a Mask, a very pale green one with black stripes on the cheeks. She didn't know what Gift green represented, but whatever it was, he clearly didn't have much of it; though obviously enough that he could see magic, or he wouldn't be able to do his job. He settled the Mask on his face, then urged the horse forward again.

Five minutes later they rounded a bend in the stream, and the mining camp came into sight.

Mara had pictured something like the Autarch's Palace, all stone walls and turrets, but the camp was surrounded only by a tall palisade of unpeeled logs bound together and driven into the ground. In area, though, it was easily the Palace's equal.

The stream ran under the palisade and into the camp

through an opening barred with rusted iron. At the corners of the compound rose wooden towers, a peaked roof forming a kind of open hut atop each. She could see guards inside the "huts," but they didn't seem to be looking out: instead, all their attention was focused inward.

She felt another chill. *The walls are to keep people in, not keep attackers out.*

They were within fifty yards of the camp before a Watcher, only his black-Masked face and shoulders visible above the rough-hewn spiky tips of the palisade's poles, glanced their way. She saw him point, then heard a shout. The man who had captured her gave a wave. "Gate's around to the south," he said, and led the mule to the right, away from the stream, down to the end of the long wall of logs, then left and down another equally long wall to two enormous, iron-bound wooden doors flanked on either side by two more guard towers.

Those doors swung open, creaking and groaning, as they approached. Mara's guide pulled up short and waited as two Watchers came out. One took the horse's reins while the other just stood to one side, Mask turned in their direction, a crossbow cradled in his arms.

Mara's captor slid out of his saddle. "The Warden?" he said.

The man who had taken the reins nodded toward the gate, and as if on cue, another man emerged. He wasn't a Watcher: though his trousers and boots were black, his long coat, trimmed with glossy brown fur, was red: his Mask was Watcher-black, but spiral patterns of red marked each cheek.

Behind the Warden she could see a broad, straight path of crushed stone leading between rows of long, low log buildings toward a few larger structures at the far end of the camp, including an impressive stone house with tall glass windows and a colonnaded porch. Halfway down the camp, off to the right of the low arched bridge that she guessed carried the road over the stream, she saw a wood-and-metal framework and thought she caught the white splash of water. A sound like continuous distant thunder rumbled through the camp.

Half a dozen Watchers walked slowly up and down the central path. She saw no one else.

Dread made her stomach clench. *What's it like inside those low buildings? And what is that strange tower?*

"Cantic," said the Warden, and for the first time she knew the name of the man who had found her in the hut. "I see you brought me more than just the . . ." He glanced at Mara. ". . . *harvest* from Rocky Top."

Cantic grunted. "I brought you *less*. There was no 'harvest' at Rocky Top."

Behind his Mask, the Warden's mouth twisted into a frown. "The harvest has never failed on Rocky Top."

"It did this time." Cantic pointed at Mara. "I found *her* instead. She's one of your runaways from the wagon."

The Warden's lips pressed together, then he spat, "Get her down."

Cantic turned to Mara, but before he could pull her down from the mule, she slid down herself, gasping a little from the pain of her abused legs, buttocks, and thighs, but determined to stand on her own.

The Warden strode forward and grabbed her arm so hard she gasped again. "Where are the others? Where are they hiding?"

"I–I don't know," Mara stuttered. She remembered what Catilla had said about the impression the un-Masked Army had hoped to leave. "We were attacked. The wagon turned over, the doors came open . . . we got out, and we saw these . . . wild men. Without Masks, all dressed in furs and rags, like . . . something out of olden times. They murdered the Watchers. It was horrible. We all scattered. I ran into the woods. I don't know if anyone else got away. If they didn't, those wild men . . ." She shuddered, she hoped convincingly. "I hope they got away," she finished in a small voice, trying to sound as young as she could. "But even if they did, they could be dead. If I hadn't seen the hut up on top of that ridge, I'd have frozen to death."

She gave the Warden her best innocent-little-girl look, one she'd practiced often on her father. Although she had to admit it hadn't ever worked very well on him.

It didn't work on the Warden, either. "Your clothes," he said. "They are not what the unMasked wear when they are sent here."

Her heart leaped and she was suddenly glad for the day's muddy ride. The clothes the unMasked Army had given her couldn't look like much, not in the fading light and splattered with muck. "They're what I was given," she said. "I don't know why. You'd have to ask the fat man"—she gave another shudder; this time it wasn't at all hard to make it convincing—"in the warehouse in Tamita. He said he wanted to draw me wearing them."

The Watcher studied her for a moment. She couldn't tell if he believed her. "What's your name?"

For a moment Mara considered lying; but there seemed little point. *Besides*, she thought, *maybe if he realizes I'm the daughter of the Master Maskmaker, he'll...*

... what? Give me special treatment?

The thought made her feel oddly ashamed. But she couldn't help hoping it was true.

"Mara," she said.

"Mara Holdfast, Daughter of the Master Maskmaker," the Warden corrected. He leaned close. "You were wise not to lie to me," he said, voice cool. "Your face is unmarked. I knew who you were the moment I saw you up close. I had word ahead of the wagon."

Mara nodded, her throat closed off by sudden fright.

The Warden straightened again. "And the others? Alita? Prella? Kirika? Simona? Grute? What of them?"

"I don't know," Mara said. "After I ran... in the woods... I got lost... I couldn't find any of the others..." She let her lip tremble, let the beginning of a sob creep into her voice, found it was far too easy, and had to fight hard to keep it from turning into full-on weeping. If she started bawling, she might never stop.

"Hmmm." The Warden released her arm and stepped back. "Building three," he said to the nearest Watcher. "Tell Hayka to look after her."

"Come on, you," the Watcher commanded, and pulled her through the gate into the camp.

The sun had just slipped behind the hills, plunging the camp into chilly shadow. Lights glowed in the windows and smoke rose from the chimneys of the long, low log buildings that Mara passed between, a dozen in all, six on one side and six on the other of the central path. A few other buildings, on the far side of the stream, loomed dark and unlit in the twilight, but bright lamplight gleamed through the big glass windows of the stone house at the path's far end and the two-story wooden structures to either side of it. It all looked peaceful and cozy, but Mara was quite certain it wasn't.

Lamps also hung from the strange framework of wood and iron, and in their light Mara could now see that the frame suspended the largest water wheel she'd ever seen, the source of the strange rumbling sound. Set inside a deep trench, it slowly revolved as the stream poured over it in a constant foaming waterfall.

But she only caught a glimpse of it, for just as it came into sight, they reached the longhouse on the right that was the third building south of the stream. Her guard took a ring of keys from his belt, selected one, and unlocked the door. He pulled it open, then grabbed her arm and shoved her inside.

She found herself in a small square room containing two bunk beds, a rotund black stove, a tiny table, and a chair. Directly across from the door to the outside was another door, barred shut.

A woman lay in the upper bunk, sound asleep, only her long, tangled black hair visible. A second woman sat at the tiny table, knitting a woolen scarf. She looked up, needles frozen, as Mara made her abrupt entrance. Her lined, pinched face made Mara think at first glance she was elderly; but her brown hair, drawn back in a loose ponytail, had no gray in it Mara could see, and her eyes were clear.

She put down the needles and got to her feet. "Who's this?"

The Watcher nodded at Mara. "New arrival, Hayka. Cantic just brought her in. Name's Mara. Warden said to give her to you. And now I done it." He turned and went out, closing and locking the door behind him.

Hayka came around the table. "New arrival, all by yourself? And brought in by a harvester?" She looked Mara up and down, taking in her mud-spattered clothes. Her eyes returned to Mara's face, and narrowed. "You're one of *them*, ain't you?" she said sharply. "One of them what escaped?"

"Didn't escape, did I," Mara muttered. She'd only just met Hayka and already she didn't like her, or trust her.

Hayka snorted. "You can say that again, baby girl. Nor will you." She leaned closer, squinting in the dim yellow light. Her breath smelled of onions. "Your face . . ." She reached out a hand and cupped Mara's chin; Mara tried to pull her head away, but Hayka's grip tightened. "Unmarked! Lucky you. Or maybe not so lucky." She leered. "Warden himself might be calling for *you* to warm his bed one of these cold nights."

With a convulsive jerk, Mara pulled her chin free. Hayka laughed at her. "Fiery, are you? Won't help. Watchers *like* that sort of thing. They'll find you *interesting*. And interesting is always . . . *exciting*."

She put her hands on her hips. "Here's what's what, girl. Me and Skriva, who's up there"—she jerked her head at the woman in the bunk, who hadn't stirred—"are trustees. We get this cozy little room, we get better food, we get warmer clothes, we get left alone by the Watchers, but only as long as there's no trouble from anybody in *there*." She jerked a thumb at the inner door, then leaned forward again, placing her face only inches from Mara's.

"So there won't be any trouble. You understand? You'll do what you're told, when you're told. You don't talk back, to the Watchers, to me, to nobody. You work your skinny little butt off, is what you do, and if the Watchers want you up at the barracks or the Warden wants you up at the big house, you'll go and make them very, very happy, and you'll never complain, not to them, not to me, not to anyone. Because if you do . . ." Hayka's hand came off her hip and lashed across Mara's face, the slap knocking her head to one side and making her ears ring. She jerked her head back around, furious, hand clutching her stinging cheek. Hayka stuck a finger in her face. "Because if you do," she snarled, "I'll make your life even more of a hell than it's going to be anyway." She straightened. "But cheer up," she said, showing her teeth in a death's-head grin. "If you're really good and cooperative for, oh, the next ten years or so—keep the Watchers and the Warden happy—maybe you'll be made a trustee, too." Bitterness tightened her voice. "Then you can enjoy *these* luxurious accommodations. More likely, of course, you'll be dead before winter's end."

Mara felt herself trembling, but she kept her lips pressed together and said nothing. Hayka was of the same ilk as Grute, she understood that. *And look what happened to* him, she thought savagely. Her own cold-blooded fury surprised her.

"All right," Hayka said. "First things first. Take off them clothes. They look pretty warm. They're mine now. Won't fit me, but there's another trustee I know'll trade me for 'em."

Mara stared. "But I'll freeze."

Hayka snorted. "Not planning to send you naked into the mine. You'll wear these." She knelt beside the bunk and pulled out from under it a rough wooden box. She rummaged in it, then held up a gray tunic and trousers. "Strip, and put 'em on. You can keep whatever underwear you've got. After the first snow, you'll get a coat. Not before."

Cheeks flaming, Mara took off the mud-caked clothes that she'd donned fresh and clean in the Secret City what seemed like a lifetime ago. The rough gray cloth of the prison clothes scratched her arms and legs as she pulled the tunic and trousers on over her drawers and undershirt. At least her new clothes seemed to be clean. Hayka tossed her dirty clothes in a corner. "Now we'll find you a bunk." She turned and unbarred the inner door, then swung it open. "In you go."

Mara stepped through into a long, shadowy, *cold* room lined with bunk beds. At its center a small fire flickered in a round fire pit. Girls and women huddled around the pitiful flames. Most looked young, a few years older than Mara at most. Only one or two looked as old as Hayka. And she saw no one older.

She didn't think that was a good sign.

A low murmur of conversation died away. Thin, pale faces turned to stare at her: not exactly hostile, but not exactly friendly, either. More like they were sizing her up. Judging her.

Trying to decide how I'm going to shake things up, she thought. *Trying to decide if I'm friend or foe.*

She didn't feel like either friend or foe at the moment: all she felt was sore, hungry, cold, thirsty, frightened, and tired. Tired to the depths of her soul.

Hayka grabbed her arm and dragged her to the fire pit. "This here's Mara," she said. "I'm sure you'll make her welcome."

A woman just a little younger than Hayka, but a lot thinner and uglier, with deep red scars slashing across her face, grabbed Mara by the upper arms. "I'll make her welcome." Her callused hands flicked all over Mara's body, as though looking for something to steal, but the pockets of Mara's new clothes were as empty as her stomach. "Dammit, she's got nothing." The woman poked at Mara's rather flat chest and laughed. "Nothing at all."

"Don't think that'll save you," said a third woman, a

little younger, with a face that might once have been pretty but now had the hard-edged look of something carved out of ice.

Mara looked around at the other women. Some openly sneered at her, but a few, the youngest, the ones closest to her own age, wouldn't meet her eyes at all. One girl, sitting cross-legged on the floor with her hands on her ankles, rocked back and forth, eyes closed, humming a tune Mara recognized as a lullaby . . .

A lullaby Mara's mother used to sing to her when she couldn't sleep.

She swallowed a sudden lump in her throat, then was jerked around to face Hayka again. "You take the bunk down there." She pointed to the far end of the long building, where there was another door. "Farthest from the fire, so it's coldest. Closest to the latrine—through that door—so it smells. You want a better bunk, you earn it." She pointed to herself. "By keeping me happy. We get meat once a week. Say you gave me your meat portion for a month. I might be able to find you a bed closer to the fire. Maybe you hear something, somebody saying something against me. You let me know so I can deal with it. Could earn you an extra blanket. You get the idea?"

Mara got it, all right. Like Grute, Hayka was somehow *broken* inside, and the Mask had known it when she was just fifteen. *This is what most of those whose Masks failed used to be like*, she thought. *But now . . .*

She looked at the others. They couldn't all be like Hayka and Grute. She remembered what Catilla had told her, how some of those whose Maskings failed had simply been . . . different. And then there were the youngest, the ones within a year or so of her age. Some of them must be like her, torn away from their parents on the biggest day of their lives, utterly shocked, utterly devastated, utterly bewildered by the failure of their Masks, not knowing why, not knowing the Masks had changed.

The rocking girl's endlessly repeating lullaby hummed in her ears.

She wanted to tell Hayka to take a flying leap into the latrine, but instead she bit her lip and swallowed her pride and said, "I get it."

"Good." Hayka straightened. "Then let me give you the rest of the grand tour."

There wasn't much to the tour and what there was was hard to see. The only light came from one smoke-blackened lantern by the door, another by the latrine door, and the fire, which had barely been showing flames when she entered and had now burned down to glowing embers, plunging most of the building into gloom. A long, shallow basin, with the spout and handle of a water pump at one end, stretched along the wall to the south of the fire pit. The latrine, lit by the tiniest of lanterns, smelled as bad as promised. It had two wooden benches, one on either side, with three holes apiece, and it was ice cold, since there was a hole in the roof to bring in fresh air and let out some of the stink. Mara grimaced, but when you had to go, you had to go, and she had to go. Fortunately she was left alone, shivering, to do it.

When she came out, Hayka had disappeared back into her own cozy room, and the women and girls who had been gathered by the fire pit were getting into their bunks. They didn't get undressed first, and considering she was already chilled to the bone, Mara understood why.

She lingered by the fire pit, trying to warm herself, but the older woman who had poked at her earlier grabbed her arm and spun her around. "Get to bed," she snapped. "Lights out in two minutes. A Watcher checks. If anybody's out of bed, we *all* get punished. Go!"

Startled, Mara hurried down to her bunk and climbed in. There was no pillow, and the thin, threadbare blanket promised little comfort. She'd barely pulled it up to her chin when the door banged open. While Hayka stood in the doorway, a Watcher carrying a lantern strolled down the middle of the longhouse, and Mara realized there was another reason besides warmth not to undress for bed as he pulled back blankets one by one, though what he was checking for, she couldn't imagine. He reached her end of the longhouse, but ignored her for a moment, first pulling open the door to the latrine. He took a quick look, made a gagging sound, and slammed the door shut.

Then he looked down at her. He reached out and pulled the blanket off her as he had the others, looked into her bunk, and tossed the blanket back. He started to turn away, but then stopped, turned back, and leaned closer, holding the lamp so near she could feel the heat from its flickering oil flame. His eyes glittered behind the black, blank Mask. "A new one," he said. "And a pretty one, not a scar to be seen. I think we'll *all* want to get to know you better, baby girl. A *lot* better." He stared another long moment, then straightened, turned away, and strode back toward Hayka, taking the light with him. A moment later Hayka's door swung shut, plunging the longhouse into darkness.

Mara wished she were Prella, naïve enough to have to ask, "What did he mean?" but she knew *exactly* what he had meant.

Her heart fluttered in her chest and despite the cold, her palms felt sweaty.

Keltan, she thought. *Hyram. Edrik. Where are you?*

No rescuers suddenly burst through the door. Instead, there was only the fading red glow of the fire pit, the creak of beds as women rolled over, and the slowly growing, ever-more-horrifying realization that she might not be rescued before . . .

Before.

Shuddering, she pulled the blanket over her head and tried to shut out the low grumble of the water wheel, tried hard to imagine she was in her own attic room, cuddling with Stoofy, hearing the murmur of her parents' voices downstairs, waiting to drift off to sleep knowing she was safe and warm and loved . . .

But although she'd always been told she had a good imagination, imagining *that* proved to be beyond her.

THIRTEEN

Descent into Darkness

THE ONLY GOOD THING about absolute exhaustion was that, despite everything, Mara fell asleep shortly after the Watcher left the longhouse. She woke to the smell of smoke. Rolling over, she saw a dark figure crouched by the fire pit, urging another small fire to life. She closed her eyes again, but had no time to drift back to sleep before Hayka's door crashed open, though it wasn't Hayka who yelled, "Up, slugs. Breakfast in half an hour. Shift change in an hour."

Mara blinked up at the rough wooden underside of the bunk over her head. It wasn't until she tried to sit up that she realized just how stiff and sore she was from the previous day's mule ride, not to mention the long, cold night in the hard little bed. It took all her strength and a lot of teeth-gritting just to swing her legs over the side.

She rubbed her hands on her gray trousers, and looked around.

The other girls and women were also getting out of bed, and a line had already formed at the latrine, stretching past her bunk. Mara joined it, and found herself standing next to a girl just a little bit older. The girl looked sideways at her. A pale ghost of a smile flicked briefly over her face. "Hi," she said. "I'm Katia."

Mara managed to smile back. "Hi," she said. "I'm Mara."

Katia lowered her voice. "Is it true? Someone attacked the wagon? You got out?"

"It's true," Mara said. Bitterness crept into her voice as she added, "But I didn't get out to stay."

"I'm sorry," Katia said. She shook her head. "This place is terrible. The mines are — " She fell silent as, from out of nowhere, Hayka appeared, shoving her way through the women who had joined the line behind Mara and Katia.

"Get into the latrine," Hayka said to Mara, ignoring Katia. "I'm supposed to take you to the Warden before breakfast."

Heart fluttering, Mara pushed to the head of the line, keeping her head down to avoid the accusing glares. Hayka was waiting for her when she came out and dragged her out of the longhouse by her arm. Skriva, the trustee who had rousted the women out of their bunks, sat at the table eating steaming porridge from a wooden bowl. She glanced up. "*You'll* have to chivvy them to the mess hall," Hayka told her.

Skriva just grunted, and went back to shoveling porridge into her mouth.

Hayka took Mara outside into a cold, cloudy morning, the sky just beginning to gray. A chill wind from the towering mountains to the north swept swirling dust through the camp. Mara shivered and wondered if she'd ever be warm again. Hayka had said she wouldn't get a coat until after the first snow. Mara looked up at the clouds hopefully, but they remained stubbornly precipitation-free.

Hayka led her up the crushed-rock path toward the big stone house, whose glazed windows glowed with light and from whose many chimneys issued tendrils of smoke, blown sideways and shredded by the wind. They passed over the low arch of the stone bridge that crossed the stream, and Mara glanced right at the top of the giant water wheel, turning in the constant flow of water. *What's it for?* she wondered. *Some sort of mill? What do they mine here, anyway?*

She glanced at Hayka's scowling face and decided not to ask.

On the far side of the bridge they passed the other wooden structures, larger and squarer than the long-houses, which had been dark the night before. From one came the smell of baking bread, and Mara's mouth watered. The dining hall, presumably. She hoped whatever the Warden wanted, he'd let her eat soon.

And what does *he want?* she thought uneasily. *Surely not . . . that. Not yet. He wouldn't, would he?*

He might. She was only fifteen, but she'd lived her life in the largest city of the Autarchy, mingling with children from all walks of life on the streets. She knew very well what went on behind some closed doors in the city, knew there were men who liked to prey on the young: knew that the Masks didn't seem to care about *that*, though there were laws against it. If the Warden were one of that sort . . .

If he were, there was nothing she could do about it.

Unless he's got a basin of magic in his room, she thought with a flare of defiance, remembering Grute.

Hayka led her up the broad stone steps onto the porch. A brass knocker hung from the shining black door. Hayka rapped sharply, and the door opened almost at once to reveal the impassive Mask of a towering Watcher. "Mara," Hayka said. "Warden wants her."

The Watcher nodded and moved to one side. Hayka left without a word as Mara stepped into the entry hall. Gold and silver sparkled at her from bright flecks in the white stone floor, reflecting the light from the oil-lamp chandelier hanging overhead. Broad stairs straight ahead led up to the second floor; on either side of the stairs, hallways led deeper into the house, doors to right and left and at the far end of each. The butter-yellow walls were crowded with paintings large and small, mostly of mountains and waterfalls and trees. They had an amateurish quality about them. *Warden probably painted them himself*, Mara thought.

Though chilly, the hallway was far warmer than the longhouse, and the dark-paneled room to the right into which the Watcher took her was warmer yet, thanks to the fire blazing in a red-tiled hearth beneath a mantelpiece made of the same gold-flecked stone as the floor. Mara hurried over to it to crouch and warm herself, while the Watcher remained in the doorway. She straightened and turned as she heard someone come in, and saw the Warden, today dressed in thick blue trousers and a thigh-length blue tunic, snowy linen showing at neck and wrists. From a chain of gold around his neck dangled a golden disk, inset with a red spiral that matched the ones on the cheeks of his black Mask. Above the Mask, his silver hair picked up highlights of yellow and red from the lamps and the fire. "Mara, good," he said brusquely. He seated himself in the big leather armchair behind the desk. Two white-upholstered chairs faced the desk, but he made no offer to her to sit.

A single piece of paper lay in the center of the desk's shining stone surface, otherwise bare apart from a pen and an inkwell inside a small wooden tray. The Warden looked down at it. "Mara," he said. "Daughter of Charlton Holdfast." He looked up at her. "I am astonished to see you here."

Mara said nothing, unsure how to respond.

The Warden pulled the sheet of paper toward him. "The failure of your Mask was considered unusual enough that I was asked to question you about it when you arrived." He perused the paper. "The Healer Ethelda attended your Masking?"

Mara nodded. "Yes," she said. "My mother expected the Autarch himself to be there, but . . ."

"No doubt he had more pressing matters to attend to." The Warden lifted his head again to meet her eyes. "Fortunately for you. Your face is unmarked, thanks to Ethelda's ministrations."

Mara swallowed. "I know. I'm . . . very lucky."

The Warden folded his hands on top of the piece of paper. "Mara," he said. "As Warden, I am in a position to make your life here much more comfortable than it might otherwise be. But I need your . . . cooperation."

Mara's heart fluttered in her chest like a caged bird. "I don't understand."

"It's very simple," said the Warden. "I need to know what happened to the wagon."

"I–I told you. Wild men attacked us. I ran away. I'd be dead if I hadn't found the hut with the magic—" she bit that off. She didn't want to talk about what had happened in the hut.

The Warden stared at her a long moment. "Yes," he said at last. "You told me. The problem is, I don't believe you."

Mara's face felt frozen as a Mask. She didn't dare say anything. She just stood, still as a statue.

"It's the clothes you were wearing, you see," the Warden continued. "You said you were sent out from the warehouse wearing them. You said the fat man wanted you to wear them while he drew you. But the fat man in the warehouse wouldn't draw you wearing those. He'd more likely draw you nude. I should know: I have several of his better pieces in my collection." He leaned forward. "This is the cooperation I need," he said softly. "I want you to tell me everything—everything—that happened on that trip here. I want you to tell me the *truth*. I want to know who attacked you. I want to know why. What were they after? You? The unmarked, unMasked daughter of the Master Maskmaker of Tamita? Or perhaps one of the other children? What do you know about *them?*"

"Nothing! We barely talked—"

"Really? Over four days? It must have been a very silent journey."

"I'm telling the truth!" Mara said desperately. "About the clothes, about everything! Please, you've got to—"

"Believe you? Well, no, I don't." The Warden leaned back, picked up the pen, dipped it in the inkwell, and scribbled something on the paper. "You're going down into the mines today," he said. "Everyone starts in the mines. But not everyone has to *stay* in the mines." He dipped and wrote again. "If you remembered something else about what happened to the wagon, about the unMasked who were in it, or the people who attacked—the people who gave you those clothes—I might be able to find a place for you aboveground." More ink, more scribbling. "Think about it." He put down the pen, raised his head, and called, "Watcher Stanlis!"

The door swung open at once and Mara's escort re-entered, took her by the arm, and led her out. The sick twisting in her stomach grew worse as he led her down the steps of the colonnaded porch. The mines? Underground?

How bad can it be? she told herself with false bravado. She soon found out.

The constant grumbling of the water wheel grew louder as the Watcher took her toward its giant framework. They crossed the stone arch of the bridge, then turned left, parallel to the water wheel and the endlessly cascading water, walking on a boardwalk alongside the deep trench in which the water wheel was set. Mara looked down. Past the water wheel, the stream foamed on over a rocky bed, but almost at once was directed away into a dark opening in the trench wall, presumably leading to a channel that would empty somewhere outside the walls. The trench itself continued toward a structure at the far end that, when she'd glimpsed it the night before, Mara had thought an ordinary shed. Instead, she now saw that it was actually the tallest building in the camp, four stories high—but most of it was below ground level, inside the trench.

Running down the middle of that trench was a long wooden beam, attached off center to the water wheel at one end so that the wheel's constant turning first pushed it forward, then pulled it back. The beam stretched across a series of posts driven into the ground. At each post the beam was attached to a shorter, vertical beam that swiveled back and forth with the horizontal beam's motion. Each vertical beam was attached at the bottom to another horizontal beam, as massive as the one attached to the wheel. As the top beam thrust forward, the motion pushed the tops of the vertical beams in that direction and their bottoms back toward the wheel, drawing the second horizontal beam with them. Then the top beam drew back and the bottom beam was thrust forward. Over and over the motion repeated, one beam swinging forward, the other back. Both beams disappeared at their far end into the wooden building.

Men, women, boys, and girls were shuffling into that building at ground level. The shed only looked large enough to hold about twenty people, but the line of people, which stretched out of sight between the nearest longhouse and the wall, kept moving forward, regular as clockwork. Mara could see nobody coming out, although, when she glanced back over her shoulder, she spotted tired, dirty-looking workers in a different line on the opposite side of the camp, shuffling into the building she had identified as the mess hall.

When she and the Watcher reached the line—there were still at least thirty people in it, Mara saw, glancing right—the Watcher shoved the other workers aside and pulled her through the door into the building's dim, cavernous interior. An open skylight in the heavy-beamed ceiling provided the only light, and the constant rumble and crash of wood on wood beat on her ears. Mara, looking down as the Watcher elbowed open their path down the long flight of stairs from ground level to the building's floor, saw that the two massive horizontal beams that ran along the trench were here attached to the ends of one cross-piece of a massive X-shape. The ends of the other cross-piece were attached to long vertical beams that, seesawing up and down, disappeared into a gaping hole in the shed's floor. Two wooden platforms, one on each vertical beam, appeared and disappeared in a regular, alternating rhythm. A worker would step onto the platform as it appeared, then disappear into the Earth with the next stroke . . . and not reappear.

It looked to Mara like the unMasked were being fed into the maw of some giant underground mechanism, and her stomach clenched in fear. It clenched again when they reached the bottom of the stairs and she saw exactly how that mechanism worked.

A worker, a grim-looking man with a patch over one eye, stepped onto the platform that appeared at the top. It descended as the other platform rose: but as the stroke ended and the platform he was on started to ascend, the one-eyed worker stepped to another farther down the other beam, which was on its downward stroke. And presumably he continued stepping from platform to platform until he reached wherever he was going in the shaft . . .

. . . however far underground that might be.

A girl only two or three years older than Mara, face blank and set, stepped onto the top platform and began her own journey into the depths.

Mara shuddered. She couldn't do that. She couldn't go down there. She *couldn't!*

But, it seemed, she would have to.

More than just the beams with their alternating wooden platforms descended into the shaft, one half of which was completely open. A rope hung down into the darkness from somewhere high overhead, and looking up, Mara saw that it was wrapped around a windlass. As she watched, two burly unMasked men began cranking it, the rope rising steadily. From their strained expressions, she gathered something very heavy was on the other end of the rope that began rising from the depths, bits of colored cloth tied around it at regular intervals.

Overseeing all of this from a tall desk were two unMasked men, though their faces were so hard and set they might as well have been Masked. "New worker," the Watcher called up to them, hands heavy on Mara's shoulders. "Name's Mara."

The two unMasked peered down at her. Vivid pink scars crisscrossed their cheeks and foreheads. "Skinny," said one. "Nice and skinny." He gave Mara a nasty grin lacking more than a few teeth. "Your timing's perfect, girl. We've been needing someone skinny ever since the roof fell in on Shimma." His grin grew even nastier. "If you find any of her bits, be sure to send them up." He looked down, scribbled something on a piece of paper, and reached it down to her. "You're going all the way to the bottom. Give this to the shift supervisor. He'll be the first person you see."

The Watcher took her over to the reciprocating platforms just as a huge iron bucket full of black rock rose from the shaft on the end of the rope. Mara didn't bother to follow its ascent, presumably to the windlass far above. She had eyes only for the endlessly appearing and disappearing platforms. The wood of each was stained with what looked suspiciously like blood. She saw that there were handholds on the beams, though the workers mostly ignored them. "You see how it works?" said the Watcher.

"Ye–yes," Mara said, through a throat so suddenly dry and tight she could hardly speak.

"Don't fall into the gap between the platforms," the Watcher said indifferently. "It makes a hell of a mess and jams up the mechanism."

He put out a hand to stop the next worker in line

from stepping onto the platform. Mara's eyes caught the startled gaze of Katia, who gave her a weak smile. "You'll be all right," she said. "It's easy, really."

"Shut up, you!" The Watcher gave Katia a shove that made her stagger back into the older woman behind her, who cursed and pushed her back again. The Watcher turned back to Mara. "You're holding things up. Go."

Mara saw the platform rising in front of her. Terror coursing through her, she stepped onto it, and gripped the handhold. She sank into the shaft. The platform descended a few feet and slowed just as a platform on the other beam rose to meet it. She stepped convulsively over the three-foot gap, teetered, grabbed the next handhold . . . and descended.

The journey seemed to take forever. Lanterns hung on the beam every four platforms or so, but at times she had to step from one platform to the next as much by feel as by sight. Rock walls, damp and glistening, rose around her. Horizontal tunnels appeared. At each one, an older unMasked man or woman stood, clipboard in hand. They watched her pass with dull, disinterested gazes. The shift supervisors, she supposed . . . but still the shaft descended.

An eternity later she at last reached the bottom, the reciprocating beams ending below her in a pit where another horizontal beam joined them together, seesawing. She stepped off onto solid stone, and found her legs so shaky she stumbled and fell against the damp wall.

A young man with a horribly scarred face squinted at her. "Who are you?"

Mara fumbled for her pocket and pulled out the crumpled piece of paper the trustee had given her. The young man opened it up, perused it, and grunted. "Good," he said. "We've been short-handed."

Ever since the roof fell in on Shimma, Mara thought sickly.

Someone else stepped off the platform behind her.

She turned, and relief flooded her at the sight of Katia's pale face. She wouldn't be alone down here after all.

"Good," the supervisor said again. "Katia, take Mara into six. She's your new partner."

Feeling more hopeful, Mara gave Katia a weak smile, but this time Katia did not return it. "This way," she said, her voice, like her expression, tight and strained.

Katia led her into a narrow tunnel, only two armspans wide, but turned at once through a rough-hewn arch to the right into a large, crudely shaped chamber. Wicker baskets were stacked along one wall; sharpened steel rods, picks, metal wedges, and hammers were arranged on shelves on another, along with candle lanterns and water flasks. "Take one of everything," Katia said, suiting actions to words. The baskets had leather straps into which she shoved her arms, making the basket into an awkward backpack. Mara copied her. The wicker bounced lightly on her back as she continued to move around the room. She tried to imagine carrying it, full of rock, through underground tunnels. Would she even be able to move?

Leather loops on the outside of the baskets held the hammers, wedges, and water flasks. That left Mara's hands free to carry a candle lantern in one hand and a steel rod in the other. Thus laden, she followed Katia back out into the main tunnel, and then deeper into the mine.

Side tunnels branched off at intervals. Mara saw nothing but blackness down any of them, though the distant ringing of steel on stone spoke of someone at work. The air, warmer than she'd expected, was so muggy that sweat soaked her clothes before they'd traveled a hundred yards. Wooden beams and posts propped up the roof. Mara was uneasily aware of the enormous weight of rock hanging above their heads. The timbers, wet and dark, beams sagging, posts cracked, hardly seemed adequate to support it. "Did you know Shimma?" Mara said to Katia's back, as the other girl led her deeper and deeper into the mine.

"She arrived in the same wagon as me," Katia said without looking back. "We were partnered. I was at the shaft with a basket of ore when the cave-in happened." She jerked her head. "Up here, on the right."

They passed another side tunnel. Katia didn't look down it, but Mara did. Tons of fallen rock, splintered timbers jutting out like the broken fangs of some slain, giant beast, blocked the tunnel just at the edge of the light. "Did anyone . . . try to dig her out?"

"No," Katia said. "Nobody cared. Even if she survived the cave-in, she's dead now. That was a month ago."

Mara pictured a girl like herself, trapped in darkness, screaming, tearing at the stone with her fingernails, growing weaker and weaker until, finally . . .

She swallowed hard and said nothing more.

They trudged on another hundred feet. The ceiling got lower and lower, until they had to bend almost double. Mara couldn't imagine a grown man making it this far. And then, horrifyingly, the tunnel narrowed again, to a hole they would have to enter on hands and knees. "In there?" Mara said, her voice quavering.

"In there," Katia said grimly. For the first time she turned around and looked at Mara. Her face, pale in the light of their candle lanterns, looked far older than her fifteen or so years: she looked, Mara thought, like an old woman. "Welcome to hell."

She slipped her arms out of the straps of the basket and attached the candle lantern to a hook Mara had seen but hadn't understood the purpose of until then. Then, still clutching the iron bar in one hand, shoving the basket ahead of her with the other, she got down on her hands and knees and crawled into the tunnel. Mara took a deep breath that did nothing to steady her shaking hands, took off her own basket, attached the candle lantern, pushed it into the tunnel after Katia, and followed.

FOURTEEN

Blood, Sweat, and Fears

EVEN ON HER HANDS AND KNEES, even without the basket on her back, the tunnel was so low Mara cracked her head twice on supporting timbers she failed to see in the flickering light of the lanterns, what little made it past the bulk of the basket in front of her. As well, it was incredibly awkward crawling with the steel bar in one hand: she bashed her knuckles on the stone with every sliding movement forward.

She gulped great ragged gasps of breath that roared in her ears but seemed to do nothing to fill her lungs, as though there were a shortage of air. *Maybe there is*, she thought, panic edging her thoughts. *Maybe we'll suffocate.* She'd heard of such things happening in mines. But she'd also heard that in bad air candles would dim or die, and although she could only catch glimpses of its light, her lantern seemed to be burning normally.

It's not a lack of air, she told herself. *It's fear. Terror.*

Horror, if it came to that; horror at being where she was, hundreds of feet underground, tons of rock pressing in on every side; horror at being a prisoner of the Watchers, unMasked and hence not even a real person. She had become a shadow, and like a shadow, she might vanish at any instant. A shrug of the earth, the tiniest twitch, and a million tons of rock would squash her like an ant beneath the boot heel of a careless passerby on the cobblestones of Tamita.

Would they even tell her parents?

Her heart pounded in her ears, and a scream built in her throat. But just when she thought she couldn't bear it any longer, the tunnel widened. It still wasn't tall enough to stand up in, but it was at least wide enough she could crawl up alongside Katia, and high enough she could kneel. "That was awful," she said, her voice thin and breathless in her ears. Blood from her battered knuckles covered the shaking hand she lifted to wipe sweat from her face.

Katia started to say something, then broke into a fit of coughing. She covered her mouth with her hand; when she took it away, Mara saw blood at the corner of her lips. "It gets worse," she said hoarsely when she had caught her breath. "Now we have to work."

Mara looked at the rock face. "What do we do?"

Katia pulled her arms free of her basket's straps. "We have to produce six baskets of ore by the end of the shift."

"Six?" Mara looked at the Katia's basket. "That's . . ."

"Impossible?" Katia shook her head. "You can't think like that. You *can't*. If you don't make your quota, you get sent to the Watchers. For entertainment."

Mara felt sick. "You mean . . . ?"

"Yeah," Katia said. "I mean."

"Have you . . . ?"

"Not yet," Katia said. "Shimma and I always managed to make quota. And when I was on my own, they took me off quota. But now I have you. And that means the quota is back in effect. And that means . . ." She let the sentence trail off, but it didn't take a mind reader to finish it.

"That means we'd better get to work," Mara said. She took a deep breath and shrugged her own basket off her back. "All right. Show me."

Katia showed her: how to pound the steel rod into the rock, splitting it; how to drive the metal wedge into the crack with the hammer and pound on it until pieces broke off the rock face; how to gather the chunks of stone into the basket. Mara, drenched with sweat, reached for her water bottle almost at once, but Katia stopped her. "That's all the water you get," she said. "All day. You have to make it last."

"What about food?" Mara said.

"You didn't bring any?"

Mara shook her head. "I didn't even get breakfast," she said.

"You have to save some of your breakfast for your lunch," Katia said. "I'll share today. But only this once."

Mara nodded, abashed, and got back to work.

The ringing of steel on stone deafened her, the hammer seemed almost too heavy to lift, the flying chips threatened her eyesight, the dust choked her. She remembered the drop of blood at the corner of Katia's mouth. *From breathing rock dust*, she thought. *Day after day after day.*

She resolved to find some way to cover her nose and mouth before the next day's work. But even thinking that, "next day's work," made her feel weak. How could she do *this* day after day? How would she survive?

Would she?

The Warden's offer hung in the back of her mind, a ray of light in a dark future. All she had to do was . . .

. . . betray the people who rescued me. Betray my friends.

No! She clenched her jaw and redoubled her efforts.

When at last they had filled a basket of ore, Katia looked at her lantern, and shook her head. "Too slow."

Mara glanced at the flickering candle and for the first time saw the dark lines on it to mark the passage of time. "I'll get faster," she promised, but in fact she'd slowed considerably since starting.

Katia said nothing; just hung her lantern on the basket of ore, shoved the basket into the tunnel, then crawled in after it. Mara got down on her hands and knees and followed.

Back at the shaft, an older boy, maybe seventeen, waited. The shift supervisor was leaning out into the empty space to the right of the constantly moving man-engine, staring up into the darkness. The boy glanced at them, his scarred, pimply face contemptuous. "*You'll* never make quota," he said, his tone maliciously amused. "Gonna be a party in the Watchers' barracks tonight. Wish *I* could be there."

But the shift supervisor, without looking down, said, "They're not on quota. Not for a week. Not until the new girl's settled in."

"What?" The boy's face slumped into a pout. It didn't improve his looks. "Why should *they* get a break?"

"Because the Warden says so," the shift supervisor snapped. He looked at Mara, then. "*And* he told me to tell you that," he added. "You think about that, girl. He's giving you a few days' grace because he wants something from you. If I were you, I'd give it to him." He looked back up. "Here comes the bucket."

Katia said nothing then, but as they made their way back down the tunnel with a new, empty basket, while behind them the rock they'd delivered rattled into the iron bucket that would take it to the surface, she glanced at Mara. "The *Warden* wants something from you?"

"Not *that*," Mara said uncomfortably. "He thinks I must know something else about the attack on the wagon. Something I haven't told him."

"And do you?" Katia said.

For an instant, Mara wanted to tell her everything: about the rescue by the unMasked Army, about the Secret City, about the plan to have her make counterfeit Masks; wanted to offer Katia *hope*, hope that the unMasked Army might one day appear at the gates of the camp and free all the unMasked tortured and toiling within it.

Instead she bit her lip, and said nothing. *It's no kindness to give false hope*, she told herself, and that was part of the reason: but another was that she already knew, or at least sensed, that in this place, you could never be certain whom you could trust. Katia might seem like a friend now, but if Mara told her the truth, then *Katia* would have the information the Warden wanted, and Katia wouldn't be human if she weren't sorely tempted to sell it to the Warden to buy her own escape from these hellish depths.

Depths that are killing her, Mara thought, as Katia burst into another fit of coughing. *That will kill me, too, if I can't get out of here.*

Would the unMasked Army appear at the gates of the camp? They had rescued her once, when they had never rescued anyone before. Was she important enough to them for them to risk revealing their existence with a rescue? The Warden, despite his suspicions, might eventually be convinced that the wagon had been attacked by one of the small bands of rogue unMasked already known to roam the Wild. But he'd never believe—and more importantly, the *Autarch* would never believe—that an all-out attack on the camp itself was the work of mere bandits. The Autarch would know then that an organized force opposed to his reign hid somewhere in the Wilderness. How long could the Secret City remain Secret if the Autarch bent all his resources to finding it?

Am I important enough for them to risk that? Mara asked herself.

She was deathly afraid that the answer was no.

Once she and Katia had crawled back to the rock face, Mara straightened and stretched. She glared at the black stone wall. "There's nothing here that looks like it contains metal," she complained. "What exactly are we mining, anyway?"

Katia shook her head. "No one knows," she said. "We've all wondered, believe me. If it were precious metal or even gems, there'd be a crusher and maybe a smelter in the camp. But there isn't."

"So where does the ore go?"

"There's a building, tucked up against the wall in the northeast corner of the camp, behind the Warden's palace and the Watcher barracks," Katia said. "Not a very big building. A gate opens from it through the palisade. The rocks go into that building for a while. Then they're taken outside the walls and dumped into a ravine about a quarter of a mile from here. They look exactly the same when they're dumped as they did when they were hauled out of here." She gestured at the chamber. "But every once in a while, a wagon is driven up to that back gate and loaded with something other than rocks. And *those* wagons head off down the road toward Tamita."

Mara had a horrible thought. "Maybe there *is* no ore," she said. "Maybe this is all just a ruse, just a scheme to keep the unMasked occupied, keep them from rebelling." She looked up at the rock ceiling just above her head. "The Watchers are outnumbered. Surely we could—"

"The Watchers are armed. We aren't," Katia said. "And it's not just the Watchers keeping us in our place. The trustees *like* it here. They're unMasked. They can't go home. But here they get . . . privileges." She leaned toward Mara. "If you're a girl, some of the trustees are *worse* than the Watchers. If they like your looks . . ." Her voice trailed off, her gaze sliding to Mara's smooth, unscarred face. "And even if we did somehow overpower the Watchers and the trustees and escape the camp, what good would it do us? We can't go home, either. There's nothing for any of the unMasked outside the walls of this camp except death: a slow death in the Wilderness, or a quick death at the hands of the Watchers." She turned away, and angrily slammed her steel bar into the black stone wall.

There's the unMasked Army, Mara again wanted to say. But was there? They'd done nothing to save the children being brought to the camp. They'd even kept themselves secret from the bandit bands. *They wouldn't welcome a flood of unMasked fleeing this camp*, she thought. *Or they would have attacked it long ago.*

And so once again she had to face the truth: more than likely, they wouldn't rescue *her*, either.

Mara swallowed an upsurge of bile in the back of her throat and grabbed her own steel bar. Pounding away at the black stone suddenly seemed attractive. It was hard to think with that noise in her ears, and thinking was the last thing she wanted to do. But despite the crash of steel on stone, despite the growing ache in her arms and shoulders and the sting of sweat in her eyes, she couldn't shut off her mind entirely.

Eventually they produced another basket of ore. Katia sent her back to the shaft with it alone, this time, and as she pushed it ahead of her through the low tunnels, she couldn't *help* thinking. But rather than let herself imagine her own bleak future, she instead turned her mind to the puzzle of what they were mining. What could be extracted from rocks without crushing, panning, or smelting? It didn't make sense.

The ugly boy took her full basket and handed her an empty one, without comment this time. She headed back to the tunnel, attached her lantern to the front of the basket, shoved it into the hole in the rock, and began pushing it ahead of her.

Halfway back to the chamber where she and Katia were working, the basket banged hard into a timber. The lantern fell off, crashed to the floor . . .

. . . and went out.

The darkness slammed down on her like a cave-in. She couldn't move, couldn't breathe, couldn't think: just crouched there, frozen, as if she were already dead.

But of course she wasn't, and after a long moment, when nothing else happened, she managed to draw a deep, shuddering breath. *Katia is up ahead somewhere. All I have to do is keep crawling. There aren't any side tunnels. I'll see her light when I get closer. I'm not trapped. I'm not dead. Everything is all right.*

All right, as long as she didn't let panic get the better of her.

She forced herself to resume crawling. Push the basket, then move knee, hand, knee, hand; push the basket, knee, hand, knee, hand. She didn't find the lantern, but she had no way to light it anyway. Presumably she was shoving it ahead of her with the basket.

Something brushed her hair; a rock or timber. Her breath caught, and she ducked lower.

And it was then, in the dark with her head down, that she discovered what they were mining.

It was faint, almost invisible. Even the dim light of the candle lantern had been enough to mask it every other time she'd crawled through the tunnel. But now, in absolute darkness, there could be no doubt:

In the rock beneath her ran a thread-thin filament of color, color that changed from moment to moment, red, gold, blue, violet, green.

Magic!

She jerked her head up, and paid the price as her skull cracked the rock. She winced, but kept her head raised, peering into the darkness.

There . . . and *there.* Like a cobweb of color splayed across the rock. Now she knew why the rocks weren't crushed or melted. This wasn't a mine for silver or gold, iron or coal.

This was a mine for magic. *They were mining magic!* And that meant there was magic all around them!

She felt a moment's euphoria, but it faded quickly.

Those slender threads of magic offered nothing she could use. There were no glowing puddles like she had seen in the cave with the unMasked Army, or in the basin in the hut on the ridge.

But somewhere, she thought, *somewhere there's a store of the magic taken from the mine, waiting for the wagon to Tamita. A lot of magic. And maybe, just maybe, I'll get a chance to use it.*

The magical illumination from the rocks was too faint to light her path down the tunnel. She still had to feel her way, still had to keep her head low to avoid cracking it on the stone. But at least the filmy web alleviated the darkness enough that she didn't *quite* feel like she'd been buried alive, and as it turned out, she didn't have to crawl all that much farther before she lost the glow of magic entirely in the faint glimmer of Katia's light.

She emerged into the dimly lit chamber where they had been working and found it almost blinding. Blinking, she held out her candle lantern to Katia. "It went out," she said.

"Happens," Katia said. She took out the candle, relit it from her own lantern, and handed it back to Mara. "I had to crawl all the way to the shaft in the dark a couple of days ago. Half convinced myself there'd been a cavein and I'd never get out. My throat's still a little raw from screaming." She said it not matter-of-factly, but with the dull, dead voice of someone who expected such things to happen and knew there was nothing she could do about it.

Mara didn't know what to say. She'd only been down here a few hours. What would she be like after days . . . weeks?

It won't happen, she thought fiercely. *The unMasked Army . . . and if not them, then . . .*

Magic. Back in the light of the candle lanterns, she could no longer see its faint glimmer in the black stone, but she knew it was there. Minute amounts, too diffuse for her to do anything with, but it was *there*.

If only she knew more about the Gift. If only the Gifted were trained in the use of magic before their Masking, instead of after. She'd used magic three times now, and every time, it had hurt. That couldn't be right. She had to be doing something wrong. But what?

Her father had once given her a complicated little automaton, a wind-up drummer who would beat different rhythms on his tiny instrument depending on how you set the knobs on his back. The gift had come with a handwritten set of instructions from the craftsman who had built it. *Too bad* this *Gift doesn't*, she thought.

She didn't tell Katia about the magic. She wasn't supposed to have it anymore, not after her Masking failed. And what good would it do Katia to know the truth of what they were mining? She couldn't even *see* the magic.

But at least she'd know there was some point to all this, Mara argued with herself. *That we're not just breaking rock—and our backs—to no purpose.*

But though it half-shamed her, her strong sense that she had to keep her secrets to herself, for her own benefit, her conviction that in this place she couldn't trust *anyone*, even Katia, kept her silent.

"Let's get back to work," Katia said. "We may not be on quota, but if we don't show signs we can meet it soon, the supervisor may decide we need *motivation* all the same."

By the time the seemingly endless shift was over, Mara's back and shoulders burned as if she'd been whipped, her fingers bled, and broken blisters stung her palms. Her head throbbed from banging it against the rock—not only when her candle went out and she saw the magic, but again the next time she took ore back to the shaft: staring at the floor, trying to see the veins of magic in the light, she had failed to see the low spot in the roof. She'd drunk her water too fast and hadn't had any for an hour now, and all that time she'd been swimming in her own sweat, so that her mouth and throat felt raw as new-butchered pork. Dust gritted between her teeth. And she still had to face the terrifying ascent on the thing they called a "man-engine."

When she finally stepped off of the horrible contraption, her legs shook so much she almost fell back down the shaft to her death. Fortunately, a trustee standing close at hand grabbed her arm and pulled her to safety. "First day's the best, girl," he sneered. Then he shoved her toward the stairs so hard she slammed down onto her hands and knees, adding new bruises and stinging scrapes to her already impressive collection.

Katia came off the platform a moment later and helped her to her feet. "Let's get out of here," she muttered. She helped Mara climb the three flights of stairs, up past the constantly moving beams of the man-engine, but another trustee stopped them at the exit. "Supervisor sent up a note with your last bucket," he said to Katia. "Says you aren't trying hard enough to meet quota."

"Supervisor also told us we're not *on* quota," Katia shot back. "Not until Mara has—"

"Supervisor thinks you need to try harder *now*," the trustee said. He grinned at her. He had a patchy black beard that hadn't grown where his face was scarred, and was missing five teeth. "You're for the Watchers tonight. Barracks B. Go."

Katia had been holding onto Mara's arm. She released it. "That's not fair!" The words sounded *squeezed*, as though she'd had to force them through a throat suddenly too small for them. "We were off quota. The supervisor *said*—"

"It's fair if we say it's fair." The trustee's grin twisted to a scowl. "Go! Or I'll drag you by your hair."

Katia's fists clenched. Mara saw them tremble. But then, convulsively, she pushed past the trustee and disappeared.

Mara's heart banged against her ribs. "Me—me, too?" Her voice sounded as strange and tight in her ears as Katia's had.

The trustee turned his piggish eyes back on her. "No,"

he said. "You're lucky." The leering grin returned. "Or maybe not. *Warden* wants to see you." He jerked his head toward the outside, and Mara, looking past him, saw a Watcher standing on the boardwalk that ran along the top of the trench. Whether it was the same man who had escorted her that morning, she had no clue. All Watchers looked alike, except in size.

Escorted by the Watcher, she retraced the steps she had taken that morning, though she hurt so much she felt as if she had aged a hundred years in those few hours. Then, the sun's light had barely begun to brighten the gray clouds. The clouds had blown away, but she still couldn't see the sun: it had slipped behind the ridges to the west, down into the hidden ocean, and stars already pricked the clear, dark-blue sky. All winter, Mara realized, the day shift would see no light at all. They would wake in darkness, descend into darkness, rise into darkness, fall asleep in darkness . . . over and over through the endless, frozen months.

How long has this been going on? Mara thought numbly as she stumbled along after the Watcher. *How many years—decades—has this camp been here?*

How long had the unMasked been digging in darkness like worms, eking out a few miserable years of existence after the failure of their Masks, until malnutrition, mistreatment, or the menacing mine itself brought their miserable lives to a miserable end? And all to gather the bits of magic that clung to the black stone, shipping it off to serve the Autarch, sitting in his palace like a bloated black spider at the dark heart of a tangled web.

The magic in my father's basin, she thought sickly. *The magic I thought so beautiful. Did it come from here? From the sweat and blood of the unMasked?*

Fury suddenly gripped her heart, fury such as she had never felt . . . fury, and fear. If the unMasked Army did *not* come for her, if Catilla decided she wasn't worth the risk, then she, too, would live and die in this hellhole. And soon enough, it would be *her* turn to make the walk to the Watchers' barracks, maybe because she'd missed quota, maybe because she'd said the wrong thing ... or maybe just because, behind his black mask, one of the Watchers saw her unmarked face and lusted after her.

Or would it be one of the trustees who took her first? One of the old ones, rejected by his Mask because of some already blossoming nastiness inside, like hidden rot at the core of an apple. The one with the patchwork beard and missing teeth, maybe — Grute, all grown up.

Unbidden, the image of Grute's face in his last moment of life appeared in her mind: the face that an instant later had vanished in a red-and-gray explosion. *I did that*, she thought. *I killed him. I touched him with magic, and I killed him.*

It had happened three days ago, but the memory suddenly hit her with as much force as if it had been three minutes. Her knees turned to jelly and the Watcher had to grab her to hold her upright. She felt her gorge rise, and swallowed hard to keep from throwing up all over his shiny black boots.

She pushed away all the images from that night, Grute, naked, coming toward her, Grute's headless body falling to the floor, the thump it made as it hit, the bits of flesh and bone on her skin, on her clothes, in her hair, on the walls, and everywhere the blood, the blood, the blood ...

But the images *wouldn't* go away. Now that they had broken through whatever tissue-thin veil her mind had wrapped them in, they were just *there*, as fresh as though they had just happened. She swallowed and straightened and tried to walk tall, tried to be brave. But the memories of Grute's death danced around in her mind's backstage, ready to come down center at any moment.

The interview with the Warden was mercifully brief. He asked her again if she had anything to tell him. She told him again she didn't. He asked her how she had found her first day in the mine. She lied and said it hadn't been as bad as she'd thought it would be. He frowned and his eyes narrowed: then they widened again and she saw his lips curl into a cruel smile behind the Mask. "In that case," he said, "I will not ask you again for some time. Let's say . . . three days. In three days, I will call for you." The smile widened, white teeth flashing. "It will be the last time—one way or the other." He nodded to the Watcher, who took Mara back out into the camp. But he didn't take her to either the longhouse or the mess hall. Instead, he stopped at another large square building, smoke rising from its tall chimney. "Women's bath," he said. "From here you go to the mess hall. From there you go to your longhouse. Got it?"

She nodded numbly. He opened the door for her, and she stepped into warm, damp air that puffed out into the cold in a cloud of steam.

The door closed behind her, and she stood still for a moment to get her bearings. The wall in front of her ended a few steps to both left and right: it was really just a barrier to block cold drafts—and possibly prying eyes, though she doubted in this place anyone had much concern for privacy.

She could hear voices, quiet, subdued. She walked to her left and stepped out into the main body of the building.

A large pool filled the middle of the room. At the far side flames flickered behind the metal grillwork of a huge cast-iron oven set in a red-brick hearth. A pipe extruded from the brickwork, steaming water pouring from it into the pool.

A dozen women of varying ages were scattered around the pool, some wrapped in toweling and sitting on the edge, others soaking in the middle. All were painfully thin, ribs standing out beneath their breasts. Near the hearth two fully dressed women scrubbed clothes in a wooden tub. As Mara watched, one of them picked up an armful of gray cloth and spread it on racks attached to the oven's bricks.

An older girl, maybe eighteen, entered the bathhouse

behind Mara and brushed past her without a second glance, hobbling around the pool to where the women were washing clothes. She stripped, dropped her clothes into a basket next to the washtub, then limped to the water and let herself down into it with a sigh.

Mara, feeling self-conscious but desperate to be clean, followed her example, walking around the slippery stones to the washwomen, who didn't even look up from their work as she struggled out of her own clothes and underwear, dropped them into the basket, and then hurried to the pool, sure everyone must be staring at her even though in fact nobody was.

The warm water felt wonderful to her aching arms and legs, though it stung the scrapes and cuts, and she relaxed into it. "I didn't expect this," she said, really to herself, but the older girl close by glanced at her.

"They give us baths," she said. "They give us food. But only so they can get as much out of us as they can get."

"As much work?" Mara said.

"Not just work," the girl said bitterly. And with that she closed her eyes and sank down so that her ears were below the water, effectively ending the conversation.

Mara soaked in the warmth for a few moments longer; then a harsh gong sounded outside. The women, variously groaning or silent—one wept quietly—got out of the water, toweled off, and began pulling on their clothes.

Mara's had never made it into the wash tub, and the washerwomen had simply stopped work and walked away when the gong had sounded. She had no choice but to pull back on the filthy, sweat-soaked drawers, undershirt, tunic, and trousers. The girl she'd spoken to was in the same boat. "Are the washerwomen here every day?" Mara asked.

"No," said the girl, tugging on her trousers. Both knees were torn out, the cloth around the holes stained rust-red, and scabs covered the skin the holes exposed.

"No?" Mara looked down at herself in dismay. "Then how often?"

"Once a week," the girl said, and limped away.

Mara followed the other women to the mess hall, the cold wrapping itself around her wet hair like a vise as she left the baths. Like everything else in the camp, it seemed, eating was segregated by gender: a wall separated the men and boys from the women and girls. The only time the two sexes met was in the mines . . .

. . . *or wherever the trustees and Wardens live*, Mara thought uneasily.

Without Katia, she had no one to talk to. She sat by herself at the end of one of the long tables and devoured the too-small portions of coarse bread and black bean soup she'd been given. The soup had bits of fat floating in it. She hated the texture and the slightly rancid taste, but she ate it anyway. Her body demanded it. She remembered what Hayka had told her. "Once a week, they give us meat." It seemed this, unfortunately, was not meat night.

For drink, there was tepid water. And then the gong sounded again, and it was back to the longhouse.

There was little conversation before lights out, and what there was seemed to be private, between pairs of women, some of whom went on to share bunks once the Watcher had come and gone. Katia did not come back that night. Three other girls Mara had seen the previous night weren't there, either. Four she *hadn't* seen before, all barely older than she, were.

Mara lay beneath her thin blanket, cold, lonely, homesick, hurting, more miserable and frightened than she had ever been in her life: but exhausted by her day in the mine, her body plunged her into unconsciousness before she could even summon the energy to cry herself to sleep.

In sleep, however, she could no longer push away the images of Grute. He came toward her again, naked; again she seized magic and flung it against his head; again his head burst like an overripe fruit . . . again, and again, and again, and each time she screamed and screamed and . . .

She woke to a stinging slap across her face and jerked upright, gasping. In the dim light of the fire pit's dying coals she could just make out the face of the oldest woman in the longhouse; Mara didn't know her name. "Stop it!" she hissed. "Stop screaming or I'll suffocate you where you lie!"

Mara gasped. "It was—I was . . ."

"A nightmare. I don't care. Keep it to yourself. Sleep is precious. You hear me? Precious as food and water. You steal our sleep, and we won't stand for it. None of us!"

How can I keep myself from screaming in my sleep? Mara thought, but, terrified, all she could do was nod.

The woman padded away to her bed. Other beds creaked as their owners rolled over. She heard a few muttered curses.

Burying her face in her pillow, she waited for sleep to come again, but the image of Grute swam up before her once more, and the horror of that memory and her fear of what would happen if she cried out again kept her from sleep for a very long time.

And then, of course, the gong sounded, and she jerked awake to the awful realization that ahead lay another day in the mines, and beyond that another, and beyond that another.

It was all she could do to force herself upright, fighting not just fear but the pain and stiffness of her battered body and aching hands. It was almost *more* than she could do to stand in line for the latrine, to slop down porridge for breakfast and tuck black bread and hard white cheese into a napkin for lunch, to join the long line of the day shift waiting its turn on the man-engine under the hard, watchful eyes of the trustees, while the weary night shift shuffled away toward the baths and mess hall and their own day-long rest.

Katia had not been at breakfast, but she was waiting at the top of the stairs and fell into line beside Mara. She looked even paler and somehow thinner than the day before, almost transparent, as though a puff of wind would blow her away. She didn't meet Mara's eyes, and held her upper arms with her hands, hugging herself; and while it was certainly chilly in the early morning air, with their breaths coming in white clouds, Mara did not think the chill she sought to ward off had anything to do with the temperature.

She didn't know what to say to Katia about what must have happened to her the night before, didn't know how to bring up the subject, and strongly suspected Katia would just as soon she didn't. So all she said was, "Hello." She got a tiny, barely visible nod back, and then they both sank back into their own weary misery as the line inched forward.

The terror of the descent on the man-engine and the necessity to carefully judge each step from platform to platform sharpened Mara's senses temporarily, but as she pushed her basket and candle lantern through the tunnels to the rock face, she could feel that false energy slipping away. With both of them suffering from lack of sleep and preoccupied with their own dark thoughts, the accident was perhaps inevitable. The only wonder, Mara thought later, was that it had not happened sooner; because in fact they grimly pounded away at the rock for seven hours without incident.

Truth be told, though, Mara was hardly conscious during that last hour, swinging the steel bar almost without thinking, her body an undifferentiated mass of pain, her brain fogged, her memories locked on her murder of Grute, her sleep-deprived mind for some reason dwelling on the incongruous juxtaposition of the beautiful, shimmering, multicolored liquid light that was her sense of magic with the red and ruined horror of the headless, naked Grute. It was that image that filled her mind, not the faint outlines of the chamber in which they labored, when a lucky blow with her iron bar broke off a large chunk of rock that fell toward Katia, and she reached for it without noticing what Katia was doing—

—with the result that Katia's iron bar slammed into her forearm with all the force she'd intended to use to slam it against the rock.

Mara heard a sound like a green branch snapping, and then came the pain, an agonizing wave of it up her shoulder and into her body. She jerked her arm back with a strangled scream. *Now*, too late, she was fully present in the chamber, all thoughts of Grute fleeing as she stared in horror at her suddenly misshapen arm, her wrist bending where it shouldn't bend, her hand useless, white bone poking through skin, blood pouring out around it. Katia gasped. "Mara, I'm sorry—we've got to get you back to the surface—"

"How?" Mara wanted to ask. She wanted to point out that she couldn't crawl. She wanted to scream and sob. But what she really did, as shock drained the blood from her head and filled her ears with roaring, was pass out.

FIFTEEN

An Unexpected Visitor

GRUTE STOOD BEFORE HER, naked. Again she
reached out with magic-covered hands, again his
head burst apart at her touch. But this time he didn't fall,
he kept coming, reaching for her, and then she heard
laughter off to one side and looked down to see that his
head hadn't exploded at all, it had simply fallen off, and
it was laughing at her, maniacal, crazed laughter pouring
from parted lips beneath staring, blood-filled eyes . . .

Mara tried to scream, but couldn't, and the effort to
make a noise brought her suddenly awake, gasping and
choking.

She stared up at a strange ceiling of whitewashed
planks. She had no idea where she was. She lay on a narrow bed, but that ceiling belonged neither to her room
in her father's house, nor the longhouse.

The flickering yellow light meant candles, and when she turned her head, that was all she could see at first: a candle, its light blotting out everything beyond it. For a long time she just stared at its flame, mesmerized. But gradually, like a bowl gathering raindrops, she began to fill with more sense of herself, and finally the bowl filled to the point where she jerked, blinked hard, and sat up to look around . . .

. . . or tried to. Her left arm was bound tight across her belly. She used her right to lift the gray blanket that covered her and saw that she wore a white—and blessedly clean—shift. And beneath it . . . she explored, and her cheeks flamed. Was that a *diaper?*

Her scalp felt odd, too, and she raised a hand to discover a bandage wrapped around her head.

She levered herself up with her good arm. Her head swam for a moment, but then steadied. She looked around.

She lay in a bed, one of thirty arranged, fifteen to a side, down the length of a long room: another longhouse, although quite unlike the one in which she'd spent two nights. For one thing, it was a lot warmer, with proper iron stoves at both ends and in the middle.

Most of the beds were occupied. Across from her lay a woman, silent and pale, eyes closed, face slack, black hair spread across her pillow. From the bed to Mara's left came a constant, low moaning, rhythmic and hopeless, and Mara, looking that way, saw a young woman curled on her side like a baby, rocking. Not all the patients were women: a teenage boy sat up bare-chested two beds down, bandages wrapped around his torso; he glanced her way, face expressionless, then looked away again, staring down at his hands, folded in his lap. She saw a few other boys and men farther down.

A man in a pale-blue Mask moved slowly down the length of the longhouse, stopping at each bed. Beside him walked a white-Masked woman, pushing a wheeled table with an opening in the top into which was set a bowl of black stone. Mara saw a multicolored shimmer of light around its rim.

Magic! she thought. *That man must be a Healer. And this must be the camp hospital.*

She was almost surprised there *was* a hospital. But then, she'd been surprised there were baths, too. *They don't want to kill us*, she thought. *They want to* use *us. In more ways than one. And the best way to keep us useful is to keep us reasonably healthy . . .*

. . . for a few years, anyway.

The Healer had reached the moaning woman. He looked at her, shook his head, and then came over to Mara, ignoring the motionless woman in the bed across from her. Neither his eyes nor what she could see of his mouth betrayed any expression. "Good," he said. "You're awake. My name is Athol. And you are . . . ?" He glanced at his assistant.

"Mara," the woman supplied.

"Mara," Athol said. He looked back at Mara. "Are you in pain?"

Mara considered that. "No," she said in some surprise. "But I don't understand why not. My arm is broken, isn't it?"

"It is," Athol said. "You also have multiple bruises and scrapes, and you suffered an injury to your head that required five stitches."

"But I don't feel anything!"

"I took away the pain," Athol said. "I also set your arm, and bandaged you, and stitched your head. Finally, I placed you in an induced sleep. You have been unconscious for three days."

"But . . ." Mara couldn't believe it. "I'm not hungry or thirsty."

"I brought you to semiconsciousness on several occasions to give you water," Athol said. "As for hunger, I have simply masked that sensation. We'll provide you with a light meal shortly, and your appetite will return to normal soon thereafter."

Mara didn't ask about the diaper; she didn't want to know. "But if you did all that, why do I still have bandages? Why didn't you Heal me completely?"

"I am not a particularly good Healer," Athol said. "Or I would not be here." He made no effort to hide the bitterness in his voice. His eyes glittered behind his Mask as he studied her. "You also scream in your sleep."

"I have . . . bad dreams," Mara said.

"To stop bad dreams is beyond my skill." And with that he turned away, walking back down the length of the hospital to the door at its far end, the assistant trundling the cart with its basin of magic in his wake. They disappeared into a back room, leaving Mara with a thousand unanswered questions, starting with: How had she ended up with a concussion and five stitches in her scalp? She remembered the iron bar slamming into her arm, the horrible sound as the bone snapped, but the bar hadn't touched her head. Unless, when she'd fainted, she'd struck it on a rock?

She learned the truth a little later when Katia arrived at her bedside, the skin of her face white and somehow stretched, dark circles under her eyes. "You look worse than I feel," Mara said, hoping to evoke a smile.

But Katia's expression didn't lighten. "It's my fault," she said in a low voice. "I broke your arm."

"No," Mara said. "It was my fault. I was an idiot for reaching across like that." She touched her bandaged scalp. "But I don't remember anything after that. Did I hit my head when I fainted?"

"Not exactly," Katia said. "I couldn't drag you out by myself—I had to go back to the shaft. The shift supervisor sent the bucket boy back with me. He banged your head on a rock pulling you out." She grimaced. "Blood everywhere. I thought he'd killed you."

Mara winced. "I'm glad I missed it." Then she frowned. "But how did you get me up the shaft? The man-engine can't—"

"You went up in the ore bucket," Katia said. "That's

how casualties are always taken up. Or the pieces of them," she added under her breath.

Shimma. "I guess you'll need another partner for a while."

Katia shook her head. "I'm out of the mine."

Mara stared at her, wondering why she'd said it in that tone of voice, as though it were a death sentence. "That's good, isn't it?"

"It means . . ." Katia stopped, and looked down. Her hands convulsively twisted the gray blanket on Mara's bed. "It means I'm now a barracks maid," she continued in a low voice. "I've spent three nights in there already, since the accident."

"Oh, Katia . . ." Mara whispered. "Punishment?"

Katia nodded, eyes still on the blanket. "For carelessness. They blame me for Shimma. And now for you."

"How long . . . ?"

Katia's head shot up and Mara drew back involuntarily at the fury in her face. "How long will I be the Watchers' nightly plaything?" she snarled. "Not long. I'll—" She bit off the remaining words, took a deep breath. "Never mind me. At least *you're* in luck. A *real* Healer arrived today from Tamita. She'll fix you up and you'll be back in the mines in no time."

"That's luck?" Mara said, trying to make a joke of it, though she felt sick at the thought.

Katia's eyes narrowed. "It's the mines or the barracks."

"What if I told them it was my fault, what happened?"

"Shimma wasn't your fault." Katia somehow dredged up a small smile, or, at least, the phantom of a ghost of a wisp of a smile. "Don't worry, Mara. I told you. I won't be in the barracks long." She reached out and squeezed Mara's good hand. "I'm glad we met. Think kindly of me." And with that she turned and walked away.

"Katia?" Mara called after her.

Katia didn't look back.

Mara worried about the other girl's strange statement for the rest of the afternoon, though it didn't stop her from devouring, awkwardly and one-handed, the much-better food she received (mashed redroots again, at last, plus a plump chicken breast and a bowl of dried apricots). After that, Athol allowed her to get up and use the latrine (much cleaner and slightly less smelly than the one by her bed in the longhouse) and remove the embarrassing diaper. Back in bed, she continued to worry . . . right up until the Healer arrived.

She had just dozed off when she jerked awake to a hubbub of voices through the door to her right. Then the door swung open, letting in cold air from the entry room beyond, and three people entered: Athol, a Watcher—and a short, round woman wearing a bright-blue Mask decorated with green gems. Mara's heart leaped.

Ethelda!

The Palace Healer ignored her. Athol's assistant had just emerged from the door at the room's far end with the trolley bearing the basin of magic. Its wheels rattled over the floor's uneven planking as she pushed it toward Ethelda, whose attention was on the unmoving woman in the bed across the aisle. "Condition?"

Athol shook his head. "She breathes. But that is all she does. She has been unconscious for six days. I have not been told how she came to be in this state, but her neck is bruised. I suspect strangulation and a destructive interruption in the flow of blood to the brain."

"Strangulation?" Ethelda leaned forward to examine the woman's neck. When she straightened, her own voice sounded strangled. "Those are handprints. Someone choked her. Has someone been punished for this?"

"No," Athol said. He sounded uncomfortable. "She was not . . . she has not been in the mines. She has been in the barracks. For . . . several weeks."

Ethelda stood stock-still for a moment. The Watcher who waited nearby was likewise as still as a statue, but even without being able to see his eyes, Mara could tell all his attention was focused on the Healer to see how she would react.

In the end, she simply . . . didn't. When she spoke, her voice remained calm, but it had an edge to it, a hint of strain, revealed by the pitch, just a little bit higher than it had been before. "Does she take fluids?"

"No," Athol said. "She will not swallow."

Ethelda nodded. "What is her name?"

"Nola," said Athol. "Her name is Nola."

Ethelda leaned forward and peeled open the unconscious woman's eyes. "Nola!" she shouted. "Nola!" She lifted the woman's arm and pinched it, hard. The woman didn't stir. Ethelda studied her for a moment, then turned to the basin of magic. She dipped one finger into the bowl, drawing it out sheathed in blue light, then turned and touched Nola's forehead. The light slid from her finger into the woman's skull but nothing changed. No expression flickered across Nola's slack face. Ethelda took a deep breath, and straightened. "This woman is dead."

"She still breathes," Athol said.

"She is dead nonetheless. Her body is an empty shell. There is no mind left within her." She dipped her finger into the basin of magic again, drew it out glowing blue, and this time touched it to the woman's chest. The light flowed into her body.

Her chest rose once more, then a second time, then stopped. Mara felt a chill. Ethelda looked at the assistant, who nodded and hurried away.

"Let's move on," Ethelda said, still in that calm-but-strained voice.

Mara expected Ethelda to cross the aisle to her bed, but instead the Healer went to the next bed on the other side. She continued in that pattern, going all the way down the row of beds on the far side of the longhouse before working her way back toward Mara, making her the last to be examined.

While Ethelda spoke to patient after patient, and occasionally drew blue light from the bowl, and Athol followed along, pushing the wheeled table, Athol's assistant returned to the bed opposite Mara with two male trust-ees. The assistant pulled the covers off of the dead woman and stripped her of her linen shift and the soiled diaper beneath it. Then, with much grunting and muffled curses, the men maneuvered her nude, emaciated body into a bag made of rough hemp, pulling tight the draw-string at its mouth. Carrying the bag between them, they banged out through the door to Mara's right. A moment later she heard the outside door open and close.

Mara watched it all in silent horror, made worse by the realization that the woman had been choked to death by some Watcher or other in the barracks—the barracks to which Katia had just been consigned. How long before *Katia's* nude corpse was hauled away in a cloth bag?

How long before it would be *hers?*

Except . . . *she* had another way out. All she had to do was tell the Warden the truth about her rescue by the unMasked Army; cooperate, just a little. *I wouldn't have to tell him where the Secret City is,* she thought. *I could lie, tell him Grute escaped and took me with him before they ever reached their camp.*

She recoiled in horror from her own cravenness. *No! If I tell the Warden anything about the unMasked Army, the Autarch will send a thousand Watchers into the Wild to track them down. They'll find the Secret City. And everyone will end up here—or dead. Hyram. Keltan. Al-ita. Prella. Simona. Kirika. Tishka. Edrik. Catilla. All of them.*

I can't do that. I won't do that! Better to die than to help the Warden or the Autarch or the Watchers. Better to die . . .

Easy to *think.* Taking the secret of the unMasked Army to her grave would be the heroic thing to do, the right thing to do, the noble thing to do, the–the *story-book* thing to do. But as she watched Athol's assistant change the stained linen of the bed where the woman strangled by the Watchers had died, she wasn't at all sure she had the strength.

She turned her head to watch Ethelda's approach, wondering what the Healer would say to her, wondering if she had brought a message from Mara's father, her mother. *Maybe she'll take me away from here*, she thought. *Maybe it's all been a mistake.*

And then, suddenly, Ethelda reached her. Mara stared into the blue Mask. The matching blue eyes behind the eyeholes revealed nothing; the pale lips behind the mouth opening neither smiled nor frowned. "Hello, Mara," Ethelda said, as if they had just met in the Outside Market at high noon.

"You know her?" said Athol.

"I represented the Autarch at her Masking. I was there when her Mask failed." Ethelda cupped Mara's chin in her hand and turned her head from side to side. "Why do you think her face is unblemished?"

"She was Gifted?" Athol said, sounding surprised.

"She was." Ethelda released Mara's chin, and touched the bandages on her head. "What happened to her?"

"Accident in the mine," said Athol. "Compound fracture of the left forearm, with puncturing of the skin. Multiple bruises and scrapes. Minor concussion, and a scalp laceration. I kept her in an induced coma for three days, allowing her to wake late this morning."

Ethelda nodded. "Let me look at you, Mara. Sit up, please."

Mara sat up. Ethelda unbound her broken arm from its sling and unwrapped it. Mara glanced at it, then looked away, swallowing hard. A bloodstained bandage wrapped her splinted forearm, blue-and-green bruises mottled the rest of her arm, and a red streak ran from the wound halfway to her shoulder. Ethelda's eyes narrowed. "Did you clean this wound?" she snapped at Athol.

"Yes, Healer," he said. "To the best of my ability. But . . ."

Ethelda sighed. "But the best of your ability is not quite good enough." She turned to the wheeled table.

Magic still glowed within the black basin, but it seemed much diminished. "We're almost out of magic," she said.

"I cannot get more until the first day of next week," Athol said.

"What?" Ethelda rounded on him. "That's two days! What if someone else is hurt before then? What if one of *these* patients suffers a crisis?"

"I cannot get more magic until the first of the week," Athol repeated. "I do not control the supply, Healer Ethelda."

Ethelda gripped the edges of the wheeled table. "This place is barbaric," she grated. She turned her Masked face toward the Watcher. "It is a horror. When I return to Tamita, I will report to the Circle exactly what I have found here. These people —"

"These 'people' are unMasked," said the Watcher, speaking for the first time. "They are lucky to be alive, and it is the Autarch's will that they be here. Do you question the Autarch's will?" The Watcher took a step toward her. "Have a care, if you do," he said in a voice low and rough as the warning growl of a dog. "You risk your Mask. And not all who end up here failed their Masking. Some arrive later in life. *Much* later."

Ethelda stood silent and frozen for a long moment. Finally she released the edges of the table and turned back to Mara. "I will heal the bone, and stop the infection from spreading, if I have enough magic." She glared at Athol. "I will have none to spare to remove the pain of that process. And so this will hurt." She plunged her hands into the bowl, turned back to Mara with blue-coated hands, and touched Mara's arm.

Mara screamed as searing pain enveloped her arm, as though skin and bone had burst together into flame. But as suddenly as it had come, the pain vanished. Sobbing, she stared wide-eyed down at her injured limb. If the flesh on it had been blackened and sizzling, dropping off the bone like cooked meat, she would not have been surprised, but in fact it looked normal: completely normal, with the bruises and the red streak alike gone as though they had never been.

Ethelda patted her on the shoulder. "Try moving it," she said, and Mara did. Nothing hurt, though her arm felt weak. Ethelda watched. "Good," she said. "I am sorry about the pain. But the magic"—she glanced at the empty basin— "has run out. Let us hope the head wound is healing on its own." She leaned forward and unwound the bandage around Mara's skull. Mara felt her gentle fingers probing her scalp and winced as she touched a tender spot. Then she straightened. "You are fortunate," she said to Mara. "I see no sign of infection, and the stitches are ... adequate. It should heal without further intervention. There will be a scar, but your hair should hide it. Rebandage that, please." She stepped back. "Anything else?"

"She screams in the night, Healer," Athol said. "It disturbs the other patients. She says she has bad dreams."

Ethelda snorted. "I'm not surprised in this place. I suspect I'll have them myself after I leave it." She sighed. "But perhaps I can help. Is there somewhere I can speak to her alone?"

"Why?" said the Watcher bluntly. "To protect her privacy? She has none."

"Do you presume to tell me my job, Watcher?" Ethelda said, turning to face him so fiercely that he took an involuntary step back, though she barely came up to his shoulder. "If I am to stop her night terrors, I must work with her someplace completely quiet. It has nothing to do with protecting her privacy; it has everything to do with allowing me to do the work I was sent here to do. If you want these workers back on the ..." She glanced at the empty bed across from Mara. "... *job* any time soon, then we must stop *this* one"—she jerked her head in Mara's direction—"from waking them up night after night with screaming."

The Watcher glanced at Mara. "Very well," he said. "There is a room we use for questioning. In the Warden's house. You will not be disturbed there."

Ethelda nodded, and turned back to Mara. "Can you walk?"

"I haven't tried, but I think so."

"Then get up." To Athol, Ethelda said, "She'll need something warm to wear. And she can't go barefoot."

Athol nodded to his assistant. "Bring a cloak," he said. "And her own shoes."

A few moments later, wrapped in a woolen cloak that scratched her bare arms, feet stuffed into the worn boots the unMasked Army had given her—the only thing she had brought to the camp that had not been taken away—Mara shuffled through the darkened camp, the Watcher on one side of her, the Healer on the other. Ahead, the Warden's house glowed with light. The rumble of the always-turning water wheel sounded to her right. And beyond the Warden's building, and off to the right, in the corner of the palisade, where the land sloped up . . . Mara blinked. Had she really seen that flash, like lightning?

It came again, a different color this time; and then again, and suddenly she recognized it as the light of magic. *Up there*, she thought. *That must be the building Katia told me about, where they take the rock. That's where they collect the magic to be shipped to Tamita.*

If I could get in there, how much magic would I find?

The Watcher took them in through the big front doors of the Warden's house, but instead of turning toward the Warden's office, where Mara had been twice before, he led them past the stairs to a door near the end of the hall. He opened it, revealing nothing but blackness. "Wait," he told them, and stepped into the darkness. Light flared. The Watcher placed the candle he had just lit in the middle of a small round table. It and two straight-backed chairs were the only furniture in the tiny windowless chamber. Empty shelves lined the dark walls, as though it had once been a storeroom, perhaps a pantry: the kitchen must be close by.

"I'll wait in the hall," the Watcher said as he stepped out.

Ethelda nodded, said, "Come," briskly to Mara, and entered the room. Mara shuffled in after her, and the Healer turned and closed the door firmly.

She indicated the chairs. Mara slumped with relief into the one farthest from the door. She felt dreadfully tired after just the short walk from the hospital, and whatever Athol had done to take away her pain seemed to be wearing off. Her newly healed arm ached, her unhealed head *really* ached, and the other scrapes and bruises on her body sang their own chorus of pain. She felt the way she imagined it felt to be old.

Not just physically, either. Had it really only been a little over two weeks since she turned fifteen? She no longer felt at all like the all-but-carefree girl she had been before her Masking. *Donning the Mask is supposed to make you a grown-up*, she thought. *Apparently failing to don a Mask makes you grow up even faster.*

The thoughts of her Masking, her lost parents, her lost life, suddenly filled her eyes with tears. She scrubbed them away with the back of her good hand, and sniffled.

Maybe she wasn't so grown up after all.

Ethelda sat down opposite her. In the lantern light, her blue eyes glittered above the white flowers on the cheeks of her immovable Mask. "Mara," she said in a soft voice. "I am pleased to see you alive, but not at all pleased to see you *here*."

Mara blinked. "What? But . . . you knew I . . ."

Ethelda shook her head slightly. "In the hospital, injured," she said, but that hadn't been what she'd meant, and Mara knew it. She opened her mouth to protest, thought of the Watcher outside the door, and closed it again.

"It was an accident," she said at last. But her heart raced. Had Ethelda just told her that she had *known* the unMasked Army would attempt to rescue her? Had her *father* known? Was one of *them* the unMasked Army's unnamed contact in Tamita?

Then why is Ethelda's Mask still intact?

All those things ran through her head, but she couldn't say anything out loud.

Ethelda smoothly continued, "Tell me about your nightmares."

Mara hesitated again. She would have to tell Ethelda at least a portion of the truth if she were to gain any relief from the dreams of Grute. And she needed relief: not just to spend her nights free of the nightmares, but so that she did not wake the others in the longhouse. The threat of being smothered in her bed she took completely seriously.

"I . . ." Mara paused to gather her thoughts. "I killed someone. A boy. One of those in the wagon with me."

Ethelda betrayed no emotion Mara could see. Her voice remained calm. "How?"

Mara hesitated again. She could lie, say she had bashed his head in with a rock or pushed him off a cliff, but she knew the nightmares she suffered were not the ordinary kind of bad dreams. Somehow they were tied up with *how* she had killed Grute. What made them so soul-drainingly vivid had to have something to do with . . .

"Magic," she said at last, barely whispering. "I killed him with magic."

Ethelda froze. Her wide eyes stared at Mara.

"My Gift survived. *Survives*," Mara whispered, horribly aware that somewhere outside the door the Watcher lurked.

Ethelda got up then, and rounded the table. She leaned down, her mouth close to Mara's ear. "I knew your Gift survived," she whispered. "Have you not guessed, child? Your father *made* your Mask to fail. He *wanted* you unMasked. And that being the case, he also wanted your Gift to survive. But, child, you *killed* with magic? How?"

She turned her ear toward Mara to hear her whispered answer, but Mara could not speak. Her father had *made* her Mask to fail? He had put her through that agony *on purpose?* He had *deliberately* sent her off into exile?

And arranged for the unMasked Army to rescue you, she reminded herself.

But why didn't he tell me? Why didn't he trust me?

He couldn't. You might have betrayed something, somehow. To the Masker. To the fat man in the warehouse.

The fat man who drew pictures of young naked girls . . .

Did my father know about that, too? How could he do that? How could he put me through that pain and degradation?

Unless . . .

She swallowed. *Unless he thought he was saving me from something far worse.*

What was going on with the Masks? With the Autarch? What did her father and Ethelda know or suspect?

She couldn't ask Ethelda—not here, in the very heart of the camp. Ethelda couldn't tell her. She must already be on the very brink of betraying the Autarch and having that betrayal revealed to the Watchers by her Mask . . . walking a knife's edge, at constant risk of a fatal slip.

She swallowed again, then focused on the question Ethelda had asked her. In a hurried whisper she told Ethelda what had happened to her, the images from that horrific night springing to life inside her mind as she did so, so that her voice shook.

When she was done, Ethelda drew back and stared at her. Then she went to the door and opened it a crack. She peered out, then opened the door wider, put her head through it, and looked both ways. "A few more minutes," she called loudly to her left, then pulled her head back in and closed the door.

She rounded the table and sat down opposite Mara. "The Watcher is at the end of the hall," she said softly. "We can talk a little—a very little—more openly." She put her hands on the table, and Mara, to her astonishment, saw that they were trembling. "Tell me again," she said urgently. "When you saw the magic in the basin in the hut, what color was it?"

"All colors," Mara said. "Constantly changing. All the colors of the rainbow, and then some. That's what I've always seen. I told the Tester I saw red-gold, but really I saw them all. I thought, as I got older, that ability would fade away. That's what I've always been told."

Ethelda glanced down at her trembling hands and clasped them tightly together. "I have never heard," she said, "of someone who, at the Second Test on their thirteenth birthday, still saw all colors. And now you are fifteen, and you tell me you are *still* seeing all colors? And not only that, you used magic to slay an attacker? The implications are alarming."

"I didn't mean to kill him," Mara said in a small voice.

"Don't misunderstand," Ethelda said. "I don't care about the fact you killed a would-be rapist. Good riddance. But the *way* you did it . . . you exerted an enormous amount of power, *without any training at all*. You did it instinctively. And you did it *again* when you cleaned away the evidence. With my Gift I could *theoretically* do what you did, pulverize bone and flesh and brain"—Mara winced—"but even if I *could* do it, which I am not at all certain of, I know I absolutely could *not* have done it when I was just fifteen and newly Masked. It took me years of training to do anything with my Gift at all. And you did it without thought!" Ethelda sat back again and unclasped her hands. They still trembled, until she pressed them flat against the tabletop. "The Gift is vanishingly small. Perhaps ten children in a thousand are born with it. Perhaps a quarter of those have enough of the Gift to use magic to affect the world around them. But someone with the power you have shown, someone who can see all the potential of magic and use it in multiple ways, it's like . . ." Her voice trailed off, and she shook her head. "If the Autarch knew . . ."

Mara felt cold. "Will you tell him?"

"No!" Ethelda snapped, so instantly and violently that Mara felt ashamed to have asked. Ethelda sat silent for a moment. "No," she said again, much softer. "No, I will not tell anyone you can see all colors of magic. But, Mara . . ." She hesitated. "I do not make this suggestion lightly," she continued after a moment. "It cuts against my grain, for certain. But I think you should consider telling the *Warden* that you still have some measure of the Gift."

Mara gasped, and Ethelda held up her hand.

"*Some* measure of it, I said. Not how much of it."

"But why? Why would I want to do that?"

"Because," Ethelda said, "I happen to know that the Warden might have a good use for an unMasked girl who can still see magic." She regarded Mara. "Do you know what is mined here?"

Mara nodded. "Magic. I saw threads of it running through the stone in the mines. *This* is where the Autarch's magic comes from."

"Some of it, yes," said Ethelda.

"But I don't understand. It's just black stone. Why does it contain magic?"

"More a question for theologians than Healers. But I will tell you what I know." Ethelda folded her hands on the table again and said, as though beginning a lecture, "Magic comes from life."

"My father told me that," Mara interjected, remembering. "'All living things produce it,' he said."

Ethelda nodded. "Exactly. And when they die, the magic seeps away, vanishes, unless it is near the black stone that is mined here, the stone they call black lodestone. Yes, I know"—she raised her hands, palms out—"there is another lodestone that attracts iron. But *black* lodestone attracts magic: draws it out of the world. In all of Aygrima, in all the world, it is found only in these mountains. Where it came from, no one knows. In fact, it is so strange some claim it fell from the sky and does not belong to our world at all.

"There are two ways to gather magic. One is through wells, I suppose you would call them. Places where the black lodestone is close to the surface. A specially crafted basin of black lodestone, set atop a mass of black lodestone plunging deep into the earth, will slowly draw out the magic in the larger mass, so that it fills of its own accord.

"That is what you found in the hut. There are similar huts throughout these mountains. Men like the one who found you, who have Gift enough to see magic but not enough to use it, travel the huts to gather the magic the huts harvest.

"The other way to gather magic is to mine black lodestone and extract the magic it has already gathered to itself, deep under the earth. That is what happens here. The magic extracted from the rocks, by those who have the Gift to do it, is placed in urns, also made from black lodestone, which are then shipped to the Autarch. Deep beneath the Palace lie vast storerooms of magic, from which the Autarch draws what he needs and from which magic is allocated to the practitioners of various sorts within the city—such as myself and your father." She hesitated. "And this is why I think you should consider telling the Warden you still have the Gift. I've heard rumors that the flow of magic from this mine has greatly diminished. The limited amount of magic I was allowed to use in the hospital supports that. Rumor also says that the Warden is concerned the mine may play out completely in relatively short order, and that he is increasingly desperate to find a new source of magic before this one fails and the camp is closed forever."

Closed forever? Mara's heart leaped at the thought; then a second thought clamped it in an iron fist. "But if they close the camp," she whispered, "what will happen to the unMasked?"

Ethelda regarded her steadily. "I think you know the answer to that."

And, sickly, Mara did. If the mine failed and the camp closed, those unMasked already here—and any new un-

Masked that resulted from the apparently increasingly common failures of Maskings—would most likely simply be executed. They had no place in Tamita, no place in all of Aygrima, except here, hellish though "here" was. "What does all that have to do with my Gift?"

"Rumor also says," Ethelda continued in a low voice, "that the Warden has been requesting a young Gifted to help prospect for a new mine, young because the young are more sensitive to magic; young also because he needs someone small, presumably to better slip through narrow passages in the rock."

Mara felt a chill despite the near-stifling warmth of the windowless storeroom. "And you think he might want to use *me* for that?"

"He might," Ethelda said. "Particularly since the Palace has steadfastly denied his request."

"But . . ." Mara felt confused. "Why would the Autarch deny it? Surely he *needs* the magic from the mine?"

"He does," Ethelda said. "He needs all the magic he can . . ." She bit off what she was about to say and raised a hand that still trembled slightly to her Mask. "I suspect the Autarch himself has never even heard of the request, or that the mine is in jeopardy. The members of the Circle and their subordinates generally find it prudent to deal with such matters on their own rather than trouble the Autarch with trivialities."

Another shock for Mara. Ethelda seemed to be implying the Autarch was not the all-seeing, all-knowing ruler she had always imagined, that she had always been told. She felt a sudden flash of hope that maybe Catilla's scheme to have her make counterfeit Masks wasn't as mad as it had first sounded to her—a flash of hope instantly extinguished by the all-encompassing darkness of where and what she was.

But then a flicker of that hope rekindled. Ethelda was offering her a way to, just possibly, stay out of the mines. She'd be helping the Warden, yes, and the Autarch, but she'd also be helping the unMasked trapped in the camp, whose very lives, miserable though they might be, depended on the mining of magic continuing.

But would they thank me, if they knew? she wondered. *If I step forward, and a new lode of magic is found, how many more unMasked will I potentially be sentencing to a long, lingering, miserable death in the mines? Wouldn't they be better off dead?*

She had no answer.

"Will *you* tell the Warden if I don't?" she asked finally. "Is this really my decision, or are you going to make it for me . . . for my own good?"

Ethelda looked down at the table. "I made this trip," she said softly, "because the Warden sent word that you were here, where you were never intended to be."

Mara blinked. "How? There hasn't been time for a messenger to make it all the way to the Palace and you to make the trip here."

"Child," Ethelda said, "this mine produces magic. There are Gifted here, and among them are those whose Gift is to use magic to communicate with others who share their Gift. Distance is no object. The moment the Warden realized the wagon had been attacked, he sent a message; and your father's position as Master Maskmaker is exalted enough that Stanik himself informed him of your capture. Naturally, Stanik also informed your father that you had found your way to the camp after all. And your father told *me*.

"I promised him then that I would come, and tell you that you aren't forgotten, that you are still loved. More, I promised I would do everything I could to protect you from the horrors of the camp. Horrors I didn't even fully grasp until I released that poor destroyed woman in the bed opposite yours." She hesitated. "By my promise to your father, I should tell the Warden what I know, Mara, in the hope that knowledge will save you from the mine. But I will not. Your father thinks of you as a child to be protected, but you are past the age of Masking, and that makes you an adult. As has what you have experienced these past two weeks. I will not take that choice from you." She touched her Mask again. "I cannot lie if I am asked a direct question. But there is no reason I should be. No one but your father and I know you still have the Gift. No one knows you can still see—and apparently use!—all colors of magic. No one knows you killed Grute with magic." She leaned forward and spoke urgently. "And whatever, if anything, you tell the Warden, do *not* tell him *that*. I do not know how the Warden, or the Circle, or the Autarch himself, would try to use your power, if they knew of it, but I do not think you would like it. They would see you as a weapon to wield against their enemies, and they wouldn't worry overmuch if the weapon shattered in the wielding.

"Or they might not try to use you at all. If any of the powerful, from the Warden to the members of the Circle to the Autarch himself, decided you were a threat to their power . . ." She left the warning unspoken.

"I understand," Mara said.

Ethelda leaned back in her chair and became businesslike again. "I cannot take the nightmares away. I suspect they are a function of having used magic in such a fashion. With enough magic of my own to draw on I could perhaps attempt to draw a veil over those memories, blunt their impact, but as you saw in the hospital, my resources are sadly limited here. The only magic I have to offer you is time." She shook her head. "If you are given it." She lowered her voice to barely a whisper. "I will take word of you to your father. He loves you, Mara. More than you know. He never intended . . ." Her voice trailed off.

And yet, whatever he intended, *he's the one that condemned me to* this, Mara thought bitterly, and said nothing.

Ethelda studied her face for a moment, but did not press for a response. She got to her feet. "I must see the Warden. I have a few comments to make on his treatment of prisoners."

She turned toward the door, but Mara said, "Wait!"

Ethelda turned back. "Yes?"

"Thank you for keeping my secret," Mara said. "For–for respecting me enough to leave the decision up to me. And thank you . . ." Her throat closed. "Thank you for coming. To check on me."

"You're welcome," said Ethelda softly. "I wish you luck, whatever you decide." She went to the door and opened it. "We're done," she called into the hall.

The Watcher separated them at once. Ethelda was shown into the Warden's office, Mara escorted back to the hospital. There she lay in her bed and stared at the white ceiling, torn by indecision. If she confessed that she retained her Gift, would she be saving herself but condemning unknown hundreds of unMasked to the horrors of this and any future labor camp? Or would she actually be saving their lives?

Would they *want* her to?

That was assuming, of course, that Ethelda had even guessed right about the Warden's need for a child with the Gift. She might be mistaken.

Or she might have been lying, Mara thought darkly. *Maybe she's telling the Warden the truth right now!*

She didn't really believe that.

She should have.

SIXTEEN

The Bargain

MARA WOKE TO VOICES, and discovered the Warden standing at the foot of her bed. Two Watchers flanked him.

"Hello, Mara," he said quietly. "Why didn't you tell me you still have your Gift?"

Startled and sleep-fogged, she didn't even think of denying it. "How did you find out?"

The Warden shrugged. "I asked the Healer, Ethelda. I had my suspicions before that. When I talked to you in my office, you referred to the 'hut of magic,' but you shouldn't have known that was what the hut was for. Cantic would have been as careful not to tell you as I was. The sources of magic are well-guarded secrets in the Autarchy. I intended to question Cantic about it the next time he was in camp, but it did occur to me that you would know the hut collected magic if you were still able to see it.

"So I asked Ethelda. I could already see in her Mask that she was hiding something from me, and I suspected it had something to do with you." Mara's eyes widened. "Yes," he said, "I have the Watcher's skill in considerable measure. And once I had asked her, she had no choice but to tell the truth or risk her Mask."

Mara felt a flash of anger, but it ebbed away almost at once. *Ethelda warned me she would have to answer a direct question*, she thought. *She just didn't expect to receive one.*

I guess she was wrong.

"She volunteered additional information," the Warden continued. "She told me what you thought to hide from me: what really happened when the wagon was attacked."

The bottom fell out of Mara's stomach.

"Let's see if I have it right," the Warden said, mouth curved into a smile. Clearly, he was enjoying himself, enjoying his power over her, his ability to cut through her childish prevarications. "Brigands attacked the wagon. No doubt desperate: winter is coming. Perhaps they thought the wagon carried food. Instead, all they found were unMasked children. But rather than running away then, as you claimed to me, you were dragged into the forest. They gave you those clothes—probably figured you'd freeze in those prison smocks they put the unMasked in, and they were probably right, too. Grute, a sturdy lad by all accounts, managed to escape, and was smart enough to grab you. Unmarked face, daughter of the Master Maskmaker—you stood out. You were in the woods for some days, lost, avoiding the brigands, while Grute tried to find his way to the camp. And then, up at the hut, Grute attempted to force himself on you. Understandable, really, strapping young boy, lovely young girl, all alone . . ." The smile turned to a stern frown. "And you killed him."

Mara felt the blood drain from her face. *He knows! He knows I used magic to kill Grute! Ethelda—*

"He chased you outside. You struggled. It was snowing, the rocks were icy. Perhaps it was an accident, perhaps you pushed him. Either way, he fell to his death, leaving you alone and frightened . . . and remorseful, I've no doubt; Grute's unwanted attentions surely did not justify his death. It's no wonder you continue to have nightmares.

"There Cantic found you the next day. He brought you here." The frown slid back into that insincere smile. "That's it, is it not?"

Mara gasped, releasing the breath she hadn't realized she'd been holding. "I–I was afraid . . ." She didn't have to feign a trembling voice. She *had* been afraid; terrified Ethelda had betrayed not only her secret but the un-Masked Army. But she hadn't. *Because she wasn't asked a direct question?* she wondered. *He said she "volunteered" the information. Did that make a difference?*

She didn't know; she was beginning to realize she knew far less about the Masks than she realized. *Who made Ethelda's Mask?* she suddenly wondered. *Father?*

And if he did, did he change it? Weaken it in some way?

What about his own?

And if he could do that, what about mine*? Why couldn't he make me one I could wear that wouldn't change me? Why did he put me through this?*

"Afraid you would face punishment for killing Grute?" The Warden interrupted the confused swirl of her thoughts. "Well, it was unfortunate, but these things happen in the heat of the moment. Perhaps we will retrieve his remains in the spring, if the scavengers have left anything of him." The Warden sat on the end of her bed. "It is true, however, that you have deprived me of a valuable asset: Grute would have made a fine, strong worker and eventually, I suspect, a trustee. That would weigh against you if not for the fact you offer me something I need even more." Teeth flashed in a predatory smile. "Someone with the Gift. Someone young. Someone . . . slim."

Remembering just in time she officially knew nothing of his plans, Mara said, "Why?"

"In good time," said the Warden. He stood up again. "I am going to move you into my house until you are fully healed. And then I will tell you what use I have for you." He nodded to the Watchers, then turned and strode out.

And so Mara found herself living in luxury while the rest of the unMasked continued to suffer and die in the mines and the barracks. Not that she thought of it that way at first. For the first day or so she simply reveled in the softness of her new bed, the clean clothes, the plentiful food. Her body knew what it wanted, and her brain more or less shut down and got out of the way while it got it. She slept, woke, ate, and slept again, there in the room at the back of the big house, up on the third floor. From the window she could actually see over the palisade and into the forest that sloped up toward the next ridge, beyond which shone the mountains' icy peaks.

But when she woke on the second morning, feeling more like herself than she had for some time, she stared up at the high wooden ceiling and thought, *What about Katia?*

Katia had now been in the barracks for several days. Mara could imagine her life there all too well, though she had no personal experience to tell her whether her imagination bore any relationship to reality. *Not yet*, she thought uneasily. She could also imagine, all *too* accurately, Katia lying in the hospital, maybe in the same bed *she* had been in, bruised, bloodied . . . or worse, still and pale like the woman the Healer had "released."

She looked around her spacious room, from the tapestries on the walls to the carved beams overhead, and guilt crashed down on her like a cave-in. She felt almost physically ill. *I have to help. I have to!*

Another thought followed, one that lit a fierce little spark in her soul. *And maybe I can if the Warden really needs me to use my Gift for him.*

An unMasked trustee, a middle-aged woman with a face like a hatchet and salt-and-pepper hair tied up in a severe bun, brought in her breakfast: a bowl of porridge, a good-sized piece of bread dripping with honey and butter, and a moisture-dewed glass filled with redcherry juice. The trustee put the platter down, with far more force than necessary, on the little table by the door, so that the juice slopped over the side of the glass. Then she gave Mara a look of pure poison. "Warden's coming to see you," she croaked. "I'd get dressed, were I you." She went out, slamming the door behind her.

Mara took the hint and quickly slipped off her white nightgown and put on the long brown woolen skirt and pale yellow blouse with which she'd been provided. Like the nightgown, they were both a bit large, but they were clean and they weren't gray prisonwear, and they made her feel more like her old self than even the food and the sleep had managed. Then she sat at the table, spooning the steaming, honey-sweetened porridge into her mouth, until the door opened and the Warden came in, smiling behind his Mask.

"Up and about, I see," he said. He glanced over his shoulder and nodded at the Watcher in the hall behind him. The Watcher closed the door, leaving them alone.

"Ethelda healed my arm well," Mara said. She held it up, wriggling the fingers.

"And your head?" the Warden asked.

"A slight ache. But I'm thinking more clearly." *At least, I hope I am.* She deliberately looked away from the Warden as she reached for her glass of juice. *Considering what I'm about to attempt.*

"Good." The Warden sat on the end of the bed, facing her, and his smile slipped away into a neutral expression. His eyes were unreadable. He twitched the corner of his cloak out from under his rear end, then leaned forward, gloved hands clasped, elbows resting on his knees. "As I told you in the hospital," he said, "I have need for someone young, like you, someone slim, like you, someone with the Gift, like you. I have asked the Palace several times for such a person."

Mara, remembering she was supposed to know none of this, kept her face carefully expressionless.

"The Palace has always refused." His lips compressed. "'Those with the Gift in sufficient measure to do what I require are rare and precious,'" he said, as if reciting something he'd been told. "The Palace is reluctant to risk a Masked citizen in the performance of the task I need done. You, however . . ." He shrugged.

I might be rare but I'm certainly not precious, Mara interpreted that to mean.

"So," the Warden continued, "the survival of your Gift is incredibly propitious." He studied her. "If you truly have the Gift," he said softly, "you know what we mine here."

"Magic," she said. "I saw it in the rocks." She remembered she was only supposed to be able to see one color of magic. "Red-gold, like liquid copper."

"But not much of it, I'll wager."

"No. Barely a glimmer."

"Once, the rocks in the mine glowed in the vision of the Gifted as bright as the full moon. Now—as you saw." He sighed. "You know Magic is only found in black lodestone?"

Mara nodded.

"Unfortunately, it is not found in *all* black lodestone. Too often we have dug new shafts or new levels, only to discover there is no magic in the stone we exposed. There is a cost to such failures, in both money and lives."

The lives of the unMasked, Mara thought. *Not that you really care about* those.

"We have men—like Cantic, who brought you to us— who have a small measure of the Gift, enough to enable them to see and collect magic from the rare and precious magical wells, like the one in the hut where you were found. But they are stretched to the limit, and their Gifts are so slight that they cannot see the tiny traces of magic in the black lodestone we mine. But you, you are young, and your Test found you to have the Gift in measure sufficient enough that you were to become a Maskmaker like your father. That means you can see magic where someone with a lesser Gift might not."

Mara decided he had told her enough for her to make the obvious leap to his conclusion. "You want to use me to find new sources of magic. Your mine is playing out."

The Warden inclined his head. "You *are* a clever girl. Yes, that is exactly the use to which I intend to put you." He nodded toward the window, where the snowy peaks showed against a sky of pale blue. "Black lodestone is found only in these mountains. We send out prospectors regularly to look for it. For years they have had little success ... until recently. A promising deposit, but how rich in magic, if it contains any at all, is yet to be determined. If it is very rich, we might begin a new mine, and eventually move this camp. *This* mine ..." He spread his hands. "We keep mining it, of course, since we must have *something* for the unMasked to do. But the amount of magic taken from it has dwindled to almost nothing. Most of the magic we ship to the city now comes from the magic-wells, not the mine."

Mara felt shock, followed by surging anger. The amount of magic taken from the mine *had dwindled to almost nothing*, and yet the Warden continued to send the unMasked into its deadly depths, just to *give them something to do?*

The unMasked aren't really people to him—to any of them, she reminded herself fiercely. *At best we're tools— beasts of burden—ambulatory engines.* She thought of Katia. *Playthings!*

And however softly I'm being treated now, I'm nothing different: a particularly valuable piece of livestock. A prize cow!

"What will I have to do?" she said, to avoid saying something else.

The Warden shrugged. "Accompany a party of prospectors into the mountains, to this recently discovered deposit of black lodestone. There is a natural opening which will allow you to penetrate it deeply."

"You haven't sent anyone in to look already?"

"The opening," the Warden said, "is very small."

Mara felt a chill. "You want me to crawl, alone, into a crack in the side of a mountain, to see if there is magic inside?"

"You will be roped," he said. "If there is a problem, we will simply pull you out."

Unless the mountain falls on me, she thought. She shuddered, remembering the tunnel deep in the mine she had had to crawl through to get to the rock face she and Katia had been working. And *then* she had known what lay ahead. In a Wilderness cave anything might lurk in the darkness. There might be a precipice. A wild animal. Poisonous gas. Or some hazard she'd never even dreamed of.

Monsters? she thought, trying to scorn herself out of her own fear. It didn't really work. For all she knew of the Wild, there really *might* be monsters.

But whatever might lurk in the cave, something *else* might also be lurking in the Wilderness outside the camp, something the Warden knew nothing about (she hoped): the unMasked Army.

Maybe all they're waiting for is for me to get out from behind these walls.

"I'll help you," she said at last.

The Warden chuckled. "Yes, you will. What made you think you had a choice?"

Mara had not been, by nature, a rebellious child. Her parents had made it clear from the moment she was aware of their guidance that she was to treat all grownups with respect. That was not only polite, her father had emphasized, it was also good practice for when she would be Masked and under the constant eye of the Watchers. And, he'd added honestly, it was good for business, too, since there were other Maskmakers to whom customers—at least of the unGifted variety—could turn: Maskmakers *without* rude children.

But Mara was not the polite, well-brought-up child she had been weeks before, and the smug certainty of the Warden that she would do *exactly* as he said, that all her efforts to avoid doing so were nothing more than the playacting of a silly little girl, fanned the spark in her soul lit by her early morning thoughts of Katia. Something inside her ignited and burst into a hot little fire of rage. She stood up, face flushed, and if she had had magic close at hand the Warden might have suffered Grute's messy fate and decorated the walls of her chamber with the contents of his skull. *"Because I am my own person!"* she snarled. "I can *choose* whether to use my Gift for you or refuse. If I refuse, you can punish me, you can torture me, you can give me to your Watchers to rape and beat, you can send me underground and keep me there forever, you can do everything in your power to break me to your will, and maybe you will succeed: but that will not change the fact that I have the choice *now* to help you or *not. And even if you break me*, I will still have the power to choose whether or not to tell you the truth about what I see or don't see. And since you have admitted you have no one else with a Gift the equal of mine, you will *never* know what that deposit holds—not until you have wasted more money and more lives and more time, while all the while the Palace grows more and more unhappy about the way you perform your duties. And if *that* happens, Master Warden, sir, how long will it be before you are down in the mines yourself. And how long do you think *you* will stay alive down there with those you treat like animals now?"

She stopped, out of words though not out of anger. She felt astonished, amazed, at her own vehemence and eloquence. It had almost felt as though she had stood outside herself, watching what she was doing, wondering who that incredibly brave girl was. It couldn't be little Mara the Maskmaker's daughter, could it?

Apparently it could. The feeling vanished. She was right there inside her own head where she was supposed to be, and the Warden's mouth was set in a furious scowl, his eyes ablaze behind his Mask. "How dare—"

"You already know how I dare! And I already know all your threats, and I've already told you how little I care for them." She took a deep breath, trying to slow her racing heart. "So let's discuss my conditions for helping you."

"Conditions?" She didn't think it was possible to splutter through a Mask, but the Warden came close.

"Yes!" But then she hesitated. How much could she ask for?

I'm valuable to him, she thought. *I'm not invaluable. It may be hard to find someone else to do what he needs done, but it isn't impossible. He won't close down the camp just to win my cooperation, he won't stop sending girls to the Watchers, he won't ease conditions in the mines. But maybe, just maybe . . .*

"There's a girl," she said at last. "A friend. Her name is Katia. My partner in the mine."

The Warden's eyes narrowed. "The one who broke your arm?"

"Yes."

"What do you care about *her?*"

"I care about her. That's all you need to know."

The Warden regarded her. "What do you want me to do?"

Mara took a step toward the Warden, keeping her eyes on his. "Release her from the barracks," she said. "*Never send her there again.* And don't send her back to the mines. Bring her here. Let her work in this house as a trustee. Unmolested."

The Warden cocked his head to one side. He pursed his lips, then said, "And if I do that, you will do as I ask, and report back truthfully what you see?"

Mara nodded. "I promise."

The Warden looked at her for another long moment, then abruptly said, "Done!"

"I want to see her here, alive and well, before I help you," Mara warned.

The Warden waved his hand as though flicking away an insect. "Of course, of course," he said. "The prospecting party cannot depart before tomorrow at the earliest anyway. I'll have her brought here immediately, directly to your room." He walked to the door, but stopped there and turned back. "But understand this, young miss," he said, his voice soft and silky, his lips curved in a sinister smile. "Her continued safety depends on *you*. You are very brave when it comes to your own well-being. How brave are you when it comes to *hers?*" With that, he strode out. The Watcher in the hall slammed the door shut behind him.

Mara suddenly found her legs didn't want her to be standing up anymore. She sank back into the chair beside her half-finished breakfast, and took a long, shaking drink of her redcherry juice. Then she wiped her chin and stared at the closed door.

I just made Katia a hostage, she thought. *I wonder if she'll thank me for it?*

True to the Warden's word, a Watcher brought Katia to Mara's door within the hour. The other girl looked frail: as if she would blow away in a strong wind, as if she would break if she tripped. The Watcher pushed her into Mara's room. "We'll miss you, Katia," he said, and though his Mask could not leer, his voice more than made up for it.

Then he slammed the door on them both.

Katia stood with her head down, not looking at Mara.

Mara didn't know what to say. Almost convulsively, she turned and went to the breakfast table. Some redcherry juice remained in her goblet. She held it out to Katia.

Katia ignored it. She brushed past Mara and sat on the end of the bed, where the Warden had been just an hour before. Hands loose on her lap, she stared at the floor. "Why did they bring me here?" she said in a hoarse whisper. "Why bring me to *you?*"

Mara looked down at the unwanted juice. She turned and placed it back down on the table, then walked over to Katia and sat beside her on the bed. "Because I asked the Warden," she said.

Katia looked up, her startled look at least an improvement on the dead expression of a moment before. "What? Why would he do that for you? Why would he do *anything* for you?" She looked around as if really noticing the room for the first time. "And why are you *here?*"

"I'm not who I said I was," Mara said. And then she told Katia at least some of the truth—not about the unMasked Army, but about her Gift, about the magic clinging to the black stone the unMasked were scratching out of the mine, and about what the Warden wanted with her.

And the bargain she had struck with him.

Katia listened without speaking, her face gradually falling back into impassivity. "So if you fail," she said, after Mara's final words tumbled into silence, and after the silence had stretched to an uncomfortable length, "it will not be you who pays the price. It will be me."

"It will be both of us," Mara said.

"It will be *me*," Katia repeated. "*You* will still have some value." She stood up. "I was already less than nothing. Now you have made me less than *that*." Her dead expression suddenly contorted into fury. "*What gives you the right to involve me in this?*"

Mara's own temper flashed and she jumped to her feet. "If I hadn't, *you* would be spending another night in the barracks! And another after that, and another after *that.* Instead, you will spend tonight here, unmolested . . . *and* another after that, and another after *that!*"

"Until *you* fail to please the Warden," Katia spat. "And then I will be sent back to the barracks, and it will be worse because I temporarily escaped. And that will be the end of me, Mara. For the day I am sent back to the barracks is the day I kill myself. And my blood will be on your hands as much as on the hands of the Warden or Watchers." She strode to the door and banged on it with both fists. The Watcher outside opened it at once. "Get me out of here," Katia said. "Take me wherever I'm going next."

The Watcher glanced over Katia's shoulder at Mara, then shrugged, grabbed Katia's arm, and pulled her from the room.

As the door closed and the lock snicked shut, Mara, shaking as much as she had after the conversation with the Warden, sat down hard on the bed.

She's still better off, she told herself. *She'll realize it, in time.*

But Katia's final words seemed to echo in her ears: "My blood will be on your hands as much as on the hands of the Warden or Watchers."

She could not deny their truth. If she failed . . .

And then the full horror of what she had done struck her like a mailed fist to the stomach.

Not just if she failed . . . *if she were rescued.*

If I'm saved, Katia dies! What have I done?

Her stomach heaved, and she barely made it into the privy before spewing up the porridge and honeyed bread she had eaten two hours before, the sticky mess richly dyed with redcherry juice . . .

. . . dyed, she thought as she clung miserably to the wooden seat, the color of blood.

SEVENTEEN

Death on the Mountain

AT FIRST LIGHT the next day, Mara found herself on muleback once more, riding down the central boulevard toward the gate through which she had entered the camp as a prisoner just a little over a week before. She had more company this time—not one man, but four: two Watchers, and two other men whose Masks, white, with four black diamonds across the forehead and another on each cheek, gave no hint as to their profession to Mara, who had never seen that design before.

She also had warmer clothes: she'd been provided with new, lined boots, red woolen trousers, a rather nice blue, long-sleeved tunic, a woolen vest, a brown sheepskin coat to wear over that, and a fur-lined cloak to wear over *that*. Plus leather gloves and a warm-but-ugly hat, both lined with rabbit fur.

Watching her breath and her mule's emerging in white clouds as she rode toward the gate, she felt grateful. Every day the snow crept lower down the slopes beneath the ice-covered peaks to the north. "Winter's just around the corner," the trustee servant had told Mara as she laid out the clothes. "Snow could come to stay any day. You'll need this and more, if you're out in the mountains for long." It was the most pleasant thing the trustee had said to her since she'd arrived in the Warden's house, and Mara, staring at her, had suddenly realized the reason for her previous surliness. *She was afraid I would take her place*, she thought. *She was afraid she'd end up back in the mine or the barracks.*

Mara had donned the new clothes gratefully, but just before they reached the gate, they rode past four unMasked women, shivering in their thin gray smocks, and Mara's thankfulness for being warm soured into guilt.

Once through the gate, the white-Masked men took the lead, while the Watchers brought up the rear. One of them led a pack mule, twin to the one Mara rode. As they set out, the two Watchers exchanged ribaldries that embarrassed and disgusted Mara, who could not help thinking of Katia as she listened to their crude jokes.

Then one of the white-Masked men dropped back to ride beside her. "Hello, Mara," he said. "My name is Pixot. My colleague"—he nodded forward at the stiff back of the other white-Masked man—"is Turpit." He lowered his voice. "I'm afraid Turpit believes it is bad luck to talk to the unMasked; he's afraid it will cause his Mask to crack, or something. Personally, I think he's afraid if he so much as *smiles* it will cause his Mask to crack. Or possibly his face. He's the single most boring human being I have ever run across, but he certainly knows his rocks. I think he identifies with them."

Mara couldn't help smiling at that, and Pixot sat back. "Excellent," he said. "You're much prettier when you smile."

That, in view of what she could still hear of the conversation between the Watchers, instantly wiped her smile away. Pixot held up a hand. "Sorry, sorry, sorry," he said. "I know what that must have sounded like." He glanced back at the Watchers. "But I assure you, that's not why I am speaking to you." He leaned close, prompting a burst of laughter from the Watchers. Pixot ignored it. "I know your father," he murmured.

That simple phrase, which once would have been an everyday pleasantry, skewered her heart like a pick of ice, so painful she gasped out loud.

Pixot leaned even closer. "He and your mother are well," he whispered rapidly. "When I get back, I will tell them—"

"You! Rock-man!" one of the Watchers called. "Get away from her!"

Pixot straightened. "Rock-man?" he snapped as he twisted to face the Watchers, the friendly tone he had been using with Mara instantly replaced by one as cold and haughty as a statue of the Autarch carved in ice. "I am the Autarch's Master Geologist. In his service, I have personally discovered major new lodes of gold, silver, and copper. I am here at *his* direct request. I will speak to whom I wish, *when* I wish, and if you take issue with that, I suggest you take it up with the Autarch the next time *you* talk to him, for *I* certainly will."

The Watcher stared at him for a long moment, then shook his head, leaned over to the other Watcher, and muttered something Mara could not catch, though she was pretty sure he was not complimenting the—what had Pixot called himself?—Master Geologist.

Pixot twisted back around in his saddle and winked at Mara. "Black-britched bastards," he said. Mara laughed out loud, but very carefully did not look back to see if the Watchers had heard him.

Pixot lifted his Masked face to gaze up at the mountains; they had rounded the corner of the palisade to follow a trail that wound up the ridge to the north. "Strange stuff, black lodestone," he said conversationally. "Not just the fact that it attracts magic, though, of course, that's why we're looking for it. Strange all the way around."

"What do you mean?" Mara said, more to keep him talking than anything else. She hadn't had an ordinary conversation with anyone for days; not since Hyram had shown her around the Secret City. And Pixot knew her parents. It was as close as she'd been in a very long time to being home . . .

. . . as close as she ever would be again. The thought fell through her mind like a lump of lead tossed into a pool.

"Its density is all wrong," Pixot answered. "It's not as spongy as pumice, which actually *floats* on water, but it's only about half as dense as it looks like it should be. And it is studded with very strange crystals. It . . ." He shook his head. "Frankly, it's like nothing else to be found in the Autarchy. And it is only found *here*, on the edge of the mountains." He pointed behind them, at the camp. "As well, very little of it is found as loose stones. It's mostly found in discrete masses, *enormous* masses in some cases, like the one that has been mined in the camp for decades, but still, they're essentially giant rocks, studding the ordinary granite and gneiss and limestone and shale like currants in a bun."

Despite everything, Mara found herself interested. "So how do you prospect for it?" Her father, who used precious metals in making Masks, had told her some of how they were found. "I know you look for copper by keeping an eye out for colored rocks. Green, blue, or red, isn't it?"

"Very good," Pixot said. "Black lodestone is found the same way, except all you're looking for is black stone."

"But there must be lots of different kinds of black stone."

"There are. Hence the difficulty. Most black stone is not black lodestone. And the most obvious outcroppings of black lodestone have long since been identified."

"So why has there only ever been this one mine?"

"Because most masses of black lodestone are too small to justify a mine—or too inaccessible. Instead, whatever magic they have attracted is harvested by other means. I understand you were found in the hut of one of the magic-wells?"

Mara nodded.

"There are about a dozen of those, scattered around. They are the way magic has traditionally been gathered. Most have existed for centuries. Perhaps you could mine the rock beneath some of them, but a man would be a fool to destroy such an elegant, sure source of magic in favor of the brute-force approach being used"—he jerked his head toward his right shoulder—"back there."

"Then why . . ." Mara looked back down the slope of the ridge to the camp. Smoke from its chimneys had turned the color of gold in the rays of the sun, just clear of the ridges to the east. It looked tranquil, pastoral, like a picturesque village where jolly matrons made smelly cheese to serve on crusty bread piping hot from the oven . . .

. . . *an oven fueled by the bodies of dead children*, Mara thought savagely, and turned her back on the camp once more.

"Why is there even *one* mine?" Pixot said. "You would have to ask our ancestors. They began it—just scratchings—two centuries ago. Large-scale mining started in the time of the Autarch's father, before there were Masks. Once there *were* Masks—and therefore un-Masked—the Autarch hit upon the idea of using those whose Masks failed as workers. Over the decades, the mine has expanded significantly, and a good thing, too; if it were not for the mine, I fear execution would automatically follow the failure of a Mask." Mara shot him a sharp look, but of course his white Mask remained as impassive as ever. "During its lifetime, the mine has produced vast quantities of magic. At its peak, more than all the wells put together. But that peak is long past. It produces less each year—even as the Palace's hunger for magic grows and grows."

Since Pixot seemed so forthcoming, Mara asked a question that had been puzzling her. "*Why* does the Palace need so much magic? My father often complained that even he, Master Maskmaker of Tamita, could barely get what he needed."

"I have no idea," Pixot said. "The Autarch does not tell me such things." He leaned close to her. "Despite what I told that lump of a Watcher, I am not *quite* on such intimate terms with the Autarch as all that."

Mara laughed.

Pixot straightened again. "In any event, we have been tasked with finding a new source of magic, a place to establish a new mine. And that has meant, over the past several years, searching these mountains summer after summer—we're not fool enough to do it in the winter!—for another mass of black lodestone as large or larger than the one beneath the mining camp." He glanced back at the Wardens; they had fallen back and were well out of earshot. He turned his black-and-white Mask toward Mara again and leaned over. "Turpit and I believe we may have found just such a mass. But *we* do not have the Gift. And the Palace has been reluctant to send us anyone who does . . . again, for reasons that are mysterious to me." Although there was something about the way he said that that made Mara think they perhaps weren't as mysterious as he wanted to let on. "Which is why the, if I may use the term, *miraculous* fact you retain your Gift even after a failed Masking makes you so important to our endeavors."

Mara said nothing for a moment, mainly because they had reached the top of the ridge and had now started to descend the other side, down a narrow, back-and-forth trail, and the change in slope had been abrupt enough to make her clutch at the mule's reins. At least she *had* reins this time, unlike the last time, and proper stirrups, too, although since she'd never ridden an animal in her life until she'd been captured she couldn't decide if the reins were a good thing or not. What if she did something wrong and the mule galloped off with her and jumped off a cliff?

Although, to be honest, the mule seemed pretty much impervious to anything she did, trudging along in the wake of Turpit's horse without doing more than flicking an occasional irritated ear in her direction, as though she were an annoying insect it had no choice but to tolerate for the moment.

"The Warden said something about a small space I'll have to squeeze into . . . ?" With the narrowing of the trail, Pixot had fallen back, so she was talking to him over her shoulder.

"Yes," he said. "I'm afraid that's true. We see degraded black lodestone on the surface, but when it's as broken down as this is, it's impossible to tell how attractive it has been for magic. Fortunately, there's a natural opening, a narrow crevasse, which we think will provide access to the main body of the stone."

"Couldn't you just dig into it? Open it up?" Mara said. "Isn't that what you would have done if I hadn't come along?"

"Possibly," Pixot said. "But the location is difficult. Bringing up men and equipment would be time-consuming and expensive, and the mountainside above the opening appears unstable. We fear any attempt to widen the opening might cause a major rockslide. The risk will be worth it if the deposit proves rich enough in magic: even if the rock face collapses during mining it would be cost-effective to clear it afterward. But while there is still a risk that the lodestone deposit is worthless, we'd rather avoid that." He laughed. "Plus, I don't want to be anywhere near it if it *does* come down!"

And yet you're sending me *into it?* Mara thought, temper rising. "Well, if it happens to 'come down' while I'm *under* it, be sure to tell my parents I died for a good cause," she snapped. "Black rock!"

"Mara—"

Mara ignored him after that. Now that they were in single file, it was easier.

They reached the bottom of that first ridge and started up the ridge beyond. The pattern repeated itself all day, each ridge higher than the last. Late in the afternoon they splashed through a shallow river easily a hundred feet across. A couple of hours later, as the sky darkened, they were on the forested lower slopes of the first of the giant mountains, its high peak still pink from the setting sun, long since hidden from them by the hills to the west.

They made camp in a clearing near an icy stream that tumbled down from high above. Although the long canvas bundles of tents hung from some of the horses and mules, the Watchers didn't bother pitching them, since no clouds threatened. Instead, they spread out their bedrolls on the forest litter and slept under the open sky, Mara with her feet shackled. She lay awake for a long time, staring at the stars, so much brighter and more plentiful than they were in Tamita, listening to the night wind sighing through the trees, hoping she might also hear the sound of unMasked Army scouts creeping up on the camp; but in the end she slept, only to be shaken awake, far too soon, in the bitterly cold gray predawn light, chilled, stiff, and singularly un-rescued.

They spent the morning angling across the face of the mountain, Pixot and Turpit leading the way, Mara in the middle, the Watchers behind. At midmorning they emerged from the forest at the foot of a massive cliff face, easily two hundred feet tall. It certainly wasn't made of black stone: in fact it was such a light gray as to be almost white. Nevertheless, they rode along its base. It went on for miles, growing taller and taller, while to their right the slope became steeper and steeper, until their path was little more than a ledge between the sheer wall to their left and a not-quite-sheer-but-quite-steep-enough-thank-you drop to their right. Far below, the tops of trees swayed in the wind whistling down around them from the peak, and Mara occasionally glimpsed the glitter of the river they had crossed the day before.

Mara held onto her reins so tightly her knuckles turned white, squeezed the flanks of the mule so hard her thighs ached, and sat as still as she could for fear of waking the beast from its plodding stupor, just in case it realized it had finally found the perfect place to rid itself of the annoying lump on its back.

Periodically, huge cracks split the cliff above them, wide at the top, narrow at the bottom, as though someone had taken a giant cleaver to it. Most of the resulting narrow ravines were choked with tangled masses of undergrowth or the crisscrossing trunks of spindly trees, all fighting for the limited sunlight, but early in the afternoon they reached one that was different: larger, darker, and distinctly shy of vegetation. A stream poured out of it across their path, cascading away to their right in a long slash of white water not *quite* steep enough to qualify as a waterfall, hurrying to join the river far below.

Into that barren ravine the geologists turned, Mara's mule following. Mara saw a few stunted trees, a patch or two of scraggly weeds, and piled and crumbled stone: *black* stone.

Then something blue and red caught the corner of her vision, and Mara turned her head to see, glistening in a shadowed corner of the ravine, the color-shifting sheen of magic. "I see magic," she said to Pixot. It was the first time she'd spoken to him all day. She pointed. "Over there. Is that enough? Do I still have go underground?"

He shook his head. "The surface collection doesn't matter. We need to know what's in the body of the stone." He looked up at the slice of sky far above. "All the black lodestone we know of is like this, embedded deep in ordinary stone like a pearl in an oyster. We only find it when it is somehow exposed to the surface. Some long-ago shrug of the mountains fortuitously split the cliff right where this mass of black lodestone lurks, revealing its presence. But how much is there? And how much magic has it attracted over the millennia? That's what we need to know; what we need *you* to tell us."

Mara said nothing. She couldn't speak through a suddenly dry mouth and a throat grown tight at the sight of the cave she would be asked to enter—if you could call a crack in the rock barely as wide as her shoulders a cave. Out of it the stream poured, white and foaming, down wet black rocks. She looked up. The mountainside loomed perilously above them, tilted forward, riven with cracks. Numerous giant boulders that had obviously fallen from that tottering cliff littered the ground around the cave mouth.

She found her voice. "You can't send me in there!"

"We have to," Pixot said. He sounded both apologetic and utterly determined. "We have to know. The Palace demands—"

"I don't care what the Palace demands!" Mara yelled at his impassive Masked face. "You think I care about the Palace anymore? *I won't go in there!*"

The nearest Watcher kicked his horse forward, shouldering it between her and Pixot. "The Warden," he said, eyes cold behind his black Mask, "told me that, should you prove reluctant to do as you are told, I was to say this to you: Katia."

Mara's heart flip-flopped.

Pixot trotted his horse in front of hers so he could face her again. "You have to," he said. No warmth remained in his voice. "For all our sakes, including yours."

Mara closed her eyes and took a deep breath that shuddered through her trembling body. That narrow opening in the crumbling cliff terrified her. But she'd ridden the river out of the Secret City. She'd gone down into the mine. She'd survived. *This can't be any worse, can it?*

"Katia," the Watcher said again, softly, and she knew, as she'd really known all along, that she had no choice.

"All right," she said. "Let's do it."

"Now?" said Pixot.

"Why wait?" she snapped. "I'll crawl into that crack. I'll tell you what I see. Then you can go back and tell the Warden, and the Autarch, and you can all get together and figure out exactly how many unMasked lives it will take to mine it. Not that *you'll* care."

She got down from the mule, not without difficulty, since she felt as stiff and sore as . . . well, as someone who had ridden a mule for two days. One of the Watchers tied a rope around her waist, and gave her a small candle lantern on a loop of rope she could hang around her neck, to keep her hands free. It dangled there, uncomfortably warm but not—quite—burning hot.

She went up to the cave mouth. "I may not get far," she said to no one in particular, as she looked at the black gash through which the stream poured. "I may get stuck."

"You get stuck, we'll pull you out," the Watcher who had tied the rope around her said.

"Maybe," said the other Watcher. "Unless you're *too* stuck."

"Oh, I'm sure if we pull hard enough, we can at least get *part* of her out," the first Watcher said, and they both laughed.

Mara didn't bother looking at them. She took a deep breath, then climbed up the slippery rocks, the water instantly chilling her as it soaked her clothes. At the cave mouth, she looked back. Pixot gave her a small wave. Turpit stood with arms folded. The two Watchers watched.

Gritting her teeth, she got down on her hands and knees in the ice-cold water and crawled into the darkness.

The candle lantern, dangling at her throat, cast dancing shadows all around her. Wet black stone glistened, but only with water. She peered into the darkness ahead, took another deep, shaking breath, and crawled forward.

The biggest problem, she quickly discovered, wasn't the narrowness of the cave—though it certainly *was* narrow, her shoulders brushing the stone on both sides—but the water. It sucked heat from her body as it rushed over her hands and wrists and around her knees, calves, and feet. The heat of the candle lantern now felt welcome, but despite its warmth, she was shivering before she'd crawled fifty feet. Yet she could not escape the water: it filled the entire bottom of the passage.

She saw no magic, saw nothing but the ordinary yellow gleam of candlelight on wet stone, until she was, by her rough reckoning, a hundred yards into the tunnel and she could no longer feel her hands. Suddenly, there *was* no tunnel anymore.

She stopped, gasping, as the ceiling opened up above her. She found herself on the edge of an underground lake, out of which the water poured. The candle lantern only illuminated a few feet of the glassy surface, but she could see the whole vast chamber clearly . . .

. . . because it *blazed* with magic.

Auroras of blue and green and red played along the walls. The water pulsated with the ever-changing hues of magic beneath its crystalline surface. Sheets of color raced across the ceiling, a good fifty feet over her head.

Mara had never seen anything more beautiful. For a long moment she just stared, entranced: and then, like a blow, she remembered what all this beauty meant. When she went back and told Pixot what she had seen, she would be condemning this place to ruin. The Warden would drive shafts into it, tear down its soaring walls, smash the stone, extract the magic, delve deeper and deeper into the mountain: and all would come at the expense of untold numbers of unMasked, crushed, beaten, starved, tortured . . . raped.

She reached out and touched the wall, and her hand came back covered with a thin sheen of magic. She stared at it, turning her hand back and forth. *I could lie*, she thought. *I could tell the Warden there's nothing there*.

Yes, she'd promised to tell him the truth, but what of that? No promise to a man like that could hold her.

But if she did *that* it wasn't just her own life she was playing with, it was Katia's. The Warden might well decide that if there were no magic to be found here, Mara was of no further use, and therefore he no longer needed to keep his bargain regarding Katia.

"My blood will be on your hands," Katia had said, and Mara couldn't deny it.

Frozen by indecision, for a long time she simply crouched there at the mouth of that beautiful, breathtaking chamber of magic . . . until the rope around her waist twitched, tightened—and jerked her backward. She flung herself belly-down, the candle lantern hissing and going out as it hit the water, and grabbed at the rock beneath the stream, but couldn't stop her slide. She banged back along the tunnel helpless, face down, fighting to keep her head out of the water, fighting to get onto her back, fighting . . . and failing. She wrapped her arms around her head, trying to protect her face and skull. Her shoulder banged into a stone so hard her arm tingled; her leg scraped over a rock so sharp she felt clothes and skin tear; and then she saw daylight glimmering on the rocks and heard distant shouts. The rope went slack. She rolled over and raised her head to look at the slash of light that was the opening to the cave, then screamed as a black silhouette filled it, lunged into the tunnel, and grabbed her ankles.

The man pulled her out and flung her into the stream, the water cushioning the fall but the impact still driving most of the air from her body. Helpless, literally breathless, she gaped up at the dark figure looming over her.

It was one of the Watchers. Something else dark and motionless lay to her left. She turned her head that way and saw, a dozen yards away, the second Watcher, staring blankly up through a Mask already crumbling away, revealing the sallow face beneath, slackened by death. Two arrows protruded from the red ruin of his neck.

"Bitch," the Watcher snarled. He straddled her, his weight pushing her down into the icy water, sharp stones digging into her back. "They killed Karx without warning, then called to give you up or they'd kill us all. But they'll kill me anyway, so the only way they'll get you is the way I'm going to give them to you—with your throat slit from ear to ear!"

He grabbed her hair and pulled it back, exposing her throat. In absolute terror, Mara shoved at him as hard as she could, desperate to get him away from her, desperate to save her life—

Only a little magic still clung to her hand. But it wasn't *that* magic that answered the silent scream for help that filled her mind, unvoiced because her lungs held too little air for her to produce a sound: instead, it was the magic inside the mountain.

It surged from the mouth of the tunnel, and this time Mara did not see it as made of many colors. This time it was pure white, white as the sun. It poured from the cave as though riding the surface of the rushing water. It enveloped her . . .

. . . and it *burned*. Pain like nothing she had ever imagined blotted out the weight of the Watcher astride her, blotted out the sight of the looming cliffs, blotted out the sky and the clouds, blotted out everything she had ever seen or done, heard or tasted, smelled or felt. Her world, her life, dissolved into burning white agony. She screamed, or thought she did, and out of desperate instinct to save her life and sanity, threw the magic away from her, threw it the only place she could—

—into the Watcher.

She didn't see what happened to him. All she knew was that suddenly, absolutely, and with finality his weight vanished . . . and so did the all-enveloping pain.

She gasped one shuddering, lung-filling breath, exhaled in a rush, and fell into darkness.

EIGHTEEN

"I Have to Rescue Her"

DARKNESS: but not the darkness of dreamless
sleep. This darkness was both less deep and more
black. Less deep, because she dreamed. More black, for
what she dreamed.

Grute. Over and over, Grute, naked, coming toward
her ... her hands on his head ... the magic dripping from
her fingers like clotted cream ... the burst of light, the
explosion of red and white and gray; Grute, headless,
dropping to the ground, blood fountaining, spreading in
a scarlet lake across the floor as his body twitched away
the last of its life ...

The Watcher, pulling her from the tunnel's mouth,
straddling her, dagger drawn, the tug of his hand in her
hair, then the rush of power, of light, of unbelievable,
searing pain ...

Those same two images, over and over, not real and yet, in some ways, *more* real than waking reality. She lay trapped in her own brain, unable to wake, unable to hear, unable to break through the thick black walls of the prison the flood of magic from the cavern had made of her skull.

But, slowly, oh so slowly, those black walls thinned. Other dreams began to creep into her mind: bad dreams, but ordinary dreams, real and terrible enough, but without the glittering, hard-edged *superreality* of the images of Grute and the Watcher.

She dreamed of the mine, darkness of a different sort, the weight of stone, the body-soaking humidity, the ache in her shoulders and back, the shock of Katia's bar slamming into her forearm, the sickening snap of the bone . . .

She dreamed of the moment of her Masking, the moment when the clay twisted and stiffened, the agony of her cheeks splitting, her nose breaking, and worse than that, the horror of her mother's scream, the knowledge she would never see her parents again . . .

Bad dreams, terrible dreams, but still, only dreams. And then, finally, she stopped dreaming altogether . . .

. . . and then she woke.

She stared up at a ceiling of whitewashed stone, tinged blue by the light of early morning or late evening. It was not the ceiling of the camp hospital. It was not the underside of the bunk above hers in the longhouse. It was not the painted ceiling of her room in the Warden's house. It was not the inside of the tent. And it most certainly was not the ceiling of her own room in her father's house in Tamita, with its loose skylight providing easy access to the roof.

So where was she?

And *how* was she?

She lay without moving for a long moment, probing her own internal workings as though poking at a loose tooth with her tongue. She felt . . . weak. Thin. *Stretched.* Like a piece of linen pulled taut to make an artist's canvas; *too* taut, so that it threatened to split down the middle at any moment.

Physically, she ached, every inch of her. Her right calf, which she remembered cutting on the rock as she was dragged from the cave, was bound in a clean white bandage. It throbbed slightly. She had other scrapes and bruises, though nothing else was bandaged.

She wore a thin white shift, and beneath that . . . a diaper. Again. *At least it's clean and dry*, she thought.

She was thirsty. Parched, in fact. She could barely summon spit enough to swallow. And her stomach cramped with emptiness, though that didn't seem nearly as important as her thirst.

How long had she been unconscious?

How long had she suffered those terrible visions of Grute and the Watcher, those horrible dreams of the mine and her Masking?

And again, *where was she?*

She took a deep breath, and by dint of enormous effort, raised her head.

Hewn out of white-painted rock, the smallish room contained three other beds, all empty, interspersed with side tables and simple wooden chairs. An earthenware pitcher and a glazed tumbler stood on the table by her bed. *Water!* She looked at them longingly, but they might as well have been in Tamita: she couldn't summon strength to reach for them.

A red curtain hung over an archway near her bed. A cool, salt-flavored breeze flowed in through a narrow, slit-like window in one wall, cut through several feet of rock. It was early morning, she decided; already the glow outside seemed brighter.

Her neck ached and her shoulders quivered from the effort of lifting her impossibly heavy head. She let it drop back to the pillow, and, bathed in cold sweat, lay there, shaking. At least, from the stone walls and narrow windows, not to mention the smell of the sea, she thought she knew where she was: the Secret City.

But how had she gotten there?

The last thing she remembered was that agonizing rush of magic. But how had it happened? She had had almost no magic on her hands, certainly not enough to do anything to the Watcher. But she hadn't needed it. The magic had simply *come*, answering her call from its chamber deep inside the mountain like an eager dog rushing to its master . . .

. . . except, like an eager dog that didn't know its own strength, it had almost killed her when it reached her.

Her father had never even *hinted* that such a thing was possible. He had said he could only use the magic from the basin—made of black lodestone, she knew now—filled for him from the stores of the Palace. And she had always heard, from her father, from her tutor, from *everyone*, that the Gifted had to *touch* magic to use it.

Maybe it didn't really happen, she thought. *Maybe I hit my head when I fell into the creek. Maybe everything else was a hallucination.*

Maybe this is.

She looked around the room. "Hello?" she called, her voice so weak and thin it sounded like it belonged to someone else. "Hello?"

A young woman in a blue dress and white apron swept in through the red-curtained archway, frowning down at a tiny green-glass bottle she carried in her right hand. When Mara said "Hello?" again, her head jerked up so suddenly she bobbled the bottle and barely managed to regain control of it before it smashed to the stone floor.

Then she turned toward Mara, brown eyes wide beneath an unruly mass of curly black hair. "You're awake!" she said. It sounded almost like an accusation.

"Shouldn't I be?" Mara croaked.

The young woman blushed. "Sorry, I . . ." She took a deep breath, and smiled, so warmly that Mara's momentary annoyance melted away like snow in the spring sun. "Sorry. My name is Asteria."

Mara smiled back. "I'm Mara," she whispered. "I'm sorry I startled you."

Asteria laughed. "I don't mind, believe me. I've been looking after you for the past two nights and I've been afraid you would never wake up at all!"

"In that case, I'm *glad* I startled you," Mara said, and Asteria laughed again. Mara worked her dry mouth. "Could I . . . could I have a drink of water, please?"

"Oh! Of course!" Asteria turned to the side table and filled the tumbler from the pitcher. She bent down with it, put her arm under Mara's head, and lifted her up so she could sip from the tumbler. She took several swallows. Her empty stomach cramped as the liquid hit it. She nodded, and Asteria put the tumbler back on the side table and lowered her to the pillow again. Mara winced as her stomach cramped again, then said, "How did I get here?"

"Edrik brought you in the day before last. He said they found you unconscious, and hadn't been able to wake you. Hyram looked mad with worry. So did that other boy, Keltan." Asteria grinned. "They're both smitten with you, you know."

"Um . . ." Mara felt her face redden. "I'll take your word for it."

"You should," Asteria said confidently. "Believe me, I know about boys. My Maris is . . ." She stopped, and now it was her turn to blush. "Well, I know, that's all." And then her hand flew to her mouth. "Oh! I forgot! I shouldn't be talking to you!"

"What?" Mara said, confused. "Why?"

"No, no, I didn't mean . . ." Asteria stopped, took a deep breath, and made a pushing-down motion with her hands. "Let me start over. What I meant was, I was told to fetch Grelda the moment you woke. *If* you woke." She paused, then added in a rush, "Um, which of course you have! Obviously."

Mara laughed. "Obviously. So who's Grelda?"

"Head Healer," Asteria said promptly and proudly.

"A Healer?" Mara felt a surge of excitement. "Then she has the Gift?" *Someone to teach me how to use it!* she thought.

"The Gift?" Asteria looked puzzled for a moment, then her face cleared. "Oh, you mean magic!" She laughed. "No, no, don't worry, there's no magic here in the Secret City. No, she's a *regular* Healer. She knows how the body works, how to fix the things that go wrong, herbs that help, that sort of thing." She leaned closer and dropped her voice to a near whisper. "I've heard she can even cut open a living man and fix what's wrong inside him, then sew him up again. But I've never seen it." She shuddered. "Don't want to!"

Mara felt more confused than ever. "But aren't you her apprentice, or something?"

"Me?" Asteria giggled. "No, no. I'm her granddaughter. I couldn't do what she does. Blood and . . . and other things. Yuck."

"Then why are you . . . ?" Mara said, bewildered. She had the feeling bewilderment might be the natural state for anyone who spent much time with Asteria.

"Sometimes I help Gran with the stuff that's not messy. She said you weren't any trouble, you'd just lie here, maybe mutter or cry out, but not to worry, and not to wake her unless you actually woke up, or, or your diaper needed, um . . ." She blushed; then she looked stricken. "Oh! And now you're awake! Look, I really must go get Gran."

"I wish you would," Mara said, but kindly; you couldn't stay mad at Asteria. It would be like kicking a puppy.

Asteria rushed out. Mara, still feeling weak, but more alert by the minute, and much better since she'd had a little water, stared up at the whitewashed ceiling. A day and a half she'd been there, Asteria had said. At least two days' travel before that. It must be six days since she'd left the camp. She felt a chill. How long would the Warden wait before he decided something was wrong and send out Watchers to look for his missing geologists?

How long would he wait before blaming Mara for it, and making Katia pay the price?

I've got to go back there, she thought in sudden desperation. *I've got to save her!*

The deaths of Grute and the Watcher already dragged on her soul. She thought it would collapse completely under the additional weight of Katia's suffering in her stead.

Asteria returned with "Gran" within a quarter of an hour. Mara heard Asteria's chatter a good twenty seconds before she swept in through the red curtain, her grandmother in tow.

Grelda proved to be a woman of the same vintage as Catilla, and, like Catilla, tiny: no taller than Mara, and a good head and a half shorter than her granddaughter, who pointed at Mara with proprietary glee, as though personally responsible for her waking up, and said, "See!"

"Yes, child," Grelda said in the tone of voice one would use to quiet a skittish horse. She came over to Mara's bedside and bent down. "Hold still," she said. For the next few moments she poked and prodded, lifting Mara's arm and letting it fall, taking her pulse in her wrist and in her neck, feeling her abdomen, feeling her forehead, peeling back an eyelid to get a good look at her eyes, making her stick out her tongue and open her mouth wide. In the end she leaned back. "There is nothing obviously wrong with you," she said. "But there has not been anything obviously wrong with you since Edrik brought you back. Except, of course, you would not wake up. So why were you unconscious? Did you suffer a blow to the head? A shortage of breath? A disruption of the rhythm of the heart?"

Mara shook her head. "No," she said. "It was the magic."

Grelda's eyes narrowed. "Magic?"

"Yes," Mara said. She told Grelda what had happened, how the rush of magic that had come from the cave had almost killed her—and presumably *had* killed the Watcher.

Grelda's lips thinned as she listened. "*No one*," she said in a low, angry voice, "told *me* you had the Gift. *No one* told me your condition might have been caused by magic." Something about the way she said "no one" made Mara think she had a very specific *someone* in mind.

Grelda turned to Asteria. "Fetch Edrik," she snapped. "And then inform Catilla that I intend to have a word with her." From the way she said it, Mara thought it clear that Grelda had no fear Catilla would refuse that word. *They're almost of an age*, Mara thought. *I wonder . . .*

"Were you one of the original ones?" she said. "One of those who founded the Secret City?"

Grelda watched Asteria bustle out of sight, then turned to Mara again. "I was," she said. "My family, and Catilla's, and three others." She frowned. "This is common knowledge. Why do you ask?"

"It's not common knowledge to *me*," Mara pointed out.

"Hmmm. Nor is the fact you have the Gift common knowledge to *me*," Grelda said. "But it should have been." She thought for a moment. "Wait here," she said. "I have something that may help."

She swished out through the hanging curtain, leaving Mara to lie in the now-bright room and wonder just where else she could possibly go.

Grelda returned after ten minutes or so, holding a steaming mug in both hands. The morning breeze blowing through the window slit wafted the scent of the mug's contents to Mara's nostrils: fresh, floral, sweet, spicy. It smelled like . . . like good things to eat, a spring morning, her mother's sun-warmed hair, all at the same time. She'd never smelled anything like it. She'd never smelled anything more wonderful.

She *wanted* it. A *lot*.

Grelda wrinkled her nose as she handed it over. "Foul stuff," she said. "But if my books are to be believed . . . can you sit up?"

"I think so." Cautiously, she raised herself up. Her skull no longer seemed made of lead, and this time she was able to sit right up in the bed without breaking into a sweat, or, at least, not much of one. The thin white shift left her arms bare, and as the blanket fell from her shoulders the cool air raised goose bumps. Grelda handed her the mug and Mara closed her hands gratefully around its warmth. "Choke it down, if you can," Grelda said doubtfully.

"What are you talking about?" Mara said absently, absorbed in the heavenly scent. "It smells *wonderful*." Grelda's eyes widened in surprise as Mara raised the mug and took her first sip of the hot liquid. It tasted as marvelous as it smelled, thirst-quenching as the freshest spring water, sweet as the sweetest redcherry juice, but with a fiery warmth that spread through her weak, stiff, bruised, and aching body in an instant. Unlike the cold water, it didn't make her empty belly cramp: in fact, it seemed to fill it, erasing the pangs of both hunger and thirst.

Mara drank the rest as quickly as she could without burning her mouth, and by the time she returned the empty mug to Grelda, she felt almost normal. The aches and stiffness remained, the bruises hadn't disappeared, her leg was still bandaged (*and I'm still wearing a diaper*, she thought), and the bad memories still lurked in her mind, but all those things, even the memories, seemed manageable now, annoying rather than debilitating.

"That was *amazing*," she told Grelda. "No wonder there's no one else in here. No one can stay sick after drinking *that*."

Grelda shook her head. "I've never made that concoction before," she said. "It looked utterly noxious. And smelled worse."

Mara blinked. "I don't understand—"

"In one of my tattered old books, this recipe was listed as a restorative 'for those with the Gift suffering from a surfeit of uncontrolled magic.' Your description of what happened to you seemed to imply that might be the cause of your coma."

"And it really smelled bad to you?"

Grelda grimaced. "Like the sickroom chamber pot after a week's run of sourbelly." She looked around the room. "And this room is empty because it's where I put the patients I expect to die," she added bluntly.

Mara blinked. "Oh," she said in a small voice.

Grelda laughed for the first time since Mara had met her. "Not to worry, girl. You might still die—"

Mara gasped.

"—but it won't be from whatever brought you in here flat on your back."

Mara let out her breath in a rush.

Footsteps sounded beyond the curtained arch. Grelda glanced that way. "Company," she said.

Edrik pushed through the curtain, Asteria peering anxiously over his shoulder as he entered. His eyes went at once to Mara, and relief, plain as the growing daylight outside, washed over his face. "You're alive!"

Mara nodded. "But I don't remember being brought here."

Edrik glanced at Grelda. "May I talk to her?"

Grelda shrugged. "As far as I can tell, she's right as a rainbow, just a little weak, a little sore." She gave Mara an appraising look. "I've seldom seen a more comprehensive set of bruises, with some nice scrapes thrown in. A particularly nasty cut on your leg. And an older, healing wound on your head. I took the stitches out of that for you."

"The mine is . . . hard on people," Mara said softly.

"Two days before I left it, I was in hospital with a concussion and a broken arm, too."

Grelda frowned. "Cracked, you mean?"

Mara shook her head. "Broken. Healer Ethelda fixed it."

Grelda's face closed down. "More magic." She turned abruptly and headed for the entrance. "Take all the time you want," she snapped at Edrik on her way out. "Asteria, with me." Her granddaughter leaped to follow. The red curtain swirled angrily in their wake.

Mara stared after them. "What did I say?"

"Magic Healing is a sore point with Grelda." Edrik grimaced. "Sorry, that sounded like I was trying to make a joke."

"Not a very good one," Mara said.

"I *said* I was sorry." Edrik pulled a chair over to Mara's bedside and sat down. He leaned toward her. "What happened?"

"You tell me."

Edrik frowned, then sighed. "Very well."

He told her how, on the day she had been kidnapped, it had been several hours before anyone realized she'd gone missing. As scouts had come back from the fruitless search for Grute, they were sent out again in search of her, uselessly. It had been Hyram—probably thinking of their conversation along the beach, Mara thought—who suggested they search along the shore, and finally, near where the water of the underground river poured into the sea, they had seen two sets of footprints in the sand, and had realized that Grute had not only evaded them, he had kidnapped Mara.

"At least, we assumed you were kidnapped," Edrik said, watching Mara's face. "Keltan, Alita, and Prella all insisted you would never have *willingly* run off with Grute."

"But *you* thought I might have?" Mara said, face heating. "Or was it your grandmother?"

"We don't really know you," Edrik said, not sounding

at all apologetic. "Or what you're capable of. As recent events have demonstrated."

"I did not run off with Grute," Mara said with finality. She told Edrik how Grute had evaded them with his improvised breathing tube, how he had surprised her in the lake, and how they had gotten out of the Secret City unseen.

When she had finished, Edrik sighed. "We were fools. It never crossed my mind that the river might offer a path of escape. Or at least," he amended, "not a path of escape that anyone could *survive*."

"We almost didn't," Mara said. "But Grute didn't seem to care whether he survived or not. Much less whether *I* did." She shuddered, remembering that terrifying, watery rush through darkness.

Edrik told her how they'd tracked her and Grute toward the mountains, and guessed they were making for the mining camp. They'd lost the trail as it climbed up into the rocks of a high ridge, and had crossed into the valley on the other side to try to pick it up again. But when they finally did find more tracks, hours later, they'd been puzzled. "The tracks we picked up were of a horse and a mule, and you'd been on foot," Edrik said. "But they were headed toward the camp, so we followed them, and finally saw some of your footprints by the stream where the animals had stopped to drink . . . along with new footprints we hadn't seen before. What we *didn't* see were any of Grute's tracks. We didn't know how to read it."

"A man from the camp found me," Mara said. "I was on the mule and he rode the horse."

"So Grute rode double with you?"

"No," Mara said. "Grute didn't ride anywhere. Grute was . . . is . . . dead."

"Dead?" Edrik looked confused. "How—?"

"I killed him." Mara hadn't intended to say it, had been planning to keep it a secret, to claim Grute had wandered off in the night and never returned, perhaps had fallen down a cliff. But the words came out before she could stop them. She needed to tell *someone*, needed to *explain* to someone . . .

. . . needed someone to tell her that what she had done was all right.

"We took shelter in a hut," Mara said, as Edrik stared at her, clearly shocked. "Grute had found some whiskey. He was drunk. He . . . he came at me. He was going to . . ." She shook her head. "I couldn't . . . I did the only thing I could. I grabbed magic. I–I killed him."

"Magic?" Edrik repeated, as if he couldn't believe what he'd heard. "You killed him with *magic?* Where did you find magic?"

"In the hut. In a basin of black stone. It's what they call a magic-well. A place where magic oozes to the surface, and can be collected."

"I've never heard of such a thing," Edrik said.

"No doubt there are many things you've never heard of, hiding in this hole all these years!" Mara snapped, anger spurred by the disbelief in his voice.

"And you claim you used this magic to kill Grute?" Edrik said, the disbelief thickening. "A boy twice your size and strong as a bear?"

"The magic didn't care how big he was."

"You just struck him dead? Poof? Just like that?"

"I grabbed his head with both hands and his head exploded!" Mara snarled. "Do you know what that feels like? It came apart in my hands like an overripe melon. I was covered in his blood, bits of his brain, chunks of skull with hair still clinging to it . . . I pulled two teeth out of my hair. Blood painted the walls, and *I did it!*" Her anger faded, her voice fading to a whisper. "I killed him with magic."

On Edrik's face, disbelief warred with horror, and then with . . .

. . . the word that came to Mara's mind was "avarice." *He looks like a greedy shopkeeper suddenly offered the bargain of the year.*

"I've never dreamed . . ." Edrik breathed. "Never dreamed *anyone* could use the Gift like that. I've never even heard *rumors* of such a thing." He stood up. "This is more important than making fake Masks. If you can do this, you can—"

Her anger roared back, full force. "Shut up!" she screamed at him. "Just shut up and listen to me!"

Edrik's eyes widened, and she wondered if it had just occurred to him that a girl who could blow Grute's head off could blow his off, too.

Not that she would. Not that she *could*, not without magic at hand.

But that had been what she'd thought when she was in the grip of the Watcher, too.

Edrik sat down again, but not comfortably; he perched on the edge of the chair as though poised to leap to his feet again at a moment's notice. "What else?"

"I also used the magic to clean up the hut," Mara went on, voice trembling. "When the Watcher came the next morning he found me, alone; no Grute and no magic left in the magic-well. He was most annoyed by that, but never even considered that I might have somehow made use of it. It's well-known the Gift doesn't survive the failure of a Mask."

Edrik's eyes narrowed. Mara went on. "He took me to the camp. The Warden was suspicious, of me and of the tale I told of how Grute and I had escaped the wagon after they were attacked by bandits. But I stuck to my story.

"He sent me down into the mines." Her throat closed as she remembered. "It's a terrible place," she managed after a moment. "And the unMasked are worked to death in it."

"Not all the unMasked," Edrik said shortly. "We know about the trustees."

The trustees. She thought of the ones she'd seen, the hardened men, the harder women, like Hayka, and their casual cruelty toward the other unMasked. How many of those suffering the mines and the barracks were of the same ilk, suffering only because they hadn't yet found a way to turn the tables and become one of the abusers instead of one of the abused? The Masks—the *old* Masks—had been very good at identifying the people who would be the dregs of any society, the bullies, the beaters, the sadists, the selfish, the predators, the perverts.

But Catilla herself had told Mara that, even before the Masks changed, not all of the unMasked were like that. Some were simply those who didn't fit in, who were different. And they were the ones the others preyed on. "Of those who are not sent to the mines—the women, the girls—many are given to the Watchers. For a night. Or . . ." Her throat closed again as she thought of Katia. "Or for longer." She remembered the woman in the bed opposite her in the hospital, the one whose heart the Healer had stopped with a touch. "For life. Which isn't very long, as a rule."

"We know about that, too," Edrik said.

Mara's anger returned. "If you know so much about what goes on in the camp, *why haven't you done anything?*"

Edrik spread his hands. "What would you have us do? Attack the camp? Kill the Watchers? Free the inmates?"

"Yes!"

"And how long would they live in the Wild? Or if they survived the Wild, how long before the Autarch's Watchers hunted them down?" He leaned closer, face hard. "Or would you have me bring them all to the Secret City? Including the trustees, and all the others who are as bad, or worse, than Grute?"

Mara pressed her lips together and said nothing.

Edrik sat back again. "We *were* considering an attack on the camp to free *you*. I am glad we did not have to carry it out."

"How did you even know for certain I was there?" Mara said.

"From the ridge to the north, you can look down into the camp," Edrik said. "We saw you: going into the mine, carried to the hospital, and then walking to the big house. *That* gave us hope we could rescue you."

"Why?"

"On the north side, it is possible to sneak up very close to the palisade without being seen—the camp is a prison, remember, not a fort. The wall and the guards are there to keep people in, not out."

Mara nodded.

"As well, on the east side, there is a hill from which it is possible to shoot arrows over the palisade wall. Our plan was to fire the hay near the stables with flaming arrows. During the resulting panic and confusion, with horses screaming and Watchers running to save them and fight the fire, we would scale the northern wall and snatch you from inside the house."

"If you're so fearful of discovery, why would you even risk that much?" Mara said bitterly. "Am I really that valuable?"

"I judged the risk acceptable," Edrik said. "If all went well, it would have been put down to another raid by bandits, a follow-up to the attack on the wagon. We would have made it look like a robbery, ransacking the house for food, clothing, and gold. Hopefully, they would have thought you were taken as nothing more than an incidental prize, just because you were there. And to answer your second question, my grandmother has deemed you that valuable, so, yes. You are." He regarded her coolly. "You should be grateful."

Mara ignored that. "But before you could try this plan . . . ?"

"You came out. We were hiding on the ridge to the north even as you rode over it."

"Then why didn't you attack *then*? Or that night, when we camped?"

"You didn't seem to be in any danger," Edrik said.

"And we were curious as to where you were riding, with two Watchers, and two others who were *not* Watchers."

Pixot and Turpit. Mara had completely forgotten about them. "The two who aren't Watchers, are they dead?"

"No," Edrik said. "Imprisoned, separately. We are still debating what to do with them."

"Don't hurt them," Mara said quickly. "They're not bad men. At least Pixot isn't. They're just geologists." She thought of the camp's gold mine along the shore. "They might even be useful."

Edrik frowned. "Geologists?" he said carefully. "I don't know that word."

"Rock-men," Mara said, remembering what the Watcher had called Pixot. "They know about rocks. That's why they were riding with us. The Warden found out that my Gift had survived. He had a use for me. He sent me out with the others to examine a find of black lodestone."

Edrik cocked his head. "Black lodestone?"

"Like regular lodestone attracts metal, black lodestone attracts magic," Mara explained. "Black lodestone is what they're mining in the camp. Or to put it another way, they're mining magic."

Edrik blinked. "Magic? Are you sure?"

Mara nodded. "Yes. But the mine is playing out. I saw it for myself: there's barely a trace of magic left in the rocks down below. It must take tons of stone to get enough magic to fill a single urn. But the place where we were when you rescued me . . ." She shook her head, remembering the wondrous beauty of the cavern with the underground lake, the auroras of magic swirling across the sparkling walls. "There's magic there, all right. More magic than fills all the store halls of the Palace. Magic to make the Autarch drool."

Edrik leaned even closer. "And now we come to it," he said. "What happened to the Watcher?"

"You killed one," Mara said.

Edrik made an impatient chopping motion with his hand. "Yes, yes. We shot him from up above when he stepped into the open. Once they made you go into the cave, we feared for you and decided we could wait no longer.

"But the second Watcher was smart. He figured out where we must be and stayed out of our line of fire. I signaled Hyram and Keltan and the rest waiting at the mouth of the ravine to attack. When they reached the cave, they saw the other Watcher straddling you. He had your head pulled back, he had his knife out, he was half a second from slitting your throat, and then . . ."

Edrik paused, as if waiting for a response, but Mara said nothing. She didn't know what to say. Edrik frowned, then continued. "And then he vanished. One instant he was there. The next—gone. Nothing but dust, swirling in a sudden, powerful whirlwind centered on *you*, flat on your back in the water, face turned into the stream, not stirring; you would have drowned if Hyram and Keltan hadn't pulled you out. You were breathing, but that was the only sign you still lived. And you were covered in fine white dust. The whole glade was covered in dust, left behind by the whirlwind."

Dust, Mara thought. *Covered in dust. The dry ash that was all that remained of the Watcher, burned away in the fury of the magical fire that almost burned me away, too. The same ash that was all the magic left of Grute, in the hut . . .*

She shuddered. "I hope somebody gave me a bath."

"Hyram and Keltan both volunteered," Edrik said, and Mara's mouth fell open. She felt herself blushing. Edrik laughed. "Don't worry. One of the women did it instead."

"Oh," she said. "Good." She forced a small laugh herself.

"Mara," Edrik said, turning serious again. "I have to know. *What happened to that Watcher?*"

She remembered Edrik's greedy look when she'd told him what she had done to Grute. *He's wondering how he can use me*, she thought. *Wondering how powerful a weapon I could be against the Autarch.*

To be fair, she was wondering that herself.

"Magic," she said.

Edrik snorted. "I know that. But where did it come from? Did you bring it out of the cavern with you?"

"No," she said. "I had a little on my hands, but not enough to . . . it was just . . . I knew he was about to kill me, I was desperate and somehow, the magic *knew*. It just *came* to me. It leaped out of the cave like a lightning bolt. It killed him." She remembered that searing agony, the way unconsciousness had been a relief. "It almost killed *me*."

"You have that much power?" Edrik breathed. "I've never . . . Mara, if we could—" He cut off as the red curtain swirled, Catilla pushing it aside as she entered, Grelda close behind her.

Edrik's grandmother hadn't changed in the slightest since Mara had first met her, which seemed odd, since Mara had changed so much. Had it really only been . . . what? Sixteen days? Seventeen? Mara had lost track of the time since she had met Catilla in her chamber. It seemed more like seventeen years.

Catilla's icy blue eyes, direct and penetrating as ever, met hers. "Good," she said softly. "Awake, alert. Undamaged. Good."

Undamaged? Mara thought. *What makes you so sure?*

"As soon as you are up and about," Catilla said, "we can get you started on the Masks you have promised to make. And then—"

"Grandmother," Edrik began. "There's something else you should—"

"No," Mara said.

Catilla had been staring at Edrik, eyes narrowed; now her head swung toward Mara, sudden as the darting glance of a hawk. "What?"

"I will not make Masks for you," Mara said as firmly as she could, though her voice showed an alarming tendency to waver. "I will not do what you want me to do unless you first do something for me."

Catilla's eyes narrowed further. "You presume—"

"I do," Mara said. "You must do what I ask or I will not help you, with either my skill at making Masks . . . or my skill with magic."

"*What* skill with magic?" Catilla said scornfully. "Your Gift survives. I knew that." She glanced at the Healer. "And yes, Grelda, we should have told you so you could better treat her." Her gaze returned to Mara. "But as I told you before, we have no magic here and without use and training, the Gift withers. Even if you have it now, you won't much longer."

"I don't think her Gift is withering," Edrik said. Catilla's cold glare switched to him, to Mara's relief. "Mara *claims*," he said, with just a slight emphasis on the word, "that she has used magic twice now to slay attackers."

Catilla's gaze snapped back to Mara. "Explain."

Mara took a deep breath, and once more told the tale of Grute's messy death, and the sudden demise of the Watcher. When she had finished, Catilla said nothing for a moment; sounding, when she finally did speak, uncertain— for the first time since Mara had met her. "I have never heard of magic that could do that, outside of the history books. 'Magic is a powerful tool for small tasks.'" She sounded as if she were reciting something she had once been told.

"Nevertheless, it happened," Mara replied. *White dust* . . . "I didn't mean to do it. It just . . . happened. Both times."

"But such power: to kill at a touch, to kill *without* a touch . . ." Catilla's face took on the same look of avaricious calculation Edrik's had borne when he'd first heard her tale.

"I've done it," Mara said. "I would not willingly do it again." An echo of the fiery agony that had filled her when she called the magic from the cave washed over her, a flash of *Grute, naked, headless*. . . . "I don't know what it would do to me."

"This last time put her into a coma," Grelda said sharply to Catilla. "One I might have pulled her out of sooner had I known it was magic-related. As a Healer—"

"Non-Gifted," said Catilla coolly.

Grelda's lips thinned. "Non-Gifted," she grated, "but still a Healer, my advice to Mara is to avoid using magic at all costs. She is untrained. That makes her dangerous—to others, and to herself."

Catilla looked at Grelda as if she would like to argue, but then nodded stiffly. "Very well," she said. "I bow to your wisdom in these matters."

Grelda smiled thinly. "Then there really is a first time for everything."

Mara glanced from one to the other. *There's a long history there*, she thought. *But are they friends, enemies, rivals, or all three?* She couldn't tell.

Catilla turned back to Mara. "Well, then," Catilla said. "If we cannot make use of your magical Gift, at least not yet"—she gave Grelda a look—"then all this is immaterial. Let us return to your skill at Maskmaking."

"The reason you rescued me in the first place," Mara said.

"Precisely," said Catilla. "What is it you insist we do before you *deign* to help us?"

Here it comes, Mara thought. "Edrik has convinced me," she said, "that it is both impossible and unwise for you to destroy the mining camp."

"Edrik is correct," Catilla said. "When the Autarch is overthrown, the camp will cease to exist. But there is nothing to be done about it now."

"I understand," Mara said. Both Catilla and Edrik looked satisfied—smug, actually—but she wasn't done yet. "I understand," she said again, locking defiant eyes on Catilla's, "that you cannot attack the camp and free everyone in it. But if you want my help, if you want me to make the Masks you say you so desperately need, then you will help me free one *particular* person from it."

Catilla's expression went cold and hard as a Mask. Edrik opened his mouth to protest, but Mara gave him no space in which to insert a word. "There is a girl in the Warden's house. She has suffered in the mines. She has been abused in the barracks. Some of her suffering can be laid at my feet. She will suffer still more if I do not return. She is a hostage to my good behavior. And I will do nothing to help you if you do not help me free her."

Now Catilla's stony expression twisted into anger. "Child, you test my patience—"

"I am not a child!" Mara said; shouted, really, anger flooding her voice, her face turning hot. "In the eyes of the law I have not been a child since the day of my failed Masking, and whatever was left of the child I was before that died in the camp." She held Catilla's fierce glare with one of her own, though her heart pounded in her chest as though she had just run the length of Maskmakers' Way. "I am the *young woman* who has the skill and knowledge to finally make your unMasked Army an army in *fact* instead of just name, to finally give you real hope of overthrowing the Autarch by giving you access to Tamita. I am the young woman whose help you need, whose help you have already killed and risked discovery to obtain, and I'm telling you now you *will not get that help* unless you help me free my friend Katia from the waking nightmare of that camp!"

Catilla's face flushed. For a moment Mara thought the old woman would slap her. But then Edrik spoke, surprising her. "Grandmother," he said, "we already had plans for rescuing Mara. Perhaps we could adapt them to free her friend?"

Thank you, Edrik, Mara thought, as Catilla's dagger-like gaze sliced toward him. She stared at him for a long moment, but he, too, held his ground. Finally she snorted.

"Very well," she snapped. "We will attempt it." She looked back to Mara. "But only on one condition of my own," she added in a growl.

Uh-oh, Mara thought. "What?"

Catilla stepped closer, her fierce gaze unwavering. "That you not only help us with the making of the Masks, you promise to serve the unMasked Army with your Gift, once you have learned to control it."

"How can I promise that?" Mara protested. "I don't even know that I *can* control my Gift." That white-hot blaze of power, that burning agony, the hallucinations . . . She shuddered.

"Let me worry about that," Catilla said. "Give me your word. I want an end to this talk of what 'you' want as opposed to what 'we' want. There is no 'you' or 'we.' There is only the unMasked Army, I command it, and you are part of it. *You have no choice*. So: if we attempt to free your friend from the camp, will you pledge your unconditional allegiance to the unMasked Army—and to *me* as its leader—and use your skills as *I* direct in our fight against the Autarch?"

Mara's heart raced even faster. If she made this promise, she could be agreeing to *anything*. Who knew what uses Catilla might find for her Gift, what horrors she might be opening herself up to?

But she had *already* made Katia a promise. And herself, too.

And besides, she thought, anger snapping through her, anger with more than a little of the feel of the white-hot fire of magic, *all of this . . . all of this . . . can be laid at the feet of the Autarch. Why wouldn't I pledge to do* whatever *I can to overthrow* him?

"I promise," she said, the words firm as the rock walls around her, though her body seemed to be vibrating like a plucked fiddle string.

Catilla's expression never changed. "Then we have a bargain."

"We have to act quickly," Mara said. "Katia . . . I don't know how long the Warden will keep her unharmed." Her throat closed on the words. *We may be too late already*.

"We will," Edrik said. He looked at Grelda. "Can she travel?"

Grelda grimaced. "She'll be weak from lying in bed. She needs to get up and eat proper food and get her strength back. I wouldn't recommend her traveling for at least three days."

"No," Mara said. Now it was Grelda giving her an angry look, but after facing Catilla she could easily ignore that. "We leave as soon as you can get your people ready to go. I'm ready now." She swung her legs over the edge of the bed and stood up. Pain stabbed her calf, the room spun around her, and for a moment her vision grayed, but she managed to stay upright, and after an instant the dizziness passed; the restorative Grelda had given her had worked wonders. "See?" she said a little breathlessly.

Edrik had taken half a step closer, hand outstretched, ready to catch her if she fell; now he let the hand drop and stepped back again. "I see." He glanced at Grelda. "But we will not be ready to leave until the day after tomorrow, in any case. She has that long to recover."

"Not long enough," Grelda grumbled. "But it seems *I* have no say."

Catilla looked at Mara with approval. "You have fire, child . . ." She stopped herself. "Young woman," she amended with what might almost have been a small smile. "More than I realized when you were first brought to me." She turned to her grandson. "Go, then, as soon as may be. Rescue this other girl if it can be done. Bring her back here." She glanced at Mara. "And Mara, too. Keep her safe. All of this is a waste if she gets herself killed."

"I'll keep her safe," Edrik promised. His mouth quirked. "I know a couple of boys who will help."

Catilla snorted and departed without another word.

Mara took a deep breath and sat down on the bed again with a feeling of relief.

Grelda stepped forward. "You endanger your health," she said with disapproval. "But the tide is against me. See me after you are dressed. I will give you a supply of the herbs for the restorative I prepared earlier, and the recipe. Just don't make it where anyone who doesn't have the Gift can smell it. Unless you're trying to ruin their appetite." She, too, went out.

Edrik was the last to leave. He swept aside the red curtain and watched the others depart, then closed the curtain and came back to Mara's side, face grim. "Though I agreed to it to bind you to our cause, this is a fool's errand. You are endangering my men and women, me — and yourself, not least of all. We may already be too late to rescue this friend of yours, and *my* friends may die in the attempt." He leaned closer, looming over her. "Training or no training, Mara, if there comes a point during this rescue mission where your Gift could save lives, you *will* use it. At *whatever* risk to yourself. Or I will throw you into that camp *myself*, to rot until the Autarch is overthrown. Am I clear?"

Mara swallowed. "Yes."

"Good." He exited in an angry swirl of red cloth.

Mara fell back on the bed and stared up at the whitewashed ceiling. *I am doing the right thing. I know I am. Katia is my responsibility. I made her a hostage. I have to rescue her.*

At any *cost?* another part of her whispered.

Any cost, she tried to tell herself firmly. But all her certainty seemed to have blown away in the gale-force winds of everything she had just set in motion.

She curled up on the bed, closed her eyes, and wished once more, wished more than anything in the world, that she *was* still the child Catilla had called her, still a little girl in her own bed in her own house in a world where everything made sense and nothing could happen that her parents couldn't make right, wished that at any moment she would hear her mother's voice outside her door, calling her down to breakfast.

But all she heard was the beating of her own heart and the cry of wild gulls in the chill salt air outside her window.

NINETEEN
The Return

THE NEXT AFTERNOON Mara lay on her back in the beach's silvery sand, staring up at the pearl-white sky. A horse's head appeared in her field of view and gazed at her quizzically. "Do you put me down here just so you can get a good look at me?" she said conversationally. "This is the third time."

A second horse's head appeared, this one accompanied by Hyram, who held its reins. "Don't blame the horse," he said severely.

"I don't think he likes me." Mara pushed herself up on her elbows and groaned. "I'm one big bruise. All the bruises I brought back with me from the camp, all the new ones I've got in the last three hours trying to learn to ride—"

"Trying to learn to stay on the horse," Hyram corrected. "You don't really learn to ride in one afternoon."

"Apparently you don't really learn to stay on a horse in one afternoon, either!" she said, and Hyram chuckled.

Keltan, leading his own horse, came over to join them.

"What about *him?*" she said, nodding at Keltan. "How long did *he* take to learn to ride?"

"Keltan knows how to stay on a horse," Hyram said. He gave Keltan a look, half-joking, half-challenging. Keltan glared back, and Mara sighed. She had seen a lot of those kinds of looks passing back and forth between the two boys all day, since midmorning when she had emerged, limping slightly, from the sickroom, where she had spent all of the previous day recuperating. They had been waiting for her—apparently they had been forbidden to visit her—and had shadowed her ever since, making sure she got a good breakfast, taking her to the stables, showing her how to saddle her own horse, and then how to ride ...

... how to stay on ...

Oh, be honest, Mara thought grouchily. *How to get used to falling off!*

She looked from one boy to the other. Flattering and kind of exciting though she had to admit she found having two boys interested in her at once, it did get rather wearying. As to which one she preferred ...

She couldn't answer that question. Not now.

Maybe later, after we get back from the camp ...

If we get back.

She shoved those thoughts out of her mind. One thing at a time. "I think I'm getting the hang of it," she said, although she didn't think any such thing. "Let me try again."

After another couple of hours, she was sorer than ever, but she really *was* getting the hang of it. Even Hyram admitted it. "You're much better," he said as the three of them sat on their horses, looking out over the ocean at the long orange streaks of clouds streaming out from the setting sun like tongues of fire. "Don't try anything silly and you should be fine."

"She'd better be," a new voice said. Mara jumped and almost fell off her horse again, then turned her head accusingly to see Edrik, on foot, standing in the sand behind the horses. "Before we see the sun again, we'll be on our way."

"How long before we can rescue Katia?" Mara asked him. *Another day lost*, she thought. *A day I spent learning to ride, laughing with Keltan and Hyram. While Katia . . .*

"Two and a half days to get there. A night and a day to reconnoiter. We might try it in five nights' time . . . *if* I deem the risk acceptable."

Mara jerked her head back around to stare blindly out at the burning sky. *Five nights! Katia . . .*

She heard Edrik's footsteps crunch away through the sand. "It's the best we can do," Hyram said softly from her left.

"I know," she said. She blinked back tears that had nothing to do with the glare of sun on water. "I just hope it's good enough."

They ensconced the horses in the stone stables, then made their way to the Great Chamber, taking their food—venison, tonight, with bitter greens and (Mara sighed happily) mashed redroots—to where Alita, Prella, Simona, and Kirika already sat at a shadowy table in the corner. It was the first time Mara had seen the other girls since her return from the camp, and she tried to ignore the sidelong glances they all—with the notable exception of the ever-sullen Kirika—shot at her while she sipped her soup. She knew they wanted to hear everything that had happened. She just wasn't sure she wanted to tell them. Especially Prella, who still seemed like such a little girl.

But she's not a little girl, she told herself. *We're all the same age. None of us have been little girls since our Masks failed. Prella . . . all of them . . . deserve to know what's out there. They deserve to know what awaited them in the camp they luckily never got to.*

And so, when she had finished eating, she told them everything: about Grute, about the mine, about Katia. They listened in silence, Prella and Simona with wide eyes, Alita impassively, Kirika without looking at her at all. Hyram and Keltan had heard some of it by then, but not all. Mara talked until her throat was sore. At first the words would hardly come; but the longer she talked, the easier it became, until the words rushed out like the waterfall that had thrown her and Grute into the sea. She felt as if a boil had been lanced, or a scab peeled away. More blood and pain might follow, but in that moment all she felt was relief.

When at last she ran out of words, the seven of them were alone, the other tables empty, the food cleared away. "And tomorrow you're going back?" Alita said.

Mara nodded.

"Of course my father agreed to rescue Katia," Hyram said. "Once he knew about—"

"He and Catilla still think the risk is too great," Mara said harshly. "I'm blackmailing them. They need me. If they didn't . . ."

"My father would have come around eventually anyway. He would have done what's right. He always does."

Mara opened her mouth to argue, then closed it again. She'd felt the same way about her father, once. It seemed a long time ago.

Kirika snorted and spoke—and looked up—for the first time. "*My* father," she said, voice venomous, "would have dragged you back to the camp himself, and sold you to the highest bidder. He would have done the same to *me*. How *he* was successfully Masked when I . . ." She broke off and looked down at the floor again, jaw clenched. Simona reached out tentatively to put her arm around Kirika's shoulder, but Kirika leaped to her feet, fast as a cat, slapping Simona's hand away with a violent swing of her arm. "Don't touch me," she snarled. "Don't *ever* touch me." And then she turned and stalked away.

"I'm sorry," Simona called after her in a stricken voice, but Kirika strode out of the Great Chamber without looking back. "I'm sorry," Simona said again, but this time to the rest of them.

Alita shook her head. "Not your fault," she said. "Blame her father."

"He must have been even worse than mine," Keltan said sourly. "And here I didn't think that was possible."

Prella said nothing, but her lower lip trembled and her eyes glistened. She was obviously thinking about her own father, who just as obviously had been nothing like theirs. Mara reached across the table and put her hand on top of the smaller girl's, who gave her a small, watery smile of gratitude.

Mara glanced at Keltan and Hyram. "Oh, and I've been meaning to thank you two," she said. A half-smile twitched up one corner of her mouth. "Your father tells me you *both* volunteered to *personally* give me a bath after the Watcher was burned to ash. That was *so* kind and selfless."

Her smile flashed to a full grin as they both turned roughly the same color as the mashed redroots and started sputtering out incoherent sounds of apology. Mara laughed, and Alita laughed with her. Prella looked a little scandalized, but then she started grinning, too, as did Simona, and soon all of them were laughing together.

The laughter felt good. Mara still felt good as she, Alita, Prella, and Simona made their way to their room, where Kirika already lay in bed, back to them all.

But she didn't feel good in the middle of the night when her decapitation of Grute and disintegration of the Watcher replayed themselves over and over and. . . .

She woke screaming, bringing the other girls gasping awake in their beds. After apologizing, she took a long time to fall back asleep, and slept poorly once she did; and when Keltan called to her from the corridor, with the sky not even graying yet outside the window slits, she didn't feel good at all. She heaved her aching body out of the bed, wincing at a throb from the raw, red scar on her forehead and a jab of pain from the wound in her calf. Though healing well, both still hurt. Alita raised her head, looked at her blearily, said, "Luck," and rolled over and went back to sleep. Prella and the others didn't even stir.

Mara wanted nothing more than to go down to the baths and soak in the warm water, but there was no time: the rescue party was to set out at first light, and first light was just around the corner. She dressed in the warm, newly repaired clothes the Warden had provided her, visited the latrine, picked up the pack she had prepared the day before, and left as quietly as she could, with a whispered "good-bye" she doubted anyone was awake to hear.

Edrik had assembled a force of eight, counting himself, Mara, Keltan, and Hyram. The other four consisted of two women and two men: Tishka, who gave Mara a warm smile; Illina, a young woman—no more than twenty, Mara judged—and twin brothers, only a little older, introduced as Skrit and Skrat. She'd seen all three around the Secret City but had never before spoken to any of them.

They led their horses out of the stables and saddled and mounted them in silence, except for the groan wrung out of Mara as she swung her wounded leg over her mount's broad back. Edrik gave her a hard look, just visible in the gray light that had seeped into the sky while they readied to ride. "All right?"

"I'm fine." She gave him what she hoped was a bright smile but suspected was more of a grimace.

He looked skeptical, but clucked to his horse, wheeled it around, and trotted off toward the ravine they had followed into the Secret City when she had first been brought there. With varying degrees of skill, the rest of them rode after him. Mara, after a brief argument with her horse, which clearly would have preferred to rejoin its stablemates rather than trot off into the chilly twilight, fell in behind Keltan. Hyram waited for her, then brought up the rear.

They rode silently up the ravine while the world brightened. After twenty minutes, the sky flushed pink. After an hour, sunlight found them, its touch bringing a little more life into Mara's chilled, stiff limbs, though the air remained cold enough to make her grateful for her gloves, vest, coat, and cloak.

Mara thought they must be heading for the cave they had passed through on their way to the Secret City, but instead, at midmorning, Edrik turned left and led the party out of the ravine, up a long defile. They rode the rest of the day through sun-dappled forest, the cold wind swirling golden leaves around the trees' black trunks.

They camped that night by a small lake. Keltan and Hyram took turns hammering in the pegs for the tent Mara would share with Illina and Tishka, competing to see who could do it faster, then sat on either side of her at the campfire as they all ate venison stew and crusty bread, washed down with a pale beer that, though weak, made Mara's head swim. She was glad to crawl into her bedroll . . .

. . . only to wake, gasping, from yet another dream of Grute.

A dark shape loomed over her and she cried out and tried to push it away, but, "Shhh, shhh," said a soothing voice, and she lay there, panting. "It's Illina. It's all right. You're safe."

On her left, Tishka muttered under her breath and rolled over, but then resumed the heavy breathing of sleep. Illina lay down close to Mara. "Bad dream?" the older girl whispered.

Mara nodded. "Every night," she whispered back. "I see Grute. He . . ." Her throat closed.

"The boy you killed? With magic?"

Mara turned her head. She couldn't see the other girl, but knew she was looking at her. "Yes," she whispered.

"He tried to rape you," Illina said. "Didn't he?"

Mara nodded. Her eyes filled with tears. "Yes." Grute, naked, leering, coming toward her; the magic on her hands, her hands on his head; the horrible burst of red and white and gray, the sickening sound, the hot slick of blood all over her—

She jerked her eyes open, gasping. She'd almost slipped back into the nightmare.

Illina moved closer in the dark, found her, wrapped her arms around her. Her body against Mara's felt warm and comforting. It brought back memories of cuddling with her mother on nights she was ill or had a bad dream, nights her mother had soothed her just as Illina soothed her now, and suddenly she found herself sobbing, trying to be silent so as not to wake Tishka, her body shaking in Illina's arms.

"Shh. Shh. It's all right," Illina whispered. "You're safe. He's gone. He can never hurt you again. Never." Her arms tightened. "You're safe. Go to sleep."

Mara took a long, shuddering breath. "Thank you," she whispered.

"I have a little sister," Illina said softly. "You remind me of her. I would do what you did—and worse—to protect her. You did the right thing. Now shh . . . and sleep. We all need rest."

Mara fell silent, then; and, wrapped in the warmth of Illina's comforting embrace, soon followed that silence into deep, dreamless sleep.

She woke to find Illina already awake and rolling up her bedroll. Tishka was nowhere to be seen. Gray light seeped through the tent flap. "Rise and shine," Illina said. "Did you sleep well the rest of the night?"

"Ye-e-ess," Mara said, stifling a yawn. "Thanks to you."

Illina smiled. "It's amazing how powerful a hug can be. You're welcome. Now get up, sleepyhead. We have many more miles to ride."

Mounting the horse again wrung a groan of pain from her. She didn't think she would have managed it at all without Hyram's help (he got to her before Keltan could), and both he and Keltan rode close throughout the day, watching her as though afraid she might drop from the animal's back at any moment. She laughed at them for it, but until a couple of hours had passed and the sun had once more loosened her joints she was secretly glad of their attention.

They went up, over, and down a series of ridges that day, and Mara realized that they were following more or less the same path she and Grute had taken on foot. On horseback, the journey didn't last as long, even though the woods were thick enough the horses could only move at a slow walk (for which she was grateful). Early in the afternoon she looked up at the next ridge—and saw the square box of the hut where she had slain Grute.

She kicked her horse in the sides and trotted ahead of Keltan and Hyram to catch up to Edrik. "We're not going up there, are we?" she demanded, thrusting her finger at the hut.

"Yes, we are," Edrik said, his eyes on the hut and not her. "There might be something we can use in it. You said there was food—"

"We *have* food," Mara snapped. "You're going there to check up on my story, aren't you?"

Edrik's gaze swung to her. "Yes," he said quietly.

"You won't find anything of Grute. The magic saw to that."

"But at least we will find the hut as you described it." Edrik's eyes locked with hers. "Won't we?"

Mara's jaw clenched. "Yes," she grated. "You will." She let her horse fall back until she rode between Keltan and Hyram again, but kept staring at Edrik, hoping he could feel her angry glare burning into his back.

Peripherally, she saw the boys exchange glances. "Um, what's wrong?" Hyram ventured at last.

"Your father *and* your great-grandmother don't trust me," Mara said. "They think I'm lying about Grute. About the magic."

"Oh." Hyram cleared his throat. "I don't think that's quite—"

"Fair?" Mara swung her angry gaze toward him, and he quailed in his saddle. "I wake up every night screaming because of what I did in that hut!" She pointed at the square stone structure, growing closer by the moment. "I never wanted to see it again. And now I'm being forced to go there, because my word isn't good enough! Is *that* fair? Would you like to be dragged to the site of your worst nightmare against your will? Is *that* fair?"

"He ..." Hyram cleared his throat and straightened. "Father has responsibilities. So does Great-Grandmother. To the unMasked Army. I'm sure they believe you. But others may not. Everyone has to understand why—"

"Oh, shut up!"

He did.

She turned her glare back on Edrik, caught a glimpse out of the corner of her eye of Keltan's face, and snapped her gaze in his direction. "And wipe that stupid smug grin off your face, Keltan—or whatever your real name is." He flinched. "Did anyone question *your* story? Did anyone wonder why you have the same name as the Autarch's *horse?* Or did they just accept what you had to say? Why am *I* the only one nobody trusts?" But she didn't wait to hear whatever feeble answers either boy might have offered. Instead, she dug her heels into her horse's flanks and trotted ahead of them until she was out of earshot.

She rode the rest of the way to the hut in black, fuming, solitary silence. Edrik held up a hand to stop them well short of the little square building, then slid from his horse and drew his sword. "We'll approach on foot," he said. "It may not be—"

Mara brushed past him. "Mara!" Edrik shouted after her, but she ignored him; limping to the hut, she threw the door open, then spun to face the rest. "Empty. As I knew it would be." And then, without waiting for Edrik's response, she went inside.

It was just as she remembered it. *Of course it would be*, she thought. She went into the room with the stone basin. At least *that* had changed: the basin was almost full of magic once more, swirling and shifting color as she watched it.

She coughed. Entering the room had stirred up the fine white dust on the floor. Acrid on her tongue, it tickled the back of her throat.

Dust.

On the floor.

Grute . . .

She ran outside, shoving Edrik out of the doorway so hard he stumbled and almost fell, then turned sharply left, dropped to her hands and knees on the cold wet stone, and heaved up the contents of her stomach. It took a long time for the spasms to pass, long after her belly was empty and all she brought up was bitter liquid. Even then she could still taste the acrid dust . . .

. . . the dust of Grute.

Edrik knelt beside her. "Here," he said gently, and handed her his waterskin. She poured water into her mouth, swirled it around and spat it out, then did it again . . . and again. "Mara, I never would have made you go in. I just wanted to see—"

"It's Grute," she said, as if he hadn't spoken. "The dust. In the hut. That's Grute. That's all that's left of him. Just like the Watcher."

"Can you stand?"

Mara nodded. Edrik helped her to her feet, then led her around to the sunny side of the hut. "Wait here," he said. Finding her legs shaky, she leaned her back against the wall, then sank down to a sitting position. The stones had soaked up enough sun to warm her aching body. She shut her eyes against the glare.

A shadow moved behind the dark red curtain of her eyelids. She opened them and blinked up at Keltan, who slid down the wall to sit at her right. He closed his own eyes. "My real name is Birik," he said, his voice low and rough. "But I'll never use it again. My father gave it to me, and I want *nothing* of his. He beat my mother to death when I was ten years old. The Autarch hung him for it. It's the only good thing the Autarch ever did. I watched him die. I wasn't supposed to be there, I was given to my mother's brother after . . . after my mother died . . . but I sneaked out. I wanted to see. And I saw. And I saw the Autarch. He was there himself that day, not for my father, there was some high-ranking City Official being hung for some offense, I don't know what. He was sitting on his beautiful white stallion. Keltan. And that's when I chose that name for my own." His eyes opened, but he didn't look at her: he gazed up at the mountains' gray-and-white peaks, wreathed in thin cloud. "I told Edrik all of this when I joined the un-Masked Army. He knows my real name. He knows why I'll never use it. And he swore he'd never tell anyone the truth." Finally, he turned his eyes on Mara. "Except for him, you're the only one who knows," he finished, his voice barely above a whisper.

Mara felt sick in a whole new way, sick for having tried to hurt Keltan with her revelation about his name, for having responded to her own hurt by trying to hurt a friend. "I'm sorry," she whispered. "I shouldn't have—"

Keltan shrugged. "It's all right." He looked back up at the mountains again, but his left hand found hers, held it. "There's an old saying: 'Be gentle, for everyone you meet is fighting a battle you know nothing of.' I think that goes double for those who have found their way to the un-Masked Army."

Mara nodded, lips pressed together.

Keltan's hand felt good in hers, so she kept it there. For about five minutes they simply sat in companionable silence; then Hyram came around the corner. "There you two are—" he began, then his face lost expression as his eyes darted to their linked hands. Suddenly embarrassed, Mara pulled free. Hyram's eyes flicked up again. "Father wants to see you," he said. His voice had gone wooden.

"But he'd like to see you in the hut. If you think you can stand it."

Mara nodded. "I can stand it." *I hope*, she thought. She left Keltan and Hyram looking at each other like tomcats circling one another stiff-legged in the street, and went around the corner of the hut to the open door. The rest of the party sat on the rocks, eating their midday meals, while the horses tugged at the sparse grasses growing among the stones. Illina gave her a friendly wave; she managed a smile in return, then ducked into the hut's dim interior.

At once she tasted the dust again. Trying not to think about what—who—it really was, she went through the front part of the hut into the back room, where magic seethed in the black stone basin.

Edrik had taken one of the empty urns from the shelves and was turning it over and over in his hands. He glanced up. "These pots," he said, "look like ordinary—"

"They're not." Mara could hardly tear her eyes from the basin, aswirl with beautiful, tempting magic. She couldn't believe Edrik couldn't see the glistening pool, the rainbow spray of colors chasing themselves around the walls, crawling over his face. "They're made of black lodestone," she said distantly. "Like the basin." Three steps took her to its side. "And this . . ." She dipped her finger into the pool, pulled it out sheathed in glimmering light. "This basin is the magic-well. It's black lodestone, too. It's drawing the magic out of a mass of the stone inside this ridge."

"There's magic in that basin right now?" Edrik set the urn aside, then leaned over the basin. He put his hand into it, his finger sliding beneath the surface of the magic but coming out clean. "I don't . . ."

"Watch," Mara said. There was so little magic on her finger, surely it would be safe to use it to . . .

She walked over to the stump of a candle set on the topmost of the shelves holding the black jars, touched her finger to it, and willed it to light.

Her finger stung as though she'd shuffled across her bedroom rug on a cold winter day and touched the metal door latch—and the wick burst into flame.

She turned back to Edrik. He was staring at the candle. "I guess ... I guess I believe you," he said.

"About time," she said tartly, and didn't feel at all sorry that he looked down, shamefaced. She turned her gaze back to the magic.

"Is there enough to fill some of these urns?" Edrik said, an odd tone in his voice.

She looked up. "Yes," she said. "Two, at least."

"Then fill them. We'll take them with us."

Mara wanted that, wanted to have magic close, just in case, but ... "Grelda said I shouldn't use magic."

"Oh, I know. She warned you against using it, and warned me against *letting* you use it," Edrik said. "But remember what *I* said?"

"That if it's necessary, I should use magic to save those who are risking their lives for me and my friend," Mara said slowly.

"Exactly." Edrik nodded at the basin. "Fill the urns. So that you have it ... as a last resort."

"All right," Mara said. The finger she had used to light the candle still hurt, sore as though stung by a bee. But she didn't tell Edrik that. Nor did she tell him that despite that pain, she longed to touch the magic again: longed to touch it, longed even more to use it. She couldn't explain it to herself, so how could she possibly explain it to him?

"I'll leave that to you, then," Edrik said. He snorted. "I can hardly help but leave it to you when I can't even *see* the stuff."

"It will only take a moment," Mara said.

Edrik nodded again, and went out.

Mara picked up the nearest urn. It was lighter than she'd expected, and she remembered what Pixot had told her about the stone being much less dense than it looked like it should be. "Now," she muttered to herself, "how does this work, exactly?"

She'd thought it would be a simple matter of dipping the urn below the surface of the pool and letting the magic flow into the urn like water. But when she took a closer look she realized that could not work, because the urn was so fat and round she would barely be able to get its mouth beneath the surface at all, certainly not enough to fill the urn.

She looked around for a ladle, or some other means of putting the magic into the jar, but saw nothing but urns, urns, and more urns, a dozen in all. *Well*, she thought, *I guess I'll get what I can.*

But the instant she dipped the urn into the pool she realized why no ladle was provided. Rather than flowing like water, the magic *crawled*, like something alive, oozing up and over the lip of the urn, slithering down inside, and then ... *coiling* was the word that came to Mara's mind, like a fat snake in a cozy gap in a rock. Mara knew magic was *not* a liquid, that it had to be something else, but her brain had insisted on seeing it as a kind of colored liquor right up until that moment. Now she swallowed, looking down in the magic-filled urn, the swirling, shifting colors as beautiful as always, but also deeply, deeply, disturbingly *weird*.

She simply set the next urn down inside the basin, and watched the magic crawl up the urn's side and pour down into its open mouth, like an overflowing milk jug in reverse. When it was done, only the faintest glimmer of magic colored the curved stone bottom of the basin.

On the lowest row of shelves lay stone lids, one per urn, with clever locking mechanisms, metal bars on hinges that lifted up and then snapped into place. With the urns sealed, Mara hefted each in turn. As far as she could tell, they weighed exactly the same as they had before the magic filled them. And yet she *knew*, without a shadow of doubt, that they were full. They might not push down harder on her hands, but they pushed down harder on her *mind*.

Also, she suddenly realized, her fingertips tingled. Not much, hardly noticeable, but the sensation was definitely there, definitely real.

She swallowed. Her Gift enabled her to use magic—but the more she was exposed to it, the more she realized that she didn't have a clue what it was, or how to control it.

The last time she *hadn't* controlled it, and it had almost killed her. What would happen if she tried to use the magic she had gathered in these black urns?

A last resort, she promised herself, carrying the urns out of the hut whose floor was white with the dust that was all that was left of Grute, whose air was thick with nightmare memories. *I'll only use it as a last resort.*

TWENTY

Waiting and Watching

THAT NIGHT, Mara did not wake screaming. She woke instead, the next morning, to Illina's gentle touch. "You slept," she said, smiling.

"I did," Mara said with pleased wonder. She yawned hugely. She felt more rested than she had in forever, it seemed. It was almost as if her return to the site that had figured so prominently in her nightmares had, at least temporarily, laid Grute's vengeful ghost to rest.

Not that I believe in ghosts, she hastened to assure herself as she got up, with a helping hand from Illina and only a *tiny* groan. *Grute is dead and gone. He is definitely not wandering around the woods as a headless spirit seeking revenge on . . .*

Stop it! She shook her head, released Illina's hand, and then went in search of the latrine and breakfast, in that order. The cut in her calf still ached, but now she was able to walk without limping. Her head didn't hurt at all, though the new scar itched.

Edrik called them all together once the horses were loaded. "We're only a few hours from the mine," he said. "We'll set up camp in the valley to the north, then reconnoiter from the same place on the ridge we used before. Once we know what's what, we can finalize plans for the actual rescue attempt." He glanced at Mara. "An attempt that will *only* be made if we are certain this friend of yours is still in the Warden's house. Are we clear on that?"

Mara nodded.

"Good." He turned and mounted. "Let's ride."

The morning passed without conversation. Everyone seemed busy with his or her own thoughts, and in any event, Edrik had made it clear that this close to the camp, with the risk of hunters or even Watchers in the woods, they must be quiet and alert. Keltan and Hyram rode behind and ahead of Mara, respectively, but neither rode beside her, and they hadn't seemed to be talking to each other even before they'd set out on the day's travel. Mara thought they were both being silly. All she'd done was hold Keltan's hand, it wasn't like she'd *kissed* him or anything, but she figured they could sort out their differences on their own. *What makes them think I'm interested in either one of them?* she told herself. *They're just friends.*

Aren't they?

She sighed.

They followed a tumbling stream along the bottom of the valley north of the camp, Edrik constantly scanning the southern slope. Shortly after noon—before they had yet stopped for their midday meal—he halted the column and pointed up the ridge. "There," he said.

Mara, peering up, saw a distinctive spire of silvery gray rock against the blue sky. Edrik turned and pointed the other way, at a clump of trees across the stream.

"Same camp as before, in the clearing in the middle of that wood." He looked back up to the spire of rock. "We'll send scouts up there on foot. I'll go first, with Mara and"—he looked around—"Hyram. He'll act as runner if I need to get word back down here in a hurry. I'll sort out watches for the rest of the day once I get back." He slid easily out of the saddle. Mara slid out a little less easily, but found the ground just the same. She hesitated, glancing at the urns of magic slung on either side of her horse. She put out a hand toward one, but Edrik shook his head. "We're just scouting," he said. "We shouldn't need any 'last resorts.'"

Hyram was off his horse, too. Grinning smugly, he handed his reins to Keltan. Keltan gave him a dirty look, but took them.

"Let's go," Edrik said, and as the column, now led by Tishka, splashed across the stream toward the clump of trees, he led Mara and Hyram up the slope.

The steep climb through stunted pines and over slippery grass and shifting stones would have left little breath for talking, even if there had been anything to say. And there wasn't, really. Mara's pulse quickened more than the climb could account for. *Was* Katia still in the Warden's house? Was she even still alive? If she wasn't, Edrik would do nothing. The camp would go on unmolested. *Unlike the women trapped in it*, she thought bitterly. Edrik's reasons for not launching a full-scale attack on the camp made perfect sense. But she still wanted desperately to bring the whole noxious hellhole crashing down around the ears of the Warden, the Watchers, and the trustees.

And how could they be certain *where* Katia was from way up here? If she didn't emerge from the Warden's house—and why should she?—how would they ever know? Edrik would do nothing without proof, and how could they possibly get it?

Unless . . .

Her foot slipped on a rock. Hyram, following her,

grabbed her waist and steadied her. His hands lingered, but she hardly noticed. The idea that had just occurred to her was possibly the most horrifying she'd ever had, more horrifying even than what she had done to Grute. But horrifying or not, she knew she would follow through with it if she had to . . .

. . . or never sleep again.

It won't come to that, she told herself, and fervently hoped it was true. Perhaps they would see Katia from their vantage point high above the camp. Perhaps their plans for rescue would work perfectly. Perhaps they'd all be safely back in the Secret City within a few days.

Perhaps.

They reached the spire of gray rock, blotched with brown, green, and orange lichen. Rounding it revealed a copse of tall pines, swaying and sighing in a chill wind Mara had hardly been aware of down in the valley but that now made her shiver despite her warm coat. Hyram noticed, and grinned at her. "If you think this is cold, just wait," he said. "Come winter, the wind up here will flay the flesh from your bones."

"I hope we're not up here *that* long," Mara said. Hyram laughed.

"Less noise," said Edrik without looking around. He pointed at the trees. "In there. Slowly." He led the way, slipping from trunk to trunk, Mara behind him, Hyram following her. About halfway through the clump of trees, Edrik said, "Now we crawl," and got down on his hands and knees. Feeling both silly and apprehensive, Mara followed suit. She watched Edrik's dusty boot heels, while the trees thinned ahead of them. Just before they reached the edge of the copse, Edrik dropped to his belly and wormed the rest of the way. Mara wriggled up beside him, and Hyram came up on her left, sandwiching her between him and his father. She lay there, panting, her leg wound throbbing slightly, and peered out through the tall grass.

Just beyond the last row of trees, the ground dropped

steeply away, all the way to the camp. Mara could see the path she remembered following with Pixot and the rest, which traveled a considerable distance to the east before beginning its switchbacking climb to the top of the ridge. Her heart raced at the sight of the palisade, the Warden's house, the longhouses, and the endlessly grinding water wheel. Even up here the constant pounding of the man-engine beat against her ears.

The morning shift change was long past and the evening one hours away, so the only people in view were a couple of Watchers patrolling the long boulevard, the trustee servant from the house — not Katia, unfortunately — digging in the gardens between the Warden's house, and a man, a tiny figure with a pitchfork, mucking out the stables at the far end of the camp. Mara glanced at Edrik. "You can't shoot arrows into the stables from here," she murmured.

"I never said we could," he replied. "But we can do it from *there*." He pointed across the camp. "See how the road to the main gate runs between two hills? From the top of the hill on the left, you can shoot into the compound. It's a blind shot — you can't actually see the stables over the wall — but it's definitely within bowshot." He glanced at her. "Let me worry about things like that. All *you've* got to worry about is spotting this friend of yours. Is that her in the gardens?"

Mara shook her head. "No. I told you, she's only a little older than me."

Edrik grunted. "Well, you'd better hope she shows herself. Every day we're this close to the camp, the more likely it is someone will spot us or stumble over us. If we can't confirm she's in there within a couple of days . . ."

"I know," Mara said. "You can't try a rescue without being sure the person you're rescuing is in there. I understand." And she felt a renewed chill.

Edrik looked at Hyram. "Go back down. Send up Skrit and Skrat. They can watch with Mara for the first shift. I'll stay here until they get back."

Hyram nodded and wriggled backward out of sight.

Mara kept staring down into the camp, willing Katia to make an appearance. But, of course, she didn't.

Nor did she for the next twenty minutes, until the twins replaced Edrik, nor for the next five hours after that, until it started to get dark and they all descended to the camp, Tishka taking their place: not with any hope of seeing Katia in the dark, but just to watch the Watchers in case they took a sudden notion to ride north.

On the journey there Mara hadn't talked much to the twins, quiet young men as alike as two kernels of wheat. She didn't talk to them much during the hours they spent together watching the camp, either (taking turns to stretch and take care of other needs as the afternoon wore away), since they seemed convinced that the Watchers far below had ears like foxes and would hear so much as a whisper. But as they began the descent to the camp in the twilight, Skrit (she thought) said, "All those people we saw, coming out of the ground, going into the ground, none of them was your friend?"

Mara shook her head. "She's in the big house," she said. *I hope.*

Skrat (probably) said, "And the camp is like that all the time? All those unMasked, disappearing underground, coming out again looking half-dead, day after day?"

Mara nodded again. "*If* they come out," she said, thinking of Shimma. "It never stops. Day after day. Until they're too sick to go down, or—if they're girls—they're sent to the Watchers in the barracks." She'd only spent two days in the mine, and the dark and the damp and the weight of stone hanging over her head had made regular appearances in her dreams since, the sense of doom and dread at least making a change from the hyperreal visions of Grute's head exploding, although not offering as much relief as she could have hoped.

Skrit shook his head. "I hope we can get your friend out. I wish we could get them *all* out."

Mara felt a surge of gratitude.

The unMasked Army's tents were tucked so far back in the thick, shadowy stand of woods that she didn't think she could have found them without the twins' guidance. The gloomy, fireless camp and the cold supper of dried meat, hard cheese, and crusty bread provided little cheer. Mara sat in the silvery light of the three-quarter moon, munching on her food with her back to a tree trunk, staring at nothing in particular. Keltan and Hyram hadn't been around when she entered the camp; now she saw them emerge from the woods together. Both were limping. They came over to her and sat down on either side of her.

She glanced from one to the other. Though it was hard to see in the moonlight, she thought Keltan had a black eye, and there seemed to be a smear of blood on Hyram's upper lip. "Run into something mean in the woods?" she said.

They exchanged looks and grinned. "You could say that," said Keltan.

"Absolutely," said Hyram.

They were fighting, Mara realized. *Over me?* It was a strange—and strangely exhilarating—thought. But she couldn't exactly ask, and they didn't volunteer to tell her. All she knew was that something had changed: the tension that had been building between the two had broken, and they joked and laughed with her for the next hour as if nothing had happened. It was all very strange, but also quite wonderful, and she relaxed and entered into the banter and didn't think about the mining camp or Katia for sometimes four or five minutes at a time.

Until that night. Headless Grute stayed away, but taking his place in the fierce competition to rob her of sleep was an interminable dream of being trapped deep underground, trying to find a way out while water rose from ankles to knees to waist to chest to neck to . . .

She woke, gasping, saw a hint of light in the sky, realized it was pointless to even try to go back to sleep, and crawled out of her tent, hoping that today would be the day she saw Katia. If she didn't, it might instead be the day she did something really, really stupid.

The wind of the day before had blown in thick, low, scudding clouds that hid the tops of the mountains even after the light grew bright enough to see them. It had turned colder, too, and without fires to warm either them or their food, everyone was out of sorts that morning. No doubt Keltan most of all, Mara thought: he had taken the midnight-to-morning watch atop the ridge and must be half frozen, though he hadn't yet descended to complain about it.

Edrik stood in the middle of the camp squinting up into the soft gray mass that had swallowed the peaks. "One more day," he said. "There could be snow in these clouds, and if it snows, we cannot spend another night without fire."

"I don't think I can spend another night without fire whether it snows or not," Illina said.

Edrik looked the other way, up the slope to the gray rock spire. "We all need warming," he said. "And hot food. This cloud is so thick and the wind so strong no smoke will clear the ridge. At night a glow might betray us, so we must still sleep in the cold and the dark, but for now . . ." He nodded to Illina. "Light a fire," he said. "Just one. Driest branches you can find."

Mara relaxed a little. She'd been afraid Edrik would declare then and there that they would have to break camp and return to the Secret City, without even given Katia a chance to make an appearance. But it looked as if she would get her second day of watching.

The wind gusted, tossing the treetops. Yellow and brown leaves cascaded around her. Mara, shivering, wrapped her arms around herself. She did not think she would get a third day.

"Once the fire is built, warm yourself while you can," Edrik told her. "You must stay on the ridge all day to watch for your friend." Mara heard an unspoken "... *if she's still alive.*"

Edrik set the watches. Tishka and Illina would join her for the first three hours. Skrit and Skrat would be her companions for the next three. And Keltan, having had the day to catch up on his sleep, would join Hyram in keeping her company during the last three hours, which would take them back to the edge of darkness. Mara didn't know whether that was good news or bad. If the day wound down with no sign of Katia, and she had to do what she *feared* she would have to do, what would Keltan and Hyram do in response?

She took full advantage of the fire Illina soon had blazing, sitting as close to it as she could to bake the chill out of her bones and ease the morning soreness that was the residue of everything that had happened to her over the past few days. She massaged her calf. The cut seemed almost fully healed, but every once in a while it would jab her with pain, as though to remind her it wasn't quite gone yet.

Illina handed her a steaming bowl of grain mush with a big dollop of butter in the middle of it, and she shoveled it down. It tasted like, well, like mush, but at least it was hot and filling. Meanwhile, Illina busied herself heating water in a pot, into which she tossed a packet of what looked like dry grass, taken from the leather pouch she wore at her side. She ladled some into a mug and handed it to Mara. Mara sipped it cautiously. It had a bitter, earthy taste. Mara made a face. "What *is* it?"

"Tellik tea," Illina said as she handed out mugs to the others.

Hyram slurped his back as though it was redcherry juice. "Just what I needed," he said. "Thanks, Illina."

Mara took a second sip. It didn't taste any better than the first. "It's ... um ..." She hesitated, searching for the right word, not wanting to hurt Illina's feelings.

But Illina just laughed. "It's absolutely awful. You

don't have to tell me that. But nothing beats it for warming and waking you on a cold morning."

Mara, who definitely felt the need for both warming *and* waking, drained her mug despite the taste, and sure enough, felt both warmer and marginally more alert once finished. Edrik stood a few paces away from the others, sipping from his mug while peering up at the sky. He drained the last of the tea and returned to the fire. "Daylight's wasting. Illina, I'll clean up. You and Tish and Mara need to get going. I'm sure Keltan is wondering where you are."

Shortly after that, Mara and the two women made the arduous climb to the stone spire. They relieved Keltan, sending him down the hill with the good news that a fire and hot food awaited him, and then buried themselves in the cover of the copse.

The morning shift change had already passed. Only a few Watchers and trustees moved around the camp. The raw wind chasing the clouds down from the mountains kept flicking Mara's hair in her face, forcing her to brush it back repeatedly until she finally got smart and tucked the stray ends under her ugly rabbit-fur hat. Unfortunately, no amount of twitching or rearranging her cloak seemed able to counter the wind's disconcerting ability to get under the collar of her coat and send cold tendrils down her back.

But despite the discomfort, which only grew as the hours crawled past, Mara stayed put all day, except for once answering the call of nature. As she hurried back from the far corner of the copse where she had relieved herself, she worried. If Katia had emerged while she wasn't present, would the others even notice her? From this distance Katia might look like an adult, like one of the trustees. Mara trusted only herself to spot her.

But Katia did not appear: not during the morning, and not during the early afternoon, when Skrit and Skrat silently replaced Illina and Tishka. Mara stayed put through their quiet watch, and on into the final watch when, with the sun already westering, Keltan and Hyram joined her. "Any sign?" Keltan said.

Mara shook her head miserably.

"Are you sure . . . ?" Hyram began, but subsided when Mara gave him a fierce look.

The late afternoon wore away. Watchers and trustees moved from building to building. The trustee servant from the house once more dug in the garden, pulling out redroots, it looked like. Once Mara saw the Warden stride down the boulevard, over the bridge, and toward the minehead. He returned half an hour later. She pointed him out to Keltan and Hyram.

Occasionally unMasked emerged from the minehead and pulled/pushed wagonloads of stone to the nondescript building, in the left-hand nearest corner from their vantage point, where the magic was extracted. She pointed that out to the boys, too. Once a wagon loaded with black stone rolled through the smaller gate behind that building, trundling out of sight along a rutted track that led around the shoulder of a hill. *Somewhere there must be an enormous waste heap*, Mara thought.

Even from such huge quantities of ore, she couldn't believe they were extracting much magic. The threads of magic she had seen when her lamp had gone out in the mine had been so minute, so insubstantial, she thought a ton of black lodestone couldn't possibly yield more than a single urn of magic.

She also wondered how they drew it out of the rock, and how much magic was stored in the extraction building. Presumably that was also where the urns from the magic-wells were stored. She wondered how long it took to collect enough magic to create a full load to ship back to Tamita. She wondered a lot of things while she lay in the trees with Hyram and Keltan; but mostly she wondered where Katia was.

She kept glancing at the sky. The sun only occasionally peeked through the scudding cloud cover, but every time she saw it, it was noticeably lower. *Maybe Edrik will give me one more day*, she thought, as the already gray day began to dim toward twilight. *Maybe . . .*

But then Edrik himself wriggled into place beside the three of them. "Any luck?" he asked.

Mara shook her head.

"I meant what I said," Edrik told her. "It's not safe for us to linger here any longer. If your friend does not make an appearance before dark tonight, then tomorrow, we return to the Secret City."

Mara said nothing.

Edrik took another long look at the camp below, grunted, and squirmed away again.

Hyram gave her an apologetic look. "Don't blame him," he said. "He has to do everything he can to keep his people safe—"

"I don't blame him," Mara said.

Keltan put a comforting hand on her shoulder. She let him.

But in truth, she was hardly aware of either of them. Her thoughts were entirely focused on what she intended to do when darkness descended.

That time came soon enough—too soon. The twilight deepened. Hyram and Keltan exchanged a look they probably thought she didn't notice, then Keltan said gently, "We need to get back. Don't want to go down that path in the dark. Tishka must already be on her way up."

"We gave it our best," Hyram said. "I hate to say it, but—"

"Then don't," Mara said shortly. She took a deep breath. "You two go on back to the rock spire. I'll be along in a minute."

Keltan looked uncomfortable. "I don't like leaving you alone up here to—"

She gave him a look. "I've been lying here for hours," she said. "What I need to do I really don't want you watching."

He reddened. Hyram gave a muffled snort of laughter. "Oh. I didn't . . . sorry . . . I'll . . . right. We'll just wait at the rock. Um, take your time."

Mara rolled over and sat up to watch them move away through the trees. The moment they were out of sight, she got to her feet, but she didn't follow them.

Instead she turned, took another deep breath, and started down the slope to the camp.

TWENTY·ONE

Fire in the Night

THROAT DRY, HEART RACING, Mara picked her
way down the ridge. She had realized the day before
what she would have to do if Katia did not appear, if she
wanted to be certain she had done everything in her
power to save her friend. But a full day of thinking about
it still hadn't prepared her for the awful reality of deliberately returning to the one place she never, ever wanted
to be again.

Yet somehow she pushed aside the choking terror
and kept going, down the slope, through the trees and
brushy undergrowth that played such an important role
in the unMasked Army's rescue plans, right up to the
palisade. Just as Edrik had predicted, no one challenged
her: the sentries were all looking in, not out.

Nor could they possibly hear her above the constant

rumbling and grinding of the big water wheel and the man-engine it drove. That suited her: the last thing she wanted to do was give the Watchers a hint as to which way she had come from, lest the Warden send out an exploratory patrol that might stumble across the others.

Staying so close to the palisade that she could only be seen by a sentry if he leaned over and looked straight down, she made her way around the camp toward the main gate. She wondered if Keltan and Hyram had yet decided she was taking too long and returned to find her gone; wondered how they would react; wondered if they were even then looking down with horror at her tiny figure creeping through the shadows.

She wondered even more what Edrik would do when he found out. She knew what she was *counting* on him to do: realize that he would have to go through with the rescue he'd originally planned, for her, if not for Katia. Her plan, such as it was, was to find Katia and make sure they both escaped when that rescue came.

Assuming Katia was alive.

But it was also possible that Edrik would refuse to risk his small band to save her after she had so deliberately flouted his orders, and would ride back to the Secret City, perhaps to plan and launch another attempt later ... or perhaps not.

In which case, when she entered the gates of the work camp for the second time, it might also be for the last time.

The thought actually brought her to a stop, back against the unpeeled logs of the palisade, chest heaving. *I could still escape*, she thought. *Get up the slope without being seen, return to the camp ...*

But if she did that she would be abandoning Katia to a terrible fate, and that she could not bear. Better to face the horrors of the camp than the horror of leaving Katia in the hands of the Warden and Watchers.

She forced herself to start moving again. She crept to the corner of the western wall, turned along the southern wall, and finally reached the main gate. There she abandoned stealth and pounded on it with both hands. She'd thought long and hard, during the endless day hiding in the woods, about what she would say. The important thing, she'd decided, was to sound frightened and breathless.

She didn't think that would be difficult.

She kept pounding on the gate until it swung inward, and then fell forward onto her hands and knees, crying, "Thank you!" She looked up then, and sure enough, both fright and breathlessness came naturally as she found two gleaming sword tips not five inches from her face, and saw beyond them the grim black Masks of Watchers. "I'm Mara," she gasped out. "Warden sent me out with the geologists ... bandits attacked us ... I escaped ... I've got to see the Warden!"

The Watchers exchanged glances. One of them sheathed his sword, stepped forward, grabbed her arm and hauled her roughly to her feet. "Close the gate," he said to his partner, and then half-led, half-dragged her up the long, broad boulevard, between the silent longhouses on either side, tattered banners of smoke streaming from their chimneys in the ever-more-bitter wind.

The Watchers patrolling the boulevard stared at her as she passed. The big house at the end of the crushed-rock path also seemed to stare at her, its glowing, diamond-paned windows like glittering insectoid eyes. The smell of woodsmoke mingled with the mouthwatering aroma of roasting meat. Her stomach growled: she'd had nothing but a little bread and water since her porridge and tellik tea that morning.

The Watcher led her up the stairs to the ironbound door, and rapped on it with his fist. After a moment, Mara heard impatient footsteps clattering across the marble floor beyond. The door swung open a crack, and a stern white Mask with black scrollwork on each cheek peered out. Mara recognized it from her time in the house; it belonged to the Warden's secretary, a man whose name she'd never learned. She heard him gasp, and then he swung the door wide. "I'll tell him you're here," he said. "Wait in the study."

The Watcher dragged Mara into the room where she had first met the Warden, blessedly warm even though the fire had burned down to embers, turned her to face the door, and stood close behind her. Too close; she was uncomfortably aware of him looming behind her. Two minutes later the Warden rushed in, still tying the belt of a long blue robe, his longish, steel-gray hair dripping water on his shoulders and down the forehead of his black-and-red Mask. *I got him out of the bath*, Mara thought with a flash of bitter amusement. *Good. Maybe he'll catch pneumonia.*

This time, the Warden didn't sit down behind the desk. He strode up to Mara and glared down at her, his eyes narrowed behind the Mask, mouth set in a stern frown. "Tell me what happened. Now!"

Mara began her carefully prepared tale. "We got to the cave where the black lodestone is. I went in, and—"

"What did you see?" the Warden interrupted. "Did you see magic?"

Mara shook her head. "Only a little," she lied. "No more than I saw in the rocks here in the mine. But I didn't have much chance to look. All of a sudden one of the Watchers started dragging me out. Then just before I reached the opening, the rope went slack. When I went out . . . they were all dead." She remembered the Watcher straddling her, the hand in her hair, that sudden rush of magic, and a convulsive swallow came naturally. "All of them. The Watchers, the geologists . . ."

"Dead?" The frown on the Warden's Mask deepened. *"How?"*

"Arrows," Mara said. "From above. And just as I came out, the ones who had shot them came howling into the ravine . . ." She shuddered. "Bandits. UnMasked. Half starved, filthy. Mostly men, but a few women. One man grabbed me. I screamed. I thought he was going to kill me, or . . ." She let the terror of the moment when the Watcher had put his knife to her throat fill her voice. "But then a woman stopped him. She said I might be useful. As a slave. Or for other things.

"They took me away. They had a camp . . . over there somewhere." She waved vaguely to the southeast, away from both the Secret City and Edrik's camp in the next valley. "It took us two days to get there."

The Warden's frown did not soften. "So how did you end up back here, alone?"

"I escaped. Two days ago. I don't think they thought I'd run away. They kept telling me I was better off with them than I was here."

The Warden's eyes reflected brief yellow sparks of candlelight as he leaned forward, until he was so close she had to crane her neck back to see his Mask. Water that had flowed from his wet hair down his Mask dripped from its gleaming black nose onto her cheek. She raised a trembling hand and wiped the moisture away. "I'm surprised you didn't agree with them," the Warden said softly.

Mara instinctively tried to step back, but all that accomplished was to press her up against the Watcher's hard, unyielding body—hardly an improvement. "No!" she said. "They were awful. *Awful.* And the men . . . they kept . . . looking at me." She shook her head violently. "No. I don't like it here, but I'm valuable to you. I have the Gift. I didn't have any value to them except as another body." She decided to let out a little bit more of the truth. "And . . . and you have Katia. As a hostage." She stared into the Warden's eyes through his Mask, and asked the all-important question. "She's still here, isn't she? In the house?"

"She's here," the Warden said. "Although she wouldn't have been much longer. A search party was heading out tomorrow to look for you. If they hadn't found you . . ." He shrugged. "She's of no value on her own except as—in your words—'another body.'"

You cold-blooded bastard, Mara thought, hate for the

man hidden behind that fancy Mask burning like acid in her chest. *None of us are of any value to you except me; and I know just how long that will last. If I lose my Gift, or I don't find you a new source of magic, then I'll be as worthless to you as Katia and all the rest of the unMasked. And then it's back to the mines.*

The uncomfortably warm bulk of the Watcher behind her, pressed into her back, reminded her of the only other possibility.

Or into the barracks.

"As to your own value," the Warden went on, "it is perhaps not as great as you think." Her body shifted from overheated to chilled as he echoed her thoughts of an instant before. "The cave you went to explore is our best hope for a new mine. Yet you tell me it is worthless. And that my geologists are dead. We have found no other deposits of black lodestone that will require your unique ability to assess. Nor do we have anyone with the expertise to resume the search."

Mara's breath caught. If the Warden decided here and now to throw her and Katia back into the general camp population, the unMasked Army wouldn't be able to rescue them: wouldn't even *try.* "I may have overstated . . . I mean, maybe there's more magic in that cavern than I thought. Than I saw. Than I *thought* I saw. I mean I only had a minute to look." *Oh, smoothly done, you idiot.*

The Warden snorted. "I suspected as much." He leaned forward. "Perhaps you have deluded yourself into believing that lying to me about the amount of magic in that deposit will, by preventing me from starting a new mine, somehow benefit the unMasked. But think again. If this mine closes, there will no longer be *any* reason for the Autarch to keep the unMasked alive. Every child whose Masking fails will thenceforth be executed that same day, as indeed they once were, in the first years of the Masks, before the Autarch realized what a waste of valuable workers that was. Do you want those future executions on your conscience?"

At least I have *a conscience*, Mara thought in fury, but out loud, she let defeat creep into her voice. "All right," she said dully. "You win. Yes, there's magic there. I don't know how much. I really did only have a moment to look. But more than here. Far more. More than enough to mine if I'm any judge."

"Hmmm." The Warden stared down at her a moment longer, as if somehow sensing she *still* wasn't telling him the whole truth, but then, to her immense relief, he stepped back. She eased herself away from the Watcher. "Very well. For the moment, I will take you at your word. But be warned. The party of Watchers I planned to send to the cave you explored will *still* be making that journey. And if they find evidence that you have lied to me . . ."

"They won't," Mara said stoutly. *Or if they do, it won't matter; because either I won't still be here or . . .*

She let that thought trail off in her own mind like the Warden's voice had trailed off at the end of his threat. After all, they both ended the same way for her: badly.

Very badly.

"Can I see Katia?" she said. "So she knows I'm back."

The Warden shrugged. "She sleeps in the room you were in. Tonight you will share it." He cinched his bathrobe tighter as he looked over her head at the Watcher. "Take her upstairs. My bathwater is getting cold." He left the office, and had vanished from view by the time the Watcher and Mara emerged into the foyer. The Watcher took her up the wooden stairs to the second floor hallway and down it to the room she had occupied before being sent on the expedition with the geologists.

Lamplight shone under the door. The Watcher unlocked it with a key from his belt, then swung it wide. Mara stepped in.

Katia stood at the window, staring out into the darkness. "I'm not hungry," she began, but then must have caught a reflection in the glass, because she spun, eyes wide. "You!" she gasped. "I thought you were dead. I thought *I* was dead."

"Not quite," Mara said. "Though it was a very near thing." She glanced at the Watcher. "Thank you," she said. "That will be all."

The Watcher took a menacing step toward her. "Don't get smart, girl," he growled. He nodded over her head at Katia. "Ask *her* what happens if you get smart." He made an obscene gesture in Katia's direction. Then he turned and went out, slamming the door behind him. A moment later the key turned in the lock with a sharp, definitive click.

The two girls stood facing each other. Mara forced herself not to look away from Katia's hard, accusing stare. "How have you been treated?" she said finally into the lengthening silence. "Since I left, I mean."

Katia's cold expression did not thaw. "Well enough. Work in the kitchen is better than the other uses they've put me to." At the first sight of Mara, Katia's voice had briefly lifted out of the curious deadness Mara had noted in her tone before she left; but now that deadness filled it once more, each word falling into the silence like a cold stone onto frozen ground. *She sounds like someone who has given up*, Mara thought. *Well, maybe I can change that.*

She went over to the window and, like Katia a moment before, gazed out into the darkness—or near darkness. On this side of the house, there were no decorative diamond panes, and though the large squares of glass in the window were a bit wavy, she could see clearly enough the lights in the magic extraction building, off to her right. Mara looked up toward where she knew the ridge towered over the camp, and wondered if Keltan or Hyram were staring down at her even then. She hoped so. She hoped they might even be able to see her standing in the window with Katia. She hoped that very much; because if the Watchers were setting out tomorrow on the trail of the vanished (except for her) prospecting party, the best chance for a rescue might be this very night.

Would Edrik act that quickly? She didn't know. But Katia needed hope, and so did she.

"We may not be here long," Mara said, speaking barely above a whisper, in case the Watcher lingered outside the door.

Katia stepped closer. "What?"

Mara turned her back on the window and motioned to the bed. They took the few steps to it and then sat down side by side, backs to the door. Mara leaned in close to the other girl. "There are a few things you don't know," she murmured. "Quite a few." And then she told Katia everything that had *really* happened since the attack on the wagon. She told her about the Secret City, though not where it was; told her about the unMasked Army, and Catilla's and Edrik's plans for her; and told her about Grute.

Katia listened silently until Mara described that horrifying moment when Grute had come after her, naked and threatening, and she had clapped her hands to his head and killed him on the spot. That made her eyes light up. "Oh!" she said. "What I wouldn't give for *that* power." The deadness in her tone lifted as she said it; in fact, she sounded so savage and fierce it was almost frightening. "I had a little of the Gift," she said, longing in her tone. "But after the Masking it was gone. Do you think it will come back?"

"I don't know," Mara said. "I still have it. But I seem to be the only one." *And maybe only because my father made a special Mask for me*, she thought. She still didn't know how she felt about that. Was she really better off here, in mortal peril, than she would have been safely Masked and apprenticed to her father, even if the new, controlling, Mask had leached all possibility of rebellion from her spirit, changed her the way it had changed her friend Sala?

She had a hard time believing it.

"Oh." Katia's excitement slipped away, her voice

sinking back down into deadness. "Then nothing's changed for me."

"Yes, it has," Mara insisted. "I'm not finished." She hurried on through the account of the prospecting trip, the attack by the unMasked Army, the magical death—disintegration!—of the Watcher . . .

. . . and then her bargain with Catilla. "I told her I wouldn't help the unMasked Army unless they rescued you. I made you hostage to the Warden to ensure my good behavior. I couldn't live with myself if you suffered because of me."

Katia looked at her with cold disbelief. "You're a fool," she said flatly. "You came back here to *save* me? Nobody can save me. I'm already lost. I'm already doomed. I have been since the moment I set foot in this camp."

"But don't you understand? If we get out of here—"

"Getting me out of here won't change what they did to me in the barracks," Katia snarled. "Take me to your 'Secret City,' take me to the end of the world, it won't change what happened. I will never be who I was before the night they . . ." Her lip trembled and her voice wavered into silence. "I will never forget," she said after a long pause. "Every night, I wake up screaming—"

"As do I!" Mara snapped. "I see Grute's head exploding, I see the Watcher turned to dust, I see—"

"It's not the same!" Katia screamed at her, showing the most life she'd shown since Mara had entered the room. "Don't you get it? *You're* having nightmares about things you've done, things you did to save yourself, things you did for a *purpose. My* nightmares . . ." She swallowed, and her voice dropped to a whisper. "*My* nightmares are about things that were *done* to me, while I lay there, helpless. I just lay there, I let them . . . do those things . . . make *me* do things . . . and I didn't try to fight back. I didn't do anything. I just took it. I gave up. *I gave up!*" And then she was weeping, hopeless, body-shaking sobs that were the most horrible thing Mara had ever heard. Mara awkwardly tried to put her arms around Katia, but the other girl pushed her away and flung herself facedown on the bed.

Mara looked helplessly at her heaving back, not knowing what to do. *Edrik will come*, she thought. *We'll both get out of here. All she needs is a fresh start. All she needs is time. All she needs . . .*

But the truth was, Mara didn't know *what* Katia needed. Katia was right: she didn't have a clue how Katia felt. How could she, without going through what Katia had gone through?

Her heart spasmed, as though someone had reached inside her chest and squeezed it with an ice-cold hand.

If Edrik doesn't come, I will *go through what Katia has gone through.*

No! she thought fiercely. *I* won't *let that happen! Not to me, and not to Katia—not again.*

But it was one thing to make such a promise, and quite another to keep it.

Katia's sobs subsided. Her breathing deepened. She'd fallen asleep. Sprawled diagonally across the bed, she'd left no room for Mara. *Well*, she thought, *I don't plan to sleep anyway*.

She got up and pulled one of the padded armchairs over to the window. No, she wouldn't sleep. She'd remain awake, vigilant, waiting for the moment when Edrik and the others came over the north wall of palisade. As they surely would.

Wouldn't they?

She grabbed a spare blanket from the wardrobe, doused the lantern, and then settled into the chair, stretching out her sore legs onto a footstool and giving her again-aching wounded calf a good rub before wrapping herself in the blanket. The glow of lights within the camp was just enough to show her the logs of the palisade some fifty yards beyond the back wall of the Warden's house.

She had no intention of going to sleep. She knew how important it was to stay awake and keep watch. But the blanket was warm and the chair was comfortable, and she had spent a long, cold, and *un*comfortable day hiding in the woods above the camp before making the terrifying descent to it. The remarkable thing, really, was not that she fell asleep, but that she stayed awake as long as she did.

An indeterminate amount of time later, she woke with a start. The sky had cleared. Moonlight silvered the logs of the palisade, but the only light in the room came from the lingering glow in the hearth.

Katia moaned in her sleep, a helpless, despairing sound. Was that what had woken her?

She listened hard. Katia moaned again. The wind, rising once more, elicited an echoing moan from the eaves. But above that, she could hear faint shouts growing louder. Someone pounded on the front door downstairs. Voices rang in the halls, questioning, yelling orders. Footsteps thundered down the stairs. She thought she heard someone shout, "Fire!"

Katia moaned again, flung herself over onto her back, gasped, and then sat bolt upright. She scrambled frantically backward until her shoulders were pressed against the carved headboard and pulled her knees tight to her chest, hugging them fiercely. She stared around the room with eyes wide and white in the faint red glow of the embers. Her gaze fell on Mara. "What's going on?" she gasped.

"If we're lucky, we're about to be rescued," Mara said.

"Rescued?"

"Shh!" Mara heard fresh footsteps in the hall outside. The door rattled as someone checked the lock, then the footsteps hurried away. Doors banged, and suddenly the house had an empty feel.

Mara turned back to the window, peered out . . . and her heart leaped as she saw shadowy figures dropping down the palisade wall like fat black spiders. "They're coming!" she breathed.

"Who's coming?" Katia said.

"The unMasked Army!" Mara ran to the door, put her ear to it, and listened hard.

A splintering crash downstairs, like a door being smashed in. Sudden shouts, breaking glass, a gurgling scream . . . silence. Mara almost pushed her head through the wood, trying to hear more. Then she heard the slap of booted feet, rushing toward her. "Check every room," said a voice, and her heart leaped.

Edrik!

"In here!" she shouted, banging on the door with her fists.

Footsteps pounded toward her. "Step away!" Edrik called. She stumbled backward, and a moment later the door crashed inward, the doorjamb splintering.

Edrik stood in the doorway, silhouetted against the lamplight in the corridor. The sword he held in his right hand glinted in a strange, dark way.

Blood, Mara realized. *It's covered with blood.*

Edrik's head turned toward Katia, her frightened eyes bright in the yellow light streaming in through the open door. "That's her?" he snapped.

Mara nodded.

"Then let's get the two of you the hell out of here." He stepped back and looked both ways along the hall. The lantern light brought his face into view for the first time. Blood had splattered one cheek. More blood stained his clothes. Mara didn't think any of it was his.

Mara rushed over to Katia. "Come on," she said. "They're going to get us out of here."

Katia hung back. "They can't," she whispered. "And if they don't—they'll catch us. The Warden will punish us. He'll send us both to the Watchers—"

"Katia," Mara said, trying to keep her voice calming, even while her brain was screaming at Katia to *move*, now, at once, before the Watchers who had run off to deal with the fire the unMasked Army had presumably set burning in the stables realized something else was happening behind their backs. "They *can* get us away. They have a safe place, their own city, the Secret City. I told you about it. They've lived safely there for decades. The Warden can't find you there. The Watchers can't find you there. Even the Autarch can't find you there." *I hope*, she thought. "But to get there, we have to go, *now*. Put your shoes on."

Katia stared at her a moment, then lunged for the edge of the bed. She got tangled in the bedspread and tumbled over the side, hitting the floor with a thud. Mara helped her up and helped her find her shoes.

"Hurry up!" Edrik snarled. "We don't know how long the fire will keep them busy. And someone may have seen or heard us. Watchers could be back here any minute."

"Coming!" Mara shouted. Katia had her shoes on and laced at last. Mara grabbed her arm and pulled her to the door.

Edrik immediately headed for the stairs. At the landing, a body lay crumpled against the blood-smeared wall. A white Mask with black scrollwork had more than half crumbled away from the slack, staring face behind it.

Averting her eyes, Mara hurried past the secretary's corpse and down the stairs in Edrik's wake. In the foyer, Keltan stood by the main door, the gleaming sword in *his* hand unbloodied. Alone of all the unMasked Army, he wore a backpack. He had the door open a crack and was peering through it.

Mara looked over her shoulder to the back door of the house. At the end of the hallway a body sprawled, half in and half out of the door, and Mara, able to see that he was unMasked, felt a pang of regret. The Warden's secretary upstairs she'd felt nothing for, but this dead man hadn't even been a Watcher, just a trustee.

One who threw in his lot with the Warden and Watchers, she reminded herself.

It didn't really make her feel any better.

Tishka straddled the body, peering out into the gardens. Illina stood behind her. She looked back, saw Mara, and flashed a brief, fierce grin.

"Where are the others?" Mara said.

"Skrit and Skrat are our best archers," Edrik said, "so I sent them up onto the hill to shoot the fire arrows. Hyram is just the other side of the wall: we need someone there for when we go back over the top. Which we're about to do. Keltan, close and lock the front door. Shove that cabinet in front of it. Illina, you lead the—"

Tishka swore and slammed the door shut. She spun to face the others. "Watchers on the walls! They just found the ropes. And cut them. They're running for the watchtowers. They'll be—"

A deep, angry gong shivered the air.

"—sounding the alarm," she finished grimly.

The gong sounded again. And again. And kept on sounding, a sound no one in the camp—no one above ground, anyway—could fail to hear.

Edrik spun to face Mara. "Any other way out?"

"I don't know," Mara said, heart fluttering in her chest like a trapped bird.

"Yes, you do," Katia said. Now she was the one who sounded calm, so strangely calm that Mara shot a glance at her, wondering what had changed. Her face in the dim yellow light gave nothing away. "Remember? There's a small gate inside the building they take the ore into. They send wagons out through it, to haul away the rock and the"—she shot a glance at Mara—"magic, I guess."

Edrik nodded. "Then that's our exit. Out the back. Stick to shadows. They'll have crossbows in the watchtowers. Keep moving. *Damn it*, I wish the sky hadn't cleared." He reached up and doused the lamp that hung in the hallway near the back door. Keltan, who had just dragged a heavy cabinet across the front door, took the hint and doused the two lanterns in the foyer.

In the sudden darkness, Tishka eased open the back door. Keeping low, she looked out, both ways.

Keltan came up close to Mara. "Take this," he said, and shoved something into her hands. She recognized it as his backpack. "It has one of the urns of magic in it. Don't know if it will do any good, but I brought it just in case."

Mara nodded. She pulled on the backpack, tightened the straps. "I just wish I knew how to use it," she whispered. *If we get out of this . . .*

"Clear," Tishka said.

"Then go," Edrik said, and Tishka dashed out into the night, Illina close behind—and, to Mara's surprise, Katia right behind her. Mara hurried after Katia, Keltan's backpack bouncing on her back; Keltan followed her, and Edrik brought up the rear.

Deep moonshadow cloaked the back of the house—but not deep enough. Mara heard a strange hissing sound and a solid "thunk!" A crossbow bolt sprouted from a timber by her head. She gasped.

"Run!" Edrik shouted. They abandoned all pretense of secrecy and dashed full-tilt through the gardens, frost-blighted plants crunching beneath their feet. Mara expected Watchers to boil out of the back doors of the barracks like termites from a rotten log, but none appeared. From the orange glow she glimpsed off to her right and the distant shouts of men, mingled with the terrified screams of horses, she suspected the stable fire had been a more successful diversion than Edrik had dared hope.

Bolts hissed past them like enormous angry insects. Ahead, the magic extraction building loomed, a black bulk hung with four lanterns, two framing the closed double doors through which the wagons full of ore from the mine entered the facility, the other two bordering a smaller door, at the top of a narrow wooden porch with four steps.

Edrik dashed past her toward that porch, sword ready. "Tishka, Illina, with me!" he shouted. Tishka matched his speed.

We're going to make it, Mara thought. *We're going to make it . . .*

Then Illina made a strange gasping noise and fell, limbs loose like a marionette whose strings had been cut. She tumbled bonelessly across the weed-covered ground. Too close behind her to stop, Mara and Katia tripped over her body. Mara hit the ground hard, rolled twice, and came up spitting dirt. Edrik and Tishka ran on, oblivious.

"No!" Mara cried. She crawled on her hands and knees back toward Illina. "Illina!"

The young woman lay on her back, gasping, staring up at the cloud-streaked sky. "Tell . . . my little sister . . ." she choked out, but whatever she wanted Mara to tell her sister remained unsaid; she gave a sighing cough, blood gushed from her mouth, she shuddered, and then her labored breathing ceased. Her eyes, already glazing over, remained open.

"No!" Mara sobbed. Keltan reached for her arms, tried to pull her up. She resisted.

"Mara!" he whispered urgently. "Crossbows—"

"The building shields us from the watchtower," Katia said. "She almost made it." She picked up Illina's fallen sword. At first it glinted silver in the moonlight, but as she turned toward Mara it caught the red glow from the stable fire and turned, for a moment, the color of blood. "But now she's dead—like the Warden will be when I find him."

And then, to Mara's horror, she dashed away—not toward the building, but toward the fire.

"Katia!" Mara screamed.

Keltan dragged her to her feet. "Let her go!" he shouted. He glanced at the extraction building. Mara followed his gaze and saw Edrik and Tishka standing on either side of the smaller door, peering back, trying to see what had happened through eyes dazzled by the lanterns. "Come on!" He tugged at her arm.

But Mara threw him off. "I'm not letting Katia get

herself killed," she said fiercely. "Not after Illina . . ." Her throat closed in sudden grief. "Do what you want," she managed to choke out. And then, though everything in her screamed that she was being an idiot—everything except for the fierce, insistent voice that told her she *had* to do this, and drowned out all else—she ran after Katia: away from the gate that would take them out of the camp, away from the unMasked who had risked everything to rescue her, away from her only real hope of safety, and toward the flickering red light of the fire . . .

. . . and all the Watchers in the camp.

TWENTY-TWO

The Edge of Destruction

KATIA, A SHADOW in the flame- and moon-lit night, ran down the hard dirt path from the extraction building to the mine, right under the eastern wall of the palisade. The path crossed a bridge that took it directly into the building at the minehead, but Katia didn't follow it that far: instead, she darted off to the right, disappearing around one of the Watchers' barracks that flanked the Warden's house. Mara followed. She heard Keltan chasing her, but she didn't look back, and the sound of his pursuit faded as she outran him; she was slowed slightly by her sore leg, but he was weighed down with sword and ring-studded leather armor.

As she rounded the barracks and pounded onto the main boulevard, the crushed rock covering it crunching beneath her feet, she saw Katia cross the main bridge by the rumbling water wheel. The other girl ran as though possessed, and she had longer legs: Mara couldn't catch her. And then, suddenly, Katia darted to the left, behind the longhouse closest to the main gate, closest to the burning stables.

The main gate stood open. Swirling smoke shrouded everything, alternately hiding and revealing scenes of men running with buckets of water, men fighting with terrified, rearing horses, one man half-dragging another away from the stables. The air, thick with the smell of burning hay and wood, rang with the shouts of Watchers and the terrified neighing of horses. Thankful for the smoke and confusion, Mara ran into the shadows of the longhouse in pursuit of Katia, and saw her at once at the building's far end, peering around the corner. Inside the longhouse she could hear women shouting questions, shouting to be let out, their voices so muffled by the thick log walls that no one who wasn't standing right next to the longhouse could possibly have heard them.

"Katia!" Mara dared call. "Wait!"

Much to her surprise, Katia stayed put. She had been crouched, looking around the corner; but now she straightened, as suddenly as though stung. The sword drooped in her hand. Mara ran up beside her, limping and gasping. "Katia, you can't—"

"We're all dead," Katia said. "All of us."

"What?" Mara stared at her.

Katia was no longer looking at the burning stables, off to the right. Instead, her eyes were locked onto a low hut right in front of them, its walls of thick stone, its roof of slate. Mara followed her gaze. The hut looked like it should have been fireproof: but by chance one of Skrit's and Skrat's fire arrows had found a chink in its armor, and Mara could see a thin line of fire licking across the peak of the roof, burning the main beam that supported it. A smooth packed trail led from the hut along the palisade toward the minehead. "What *is* that building?" Mara whispered.

"It's full of rockbreakers." Katia turned eyes that were black, flame-flecked pools in Mara's direction. "Do you understand?"

"Rockbreakers? I don't—"

"How do you think they expand the mine? Even working the unMasked to death, they could never dig those levels by hand. They use what's in that building." She pointed with the sword. "Rockbreakers. They're sticks of something, I don't know what, but they shove them into holes in the rocks, they light a fuse, and then the sticks explode. They shatter the rock. One stick can shatter a chunk of rock the size of a house. That building contains thousands of sticks. When the fire reaches them, there won't be a camp anymore. There won't be anything anymore. Not for any of us." She shoved the sword into the ground so hard it stuck there, quivering, and then began to laugh, a horrible, croaking sound that had no amusement in it. "I came down here to find the Warden and kill him, and *he's already dead*. We're all dead. This camp is about to become one big hole in the ground. We're all going to hell together."

"We have to tell the Watchers! They can—"

"No," Katia said. "They can't stop it. There's no time." Her laughter dried up as suddenly as it had begun and her voice turned sharp as the sword. "Even if there were, *I wouldn't warn them*. Better this whole camp be blasted to oblivion, better everyone in it die, than the things that have gone on here for years, for *decades*, continue. When the next wagon carrying girls and boys from the city arrives, let them find nothing but a smoking hole in the ground, soaked in the blood of Masked and unMasked alike!"

Mara stared at that growing line of fire. "There has to be something we can do!"

"There's nothing anyone can do!" Katia, face the color of blood in the firelight, stared up at the burning roof with a look of fierce reverence, as though worshipping at some strange altar.

And Mara suddenly remembered what she carried.

She shrugged out of Keltan's backpack, dropped it to the ground, and flung herself on her knees beside it. The magic urn tumbled out. She pried the lid off, and stared down at the beautiful, swirling colors, untouched by the red tinge the fire gave everything else. *But I don't know how to use it!* she cried to herself.

"Any minute now," Katia breathed behind her, and, desperately, Mara plunged first one hand and then the other into the wide-mouthed urn, drew them out again sheathed in glistening gloves. She raised her trembling fingers before her face, feeling the tingling power of the magic, took a deep breath, prepared to stand and turn to face the burning hut . . .

Then, at the end of the longhouse, she saw Keltan appear, sword in hand. He paused, panting, staring around—and suddenly a Watcher burst into sight behind him, grabbed him, and threw him to the ground. His sword flew from his hand as he thudded to the earth. The Watcher straddled him, drew his own sword—

Mara lunged to her feet. "No!" she screamed, and dashed forward.

The Watcher's head snapped around.

Keltan rolled over, tried to scramble away. The Watcher's head turned back to his prisoner. He shoved his booted foot into Keltan's back, hard. Then he placed the point of his sword at the base of Keltan's skull and turned his head to face Mara again. "One more step and I sever his spine," the Watcher snarled.

Mara skidded to a stop. "Get off him!" she shouted . . .
. . . and the magic responded.

It leaped from her hands like a bolt of lightning. She screamed with the agony of it, as searing as though she had plunged her hands into the coals of a fireplace.

The Watcher didn't scream. He had no time. The magic struck him in the middle of his chest. A gray mist erupted all around him, blowing away in an instant in the cold wind. Mara had one horrifying glimpse of the perfectly round hole that passed through his body, the white ends of severed ribs and spine gleaming within it, then the Watcher crumpled without a sound. Keltan, soaked in the sudden gush of blood from the horrific wound, frantically rolled to one side to avoid being crushed.

Mara, feeling sick, held out her still-burning hand. Keltan grabbed it, making her gasp with pain, but she gritted her teeth and pulled him upright. He stared down at the Watcher, then at her. "Thanks," he said. He sounded awed. His gaze fell on his sword, and he snatched it up from where it had fallen. "Where's Katia?"

"Down there," Mara said, pointing. "Keltan, the fire—"

"They've almost got it under control," he said. "We've got to—"

"No, not that fire!" Mara glanced toward the stables. The roof had collapsed, but long lines of men continued to pour water on the burning ruins, bucket after bucket drawn from the well by the open gate. "There's a building, where I left Katia, she says it's full of something called rockbreakers, she says—"

"Rockbreakers? And it's on fire?" Even in the uncertain light Mara saw Keltan's face go slack with shock. He spun to look at the bucket brigade. "We've got to—"

"Katia says there's no time! I was going to try to use magic, that's why I had it on my hands, but then I saw you—"

"Come on!" Keltan cried. He ran past her, into the space between the longhouses, and she dashed after him.

Katia still crouched where Mara had left her, watching the flames lick along the roof-peak of the rockbreaker hut. Keltan took one look and spun back to Mara. "We can't stop it," he gasped out. "We've got to get the rockbreakers out of there before the roof collapses. We've got to tell the Watchers—"

Katia lunged upright and back, her body slamming into Keltan, flinging him toward Mara. They both went down in a heap, Keltan's sword again flying from his hand. Mara and Keltan struggled to untangle themselves. But Keltan suddenly stopped moving. Mara rolled off him, turned her face toward him—and also froze. Katia had Illina's sword in her hand once more. The gleaming point kissed the boy's throat. "Nobody tells the Watchers," she snarled. "We let it blow."

"We'll all be killed!" Keltan cried.

"Good," Katia said. Her voice sounded thick, strange, strangled, as though she were squeezing out the word past some obstruction. "Good! I want them dead, and I'm glad to die with them!"

"But *we* don't want to die!" Mara said, pleading. "Katia, I'm your friend—"

"Friend?" Katia gave her a flat, hard look. "*You're* just a girl I was thrown into the mine with. *Shimma* was my *friend*. We grew up together in Tamita. We arrived on the same wagon. We worked that tunnel for months before the cave-in got her. You thought *you* could take her place? You were down there *two days!* And then you *conveniently* got yourself hurt, and *I* got blamed, and *I'm* the one who ended up in the barracks. And then you made me a hostage. *Friend?* A meddling fool who doesn't understand anything. *Anything.*"

"Katia—" Keltan pleaded.

For a moment, Mara couldn't speak. The ice-cold hand had once more plunged into her chest and gripped her heart, so hard and tight it could hardly beat. But the fire continued to lick the roof behind Katia's head, and somehow, she found her voice. "Katia, I came back for *you*. That's the only reason I'm here. You don't have to die. *We* don't have to die. *Nobody has to die.*"

"Everybody has to die," Katia spat. "Too bad you were fool enough to come back here to do it."

"Katia—"

Mara choked off her cry as she heard voices rise above the general hubbub. Booted feet ran toward them. Two men appeared behind Katia, but they weren't looking at the three in the shadows: they were staring up at the roof of the rockbreaker hut. One was the Warden. With him was a trustee she thought she'd seen at the desk in the minehead.

The Warden cursed. "Get the Watchers!" he shouted at the trustee. "Now! We have to get the rockbreakers out of here or we'll all be blown to paste!"

The trustee dashed away. The Warden went to the door of the hut, pulled keys from his belt, fumbled with the lock ...

And Katia jerked the blade away from Keltan's throat, spun, and dashed toward the Warden, sword raised.

The Warden, who had just gotten the door open, must have glimpsed Katia from the corner of his eye; he glanced right, yelped, and darted inside the hut. Katia reached him just as he tried to slam the door shut. Her sword thrust into the crack, stopping it from closing, and the Warden cried out again, this time in pain. Katia shoved at the door. The Warden shoved from the other direction. The sword kept the door from closing.

Impasse.

Keltan seemed oblivious. Still on his back, he stared at the roof of the hut. Tendrils of flame now ran all over it, and the wood beneath the slates glowed, limning the black rectangles of stone in lines of bright red. "If you've got any more magic," he said, voice trembling, "now's the time."

Mara scrambled on hands and knees over to the urn. It still glowed, but faintly. She'd used so much already.

She heard an ominous creaking from the hut. She grabbed the urn, scrambled to her feet, and ran toward the hut. But as she emerged from behind the longhouse, she heard shouts from her right and turned her head to see a half-dozen Watchers and three trustees, big men with soot-stained, angry faces, running toward her.

The roof creaked again—and sagged. The Watchers and trustees skidded to a halt, mouths wide in horror, then turned and ran the other way, falling over each other in their haste. Keltan shouted, "We're out of time!" Frantically, Mara plunged her hand into what remained of the magic, drew it out, but there was so little of it, *so little*—

The roof gave another alarming sigh and sagged even more. The Warden shrieked in horror and flung the door wide. Without hesitation, Katia lunged forward, sword outstretched. The blade slid into the Warden's exposed throat and burst out the back of his neck. Blood gushed, covering Katia's hand and arm and chest, giving her, in that final instant, a red Mask, her bared teeth a white, savage, skull-like grin in the middle of it. She crashed into the Warden's falling body, knocked him backward into the hut, fell on top of him ...

... and the roof caved in.

For Mara, time stopped. Everything went still and silent. She had thrust out her magic-covered hand, and her will, driven by the horror of what Katia had just done, the terror of what would happen if the rockbreakers exploded, the shock of Katia's last words to her, hurled the magic into the hut, her only thought to stop the explosion, to prevent the deaths of all those unMasked locked in the longhouses all around them, the unMasked in the mine who would be trapped there if the man-engine collapsed into the shaft, even the Watchers and the trustees.

The last bit of magic from the urn tried to carry out her will, but it was too little, far too little ...

So, as had happened to her in the ravine when she had drawn magic out of the tunnel to destroy her attacker, she drew magic from ... elsewhere.

The magic in the mine was too far away and too shielded by stone. The magic in the extraction building, if there was any, was likewise too distant.

And yet she found magic. All around her. In the longhouses. Down by the burning stables. She pulled it toward her. It resisted, but she pulled harder and harder. And then, as though she had ripped it free from some anchor, it flooded into her, and she had all she needed, and more.

Flaming coals had already fallen into the crates of rockbreakers. It was too late to stop the explosion, but not too late to do . . .

. . . this.

The rockbreakers exploded, a hundred tons of explosives turning instantly into violently expanding hot gas. But the blast wave and the gas did not rip across the camp, flattening buildings, pulverizing flesh, incinerating and destroying. It could not escape through the barrier she had flung up around it, more solid than steel, invisible but impenetrable, a cylinder that directed the force of the explosion straight up into the sky in a raging, roaring column of fire, splitting the air with the sound of a thousand thunderbolts striking at once.

For one instant, Mara gaped up at that swirling tower of flame, spreading out into black smoke a thousand feet above her, like dark leaves atop a fiery trunk. For one instant, she marveled at the swirling colors of magic mingled with the white fire of the explosion, every color imaginable, twisting, turning, and twining like jeweled vines. But only for an instant, because as the explosion spent itself and the magic released, she screamed, her body aflame with agony: a short-lived scream as the pain became so much her throat seized up. She fell like a toppled tree, gasping, lost in a world of pain such as she had never imagined, worse than when she had killed the Watcher at the tunnel, far worse, because that time she had passed out, and this time she remained horribly, horribly awake.

If the pain had gone on indefinitely, she later thought, she would have died or gone mad, but the pain began to ease almost at once: slowly, and certainly not entirely, but enough so that, some interminable time later, she managed to sit up. Though soaked in sweat, she felt chilled to the bone and weak as a kitten. Hunched on the ground, she wrapped her arms around herself and looked around, blinking away the tears blurring her vision.

Keltan lay close beside her, on his back, eyes closed, but she could see his chest rising and falling. He was alive! Relief flooded her.

By the flickering light of the burning pile of timber that was all that remained of the stables, she saw other dark figures on the ground: Watchers and trustees, unconscious or dead. She couldn't hear any sound from the longhouses. Only the rumbling of the water wheel and the unceasing creaking of the man-engine remained unchanged. *Down in the mine they don't know anything strange has happened up here at all.*

The rockbreaker hut, and Katia and the Warden, were simply *gone*. Where the hut had stood was a deep, perfectly circular hole, its bottom perhaps ten feet below the surface. Both the bottom and sides of the hole were glazed over with what looked like black glass, dark in the flickering firelight.

Mara looked up, and saw a thick, heaving cloud overhead, tinged dimly red by the fires below.

And then she heard running footsteps behind her. She turned, saw two figures charging toward her, and tried to scramble to her feet, but her arms and legs wouldn't work, and all she managed to do was push herself backward across the frosted grass until she had her back pressed against the nearest longhouse, silent now, the shouts and pleas she had heard earlier from inside it no longer audible.

The figures reached her. One bent over Keltan. The other loomed over her and held out a hand.

"Let's get out of here," Edrik said.

TWENTY-THREE

The Restless Dead

WITH TISHKA CARRYING Mara and Edrik carrying Keltan, they made their slow escape from the camp, through the wide-open front gate. There was no one to see them. Every Watcher and trustee lay motionless where he had been when the hut exploded. The stable, reduced to embers, cracked and popped; the blackened palisade wall behind it smoked. The horses had all fled in terror.

Mara clung to Tishka's back, her head resting on the woman's shoulder. Every movement hurt. Her joints seemed filled with ground glass, her skin felt raw, her blood burned like acid, her breath scraped her throat. She couldn't hope to walk. She wondered if she would ever walk again.

What had happened to Keltan and all the others?

Had the force of the explosion been great enough to knock them senseless, even though her magic had directed it upward?

Magic . . . she had a hard time remembering exactly what she had done. She'd used the magic from the urn, but that hadn't been enough. She'd gotten more from somewhere—it had seemed to be all around her—but where? There were no stores of magic in the longhouses. They'd serve no purpose. Maybe some had been stored in the hut with the rockbreakers . . . ?

But no. The magic hadn't been in the hut. It had surrounded her. She was sure of it.

Where had it come from?

She couldn't think clearly. Her head hurt, as though her aimlessly tumbling thoughts were bruising the inside of her skull as they rolled around and around. Again she wished she could pass out, be as unconscious as Keltan, but wishing didn't make it so. So she suffered, moaning when the pain became too much to bear, as the two of them were carried out into the darkness and away from the camp, finally joining Skrit and Skrat and Hyram in a hidden glade behind the shoulder of a hill. The un-Masked Army's horses shivered and rolled their eyes as they were mounted. Mara was shivering, too, so she couldn't blame them. She rode double with Edrik, remembering how the very idea of doing so had been dismissed out of hand when she'd first been rescued because it would be hard on the precious horses: no one seemed worried about that now. Keltan rode behind Skrit. Skrat and Hyram brought up the rear, Skrat leading Keltan's horse, Hyram leading Mara's . . . and Illina's.

Keltan, though still not awake, wasn't quite unconscious anymore, either. At least he seemed aware enough of his surroundings to hold on to Skrit's waist, although his wrists were bound together just to be safe.

They rode away from the camp, from the roiling mass of black smoke slowly dissipating above it, from the smell of burning wood and hay and the sound of the constant slow grinding of the water wheel. But Mara carried it all inside her, in her mind and in her aching body, and the tears she cried as they rode through the darkness had little to do with her own pain and everything to do with Katia, the girl she had tried so hard, and failed so badly, to rescue. And she grieved for Illina, the kind young woman who had helped her with her nightmares and paid the ultimate price for Mara's folly. Mixed in were even tears for the Watcher she had killed to save Keltan, and the Watcher the magic had killed in the mountains. Three lives she had taken now. *I'm only fifteen*, she thought. *I'm too young to be a killer!*

But she could not deny it: a killer she had become, not only taking lives herself but costing others theirs. The trustee in the Warden's house. The Warden's secretary.

Illina.

She sobbed and thought she would never stop, but sometime in the night she dozed off despite the swaying and jerking of the horse and the bouncing of her head against Edrik's back. Sleep didn't last: a nightmarish vision of the hole she had blown through the Watcher attacking Keltan snapped her awake almost at once, gasping.

"It's all right," Edrik said, reining the horse to a halt. "We're stopping." Mara peered blearily around in darkness more complete than before; the moon had set. They seemed to be in an open space, defined by the forest's trees on one side and a rocky bluff on the other. "They'll have their hands full at the camp without worrying about a few 'bandits.' I doubt they'll even try to track us once they wake up, *if* they wake up. Even if they do, it won't be for hours. We'll be long gone with no tracks to find by then. But we must sleep, and see to you and Keltan."

Mara straightened with a groan. The pain had faded, but not gone. Her body felt abused, and her mind somehow pale, washed out, as though, like the basin of the magic-well, it had been completely emptied and was only now beginning to slowly fill again. She wanted more sleep, desperately wanted it; but she feared what dreams might come. *And Illina is no longer here to comfort me*, she thought, a sob slipping from her throat.

Then, with a hopeful leap of her heart, she remembered the herbs Grelda had given her, to make the restorative the Healer had given her in the Secret City sickroom. "A fire," she said. "Can we have a fire?"

Edrik frowned. "A fire? Why?"

"I need a potion. Medicine. Please."

Edrik glanced over his shoulder. "All right," he said. "But only long enough to brew it. Then we douse it again."

"Where are we?" she asked as Edrik slid from his saddle, then turned and helped her down. She staggered, and he caught her arm.

"Halfway between the camp and the spot where we attacked the wagon," he said. "We will take the same path home, to ensure there is no trail to follow to the Secret City. Let them think we were just bandits, un-Masked scraping by in the Wild, who made a particularly daring raid."

"How's Keltan?" Mara turned to look around her, but with only starlight to illuminate the forest, she could see nothing but indistinct shapes of horses and people as Skrit, Skrat, Hyram, and Tishka set up camp.

"Stirring, but still not awake. What happened?" Edrik began, but then cut off his own question. "No, not now. Rest." He led her forward a few feet. "Here's your bedroll. Lie here until the fire is ready."

She knelt down, felt the familiar rough weave of her blankets, and crawled into them. They had been laid on a thick bed of pine needles, and it seemed her body, at rest, was at last able to insist on its needs being met despite the chaos in her mind. She dozed within moments; woke startled and afraid moments later when Edrik touched her shoulder to tell her the fire was ready; made her potion and drank it, while the others hung back and exchanged disgusted looks; and lay down, the pain subsiding, hoping the potion would also give her dreamless sleep.

It didn't. The dead awaited her. Grute. Both Watchers she had killed. The images of all three sharp, clear, *real*. And then, in her ordinary nightmares, Illina. The Warden. Katia . . .

When she woke at last, she struggled up from thick black depths of slumber that, like stinking mud in the bottom of a pond, kept trying to drag her back into the dreams of horror that had gripped her all night. Finally she gasped in air and forced her eyes open to stare up into a sky once more shrouded by gray, scudding cloud. Never waking, she realized, was far worse than all the nights she had woken crying out in terror. Better to wake screaming than scream silently a hundred times but never escape the hallucinations and dreams.

If her mind felt anything but rested, at least her body didn't hurt as much, presumably thanks to the potion. She sat up and looked around. Edrik, Skrit, and Skrat were saddling their horses; Tishka and Hyram were nowhere to be seen; and (her heart leaped) Keltan sat on a rock, spooning into his mouth what had to be old, cold gruel, since no fire had been lit. Dark shadows clung to the deathly pale skin beneath his eyes, and his hand trembled as he lifted each spoonful to his mouth, but at least he was awake—and alive.

In her heart she leaped up, ran to his side, and gave him a relieved, welcoming hug. In reality she struggled to her feet, hobbled over to him, and groaned as she joined him on the rock. "How are you?"

"Terrible," he said. "I feel like someone stuck a wire brush into my head and scrubbed real hard."

Mara blinked, and gave a sort of gasp of amusement that wasn't quite a laugh. "You know, that pretty much describes the way I feel, too." The proto-laugh died on her lips. "What happened to you?"

"Not a clue," Keltan said. He frowned. "I saw . . . or

think I saw . . ." His head snapped toward her. "Did Katia kill the Warden?"

Mara nodded.

"I saw that, then," he muttered. "Wish I hadn't. And then they both fell into the rockbreaker hut, and I saw the roof start to fall in, and I thought, 'This is it!' and . . . and . . ." His voice trailed off. "Something pulled me inside out." He shook his head. "That doesn't make any sense, but that's what it felt like: like someone had reached right inside me, down here, somewhere"—he gestured in the vicinity of his belly button—"and pulled everything that was inside me out through my ears." He shrugged. "Crazy. But that's what it felt like. And as it went rushing out of me, it took me—well, my consciousness—with it. Then there was kind of a long confused period of being not quite awake and not quite asleep, and then a blank stretch, and then I woke up here." He looked at her. "So why aren't we a pale pink mist floating over the camp?"

But Mara hardly heard him. *It felt like someone had pulled everything that was inside me out through my ears.* She remembered what *she* had felt, the sense of magic rushing to her from all around her, the power she had suddenly found to hurl at the rockbreaker hut, containing the explosion that would have killed them all. And she knew what had reached inside Keltan.

She had. *She* had been the force that pulled him inside out. She had drawn *magic* from him, and every other person surrounding the rockbreaker hut, stole it from them, ripped it right out of their bodies, throwing him and everyone else over the cliff of unconsciousness.

No, she told herself. *No! That's not possible!*

She couldn't tell him. She couldn't tell *anyone*. Not until she was sure.

Maybe not even then.

Magic didn't work that way, did it? You couldn't just yank it out of other people. Could you?

And even if you *could*, even if that was what she had

done, it had felt wrong. Bad. Even though it had saved all their lives. As if the magic pouring through her had been corrosive: power, but the wrong sort of power. Whatever she had done, she had a very strong feeling she shouldn't have done it, and that she should never do it again.

But the power, a part of her whispered. *All that power. You contained an explosion. What else might you be able to do with that much power?*

She kept all those thoughts tucked silently away inside her, and only said, "I used magic."

"Wow." He stared at her. "Good thing I had that urn with me."

She nodded.

"If you two can ride," Edrik said, coming over, "we should get going. Tishka has scouted back along our trail and sees no signs of pursuit, but that may not last much longer. Hyram has returned to the ridge above the camp to keep watch and race after us with warning if need be. We've left Illina's body for them"—he looked grim, and Mara felt as if someone had stabbed her in the heart—"but they know there were more of us. We want to be long gone, and the trail long cold, before they even think to begin to track us."

And so began the weary journey back to the Secret City. The first time, Mara had been anxious, concerned, excited, wondering what lay ahead. Now she felt grim and weary and far older than her fifteen years. How had everything gone so wrong? How had her noble goal of rescuing the girl she'd made a hostage to her good behavior turned into so many dead—almost so many dead they would have been uncountable, and herself among them—without her goal even being achieved?

It doesn't work that way in stories.

Skrit and Skrat and Tishka remained distant and reserved during the journey, barely speaking to her, avoiding her at meals, placing their bedrolls on the far side of the fire from her own. Keltan rode with her, but he seemed to be taking a very long time to recover from whatever had happened to him.

She still shied away from what she very much feared was the truth, that when she had needed more magic than she'd had at hand, she had ripped it from the living bodies of all those within her reach—including Keltan. She could have killed him, without even knowing what she was doing.

Magic comes from living things, her father had told her, long ago, when she had still been a child and her only concern had been whether her mother would catch her wearing her too-short tunic in the street. *But it must be carefully harvested . . .*

She hadn't *harvested* it. She had pulled it out roots and all. And if it had struck Keltan so hard, Keltan who was young and healthy, what might it have done to some of those in the longhouses, the older men and women, their health already damaged by long hours in the mine, cold nights in the barracks? Had she killed more than she knew, people she had never met, people who had done her no wrong?

She could hardly bear to think it. She found it difficult to eat, difficult to do anything but go through the necessary motions of travel. She mounted her horse, rode silently all day as they splashed through the stream and up the ravine, and rolled into her blankets in the cavern where she had discovered she could still see magic. Sleep should have offered surcease, but it offered no such thing, for in the night, the visions came: naked Grute, head bursting like overripe fruit at her touch; the Watcher blasted into dust at the cave; the Watcher with the hole in his chest, dropping soundlessly on top of the prostrate Keltan. Even when the visions of those she had killed directly faded, she saw bloody, screaming Katia, ripping out the Warden's throat, falling into the rock-breaker hut as the flaming roof collapsed, and Illina, tumbling nervelessly across the black, weed-strewn ground. The next morning she was as hollow-eyed and trembling as Keltan had been the morning after the attack on the camp.

Edrik questioned her, trying to find out what had happened after they were separated. He also told her what he and Tishka had done, how they had burst into the extraction building to find it deserted, and broken out through its gate into the darkness outside the walls, slipping through shadows until they could make a dash for the woods, the Watchers on the palisade spotting them too late to do more than waste a few arrows in their direction. They'd retrieved Hyram, then circled to where Skrit and Skrat lay in hiding on the bluff that had given them clear bow shots into the camp; had watched from there as everything unfolded. They had seen the spear of flame stab the sky, had been pounded into the ground by its shattering thunder.

When they could see and hear again, they had seen and heard nothing. Every Watcher they could spot lay on the ground, unconscious or dead. As did Mara and Keltan. And the gate stood open.

Edrik and Tishka had taken their chance, and Mara knew the rest.

What Edrik pointedly did *not* ask her was why she had run after Katia in the first place. He had to know, and he had to know that she understood the gravity of her decision. He didn't berate her for it.

She almost wished he would. When she'd gotten in trouble as a child, her father or mother would punish her, and that would be an end to it: the trouble receded into the past and cast no shadow over the future.

But *this* trouble — these actions, these memories, these dreams — were not receding into the past. And they cast a very long shadow indeed: a shadow that, as they approached the Secret City, crept out of her dreams and into her waking life.

They were riding in gathering twilight, after a second day of travel, down the last stretch of the ravine that led to the Secret City's cliff-walled cove. The purpling sky still gave enough light to see the trees and rocks, but between and beneath those rocks and trees the shadows lay thick and black . . .

Then, to Mara's breath-stopping terror, those shadows *moved*, coalesced, and stepped out into the light as the horrors of her dreams: Grute, naked and headless, blood streaming down his chest, arms outstretched, somehow still stalking toward her; the Watcher who had threatened Keltan, the forest behind him visible through the gaping red hole in his chest, face unMasked and covered with blood; Katia, her unblinking eyes blank and glazed above a grin stretched too wide by the rictus of death, the Warden's gore dripping from the lank strands of her hair; Illina, arrow piercing her breast, rage contorting her face; the Warden, head flopped to one side above the terrible red smile of his ruined throat. All of them (except for the headless Grute) had their eyes locked on her face. All had their arms outstretched, their hands curved into terrible claws . . .

Mara screamed and screamed and screamed, turning her horse around and around, but the shades surrounded her, the victims of all her stupid, childish decisions, of the so-called Gift she now knew, beyond question, to be no Gift at all, but a horrible, horrible curse.

Grute's dead arms reached up to pull her from her mount. She struck out blindly, kicking, slapping, and screamed and screamed and went on screaming . . .

. . . right up until she fell from the saddle and into darkness.

TWENTY-FOUR

Revelations and Discoveries

WHEN MARA CAME TO HERSELF AGAIN, she thought for one horrible moment that everything that had happened since Katia broke her arm in the mine had been a dream: for sitting by her bed was Healer Ethelda, her blue Mask with its green gems unmistakable.

But beyond Ethelda's Mask Mara saw, not the wood of the camp hospital's ceiling, but rough whitewashed stone, cast in sharp relief by sunlight streaming in from her left. Mara looked that way and saw a narrow opening in a stone wall, blue sky beyond, heard the cry of gulls and the rush of waves against the shore, and knew that she was in the Secret City once more, in the same sickroom in which she had awakened the last time she had returned from the camp. Everything she remembered had happened as she remembered it.

And then she gasped, a scream trying to form in her throat, because what she remembered most vividly of all was *dead people pulling her from her horse*. That hadn't been a dream! It had really happened! But—

Ethelda patted her hand. "Easy, easy," she said. "You're safe."

Am I? She turned her head this way and that. A black urn stood on the bedside table. Mara knew, even without seeing inside it, that it held magic, presumably for Ethelda's use. The magic felt like another presence in the room, but in fact, she and Ethelda were alone.

Most importantly, no dead eyes stared at her from the shadows, no bloodstained hands reached for her. She took a deep breath. *A hallucination*, she thought. *It must have been a hallucination.*

But it had seemed so real. In her memory, it *still* seemed real.

Mara found her voice. "What are you doing here?"

Ethelda snorted. "It's not by choice. I was riding back to Tamita, escorted by a Watcher, when we were attacked. They killed the Watcher. They brought me here. They locked me up. No one said a word to me until last night. Then I was told, 'You have a patient,' and they brought me to *you*." She straightened and looked down at Mara, her eyes sharp and narrow behind her Mask. "They tell me you have used magic," she said. "A *lot* of magic."

Mara nodded. The power, rushing through her but burning like acid . . . "Yes," she said. "I had to."

"Have you used it to kill again? Since Grute?" Ethelda said intently.

One Watcher blasted into dust by the magic from the cave, another's chest blown apart by the magic from the urn. "Yes," she whispered. "Twice that I know of. There may have been other deaths."

"May have been?" Ethelda's voice sharpened. "How can you not know?"

And Mara, with a sense of vast relief, poured out her

story, what she thought she had done, how she thought she had reached into everyone around her in the camp, sucking magic directly from their bodies to hurl against the force of the rockbreaker explosion. "Keltan was so weak and shaken afterward, and he's young," she said miserably. "So many people in the camp are weak and sick. I'm afraid some of them . . ." Her throat closed on the words.

"Mara, oh, Mara," Ethelda whispered. Fear and awe mingled in her voice.

"What is it?" Mara pleaded. "What's happened to me? What's *happening* to me?"

Ethelda's breath came in strange, ragged gasps. "Mara . . . what you did . . . what you are capable of doing . . ." She stopped, took one long, shuddering breath, then leaned forward. "You are not the first with this ability. But I know of only one other alive today, and he . . ." She stopped. "He does not have this ability in the same measure," she continued after a moment. "He could not have done what you did. At this moment in history, you are unique."

"What? No, I'm just an ordinary girl." But remembering what she had done in the camp, Mara knew even as she said it that it was a lie.

Ethelda ignored her protest. "You see *all* the colors of magic. I told you in the camp how unusual that was. Now I find you can also *use* all the colors of magic, combine them at will. What you did in the camp would ordinarily require a dozen Gifted, trained practitioners, and an enormous store of magic, to even attempt. And they would probably fail. You are, in short, potentially the most powerful woman in all of Aygrima."

Mara gaped.

"That alone makes you unique," Ethelda continued inexorably, "but you combine that ability with another: *you do not have to touch magic to use it.* You can draw it to you from whatever source is at hand: when you killed the Watcher in the mountains, you called the magic from the reservoir within the black lodestone deposit inside the mountain.

"But even *that* is not the end of it. You have another ability." Her voice dropped to a whisper. "And if I tell you all I know about it, my Mask will shatter."

"Then don't tell me," Mara said. A vast panic welled inside her, threatening to escape in a scream that she feared, if she let it begin, she would never be able to stop. She didn't *want* this. She didn't want any of this. She didn't want to know. "Don't tell me!"

"I must," Ethelda said, still whispering. "For until you know what you are capable of, until you learn to *control* what you are capable of, you are a danger to yourself and everyone around you." She stopped speaking. For a long moment she sat perfectly still: and then, to Mara's shock, she reached up and took off her Mask.

The woman behind that Mask was younger than Mara had thought, no older than her own mother. The Healer had a round, pleasant face, pale as a lily since no sun had touched it since childhood, with just the beginnings of wrinkles at the corners of her eyes, wrinkles that seemed related more to smiles than frowns. But no smile touched Ethelda's face now. Both her lips and her hands trembled as she set the Mask to one side.

"Don't!" Mara said again. "If you shatter your Mask, you can never go back to the Palace."

Ethelda laughed shakily. "Child," she said. "It's been clear I'll never return to the Palace since the moment I was brought here. The only reason I haven't removed the Mask until now is that . . ." She reddened. "I feel naked without it. But at the same time . . ." A slow smile spread across her face. "I have to confess it feels wonderful to set the evil thing aside forever."

Mara couldn't return the smile. "It's not too late. You don't have to . . ."

The smile faded. "I do."

I don't want to hear this! Mara thought again. *I don't—*

But Ethelda continued, in a voice that trembled only

a little, "All magic comes from living things. Ordinarily it departs them when they die, and either dissipates or is drawn to black lodestone. Most Gifted can only access magic after it is freed from the living creatures that created it, after it has collected in black lodestone in sufficient quantities." She nodded at the black urn. "But a few, a very few, a handful through all of recorded history, have had the power to draw magic right from its source: to pull it directly from living creatures. It is possible to gain enormous amounts of power that way." She paused again. "You have this rare ability. So does one other I know of, though to a much lesser degree." She swallowed, and glanced at her Mask. "The Autarch."

With a grating, screeching sound like an animal in agony, Ethelda's Mask writhed, like Mara's on the day her Masking failed, and then shattered. The shards scattered across the side table around the urn of magic, some falling to the stone floor. Ethelda made a sound halfway between a gasp and a sob. Mara stared at the Mask, then at Ethelda. "The Autarch can draw power from people?"

Ethelda turned away from the shattered Mask and said in a shaky voice, "Yes. But his ability is weak, compared to you. He cannot draw it directly as you do. He requires help." She locked her eyes with Mara's. "He does it through the Masks."

Mara gaped. "Through the Masks? Has he always ... ?"

"Not always," Ethelda said. "Just since the Masks changed. At least, that is what we believe."

"We?"

"Your father and I."

The hairs stood up on the back of Mara's neck. "Father knows?"

"Suspects, at least." Ethelda shook her head. "I had better start at the beginning.

"Some of this is only a guess, Mara. But I have been Healer to the Autarch and the Circle for twenty years. I have been called on many times by those in the Circle, for illness or injury or simply to alleviate, as best I can, the inevitable infirmities of age. Yet through all those years, my only service to the Autarch has been an annual examination. And every year, he remains healthy. Impossibly healthy. Impossibly *young*. He is almost eighty, and he looks half that. Even his hair remains the dark brown of his youth.

"It took no great insight on my part to figure out that the Autarch has the ability to use magic to maintain some semblance of youth. I thought he must be a self-Healer, an unusual Gift, but not unheard of. I cannot Heal myself, but I have known of one other who could.

"But recently I've realized there's something else going on." She paused. "You know of the Child Guards?"

"Of course," Mara said. She remembered the white-Masked youths riding behind the Autarch in the Outside Market, the young boy at the end who had looked up at her . . .

"An honor for the best, most-Gifted children of the outlying towns and villages," Ethelda said. "So it is said. So it is perceived.

"But I know differently," she continued, her voice suddenly flat and hard. "I treat those children. They do not thrive in the Palace. They weaken. They do not develop normally. If they have not reached puberty, it is unnaturally delayed. They are frequently ill. They are troubled by nightmares and headaches. And on six occasions—six, in just the five years—there has been a Child Guard who has died. Four girls. Two boys. I could do nothing for them, because I did not understand what was wrong with them.

"Your father came to me with his fears. We had known each other for years, of course, and he trusted me; trusted me enough to tell me that, at the same time that the Child Guards unit was formed, the 'recipe' for the Masks had been altered by the Palace."

Mara had learned what that was during her two years' pre-apprenticeship to her father: while some of the magic in the Masks was imbued by the Maskmaker, using his personal Gift, a portion came straight from the Palace, as vials of black dust. A small portion, a spoonful, no more, of that dust was mixed with the clay of each Mask, and suddenly Mara understood why. "The dust," she said suddenly. "The 'recipe.' It's black lodestone?"

Ethelda nodded. "Black lodestone, with carefully crafted magic clinging to it. Your father's Gift is powerful enough that, though he could not tell the purpose of the alterations, he could tell that the magic had changed. And as time passed, he realized that the Masks were also changing those who wore them. There seemed to be a strange loss of will, a flattening of personality."

Sala, Mara thought, remembering how her newly Masked friend had cut her dead in the street.

"He came to me to ask, cautiously, if I had noticed any of this in my duties as Healer. I had. Masked, we could hardly discuss our suspicions except in the most roundabout way. It's astonishing," Ethelda said bitterly, "how adept one becomes in the Palace at talking around things that cannot be said straightforwardly.

"But your father found a way around that, too. That Mask"—she nodded at the scattered shards on the side table—"was not the one I received at my Masking, nor yet the one I was given when I was made Master Healer. Instead, it was carefully crafted by your father for me, altered—as much as he could alter it without drawing the Watchers' attention—to allow me to speak more freely. He gave it to me the day I came to your house."

Mara blinked; she remembered that day well, since it was after that that she had been barred from the workshop.

"Wearing it, I still could not openly say things that violated my oath to the Autarch, but it gave me somewhat more leeway than a normal Mask would have. Your father, of course, also made one for himself and donned it that same day: and with those in place, I was able to tell him my growing conviction that the Autarch was somehow drawing magic directly from the Child Guards, drawing so much of it he was making them ill. And he was able to tell me his suspicion that the change in the Masks was designed to do two things: to change people so that they could not even begin to formulate rebellious thoughts against the Autarch, and to make it possible for the Autarch to draw minute amounts of magic from *everyone* wearing one of the new Masks. In fact, the two things were linked: by drawing magic from the new Masks, the Autarch draws off a small part of the wearers' souls; just a small part. Just the part containing the flicker of independence that might make them question their obedience to him." Ethelda's voice turned caustic as lye. "Just the part that made them fully human.

"Sharing our knowledge over the next few weeks, we suddenly understood the reasons for another disturbing trend: the increasing failure of Maskings, for Gifted and unGifted alike. Some unGifted people are presumably more resistant to having magic drawn from them than others. The Masks, already designed to weed out those who threaten the stability of the regime, interpret that resistance as a reason to reject the Wearer, and so you see more and more innocent children being sent to the mining camp." Ethelda shook her head. "I had no idea what a horror that was until I saw it for myself," she said in a low voice. "It made me ashamed of my years serving the Palace, ashamed of my use of the magic extracted at such a cost."

"And the Maskings of the Gifted?" Mara demanded. She had a nasty suspicion she knew the answer, and Ethelda confirmed it.

"The Autarch has made it a point, for two years now, to attend almost all Maskings of the Gifted," Ethelda said. "And one out of ten of those he attends fail. I believe that his need for magic is so great that, in the moment of the Masking, he often draws on it too eagerly, ripping it from the Gifted child with so much force that the Mask shatters, and the wearer's Gift is lost."

Mara felt a chill. "Then if he had come to mine . . ."

"But he didn't," Ethelda said. "I did."

"How did you arrange *that?*"

"I didn't," Ethelda said. "Oh, I had plans to—I intended to request the honor of representing the Autarch at your Masking because I was 'an old family friend'—but in fact, before I even made my request, the Autarch announced on his own he would not attend."

Mara blinked. "Why?"

"I can only guess, but I suspect he knows, at least at some level, that *he* is causing the recent failures of the Gifted's Masks. If that's the case, he may have chosen to stay away from your Masking for fear of endangering your Gift. After all, Maskmakers are crucial to feeding his need and you were to be apprenticed to your father, one day perhaps to be Master Maskmaker yourself. Whatever his reason, his decision worked perfectly for our plans."

"You and my father?"

Ethelda nodded. "Your father confided in me that, just as he had made special Masks for each of us, so he was making a special one for you: one he knew would fail, without ever letting the Autarch draw on your magic. He said he had also arranged for you to be rescued on the way into exile. He told me no more than that. I knew nothing of this place"—she gestured at the cavern walls—"or of the unMasked Army. I thought he must have bribed some of the bandits known to infest the Wild, and wondered that he seemed so confident they would uphold their end of the bargain. But again, I was Masked, and even with the special Mask your father made for me, I dared not learn too much or ask too many questions for fear of . . ." She gestured at the shattered shards of blue.

Mara felt a pang of guilt for doubting her father. An upwelling of love threatened to choke her. "Why?" she cried. "Why is the Autarch doing all this? Destroying Gifted, sucking the life out of the Child Guards, feeding on the magic of his people? Why?"

"Because he's old," Ethelda said flatly. "Old and childless. He fears death, and more than that, he fears losing his grip on the reins of state. To hold on to both youth and power, he needs more and more magic to fight the ravages of time. He's an addict, and like any addict, it takes greater and greater quantities of what he's addicted to to give him the results he wants. And to hell with those he uses and discards along the way." She leaned forward. "But it is you I'm most concerned with now, child. Tell me, using magic from the black lodestone jars *hurts*, doesn't it?"

Mara nodded. "The more I use, the more it hurts." She remembered the searing pain in her hands when she had killed the Watcher threatening Keltan.

"That is because you are untrained. You have not learned to direct it properly, and so it scrapes your nerves on its passage through your body. But the magic you tore from the people in the camp—that hurt in a different way, did it not?"

Mara shuddered, remembering that soul-shredding agony. "Like being burned alive."

Again Ethelda nodded. "The magic from the lodestone is smoothed and blended by its long passage through the rock. But the magic from a living mind is pure, strong—and not intended for use by *you* at all. It's like . . ." She paused as if trying to think of the proper simile. "Sometimes, Healers have tried to replace the blood lost by the victim of a terrible accident by injecting them with blood drawn willingly from someone else. Rarely, that saves a life. More often . . ." She sighed. "More often, the victim dies a painful death. We believe that just as there are various kinds of magic, there are different kinds of blood, though we have no way of telling them apart. And if you receive the wrong kind of blood, it causes a reaction that in many cases proves fatal.

"You received the wrong kind of magic. You received very many *different* kinds of the wrong kind of magic. You were lucky to survive. If you had held it within yourself for long, I don't believe you would have. Fortunately, you thrust it away at once, to contain the explosion." She shook her head. "An amazing feat. I wish I had seen it."

"I wish I hadn't," Mara said. "But it's not just the pain. There's something else. The . . . dreams."

Ethelda leaned closer. "More vivid than any dreams you've ever had before?" she asked.

Mara nodded.

"You see those who have died?"

Mara nodded again. "Grute was the first," she said. "The Watcher I . . . destroyed . . . with magic in the mountains. Another Watcher I–I blasted to save Keltan. They're the most vivid, the most *real*. But I'm seeing others, too, others I *didn't* kill." *Not directly, at least,* she thought bitterly. "The Warden. Katia. Illina . . ."

"Here is what I think is happening," Ethelda said. "When someone dies, their magic is released, and you have the ability to draw magic to yourself. You're like living black lodestone. So when someone dies near you, whether you killed them or not, their magic flows into you, suddenly, with enough force to leave an . . . an image, like a vivid painting; an imprint of their magic on your mind. And if you *did* kill them, using magic, that imprint is particularly strong."

"A *permanent* imprint?" Mara cried out, stiffening in terror. "Will I see them my whole life?"

She expected—needed—Ethelda to reassure her, but Ethelda hesitated. "I don't know," she said. "I'm only guessing. I can give you herbs to dull the dreams and let you sleep more calmly and perhaps, over time, the imprints will fade, like the ball of light that remains in your vision after you glance at the sun."

"*Perhaps?*" Mara felt sick. "You don't *know?*"

Ethelda shook her head. "No, child, I don't. I can only guess." She put her hand on Mara's shoulder, and squeezed it hard. "Listen to me very carefully, Mara," she said. Her eyes, wide and clear, free of the shadows of the Mask, bored into Mara's; her voice, low and intense, bored into Mara's ears and mind. "You are in a fragile state. Stable, but barely so. Those who kill with magic can grow to *like* killing. Those who pull magic from others can move past the pain and grow to like the power."

"Like the Autarch?" Mara whispered.

"Worse."

"Worse!"

Ethelda nodded. "There are tales of those with these powers commingled: the magekings and witchqueens of old. They have names: The Beast of Barak'kum. Bloody Britha. Atul the Slaughterer. Ancient names that have inspired terror for centuries. And one other, not ancient at all: The Lady of Pain and Fire."

Mara blinked. The first three names, dreadful though they sounded, meant nothing to her. But the Lady of Pain and Fire—the witch the Autarch had supposedly personally defeated—she remembered hearing about from Tutor Ancilla. In recent years Mara had begun to suspect she was a myth created to bolster the image of the Autarch as all-knowing and all-powerful. "The Lady of Pain and Fire was *real?*"

"She was," Ethelda said. "And maybe still is. Her body was never found. Whether she still lives, outside our borders, I cannot say. Perhaps the Autarch knows. But if you've heard of her, you know the things she did: whole villages wiped out, forests leveled, children snatched from their beds, men and women tortured to death for no purpose anyone could ever discern." Mara had a sudden flash of memory, a white skull grinning at her from a green mound in the ruined village where she and Grute had sheltered. Ethelda leaned closer, lowered her voice further, and said with grim certainty, "Mara, if you continue in this path you have chosen, though you chose it inadvertently and in ignorance, you could become just like her: a thing of nightmare, one of the most terrifying creatures the world has ever birthed."

Mara gasped, and tears filled her eyes. "No!" she said. "No! I could never—I wouldn't—I'm not a monster!"

"No," Ethelda agreed quickly. "No, of course you're not a monster." She touched her unscarred face. "I'm not accusing you, child. But I *am* warning you. The danger is there."

"What do I do?" Mara begged. "Ethelda, what do I do?"

"Be very careful using magic," Ethelda said. "I think, with training, you can safely use that which is collected in the usual fashion. But do not draw magic from life as you did in the camp. Above all, do not use magic to kill, not if you value your soul."

Mara's heart raced. "But–but every time, it just happened. I didn't do it on purpose. What if I can't control it?"

Ethelda's hand trembled on her shoulder, but she didn't release her. "I don't know, Mara. Somehow, we have to find a way. I must think on it." She relaxed her hand, drew it back. "For now, I'll go prepare a draught of the sleeping potion of which I spoke. It will take some time. Rest here until I get back." She gave Mara a smile, glanced at the shattered Mask, took a deep breath, and then went out, leaving the broken shards where they lay.

She also left the urn of magic. Without Ethelda to distract her, Mara was more aware of it than ever, aware of the power lurking within the simple black vessel. It called to her, urging her to use it, to touch it, to draw it to her, to . . .

She swallowed. *I could be a monster*, she thought. *Magic could make me into a monster. I've already killed three people, maybe more.*

It was a horrible thought, a terrifying thought. *Be very careful using magic*, Ethelda had said, but how? How *could* she be careful? She had no control, and Ethelda clearly had no way to teach it to her. She hadn't meant to kill Grute, or the two Watchers. But she had, magic leaping to do her bidding without conscious thought on her part. And then, in the camp, there had been searing pain as she had stripped living creatures all around her of the magic they unwittingly possessed. Already the memory of the agony was fading, and all she could remember was the power, tantalizing her, calling to her. She'd saved lives, true, but she might just as easily have taken them. If she could not control her magic, when would she kill again? The next time she got angry? And who would the victim be? Edrik? Catilla? Hyram? Keltan? Prella?

As for those she had already killed . . . Ethelda could not promise the dreams would stop. And the last time Mara had seen the shades of her victims, they had not even waited for sleep: they had come for her while she rode the waking world. How long could she live with horrors always lurking just beneath the surface of her mind, ready to invade her thoughts night and day without warning? How long before she went mad? And if she went mad, what would she do with her terrible power then?

Hot tears flooded her eyes, poured onto her cheeks. She let them lie there. She hadn't asked for this power. She didn't *want* this power. But she had it, and she couldn't see any way to be rid of it, or rid of the danger it posed to everyone around her.

Unless . . .

She remembered Ethelda reaching down one blue-sheathed finger to touch the chest of the woman in the bed across the aisle from her in the camp hospital, how the woman's breathing had simply stopped. "Release," Ethelda had called it.

There's one kind of sleep where dreams will never trouble me, Mara thought then, the idea cold and clear in her roiling mind as a shard of ice shining in a muddy pool. *One kind of sleep from which I'll never wake screaming. One kind of sleep that will keep me from harming anyone, ever again . . .*

The magic called to her. *Use me,* it seemed to cry. *Use me as you will. Use me . . .*

It would be so easy. Would she even have to open the urn? She could call for the magic, pull it into herself . . .

... and stop her heart.

Her breath went ragged in her throat. *No*, she thought. *No, it hasn't come to that.*

But the horror of the ghosts pulling her from her saddle, the terrible dreams of Grute and all the others ... she could end them. End it all. Ethelda couldn't promise she could free Mara from those horrors. But Mara could certainly free herself.

She closed her eyes. Maybe it would be best. Maybe it would. *No more troubles for me, or anyone else. No more dangers. No more deaths after this one ...*

She took a deep breath. She opened her eyes again. She turned her head to regard the urn of magic, rolled over and reached for it ...

... and jerked back as frantic shouts erupted in the next room. Sweeping aside the red curtain, Grelda burst in, shouting, "Put her there!" Simona and Keltan came next, carrying someone between them. Alita followed, weeping as if her heart would break, and behind her came Kirika, face white, eyes red, silent, staring, horror-stricken.

Simona and Keltan gently placed their burden on one of the other beds and Mara gasped as she saw who it was.

Little Prella, still so childlike, lay shuddering on the bed, blood already soaking it as it had soaked her side, pouring from a horrifying wound, a gaping slash in her side through which protruded the white ends of broken ribs. Prella's eyes had rolled back into her head so that only the whites showed, and blood bubbled from her mouth with each short, choking gasp.

"What happened?" Mara cried, sitting up in her bed.

"*She* happened!" Alita snarled, suddenly turning on Kirika and throwing her up against the wall. She held her forearm across the other girl's throat. "She's killed Prella!"

Kirika said nothing, her face a waxen mask. She didn't try to push Alita away.

"Stop it," Grelda snapped. "This is a sickroom, not a brawling ground. Mara, where's Ethelda?"

"She . . . she left. I don't know where . . . she was going to make me a sleeping potion . . ." Prella gave a shuddering groan and fresh blood bubbled from her mouth. "You've got to do something!"

"I can't," Grelda said, voice bitter. "My healing arts cannot deal with such a wound. She will die in minutes unless Ethelda has magical skill enough to heal her. Alita, leave Kirika! Find Ethelda, if you value Prella's life!"

Alita gave Kirika another angry shove, then shouldered through the red curtain and was gone.

But in that same instant, Prella gasped and stopped breathing. Grelda turned and looked down at her. "Too late," she said quietly.

"No!" Mara stared at the smaller girl. Kirika gave her own small gasp and sank down against the wall, burying her face in her hands. Keltan and Simona stood by, awkward, helpless, faces set in shock and disbelief. *This can't be happening*, Mara thought. *This* must not *happen!*

And just as it had in the camp in her moment of greatest need, magic answered her.

She did not draw it from those in the room. She did not need to. The magic in the urn poured out through the black stone sides as though they were porous as a sieve, and leaped to her. Hands sheathed in blue, she stumbled from her bed, eyes locked on Prella, who lay still and silent, face slackening into death, covered in blood, the awful hole gaping in her side. "What are you—" Grelda began, but her words died as Mara fell to her knees beside the wounded girl and touched her with her magic-covered hands. *Live*, she thought. *Oh, Prella. Live!*

She gasped as power flowed from her hands into the dying girl: not because it hurt, but because, this time, *it didn't*. It didn't feel wrong. For the first time, it felt *right*.

The gaping wound in Prella's side closed, pink flesh suddenly reappearing beneath the blood-soaked rent in her tunic. The ribs knitted, the lung sealed, the blood vessels rejoined. The heart that had stopped quivered and leaped back to thumping life. And Prella arched her back, took a huge gasping breath, then turned her head and coughed out blood. Her eyes flew open and met Mara's. She smiled a little. "Hello, Mara!" she croaked. "Welcome back." Then she looked down at herself. "Yuck! What happened?"

Mara hardly heard her. She raised her fingers in front of her face. Again she'd used magic without thinking, without proper control, despite all Ethelda's warnings. But this time . . . *this* time she had used it to heal, not kill.

And this time it hadn't hurt!

Grelda was staring down at her, eyes wide. Hyram and Keltan had similar awed expressions. By the archway, Kirika raised a face that now, at last, was as stained with tears as Alita's had been. She saw Prella sitting up, looking confused, staggered to her feet and almost flung herself on the younger girl. "Oh, Prella," she gasped out. "I'm so sorry. I'm so sorry!"

"I don't understand," Prella said, returning Kirika's hug but looking over her shoulder at Mara. "What just happened?"

"What, indeed?" said Ethelda, coming into the room with Alita.

Mara would have liked to have answered. But everything in the room seemed to be receding from her as though disappearing down a long gray tunnel, and in another moment had disappeared entirely.

The sleep that followed was without dreams.

TWENTY-FIVE

Aftermath and Beginnings

MARA SAT IN THE SAND with Keltan and Hyram, watching the sun set over the restless ocean. Five days had passed since they had returned from the camp. Two of those days had brought cold rain and the third two inches of snow; but yesterday had been warmer and today the sun shone with enough warmth to make their seaside lounging comfortable, though skiffs of white still lingered in the shadows of the cliffs.

Keltan seemed almost fully recovered, though occasionally he just *stopped*, for a moment, as if his mind were elsewhere. Mara, ever since Healing Prella, had slept, if not entirely without dreams, at least without those dreams bringing her to screaming wakefulness. She had not needed Ethelda's sleeping draught. She felt almost normal.

Prella showed no ill effects from having been dead. Keltan, who had seen the whole thing, had told Mara how the smaller girl had been hurt. "Kirika and Alita were harvesting potatoes," he said. "They each had a sharp spade. Prella had been doing something else. She came out, saw them with their backs to her, and thought it would be funny to sneak up on them. She looked at me and put a finger to her lips, then crept up behind Kirika and threw her arms around her." He'd gone pale as he'd told Mara the story. "Kirika . . . it was like when Simona touched her and she lashed out, only worse. She acted out of pure instinct. I've never seen anyone move so fast. She threw Prella off her and swung around with her spade, all in an instant. The spade smashed into Prella's side. It–it *crunched*. And the blood . . . Prella stared down at the wound, her face turned white, her eyes rolled up in her head, and then she collapsed. Simona and I hurried her up to the sickroom. The rest you know."

I Healed her, Mara thought. She still couldn't quite believe it. Prella's ribs had been smashed. Her lung punctured. She'd lost a huge amount of blood. She'd stopped breathing. Her heart had stopped. *And I brought her back.*

And in the process, Ethelda thought, Mara had partially Healed herself. "It doesn't change the risks," she'd told Mara. "Everything I warned you about still stands. You are still untrained. Still a danger to yourself and others. You should *still* avoid using magic.

"But this time, *you* controlled the magic, at least after a fashion, although since you passed out afterward, I'd say your technique needs work. As for why the dreams have eased . . ." She smiled. "Perhaps by soothing the irritated magical pathways in your mind, you softened the imprints that have given you the nightmares. Or perhaps it's simply because you've alleviated your guilt. I've noticed," she said dryly, "that you're almost as Gifted at guilt as at magic."

You don't know the half of it, Mara thought. She

hadn't told the Healer what she'd been on the verge of using the magic for just before Prella had been brought in. That dark urge had vanished. *If I'd killed myself, I wouldn't have been there for Prella*, she thought fiercely. *I wasn't able to save Katia. But at least I saved someone.*

For the moment, at least, the darkness that had been growing in her soul had retreated.

Hyram, returning from the camp two days after the others, had reported that the main gate had abruptly closed just before dawn the morning after the explosion. Shortly after that Watchers had emerged, but they had focused all their energy on finding their runaway horses. The unMasked had made it cleanly away. The Secret City remained a secret.

Mara had only spoken to Catilla briefly since awakening. She had agreed that Catilla had upheld her end of their bargain, and that she would, therefore, attempt to make the counterfeit Masks. "And learn to use your Gift," Catilla had reminded her sharply. "That was part of our bargain, too. The power you demonstrated, in the camp, and healing Prella—"

"And learn to use my Gift," Mara had agreed. "If that ever becomes possible."

Catilla had had to be content with that. Mara's Healing of Prella had exhausted the contents of the urn of magic they had brought back from the camp. "Among other things, you need to learn moderation," Ethelda had told her severely. "You could have healed that wound with only a portion of that magic, and left some for future emergencies. And maybe if you *had,* you wouldn't have knocked yourself out."

But learning moderation, or anything else about using her Gift, would have to wait until they had more magic: and for the moment, there was no prospect of that.

Ethelda had explained that to Catilla, which was why Catilla did not press the matter of Mara better learning to use her Gift. Neither Ethelda nor Mara had told Catilla— or anyone else—where the magic Mara had used to stop the explosion had come from. Her ability to draw magic directly from living things remained a secret shared only by the two of them.

Given a room in which to work on Masks, Mara had examined the supplies stolen from the village Mask-maker and confirmed everything was there. Even the "recipe," the black lodestone dust she now knew carried carefully crafted magic from the Palace had been brought, magic she would certainly *not* be incorporating into her fakes.

But what could I *do with the Masks?* she wondered now, as she stared out at the orange-and-gold water. *With the power I have . . . ?*

The power you dare not use, she reminded herself, as she did every day: every day, because with each day the memory of the pain she had felt when she'd saved the camp receded like the tide, leaving behind, like a glass float from some fisherman's net tangled in seaweed along the shore, the shining memory of the incredible power that had filled her: the unforgettable feeling that she could do *anything*. And unlike that glass ball, which lost some of its gleam as it dried, the memory of power seemed to grow more and more attractive, more and more something she'd like to experience again, no matter what the cost.

The Autarch is an addict, she remembered Ethelda saying. *Am I one, too?*

If Catilla knew where my power came from in the camp, she wouldn't worry about what using magic might do to me. She'd see me only as a weapon. She'd . . . what? Send me to Tamita to kill the Autarch?

She can't *know. I don't want to be a weapon. Not like that.* She remembered Ethelda's grim warning. *If I became a weapon, how long before I'd turn from weapon to monster, another Lady of Pain and Fire?*

But she couldn't help turning the idea over and over in her head. What if she *could* get into Tamita? What if she *could* kill the Autarch? Would that really be so bad?

How could *killing* a monster make *her* a monster? Killing monsters was something *heroes* did.

"I wonder if there really are monsters out there?" Hyram said idly, his question so close to her thoughts that she started.

"Out where?"

"Out there. In the ocean." Hyram waved a hand. "And how far do you have to go before you fall off the edge of the world?"

"Some people say the world is round," Mara said, glad to talk about something, anything, that had nothing to do with what she'd been thinking.

Hyram snorted. "And how does that work, exactly? If the world were round, all that water would drain off. And if you walked too far in one direction you'd eventually topple over and fall." He leaned back on his elbows in the sand. His bare feet were stretched out in front of him, and he wriggled his toes. "No, the world is flat. And somewhere out there is the edge."

"There are stories about other lands across the sea," Mara said, remembering books she had read in childhood. "Once upon a time, the stories say, people from other lands regularly visited Aygrima. We even traded with them. It was a long, long time ago, though. Before the Autarch. Before the days of the Autarch's great-grandfather, in fact."

"Other lands?" Hyram looked at her. "What do you mean, other lands?"

"Islands, I guess," Mara said.

"With other people on them." Hyram shook his head. "Children's tales. This is the only land. We're the only people. And the Autarch . . ." His face turned grim. "The Autarch rules us all." Then he grinned fiercely. "*For now.* Because one day, we will be rid of him and everyone will walk free and unMasked."

"I don't know," Keltan said, rather unexpectedly; he had been gazing off into space as if lost in his own head. "In Tamita everyone thinks the unMasked Army is a myth, nothing but a children's tale, that it can't possibly be real. Yet here I am, in the unMasked Army." He waved a hand at the sea. "So who's to say the children's tales about other lands beyond the waters don't have some basis in truth, too?"

Hyram snorted again. "I'll make you a wager. If we ever find out there are other lands beyond the water, I'll clean your boots and make your bed for a month."

Keltan laughed. "I'll hold you to that." Mara looked from one to the other, and smiled. *Maybe Keltan will be all right after all*, she thought. *Maybe I will, too.*

With the sun almost gone, they went back into the Secret City, Mara walking between the two boys, enjoying their easy banter, the warmth of their companionship . . .

. . . and trying not to feel, deep in her mind, the insistent call of the magic within the two young bodies at her side . . . especially from Keltan, the boy she had already pulled magic from once before, and from whom it would be so easy, so *pleasurable*, to do so again . . .

She shuddered. *I can control this*, she thought fiercely. *I* can. *I am* not *a monster.*

They entered the Secret City. Behind them, darkness descended over the endlessly rolling ocean.

Now available in hardcover from DAW,
the second in *The Masks of Aygrima*
by E. C. Blake:

SHADOWS

Read on for a special preview.

THE DAYS HAD GROWN SHORTER and shorter over the past few weeks, until now, though it was only about four hours past noon, the sun was already dipping toward the horizon, casting long blue shadows on the snowdrifts, crisscrossed by trampled paths, that filled the cove. In ten days it would be Midwinter. Just a year ago she had celebrated it with her parents, their home alight with candles and hung with evergreen boughs. She could still remember how their fragrance had mingled with the delicious smells of cooking ham and baking cakes, how everything had felt beautiful and warm and safe. This year . . .

This year, there seemed little to celebrate, even if the unMasked Army marked the day. So far she'd seen no sign of it.

The ocean thundered, tall breakers racing in to batter themselves into white spray against the stony shore, the sea still unsettled from a violent storm that had blown through the night before. Mara, seeing the height of the waves, hesitated; in storms the water sometimes reached the path along the beach she meant to travel. But she decided to walk down to the water's edge at least, and once there, looking north, she saw that the path was open. *Must be low tide*, she thought, for though the water roared against the shore, only the occasional blast of spray made it as far as the cliff face.

The path looked grim, gray, cold, and lonely.

Perfect, Mara thought, and set out along it.

Her feet crunched over the salt-rotted ice covering the sand-and-pebbles beach. Just before the curve of cliff face hid it from her, she glanced back at the Secret City. Two dark figures trudged across the open space, presumably heading to the Broad Way from the stables carved into the base of the cove's northern cliff. She recognized them instantly as Keltan and Hyram, but they had their backs to her and didn't see her . . . which suited her fine.

Ten more steps and they, and the cove, were lost to sight. Alone with her thoughts, she wended her way north along the narrow strip of land between the pounding waves to her left and the gray stone cliff to her right, past the entrance to the mine from which the Secret City drew the gold it occasionally used to purchase goods in the villages via children too young to be Masked.

I can't make the Masks Catilla wants, she thought again as she walked. Spray touched her face. She licked salt from her lips, but lowered her head and trudged on, her breath forming white clouds, the crunch of her footsteps echoing from the cliff to her right. *I don't know how. I need to talk to someone who knows more. I need to talk to . . .*

Her thoughts and her feet stumbled. She caught herself with a hand on an ice-coated outcropping of gray stone.

I need to talk to my father.

Her father had deliberately sent her into exile. At great risk to himself—uncertain if his own Mask, modified though it was, might reveal his betrayal to the Watchers—he had crafted her Mask to fail at her Masking on her fifteenth birthday . . . and then had sent word to the unMasked Army that someone with the ability to make Masks would be in the next wagonload of un-Masked children sent north from Tamita to the mining camp.

Father must have known I couldn't really make counterfeit Masks, Mara thought. *Which means he lied to the unMasked Army, tricking Catilla into saving me.*

But now that lie was unraveling. With the stolen Maskmaker's clay all but gone, she could hide the truth no longer. She would have to tell Catilla that she could not provide her with the counterfeit Masks she needed.

Unless Mara could talk to her father.

She wanted that; wanted it so much that she wondered for a moment if she had subconsciously *made* her Masks fail. *Of course not,* she told herself: but having wondered it herself, even for a moment, she knew there was little doubt Catilla would ask her about it point-blank.

No, she thought. *I did everything I could. I did. I just don't have the knowledge . . . or the magic. Catilla will have to see that. She'll* have to. *And then she'll have to figure out some way for me to go back to Tamita . . . some way for me to see my father again. She'll* have to.

Won't she?

Mara stopped her northward wandering and wiped water from her cheeks. She told herself it was spray from the sea . . . but it was warm.

She looked around. She'd gone past the narrow defile in the cliff that, providing the only access up from the beach for horses, led to the Secret City's grain fields and pastures. She'd never walked any farther. The cliff curved out to sea in front of her, and the beach narrowed, so that at the tip of the headland the waves appeared to be crashing across it. *Time to head back*, she thought. *Time to face Catilla.*

She tugged her rabbit-skin hat tighter onto her head, shrugged her coat more firmly into place, started to turn . . .

. . . and then froze as a stranger came around the shoulder of the cliff.

• • •

Mara's first instinct was to flee. But then an extra-large wave rolled in from the sea, doused the stranger in spray as it smashed into the rocks, and washed around his feet as it receded. He stumbled and fell, splashing into the water . . . and didn't get up. She hesitated, torn between fear and compassion.

Compassion won.

She hurried forward, not quite daring to run on the ice-slicked beach. As she got closer, she saw the stranger try to get to his hands and knees, but he collapsed forward, head turned, his cheek pressed against the stones.

His *unMasked* cheek, she realized with a thrill.

Another wave splashed over him, and receded.

Just because he wasn't wearing a Mask didn't necessarily mean he was *really* unMasked, of course. Like the Watcher who had found her in the magic-collection hut the morning after she had slain her kidnapper and would-be rapist, Grute, with magic—blowing off his head in a gruesome fashion that continued to haunt her dreams—this young man might merely have removed his Mask while he wandered the Wild, intending to don it again whenever he got back to civilization.

But she didn't really think so. The young man wasn't carrying anything with him, and anyone Masked would keep his Mask close at hand at all times: the Masks would crack and crumble if they were abandoned and that would be a death sentence should the wearer encounter a Watcher.

The stranger wore dark blue trousers, a heavy leather coat, and black boots, all soaked through. His pale hair — Mara had never before seen anyone young with such pale hair, so blond as to almost be white — was plastered to his head in lank, dripping strands. At his side he wore a sword with a strange, basket-shaped hilt.

She took all that in as she ran up to him. As she reached his side, she was able to see around the shoulder of the cliff for the first time. Debris lay scattered along the shore, bits and pieces of planking and rigging, clearly the remains of a wrecked boat. Debris . . .

. . . and corpses. Her breath caught. She counted five, all dressed in nondescript clothing like the young man at her feet. She didn't have to go close to them to know they were dead: her Gift told her. When living people were near, she could always — always — feel the magic within them, the magic she sometimes had to fight not to draw on. She could feel no magic from those sprawled, wave-tossed bodies.

But she could feel it in the young man. She could do nothing for the others, but him, she might still be able to save.

She knelt, the icy pebbles digging painfully into her knees. The stranger's face was white as the ice all around, his lips the color of a bruise. His eyes fluttered open, startlingly blue in his white face, framed by that astonishing pale-gold hair. "Help . . ." he whispered.

"I will," Mara assured him. *But how?* her mind whispered, as panic fluttered in her chest. If she ran for help, he might freeze to death before she returned. She had nothing with which to make a fire.

Magic, she thought. *If only I had magic . . .*

But she had none, except for what she sensed in the shivering frame of the frozen youth, and if she drew on that, she'd likely kill him.

Not to mention what it might do to her.

"I'll help you," she said again, "but you have to help me do it. You have to walk."

"Don't know . . . if I can," he said. His words were oddly shaped, vowels elongated, consonants clipped.

"You have to," Mara repeated firmly. "You can lean on me."

A brief smile flickered across his white face. "I'll t-t-t-try," he said through chattering teeth.

She helped him to a sitting position, then slipped his arm over her shoulder. "We'll stand together," she said. "On three. One . . . two . . . three!"

She struggled to rise and he struggled to rise with her. Mara's foot slipped on an icy rock and they both collapsed back into a heap, Mara on top of the youth, who grunted at the impact. "Sorry!" she said, and they tried again. This time they managed it. Another tall wave doused them both with spray and sluiced freezing water around their ankles, almost tugging them down again, but Mara held on, though she was now so thoroughly soaked that her teeth, too, were chattering. "Hold on t-t-to me," she gasped out.

"Right . . ." he mumbled.

Together, they began struggling back toward the Secret City. The young man . . . *he can't be more than twenty*, Mara thought, glancing sideways at his smooth-shaven, unlined face, *maybe younger* . . . was a head taller than her, but thin enough that she was able to support him without trouble.

Even as she thought it, his feet slipped on the ice and he fell, dragging her down with him so that she sprawled across him once again, this time over his back. Her knees had both cracked hard against the ground as she fell, and she sat up and rubbed them. "Ow," she said.

The youth rolled over. "S-s-s-sorry," he said.

"It's all right," Mara said. "We're alm-m-m-ost th-there."

"Where?" the youth said as she helped him stand again.

"The Se-secret Ci-city," Mara said, then clamped shut

her chattering teeth, wondering if she'd said more than she should.

Well, he's going to see it for himself soon enough, isn't he?

"What's your n-name?" she said as they struggled along, the going a little easier now they were past the defile leading up to the pastures. "I'm Ma-ma-mara Holdfast."

"Chell," he said. "Royal Korellian Navy." The chatter of his teeth had stopped, but his speech was slurred. "At your service. May I have this dance?" He blinked sleepily at her. "Actually, rather tired. Think I need a nap. Dance later."

The name was outlandish, the rest gibberish; clearly the cold was making him delirious. *Catilla will have to figure this one out*, Mara thought.

The youth leaned harder and harder against her, his weight dragging at her, and then, with the cove still a hundred yards away, slipped away from her entirely. She clutched at him and managed to slow his fall, but when he hit the ground he lay motionless, eyes closed, cheek pressed against the icy stone.

Mara straightened and ran for the Secret City, slipping and sliding and shouting for help.

E. C. Blake
The Masks of Aygrima

"Brilliant world-building combined with can't-put-down storytelling, *Masks* reveals its dark truths through the eyes of a girl who must learn to wield unthinkable power or watch her people succumb to evil. Bring on the next in this highly original series!"

—Julie E. Czerneda

"Mara's personal growth is a delight to follow. Sharp characterization, a fast-moving plot, and a steady unveiling of a bigger picture make this a welcome addition to the genre."

—*Publishers Weekly*

"*Masks* is simply impossible to put down."

—*RT Book Reviews*

MASKS
978-0-7564-0947-0

SHADOWS
978-0-7564-0760-5

FACES
978-0-7564-0939-5
(Coming from DAW in 2015!)

To Order Call: 1-800-788-6262
www.dawbooks.com

Michelle Sagara
The Queen of the Dead

"Brilliant storyteller Sagara heads in a new direction with her *Queen of the Dead* series. She does an excellent job of breathing life into not only her reluctant heroine, but also the supporting players in this dramatic and spellbinding series starter. There is a haunting beauty to this story of love, loss and a teenager's determination to do the right thing. Do not miss out!"

—*RT Book Reviews*

"It's rare to find a book as smart and sweet as this one."

—Sarah Rees Brennan

SILENCE
978-0-7564-0799-5

TOUCH
978-0-7564-0800-8

And watch for the third book in the series, *Grave*, coming soon from DAW!

To Order Call: 1-800-788-6262
www.dawbooks.com

DAW 192

Edward Willett

"Their moral dilemma is only on of the reasons this novel is so fascinating. The Selkie culture and infrastructure is very picturesque and easily pictured by readers who will want to visit his exotic world." —*Midwest Book Review*

"Willett is well able to keep all his juggling balls in the air at the same time....It's a good story, a great mate to the first volume." —Ian Randal Strock at *SF Scope*

The Helix War
Omnibus:
Marseguro   Terra Insegura
978-0-7564-0738-4

And don't miss:

Lost in Translation
978-0-7564-0340-9

To Order Call: 1-800-788-6262
www.dawbooks.com